Deep Cover

C. Paradee

Quest Books

Nederland, Texas

Copyright © 2004 by C. Paradee

All rights reserved. No part of this publication may be reproduced, transmitted in any form or by any means, electronic or mechanical, including photocopy, recording, or any information storage and retrieval system, without permission in writing from the publisher. The characters, incidents and dialogue herein are fictional and any resemblance to actual events or persons, living or dead, is purely coincidental.

ISBN 1-932300-23-6

First Printing 2004

9 8 7 6 5 4 3 2 1

Cover design by Donna Pawlowski

Published by:

QuestBooks
PMB 210, 8691 9th Avenue
Port Arthur, Texas 77642-8025

Find us on the World Wide Web at
http://www.regalcrest.biz

Printed in the United States of America

Acknowledgments

Special thanks to my wonderful beta readers and friends, Day, Inga, Lois, Maribel, and Pam for helping me to make this a better story with their great feedback, editing and suggestions.

Prologue

Antananarivo, Madagascar

OBLIVIOUS OF THE crosshairs centered on his forehead, the target strode confidently from a high-rise office building to a waiting black Mercedes Benz. The car, his Armani suit, the gold Rolex that flashed in the noonday sun as he impatiently checked the time, and the half dozen bodyguards surrounding him all signaled the man's wealth and position. The ostentatious trappings of power were useless though, as the sniper squeezed the trigger of the fifty-caliber rifle. Mission accomplished, the executioner calmly abandoned the weapon and exited the room before the echo of the discharge had even stilled. Within moments, the killer was on the street, one more anonymous face amongst the shocked and excited people gathering around the corpse. Ignoring the impotent bodyguards who waved large, black handguns around and screamed hoarsely at the gaping onlookers, the killer's dispassionate blue eyes verified the kill. Silently, the sniper faded back into the dense crowd, and disappeared from view.

Chapter One

CIA Headquarters

SHELBY CARSON ENTERED the sterile halls of CIA headquarters and walked to the bank of elevators on the north side of the building. She usually smiled and spoke to each person she passed along the way, but this morning she was unusually distracted and failed to voice her customary greetings. Not that anyone noticed, as they all went busily about their duties with little regard for the niceties that one might expect in a more traditional workplace. Shelby had worked at the Company for almost six months and often passed the same people in the hall daily, yet they remained strangers. Ruefully, she had decided that paranoia seemed paramount within these walls. *Well, at least a few of the people I work with are friendly.*

Getting off on the third floor, she saw a coworker. "Hey, Maggie, how's it going?"

Maggie grinned at Shelby. "Good. You?"

"Okay. Glad it's Friday, though. I hate feeling so closed in. Wouldn't be so bad if we had windows."

"I hear you. It's like working in a dungeon. Her eyes twinkling, Shelby said, "I know, let's requisition some. Can you just imagine the look on Dennis' face?" She chuckled at the image of her supervisor that her mind conjured up. "It would almost be worth doing, just to see his reaction."

Laughing at the idea, Maggie said, "Isn't that the truth!"

Anxious to verify the pattern she had found in the data she was analyzing, Shelby glanced at her watch. "Hey, I gotta run. See ya later."

Knowing how unlikely that was with their current workload, Maggie grinned and returned, "Yeah, right."

More than ten hours later, Shelby brushed back a lock of blonde hair, her tired green eyes studying the computer printouts spread across her desk and the list of names she had jotted on a tablet. After weeks of meticulous research and patient follow-up, she had uncovered a disturbing pattern in a worldwide rash of assassinations of highly placed government officials. Her normal optimism faded at the implications of the tentative connection between the killings.

It was the third time she had come up with exactly the same results: a CIA agent was definitely involved, and every operative on the list could have been on location at the time of each assassination. None of the names could be ruled out: Atlas, Astera, Blue, Celt, Dragon... She looked at the twenty-seven names until the print became blurred and the code names were burned into her memory.

Shaking her head to clear it, the young woman stood up and stretched to work the kinks out of her back. She picked up some change lying on the desk and walked through the doorway, automatically smiling up at the Marine guard posted in the hall just outside of her office. Unable to ignore her warm smile, his mouth turned up in a fleeting response before his official implacable military face fell back into place.

Shelby felt sorry for the serviceman, who towered over her own 5'5" by a good six inches. How boring to be required to stand outside a doorway for hours on end. She understood the necessity of the guard, but couldn't imagine ever being still or quiet hour after hour. She walked to the vending machine, inserted four quarters and plucked a can of cranberry juice from the tray before reluctantly returning to her desk in Section 5.

A psychological analyst for the Company, Shelby's responsibility was to analyze information on individuals or groups, look for patterns in behaviors, and then, once an archetype was identified, render a psychological profile to be disseminated to agents. In some ways her job was similar to that of FBI profilers, but Shelby's duties were wider in scope. Her superiors had quickly discovered she had an uncanny knack for spotting tiny clues frequently overlooked by her peers. Consequently, she was assigned more divergent challenges and now worked on the Company's most sensitive cases, such as her current assignment.

The profile she had been developing concerned a series of assassinations which seemed to point toward the perpetrator being a CIA agent doing unsanctioned wetwork. She knew the only reason she'd detected the pattern was because she'd been granted unlimited access to all of the Company's data banks. Being logical, she knew that there was almost no chance her discoveries could be explained by coincidence, but still wasn't looking forward to telling her boss what she'd uncovered. This was one time Shelby sincerely wanted her conclusions to be wrong. If the proximity of any of the field operatives was not happenstance, it meant one of three things, and Shelby was loath to speak any of them aloud.

Dennis McNabb watched assessingly as one of his rising new stars walked into his office. Her blonde hair was cut in a very attractive shaggy style that accentuated the curves of her face and lent age to an otherwise youthful appearance. Bangs ended just above well-shaped eyebrows, and intelligent green eyes gazed back at him. He considered himself an expert on reading people, but she had continually surprised him from the day he'd met her. She possessed maturity beyond her years, and despite the inherently dark and suspicious nature of her work, the normally laid-back young woman had maintained a sunny demeanor and optimistic attitude. So, he had been concerned when she uncharacteristically requested an urgent meeting.

His stomach sank as he saw the lines of worry etched across her face and the usual bounce missing from her step. Keeping his expression neutral, he nodded. "Shelby."

Smiling, Shelby said, "Hi, Dennis. Sorry to bother you on such short notice, but I think I've found a pattern relative to those assassinations."

Dennis' eyes riveted on the analyst. "And that would be?"

An hour later, after painstakingly reviewing her findings and being unable to fault her reasoning, he sat back in his chair and gazed at her. "Given this data, what are your conclusions?"

Faced with the question she had known he would ask, Shelby met his brown eyes and answered confidently, "If it's not just a bizarre coincidence, I'd say rogue, mole, or double."

Dennis sighed. "Unfortunately, I agree." He suddenly stood up and began pacing the room. "Just what we need, another scandal."

Tentatively, Shelby said, "Maybe it doesn't have to escalate to that level. If the investigation team is small enough, word might not get out."

His snort of disbelief spoke volumes. "As classified as this place is, there is always some disgruntled employee just waiting for something they can run to the papers with. Each time you request information from someone as you pursue this investigation, you'll run that risk. And I need to assign an operative to work this case with you."

Sitting, Dennis shook his head. "Field operatives hate this kind of work. They're used to working on their own, and assigning them a desk job always causes a lot of friction. More than one of them has dropped a dime to the media to get out of an assignment like this. It could get ugly real fast."

"Why do I have to work with a field operative, because I'm new?"

"That's only part of it. I'd probably assign one, regardless. We've got to eliminate some of the names on your list. There's no one better than one of our own to determine what is and isn't possible in the field. What's feasible on paper isn't always possible in actuality."

At least he isn't pulling me off the case. Shelby had been worried about that, and her mind worked quickly trying to come up with a solution that would forestall a public debacle. "Why not choose one of the operatives on the list? Can't very well run to the papers if they're under suspicion."

Dennis' eyes drilled into his subordinate's. "And what if *they* are the guilty party?"

"It's possible, but come on, Dennis. There are twenty-seven operatives that were within traveling distance of each of those assassinations. Twenty-seven to one are pretty good odds."

Leaning back in his chair, Dennis thought over his very limited options before nodding. "It would be a long shot."

"I'm willing to take the chance. We don't know for sure it's anyone on that list, anyway."

Dennis was warming to the idea. If it were one of the Company's own, this maneuver would possibly prevent a scandal, and the likelihood of Shelby being paired with the killer was statistically small. "I'll talk to Jeb and get back to you. Now go on home. You've already been here twelve hours."

Shelby smiled, pleased that her lead was being taken up the chain of command. Jeb was short for James Evan Benton, the Director of Coordinated Operations. "Thanks, Dennis."

"If he approves this, you might not be thanking me later. Not all of our field operatives have well-developed social skills."

Shelby shoved his warning to the back of her mind. She had considered the risks before making the suggestion, and had offered it only because Dennis almost seemed willing to ignore the threat rather than risk a scandal. She did have some private concerns about working with a field agent who could turn out to be the unsanctioned killer, and sent up a brief prayer that she and her new partner would both be on the same side.

A Desert Camp in Saudi Arabia

KRISTINE BARTLEY RAISED the antenna on the portable receiver and directed it toward a satellite south of her position. Within five minutes, an encrypted message she had intercepted began downloading into her self-modified hand-held receiver without leaving any trace of having done so. The message was automatically decoded and displayed across the three-inch screen in timed bursts. As the import of the words registered, her eyes narrowed in speculation. She quickly returned to her quarters and waited for her

Saudi liaison.

Ahmed received his new instructions and slowly made his way across the camp to the American woman's location. He didn't like her, and was relieved this would be the last message he would have to deliver to her. He would miss her skills, but she didn't know her place, and when he had challenged her, he had barely escaped with his life. He would never forget the emotionless, ice-blue eyes as she threatened to strike the fatal blow. If Henri's arrival hadn't been so timely, he was sure she would've killed him. No, skilled or not, he would be glad to see her go.

Kris sat on the bedroll against the canvas wall, seemingly relaxed and unconcerned as she called out in Arabic, "Come in," the foreign language rolling smoothly off her tongue.

Actually, every muscle in her tall body was prepared to move at the slightest threat or provocation. She didn't trust her Saudi counterpart, but then she didn't trust anyone, so it wasn't an alien feeling. In her business, trust could mean death, and Kris had no intentions of becoming worm food any time soon.

When Ahmed entered, Kris grinned sardonically, fully aware of how intimidated he was, and how much he despised her for that very reason. She snorted to herself. He had determined the parameters of their association by strutting up to her shortly after her arrival and informing her that as long as she was in his country, she would be subordinate to him. Most men, and women too, usually succumbed to her natural charisma when she chose to use it, but he had been totally oblivious to it and so she had been forced to physically correct his misperception of their working relationship.

"Hawk just called a Code Yellow." Ahmed looked closely at the beautiful woman for any reaction to his words. He knew Code Yellow meant that the mission was aborted and operatives were to return to headquarters. The Saudi also knew it was highly unusual, yet the American's face remained impassive. He knew it was impossible, but it seemed as if she had already known. Angered by yet another display of her total self-control, he barked, "You will depart now!"

Ahmed felt his intake of air cut off and fleetingly wondered how she could move so quickly. He heard a quiet chuckle and his blood ran cold. She had to be crazy. She whispered in his ear, "I'll leave when I'm ready. Understand?" Then, as if talking to a child, she repeated the words in Arabic. Ahmed nodded his head, unable to speak through the vise gripping his throat.

"Good. I'm glad we understand each other. So, you want to tell me what that was all about? We both know there are no flights to the States until morning." Kris loosened her hold on his neck so that he could answer.

"I thought you might want to wait at the airport."

Her voice steely, Kris growled, "You are a poor liar, Ahmed. And a poor excuse for a soldier. Get out of here while you still can."

Ahmed strode out of her quarters in what he hoped was a dignified manner, consoling himself with the fact that she was most assuredly in trouble with her superiors.

Kris remained awake until she departed for the airport the following morning. She could sleep on the plane. Contrary to what Ahmed thought, the operative was actually very concerned about being recalled. It was a first in her career, and she doubted it boded well for her. Her mind processed a multitude of possible reasons, none of which were reassuring; one was downright terrifying.

Fairfax, Virginia

SHELBY WALKED INTO her second floor garden apartment, tossed her purse on the floor by the couch, and kicked off her shoes before sinking into a large, mauve, overstuffed chair. She glanced over and checked the answering machine, but the light wasn't blinking. Surprised that her mother hadn't called, she got up and began shedding her clothing one piece at a time. Her blouse ended up on the bathroom doorknob, the skirt on the bed, and her underwear in the hamper. All she could think of was a warm shower to wash the stress from her tense muscles.

Shelby took a long, leisurely shower, then donned her pajamas and made her way into the living room. She curled up on the couch in her long, red, sleeping T-shirt with its picture of kittens playing on the front. Tonight all she wanted to do was relax. *Maybe I'll watch The Fugitive. Kim seems to think it's good.* Shelby didn't want to think about what Monday would bring. If Jeb approved her suggestion, she was going to be working with a field operative who could just possibly be an assassin, and that made Shelby decidedly uneasy.

She still couldn't believe she was working for the CIA. After graduating from college with degrees in both computer science and psychology, Shelby accepted a position as a computer programmer with a local head-hunter company. She quickly mastered the job, but found the work tedious and boring. Increasingly dissatisfied, she enrolled part-time in graduate school, and had just finished her last course when Shawn Burgess became her supervisor. His interest in her had extended beyond the job, and things quickly deteriorated when she rebuffed his advances. Going up the supervisory chain with her complaint only made matters worse, so, unwilling to put up with the constant harassment, she had started looking for another job while she waited for her degree to be conferred.

Shelby clearly remembered the day she had sent her resumé to a post office box address in response to an advertisement in a local paper. Her Master's degree in psychology had qualified her for the position, and she was excited about an opportunity to put it to use. Smiling inwardly, Shelby reflected that, had she known it was a CIA recruitment ad, she might not have answered it. The Company had a poor public image because of past scandals and a common misconception was that many CIA operatives were government-sanctioned killers. Shelby had never believed that, although she was not naïve enough to doubt that the Company would do whatever was necessary to protect the interests of the United States. She accepted the job they offered, and, so far, had no regrets. Her new job was interesting and challenging, a distinct improvement over the previous one.

After her promotion, Shelby began working on highly classified cases and came across the term "wet operative" in a few cases that had deadly outcomes. She intuitively made the connection and noted that the title was gruesomely appropriate. For her, the biggest downside of the job was the loneliness of the work. There was very little opportunity to interact with other employees. Being gregarious by nature, Shelby missed that.

Forcing work from her mind, she decided to call Kim. Most of her friends were married or had ongoing relationships, but her best friend was single like she was and usually available for a night out. She punched in the number, and waited for Kim to answer.

"Hello."

"Hiya."

"Hey, Shelby. Whazup?"

"Not too much. Wanna see *Charlie's Angels* tomorrow? The write-up's pretty good."

"Sure. What time?"

"Well, we could get something to eat and catch the 9:30. Want me to pick you up?"

"Yeah. That'd be good. It's your turn to drive."

Shelby laughed. "What're you doing, keeping track?"

"No. I just hate to drive in this city. Maybe someday I'll get used to it."

"I hear you. Doesn't bother me that much, though."

Eating out being one of her favorite things, Kim asked, "So, where are we going to eat?"

"You pick. I picked the movie."

"Umm, how 'bout Chesapeake Bay Seafood House?"

"Sounds good. See you tomorrow."

Shelby hung up the phone and relaxed. Their outing tomorrow would be a nice mental diversion from the worrisome events that were starting to become way too commonplace.

CIA Headquarters

STRICTLY A REMF (Rear Echelon MFer), Jeb accepted the intended slur proudly. He commanded from a desk, and that was the way he liked it. Lots of power, but he stayed nice and safe. He had no intention of getting his ass shot off, or being tortured in some foreign country while the government disavowed any knowledge of him. So he almost sighed with relief as he left the office of the head honcho of covert ops, Earl Mason. Having met with Dennis the evening before, Jeb agreed it was necessary to pull an operative from the field, but he didn't have the authority. Earl Mason, who he quite frankly thought of as one scary guy, did.

Returning to his own office, he called Dennis. "It's a go. Earl is pulling Blue." His lips twitched in a slight grin as he heard the sharp intake of breath through the phone. That had been his reaction, too.

Dennis had heard rumors about just how ruthless Blue was; the operative had a reputation for never failing, regardless of how long the mission took. It was the "ruthless" part that bothered him if there were any truth to the tales he had heard, and experience had taught him that there was always some truth in the rumor mill. "Why Blue?"

"You'll have to ask Earl that."

Dennis snorted. "Yeah, right. He's real amenable to having his decisions questioned."

"My point exactly. Blue's already been recalled and will be meeting with Earl at ten. He told me to tell you to be standing by from eleven on."

"Thanks for going to bat for me, Jim."

"Let's just hope we solve this case real fast."

Dennis hung up the phone and issued an apology that would never be spoken aloud. *I'm sorry, Shelby. This guy is probably some cold fish with dead eyes, and you're stuck with him.*

KRIS IGNORED THE admiring glances cast her way as she walked down the main corridor of CIA headquarters en route to a Sunday meeting with her boss. She was used to the attention—it had served her, and her employer, exceptionally well.

She was tall, lithe and strikingly attractive. Her black hair flowed over her shoulders and down her back. Longish bangs in need of a trim were brushed aside, contrasting nicely with an olive complexion. High cheekbones and a full mouth gave her an almost exotic appearance, but it was her sapphire blue eyes that were her most memorable feature.

Over the years, on the few occasions that the operative had been spotted, the witness would cite mesmerizing blue eyes, but beyond that, their memory seemed to fail. Her code name was, appropriately, Blue. And it was for just that very reason that dark sunglasses usually hid her eyes from casual onlookers.

At the moment, the operative looked every bit an executive within the Agency. She wore a fashionable gray, moderately cut suit with a crisp white blouse. Tasteful gold earrings, a matching brooch and a light smattering of make up, tastefully applied, accented her attire. The strap of a black purse was slung over her right shoulder, and the handle of a black leather briefcase was secured in her left hand. Kris excelled at role-playing. She had been doing it for years.

She had arrived in Washington the previous evening and had wanted to be well rested for her meeting, but troubling thoughts had thwarted those plans; she was operating on sheer adrenaline, worry vying with curiosity.

Arriving at her destination, Kris knocked once and entered the outer office of the Director of Strategic Planning, commonly referred to as Covert Ops. She passed the empty secretary's desk on the way to the inner office door, knowing she'd been told to report on Sunday so there would be a limited number of people around. She knocked, and the door immediately opened.

Earl backed away from the door far enough to allow Kris entry, and then closed it. "Long time, no see."

"I would say 'charmed,' except that I'm not."

"That's not very friendly of you."

"What's going on, Earl? You trash an ongoing operation and call me back here at the risk of blowing my cover. What is so damned important it couldn't have waited a few more weeks?"

Earl studied the woman silently, hoping that would give him the upper hand in this meeting, but the tactic had no effect on her demeanor. "We have a potential security breach, and you're being reassigned here to work with one of our top analysts to get to the bottom of it."

Kris fought against reacting to the news. She was a field agent, not a desk jockey. In her mind, there was only one thing worse than being chained to a desk; being dead.

"Potential security breach?" She raised an eyebrow to indicate her disdain for the deliberately vague language. "Do we or don't we have one?"

"That's your job. You tell me." Earl handed Kris a copy of the typed report he'd gotten from Jeb, and sat back in his chair while she read it.

Kris read the report quickly. The evidence was solid, but there was no explicit proof of any wrongdoing by any operative listed. "Strictly circumstantial. Could be coincidence." She wasn't the least bit pleased that her name had been included in the list of suspects.

"Right. That's where you come in. I need you to work with the analyst and narrow that list down. I figure it should take you a couple of weeks to accurately account for each operative's location. You will have full access to copies of the time-pertinent satellite transmissions for each person on that list, where they were sent to and received from. Use every means at your disposal to verify where each one was when the assassinations went down. Best case scenario—all the names are eliminated."

"I can't accept this assignment, I'm on the list. That's a conflict of interest." Kris smiled sardonically. "Besides, what if it's me? I could stymie you at every turn."

The hairs on the back of Earl's neck stood on end. He'd considered that possibility, and hoped for all of their sakes that it wasn't true. To have her as an opponent would be catastrophic.

"First off, you don't have a choice. You're the best we have, and I want you on this. Second, you're too smart to do anything as dumb as interfere with an investigation." Earl returned her smile. "Nice try, Kris."

Kris bit off a retort. This was quickly turning into the assignment from hell.

He stood up. "Dennis McNabb is standing by. He'll answer any other questions you have, and set you up with the analyst. Any questions?"

"No. But I want you to know that I am accepting this assignment under duress."

"Duly noted." Earl ran a hand through his thinning gray hair. "I probably don't need to tell you that if word of this investigation gets out, it could get dicey."

Kris rolled her eyes, the action hidden behind her sunglasses. "Yeah, Earl. So what else is new?"

Earl routinely dealt with some of the most cold-blooded men and women in the world, but this one had to be the deadliest of the lot. Her ability to turn her charm on and off at will put people, himself included, at a distinct disadvantage, and it wasn't a position he liked being in. Earl had pulled her because he wanted a quick resolution to the case, but he felt a pang of sympathy for the analyst she'd be working with.

EARL HAD MADE his introductions and his exit five minutes earlier, and Dennis was still trying to recover. And it didn't help that the agent sat there watching him with an unreadable smile on her face and her eyes covered by sunglasses. You couldn't very well gauge a person if you couldn't see their eyes. *Damn, Earl could've at least warned me.*

When Earl had introduced her as Blue, Dennis had been unable to hide his shock, and his mouth had dropped open. Since she was being saddled with a desk assignment, Kris intended to find amusement wherever she could, and she was thoroughly enjoying the effect she was having on Dennis. She would've loved to know what image his mind's eye had conjured up prior to meeting her. She was well aware of the exaggerated rumors floating around headquarters regarding her and a few of her peers.

Deciding to keep their meeting brief, Dennis quickly explained how Shelby had come up with the information, totally unaware that Kris had already seen the report. Finished, he said, "Um. If you could be back here tomorrow at nine, I'll introduce you to Shelby."

Kris nodded. "I'll be here." And she walked out the door.

Dennis watched her admiringly, but knew that was all he'd ever do.

KRIS PAID THE cab driver and walked into the Sheraton. She was totally aware of her surroundings and everyone in the immediate vicinity, although she scanned the area so unobtrusively only someone similarly trained would have noticed her scrutiny.

Satisfied that there was nothing out of the ordinary, she took the elevator to the fourth floor and entered a room near the far end. Kris was emotionally and mentally exhausted. The constant stress of worrying about why her assignment had been terminated and keeping her public persona in place had taken its toll. She quickly removed her suit, hanging it on one of the hangers provided. Most of her clothes were being stored at the Company's expense, and a visit to the storage unit was going to be necessary very soon if she was to blend in with the Company's support staff.

After a quick shower, Kris exited the bathroom and donned a bathrobe before sinking onto the bed. She called room service and ordered a chef's salad, only because she knew she should eat something.

Her thoughts turned back to the events of the past three days. She wasn't the least bit happy to be back at headquarters, although her worst fears had not been realized, and that in itself was a tremendous weight lifted from her shoulders.

The analyst she would be working with had to be fairly sharp to have picked up the pattern on the assassinations. That could be both good and bad. Time would tell.

After eating, Kris checked her gun and laid it on the nightstand next to her bed. She never went anywhere without it. It was the only friend she had. Turning off the light, the tall woman was asleep almost before her head hit the pillow.

KRIS JERKED UPRIGHT in bed, then breathed a sigh of relief when she discovered the disturbance was the ringing of the phone. She glanced at the clock and saw it was eleven. Having absolutely no idea why anyone would be calling her, she answered the phone more out of curiosity than anything else. "Yes?"

"Your uncle wants to talk to you."

Still brushing the cobwebs from her mind, Kris said, "You've got the wrong number."

"I don't think so, Natasha Lubinyenka."

Kris' head began throbbing, and she squeezed the phone until her knuckles turned white, matching her equally pale face. She felt like she'd been punched in the solar plexus. *No. Not now. Not here. Not while I'm under such close scrutiny.*

Chapter Two

SHELBY SLEEPILY EXTENDED an arm from beneath the covers and turned off the alarm clock on her nightstand, bright green eyes suddenly popping open when she realized it was finally Monday.

Tossing back the covers, she sat up, wondering, for what had to be the hundredth time, whether Jeb had decided to assign her the case. On the few occasions that she'd uncovered data concerning a field operative, Dennis had forwarded it to Central Affairs, and her part in it was over. She relished the challenge the case would offer, but was uneasy, too.

Shelby had an excellent memory and had recognized some of the names on the list, but five stood out starkly in her mind: Atlas, Blue, Jet, Roman, and Silver. She had seen each of those names mentioned in wet operation cases she'd reviewed. Would one of them be assigned to work on the case? What would it be like to work with someone from wet ops? Even if none of those five were assigned to the case, she could still end up working with a killer, and she found that thought scary, but fascinating, too. *Must be the psychologist in me.*

Shelby began chuckling at her overactive imagination when a picture of Hannibal Lecter from *Silence of the Lambs* formed in her mind. Shaking her head, she got out of bed and made her way to the bathroom.

Shelby left her apartment a short time later, quickly descending the steps to the surface parking lot. Enjoying the warm sun on her arms, she walked to her new red Mercury Sable, turned off the alarm and unlocked the door with her handheld keypad. A couple of minutes later, she merged with the rest of the traffic for what would be a slow drive to McLean, Virginia.

KRIS SAT DRINKING coffee at the small round table in her hotel room. She seldom had access to American television and had mindlessly flipped through the cable channels before settling on

CNN. She had awakened early from a fitful sleep with a gnawing tension headache that had finally subsided to a dull throb. In the course of three short days, the carefully constructed fabric of her life had begun to unravel, one thread at a time. It was bad enough to be recalled from the field to assist in an investigation based upon circumstantial evidence, but the implications of the phone call the previous night had been disturbing.

I'd actually dared to hope...

Kris impatiently cut off that train of thought and poured another cup of coffee from the pot that room service had delivered. She had little room to maneuver in her new assignment and silently cursed the analyst who was the catalyst for her return. Knowing that type of thinking was self-defeating, she began to focus on how to eliminate the names on that list, her own included, to the satisfaction of the REMFs.

Kris donned black slacks, an off-white blouse, and a red blazer. The combination was striking on her and she knew it. Her intent was to attract attention. Kris was well aware that remaining in plain sight was often a better disguise than lurking in the shadows. After calling a cab, she tied a black silk scarf loosely around her neck, and slipped on a pair of loafer-style walking shoes. Kris touched up her hair and makeup and then, satisfied with her appearance, placed her gun in a small, out of sight holster attached to her belt, and went down to the lobby to wait for the taxi.

During the slow ride to work, Kris made a quick decision to rent a car that evening. She'd been too tired the day before to bother with it, but suddenly it had become a priority. She had places she needed to go.

SHELBY HAD BARELY gotten settled in at her desk when the phone rang. "Shelby Carson."

There was no preamble, no greeting. "Come on down to my office. Jeb gave the go ahead."

Unable to hide the excitement in her voice, Shelby answered, "I'll be right there." She hurriedly shoved her purse into the bottom drawer and walked away, then quickly went back and locked the desk. Shaking her head, she muttered, "Get a grip, already."

Shelby walked briskly up the corridor under the scrutiny of the Marine who regarded her curiously. It was the first time since her arrival that she hadn't spoken to him as she passed.

DENNIS HUNG UP the phone and leaned back in his chair. Jeb had cautioned him against using Blue's code name, which was probably just as well. He didn't know if Shelby paid any attention to the rumor mill, but there was no sense in alarming her if she did. He needed for her to be at her best, not worrying about the deadly reputation of the operative she'd be working with.

Shelby knocked, waiting impatiently for Dennis to respond. When he did, she entered, smiling. "Good morning."

"Morning. Have a seat." Dennis waited until Shelby was settled into the chair next to his desk before beginning to brief her. "I don't think I need to tell you how important this case is. With as much discretion as possible, I want you to eliminate as many of the names on that list as you can. You will be working with," unable to recall Blue's real name, Dennis glanced down at a paper on his desk. "Kris Bartley. I suggest you follow her lead. She'll know what to look for. Any data you need will be made available. I want this investigation kept very low key, but I also want no stone left unturned."

Shelby was surprised that she would be working with a woman. She had never thought of the code names in terms of gender, and had assumed that those on her list were men. On reflection, she realized how naïve of her that had been. "Okay. What happens after the list is narrowed down?"

"The remaining names will be turned over to Jeb. My guess is it'll probably be assigned to some field operatives for follow-up. Any other questions?"

"No. I'll do my best."

Dennis smiled. "I know you will. Kris will be here shortly. I'll introduce you, and then you can get started. Oh, one more thing. I want you both keeping normal hours. It's going to be hard enough to keep this case quiet once you start requesting information; I don't want you calling attention to yourself. If anyone asks, Kris just transferred in. I don't want anything done that might compromise her identity."

She was annoyed that Dennis thought it necessary to mention confidentiality. "I wouldn't do that." Shelby thought about asking what Kris' code name was, but knew Dennis would have told her if he could. He would probably just tell her he didn't want anything to affect her objectivity.

"I have to cover all the bases—" Dennis stopped speaking when a knock sounded at the door and it swung open. Irritated, he glanced up.

"I'm not interrupting anything, am I?" Kris had intended to make an entrance that would give her the upper hand, but her question had been an automatic mechanism to hide her own surprise. A very attractive woman was sitting next to Dennis' desk, watching her with unabashed curiosity and a surprise that matched her own. Kris smiled inwardly at the transparent emotions visible on the seated woman's face. It seemed she wasn't the only one who had been caught off-guard.

Shelby looked over her shoulder as a breathtakingly gorgeous woman walked into the office. The room seemed to shrink in the newcomer's commanding presence. Sunglasses hid her eyes, but Shelby immediately sensed this was not a woman to be trifled with. *This must be Kris.* She certainly wasn't what Shelby had imagined and, sensitive to people, unbidden impressions began floating through her mind: *Tall, dark, dangerous, sexy.* She almost chuckled aloud at the last. *Sexy?*

"No. We were waiting for you." Dennis couldn't believe the brazenness of the operative. Not only did she come barging in, but she was also wearing a bright red jacket. She had that damned inscrutable smile on her face again, and those sunglasses. The woman had to be nuts. And to makes matters worse, he found her incredibly alluring.

He also hadn't missed the open curiosity on Shelby's face and silently warned her, *Don't be fooled by her looks,* unaware that Shelby's own assessment had been warning enough. "Shelby, this is Kris Bartley." Glancing at the intimidating operative, he completed the introduction. "Kris, this is Shelby Carson."

Standing, Shelby extended her hand. "Pleased to meet you."

Kris grasped the extended hand. "The pleasure is mine." She held the smaller hand a little longer than was necessary, enjoying the contact. *Maybe this assignment won't be so bad after all.*

Shelby dropped her hand with mixed feelings. The larger hand covering hers had felt good, and that frightened her. *Kris could be a killer, for God's sake. What is wrong with me?* Her thoughts were interrupted by her boss' voice.

"Keep me informed of your progress."

Kris smirked at Dennis, amused by his attempt to regain control in his office. Her smirk broadened to an arctic smile when he glared at her.

Totally unnerved in the presence of the operative, Dennis just wished she'd get the hell out of his office.

Turning her attention to Shelby, Kris said, "Shall we get started?" It was a statement rather than a question.

"Sure. My office is right down the hall," Shelby hastily agreed, unsettled by the silent exchange between her boss and new partner. She was more than anxious to leave the suddenly tense office behind.

Dennis watched the two women leave. They were as different as night and day, dark and light. He hoped for a quick resolution to the case so that he could be rid of Blue. She almost scared the shit out of him.

IT WASN'T UNTIL Shelby left the office with Kris that she realized just how tall the operative was. She considered herself to be of average height, and Kris towered over her. "How tall are you?"

Kris raised an eyebrow. "Six foot."

Shelby nervously tried to think of something to talk about during the walk down what had suddenly become a very long hallway, and found her sudden loss for words troublesome. "Have you worked here long?"

"No. I've never worked here," Kris answered evasively. While she considered her attractive new partner a perk of the case, she had no intentions of sharing anything except case-related information with her.

"Oh." Shelby took the hint and remained silent until they arrived outside her office. Glancing up at the Marine, she smiled warmly, "Hi."

Nodding slightly, his eyes remained glued on Shelby's striking companion. Much to his relief, after a casual once-over, she strolled by him into the office. Though loath to admit it, he was shamed by the fact that the woman had intimidated him.

Kris' appraisal of the Marine had been anything but casual. She had sized up the guard and dismissed him as no immediate threat. She glanced around the analyst's small office. Three computers sat on a long Formica table on one side of the windowless room. A large, old wooden desk covered with computer printouts was crammed on the other side. The walls were painted institutional green, their lengths unbroken except for a clock above the doorway. *Nice working conditions*, she thought sarcastically and relayed her opinion to Shelby. "You work in here?"

"Well, yeah. You get used to it after a while."

The woman who was more used to wide open spaces had her own doubts about that. She'd never get used to working in such a confined area. "Whatever you say."

Shelby was trying to get a better feel for Kris, but was unable to expand on her initial impression and found that very disquieting. "It's kind of warm in here. They're working on the air conditioning. You can hang your jacket over there, if you want."

Kris hung up her jacket and crossed over to the large desk, waiting for Shelby to join her. "What do you have?"

Shelby knew her research was solid, and relaxed as she briefed Kris on her findings. Once she had covered the basics, she picked up a copy of the report she'd prepared for Dennis and handed it to the operative. "It's all in here."

Kris took the report and injected a slightly incredulous tone in her voice. She needed to know more about her new partner, and angering her was a good way to do that. "So, you were just looking for similarities in the assassinations and happened to notice there were operatives in each location?"

"Yes. That's exactly what happened," Shelby answered, puzzled as to why her methodology was being questioned.

"Sure you aren't just making some leaps in logic to support your theory?"

Green eyes flashing, Shelby cut her off. "If you read the report, you'll clearly see that there is a distinct connection. None of it is tenuous or non-existent. Are you questioning my research because you're on the list? Is that what this is all about?"

Kris had found out what she wanted to know. This woman had backbone and would stand up for what she believed in. Those were two highly desirable attributes in a partner, no matter how mundane the job. "Think I did it?" Kris' expression was neutral, but she was intensely curious about what Shelby's response would be.

That was the last question in the world the analyst had been expecting. Shelby glanced around the room trying to figure out how to answer the question honestly without offending the stoic woman looking at her. They were already off to a rocky start, and the last thing she wanted to do was further antagonize her new partner. She looked up at the operative, only to see her own reflection in the sunglasses. "I really don't know."

Kris quirked a half smile, pleased with Shelby's answer. She knew how uneasy the analyst was, and it had taken a lot of guts for her to answer honestly, and that was the other key ingredient she'd been looking for. "Good. No one on that list should be eliminated arbitrarily."

Shelby was confused. The fleeting smile that crossed the operative's face was puzzling, but somehow reassuring, too. It didn't make sense, but it almost seemed as if she had passed some private test. "So what now?" she asked.

"Pardon?"

"Um, I've never investigated a case involving field operatives. Dennis said to follow your lead." Shelby unconsciously took a step backward as a dark look covered the operative's face.

"You're not assigned to Central Affairs?"

Shelby couldn't imagine working with those ultra-paranoid people. "God, no."

Kris didn't like being caught off guard and asked sharply, "Then why are you working this case?"

"They want to keep it low profile to avoid a potential scandal, and I was already in the loop," Shelby stated quietly, taken aback by Kris' anger.

"Those bastards!" Kris studied Shelby intently. "Just what is your job?"

"I analyze data looking for patterns. If there is a human aspect to the pattern, I develop a psychological profile based on the available information."

"So you're a psychologist?"

"No. I have a Master's in psychology, but I'm also a computer nerd."

Kris was silent as she thought about the implications of what Shelby had told her. Her inexperience in working on cases involving field operatives was a disadvantage. What she should do was go to Earl and tell him to get an experienced analyst from Central Affairs on the case. Two things made her hesitate. She found the emerald-eyed, feisty woman facing her intriguing, and having a relative newby on the case could have some advantages—less suspicion and scrutiny being among them. And when it came right down to it, she hated Central Affairs with a passion, and would much rather work with this woman, experienced or not, than those bastards. Shelby's voice interrupted her thoughts.

"You might try giving me a chance instead of writing me off. I have worked on other cases, and this one can't be all that different."

Shelby's words cemented Kris' decision, and she asked casually, "Why are you still standing there? Let's get started. Show me your data."

Shelby's mind was whirling. This woman was an enigma. "You have it already."

"I have the report," Kris agreed. "I want to see the raw data."

Shelby retrieved a thick sheaf of green and white paper and handed it over. While it appeared that Kris was willing to work with her, Shelby got the feeling that she was on probation. Fair enough; she wasn't sure she really trusted Kris, either.

An hour later, Kris looked up, impressed. "The pattern wasn't easy to spot."

Shelby smiled, pleased at the compliment. "It took me a while."

Kris paced around the room, gathering her thoughts. "Okay, we need airline schedules for each of the airports within driving distance of each operative on that list. For those in the European theater, we also need train and bus schedules. Once we have those, we need passenger manifests. Public transportation is used a lot more over there than it is here. We'll also need to contact all car rental agencies, and, for the locals, taxis."

Impressed by the agent's immediate assessment and action plan, Shelby jotted down key words as Kris spoke. "Okay."

"I need access to the cases the operatives are working on and the location of each." Kris glanced around the room. "Is that information available on one of these computers?"

"Well, yeah, but you have to have a password." When Kris

raised a questioning eyebrow, Shelby feigned innocence and added, "Dennis got me mine."

Not going to share, huh? Smart woman. Too bad, it would've made things a lot quicker. Time to pay Earl a visit. "I'll be back."

Shelby watched Kris walk out of the office. She found the operative absolutely fascinating, and acknowledged that she wanted to know more about her than just what was required by their working relationship. At odds with her conflicting thoughts, she hoped the case would last long enough for her to be able to do that.

EARL CALLED OUT, "Come in," and watched as Kris entered. He sat back, waiting for her to speak.

"I need a password to access the other operatives' files."

"No."

"I'm not going to work blind. Either I have access to the files I need, or you can find someone else to investigate this case."

"I can't give you access. It's against the regs for one operative to be able to access another's files, and you know it."

"The closet rats do it all the time."

Earl sighed. *I should have known she'd bring up Central Affairs. Hell, I hate the sneaky bastards, too.* "That's what they do. It's their job."

"So is this case." Kris smiled sweetly, having played her ace card.

"Technically, that's true." Earl silently cursed as he weighed his options. She'd obviously found out Shelby was not attached to that directorate. He could limit her access to the twenty-seven names on the list and immediately cancel her access upon completion of the case. "Okay. I'll have your current password coded for access. Anything else?"

"No. That's it. Thanks, Earl."

He nodded. Like she had really given him any choice in the matter. Served him right for playing with fire. After all, he had trained her; Earl just hadn't counted on her skills surpassing his own, but they had, in spades.

KRIS, TIRED OF staring at the computer screen, decided Shelby was a lot more pleasing to look at. She had taken off her sunglasses and was sitting at one of the computers, watching her colleague. Shelby was wearing a light green blouse that favored her fair coloring and deepened the green of her eyes. Occasionally, as she leaned over studying the notes she was jotting down, the thin silver necklace she was wearing would fall forward. The analyst had been working at the computer on her desk since Kris had returned from Earl's office. Typing commands and writing, the pattern continued nonstop. Kris quickly diverted her eyes when the younger woman looked up.

Shelby could've sworn Kris had been watching her. She needed a break, and was hungry, but had been pushing herself relentlessly, trying to prove to the operative that she could hold her own. Her normal lunch break had passed a couple of hours earlier, and skipping meals wasn't something she was accustomed to. She decided to break the lengthy silence. "Are you hungry? The cafeteria's not too bad, and it won't be busy this late."

Kris hadn't really thought about lunch. She was beginning to go stir crazy in the tiny office, though, and it would be a welcome break from the stark green walls. A quick smile flickered across her face as she stood up. "Lead on."

Standing at the cold food bar, Kris glanced at the small salad and fruit Shelby had selected. "I thought you were hungry."

"I am, but I'm on a diet. I've gained a couple of pounds, and it's hard to lose weight when you sit at a desk all day."

Kris' eyes slowly moved down Shelby's attractive, lean body. "You look just right to me."

Her cheeks blazing, Shelby muttered, "Uh, thanks," and studied the various selections without seeing any of them. Her body was still reacting to the feel of those brilliant blue eyes as they had traveled the length of her body.

Kris hadn't intended to embarrass the younger woman, she had simply spoken her mind. She thought Shelby looked adorable with her flushed cheeks, not that she intended to voice that thought. She followed her quiet companion through the line, then led her to a corner table, preferring a clear view of any room she was in. Her caution had saved her life on more than one occasion.

Shelby had regained her composure and was quietly pondering her reaction to Kris' compliment as she pushed her salad around on her plate. She had been unable to prevent her body's reaction to Kris' frank appraisal. She tried to thrust the incident from the forefront of her mind. Feeling the operative's eyes on her, she looked up.

Kris wasn't one for small talk unless it served a purpose, but she felt responsible for Shelby's discomfort and, for some unfathomable reason, wanted to put her at ease. "What's fun to do around here besides the tourist traps?"

"You're asking the wrong person. My idea of a night out is dinner and a movie. Now, places to shop, that I can tell you about. I'm gonna stop at Fair Oaks Mall after work tonight." Impulsively, Shelby asked, "You wanna come?"

Kris hadn't expected the question, but quickly recovered.

"Thanks, but I'm not much of a shopper. Besides, I've got to pick up a car tonight."

Shelby hadn't expected Kris to accept, but she was still a little disappointed. "Seen any good movies lately?"

Kris knew Shelby was searching for a neutral topic and decided to help her out. "Nope. How about you?"

"I saw *Charlie's Angels* over the weekend. I really liked it. It was just a good, fun movie. I used to watch all the reruns of *Charlie's Angels* on cable. I loved Kate Jackson. She was really cool."

Kris was enjoying listening to Shelby talk. She had a natural warmth that the operative found endearing. In another time or place, things could have been different, but there was no sense in considering impossibilities. Abruptly dismissing all thoughts but those of the case, she asked, "Ready?" and stood up. Kris looked away from the puzzled expression on the analyst's face, and they walked back to the office in silence.

The next few hours passed quickly and when Shelby stood up at five and started gathering her belongings, Kris quickly followed suit.

Lingering behind until Shelby had left, Kris called a cab. She didn't want to have to turn Shelby down again if she offered her a ride. Kris paused with her hand on the phone. *When was the last time I cared about something like that?* Choosing to ignore her thought, she focused on all the things she had to accomplish that evening, and one of them was already leaving a distinctly foul taste in her mouth.

GREGOR KASLOV WALKED down Wisconsin Avenue en route to the Russian Federation embassy. Contact had been made, directives issued, and all the players were in place. Now all he had to do was check the drops each day. The Americans routinely followed him whenever he left the embassy, and he let them. Checking the various drops only required disappearing for a few minutes at a time. He always made sure to reappear before his shadows panicked, and was careful to systematically vary the locations he checked.

SHELBY WONDERED WHAT she could have said wrong to cause Kris' abrupt withdrawal in the cafeteria. All she'd done was talk about *Charlie's Angels*. No closer to figuring it out now than she had been earlier, her thoughts turned to her body's reaction to the operative's appraisal. The woman had only looked at her, yet her whole body had tingled with excitement. And even as she wondered why, Shelby knew that it certainly wasn't a feeling she would be forgetting any time soon. She was glad when she finally arrived at the mall. She definitely needed a diversion from Ms. Tall and Mysterious, and shopping always relaxed her.

Shelby finally tired a couple of hours and two large department store bags later. A book in the window display of Barnes and Noble caught her attention, and she approached the plate glass for a closer look. As she turned away from the window, she thought she saw Kris out of the corner of her eye, but by the time she could get a clear look, she had disappeared. *It probably wasn't even her—just wishful thinking.*

Shelby walked down the parking lane toward her car. It was a pleasant evening and other shoppers were plentiful. However, trained to caution, when she heard a slight noise she stopped. Glancing around, she tried to determine what the noise had been, but it was not repeated. *My imagination is really working overtime tonight. First I see Kris, and now I'm hearing things. A good, hot, relaxing bath is definitely in order.*

She stopped when she heard it again. Looking down, she located the source of the sound and smiled. Setting down her bags, she slowly walked between two cars then quickly knelt to capture a retreating small gray ball of fur just visible beneath one of the parked cars. As she drew the kitten toward her, a loud crack suddenly echoed through the air, and the rear passenger window of the car she had been standing in front of a microsecond earlier shattered directly above her head, raining glass all over her and the surrounding asphalt.

Shelby bent forward and tucked the ball of fur against her, shielding the kitten from the falling glass. A cold fear gripped her, and she remained frozen amidst the sounds of screams and running footsteps.

Bits of conversation drifted across the parking lot.

"Did you see that? Someone shot at her."

"Is she okay?"

"I don't know."

"There she is!"

Shelby could hear people gathering around her and felt a hand on her shoulder. She looked up to see a mall policeman.

"It's okay, Miss. Whoever fired that weapon is probably long gone. Some of the other mall officers are searching just to make sure, and the Arlington police are on the way."

Shelby slowly stood up, still hugging her living parcel and wondering which of them was shaking the worst.

Chapter Three

SHELBY SPENT THE next hour giving statements to both the mall and Arlington police. There was little she could tell them, for she hadn't seen anything suspicious, and had no idea why she'd been singled out as a target.

One of the Arlington policemen offered to call animal control to take the kitten to a local shelter, but Shelby was unwilling to turn the kitten over to such an uncertain fate. She would find a good home for the tiny creature that had almost certainly saved her life.

Shelby took some comfort from the fact that the police seemed to think the near miss was either a stray bullet or a random attack by a nut case, but remembered the parting words of the investigating officer.

"The chances of finding the perpetrator aren't very good. If we do, you may be required to come down to the station to eliminate the possibility that it's someone you know."

His words sent a chill down her spine. He must have seen her concern because he added, "Don't worry. You were probably just in the wrong place at the wrong time. It happens." As she walked away from the police and bystanders still milling around the crime scene, Shelby didn't find that particularly comforting.

Hanging onto a squirming kitten in addition to all of her packages was no easy feat, and she deposited her shopping bags in the trunk with a sigh of relief. She got into her car, closed the door, and set the kitten on the passenger seat, knowing that the likelihood of the gray fuzzball remaining there was slim to none. However, Shelby had no intention of spending one minute longer than necessary in the mall parking lot. *Better safe than sorry.*

Realizing that her new acquisition would require some necessities, she drove to a large pet supply store that allowed pets inside. Coaxing the kitten out from under the passenger seat, she carried her small friend into the store. Shelby selected a small teal-colored carrier and immediately placed the animal inside before quickly adding litter, food, a collar and some toys to her cart. Glad for the distraction after the harrowing events of the evening, she spoke softly to the complaining kitten as she maneuvered the cart through the store.

SHELBY PARKED HER car and carried her temporary companion inside before going back to retrieve her other purchases. She decided to put an ad in the paper to find a home for the tiny stray. It would be two days before it was listed, allowing her time to take the animal to the vet and get its shots. It was too young to spay or neuter. Shelby chuckled when she realized she hadn't even looked to see if the kitten was male or female.

The refugee just about inhaled the small can of food she put down, and Shelby wondered where it had come from, knowing the kitten couldn't have been born on the streets; it was too friendly. A half-hour later, she finally settled into her chair and watched the kitten explore her small apartment.

Shelby heard a noise and jumped before realizing that it had come from an adjacent apartment. *Oh, I'm in rare form tonight. Just get over it, already.* But doubts still roamed the darker corridors of her mind. *The shooting could be random, coincidence, but why now? Why on my first day working a case involving field operatives?*

She suddenly noticed the light was blinking on her answering machine and pressed the playback button. "Hi, Shelby. It's Mom. Call me later."

"Sorry, Mom, but not tonight," Shelby decided as she hit the button, erasing the message. Her mother frequently let her know in no uncertain terms what she thought of her daughter working at the CIA, and none of it was good. She knew her mother was just worried about her, but no matter how many times she'd explained that she was not a spy, it hadn't made any difference. Her mother firmly believed that you were who you ran with, and in her mind that included work, too. And Shelby knew if her mother ever found out about the shooting, she would hound her relentlessly with 'I told you so's and exert even more pressure on her to find 'more suitable work.' No, she definitely couldn't deal with her mother tonight. Instead, she picked up the phone and called Kim. "Hey."

"Hiya. What's going on? Kinda late for you to be calling, isn't it?"

"Sorry, Kim. I never even looked at the clock."

Kim's voice changed from teasing to concerned. "You know me better than that. I'm always up late. I was just surprised that you are." She paused. "You sound kind of funny. You okay?"

"Yeah. I'm fine. I had an interesting evening at the mall."

"You went shopping and didn't tell me? Did I ever tell you paybacks are a bitch? What was so interesting?"

Shelby began to relax at the sound of her friend's teasing, non-stop chatter. "Well, if you'd quit asking so many questions, I could tell you."

Kim chuckled, pleased that Shelby was sounding more like herself. "Okay, I'm all ears."

Unable to think of any way to break her news gently, Shelby said simply, "Someone shot at me in the mall parking lot."

"What!" Kim's voice was incredulous, but not disbelieving. "Are you okay? I'm coming right over."

"No, Kim, wait; I'm fine. Anyhow, it's too late to come over. We've both got to work tomorrow. I just wanted to talk to someone about it."

"But, Shelby, I think I should come over. Are you sure you're okay?"

"Kim, please calm down. There's no need, really. I'm fine."

"Calm down? My best friend gets shot at, and you want me to calm down? How can *you* be calm?"

"I'm not. That's why I called you. You're supposed to be calm and make me feel better."

"God, woman, not asking much, are you? Okay, tell me what happened. And don't leave out a thing, okay?"

Shelby got off the phone a half hour later feeling much better until, mulling over the police officer's suggestion that it might be someone she knew, she suddenly remembered thinking that she'd seen Kris at the mall. Her mind refused to explore that line of reasoning. *I don't want it to be her.* The implications were too unthinkable. *She wouldn't do that.*

Upset that the idea had even crossed her mind, Shelby decided it was an indication of just how shaken she was and thrust the thoughts from her mind. The incident was purely random, just as she'd conveyed to Kim, and it wasn't the least bit fair to Kris to suspect her of having anything to do with it.

Shelby went to bed a short time later but her sleep was fitful, as she was awakened repeatedly by odd sounds. She knew that the kitten was responsible for the noises, but Shelby could normally sleep through anything, and knew the underlying cause of her restlessness was the shooting.

KRIS ARRIVED BACK in her hotel room after eleven. Her business had taken longer than she'd anticipated because she'd been followed. That in itself irked her, but what was even more troubling was that she could only speculate as to who it had been. She could think of two possibilities, but Kris had been in the business too long to limit the possibilities to only the obvious.

Actually, she mused, *it was a good exercise.* Her tail had been driving a black Honda Accord and had picked her up as she left the Avis car rental office. Since one of her errands was more immediate than the other, Kris set out to quickly lose her pursuer, and was satisfied that it had taken only a few minutes to do so. She smiled, pleased that she hadn't lost any of her evasive driving skills while ensconced in the Middle Eastern desert.

The Accord had appeared again as she was driving down Wisconsin Avenue and Kris had led him on a leisurely sightseeing tour through northern Virginia and Washington, D.C., while at the same time familiarizing herself with the layout of the streets. It was her first trip back to the area since she'd graduated with top honors from her training course, and the operative didn't intend to be caught short by not having escape routes planned. When it was time for her meeting, she'd simply lost him again.

Kris quickly showered, settled onto the bed, and flicked on the TV. She seldom had access to American television shows and flipped through the channels, finally settling on CNN. But she found herself unable to concentrate, her thoughts focusing instead on a set of friendly but wary green eyes. *Just forget about her. She is no different than any of the others.* Closing her eyes tightly, she tried to force the image of the attractive woman from her mind. *She's nothing but danger wrapped up in a pretty package. Besides, she'd hate me if she knew what I did tonight.* Her last thought finally caused the image to fade away and, exhausted from the mentally draining activities of the past few days, she fell asleep.

FOR THE SECOND morning in a row, Shelby was up early, only this time the cause was a small kitten sitting on the pillow, playing with her hair. "Ouch." She lifted the kitten up, set it on her chest, and gently stroked its soft fur. "Just what is wrong with the toys I bought for you?" Shelby chuckled when the kitten looked right at her and meowed. "Whatsa matter? You hungry?" When her companion meowed a second response, she laughed. "Okay, already, I'm getting up."

She fed the kitten, and then played with it for a while before looking through her closet, trying to decide what to wear. Practicality exerting itself in the light of day, Shelby was feeling considerably better than she had the night before. *I probably was in the wrong place at the wrong time. Just hope I never am again.* She selected a rust-colored blouse that contrasted nicely with her light complexion, and paired it with a white skirt. Unaware that she was doing it, Shelby took a little extra care with her hair and makeup before turning away from the mirror.

Shelby bent to pick up the kitten one last time. "I'm gonna find you a great home." She turned the kitten around and looked at its backside. "So, you're a girl. I gotta go now, little one. You be good." Smiling at the purr that answered her, Shelby set her down before opening the door just enough to squeeze through, leaving the kitten inside.

KRIS ROSE EARLY, as she always did, and ordered a pot of coffee. Her mind rapidly explored avenues that would accelerate the elimination of most of the twenty-seven operatives under suspicion. She hadn't been pleased to discover she was included on the list, but wasn't particularly bothered by the fact that her own name would not be among those quickly eliminated. She doubted the case would ever be solved conclusively, regardless. Her main priority was to get out of the assignment at headquarters, and to do that she had to produce a short list of names, the sooner the better.

Try as she might, Kris was unable to keep her thoughts from turning to Shelby. She was unlike anyone the operative had worked with before, and Kris tried to analyze what was so different. When she was unable to isolate the difference logically, her emotions took over and descriptive words began appearing in her mind: *Refreshing, friendly, open, honest, warm, feisty, attractive...*

Kris snorted. "And I need to focus on the case, not the scenery." But even as she spoke the harsh words, she felt a fleeting sense of loss for what could never be. Deep down, Kris knew Shelby was different in a good way, and cursed fate for dealing her the harsh, lonely hand it had.

Consciously casting those thoughts aside, Kris cleared her mind as she continued to sip the strong black coffee. She knew "Uncle" wasn't going to wait too long before getting impatient; she needed to decide how to proceed on that front. The operative had been in tough spots before; it was the nature of her work. Still, this time, Kris knew she would need to use every bit of gray matter she possessed and every trick in her extensive repertoire to survive this dangerous new game in which she was only a pawn.

Torn by her limited options, Kris sighed and made the only decision she could; her personal code of honor would allow no less. But she was well aware that her life would be forfeit if what she was going to do were to be discovered.

An hour later, she left the hotel wearing navy-blue slacks, a pale blue blouse and a white blazer. Getting into the Buick Regal she'd rented, Kris drove toward Langley, her thoughts on how to obtain the information she needed.

SHELBY DEBATED WHETHER to go to her office first or stop to see Dennis, deciding on the latter. She knew the police would forward a report of the mall shooting since a CIA employee was involved, but because of the sensitivity of her work it was also her responsibility to report any unusual events. She grinned ruefully as she entered the director's office. *I think the shooting can definitely be classified as unusual.*

"Hi, Joanne. Is Dennis in yet?"

Joanne nodded and leaned forward conspiratorially. "I just gave him a fax from the Arlington police. I would've been scared to death!"

"Trust me, I was." Shelby waited while Joanne announced her and then entered his office.

Dennis eyed Shelby closely. "How are you?"

"Better than last night. You've already read the report?"

"Just finished." Dennis waved Shelby to a chair. "Tell me what happened." He listened as the analyst related her version of the incident, noting that it was virtually identical to the police report. "Do you have any reason to believe this is case-related?"

Shelby thought the question unfair. If someone had targeted her because of the case she was working on, they sure weren't going to advertise it. "No. But I don't have any reason to believe it's not, either."

Dennis knew she had a point and said, "Have Joanne give you an incident report to fill out. Once I have that, I'll talk to Jeb."

"Okay."

SHELBY FILLED OUT the report quickly and thoroughly, then handed it to Joanne. "Dennis is waiting for this."

Joanne smiled. "I figured."

Shelby rolled her eyes at having stated the obvious. "Sorry. I wasn't thinking."

"No problem. You're doing a lot better than I would be."

After Shelby left his office, Dennis read the police report again. The police seemed to think the incident was simply a random shooting, and he tended to agree. There was a remote possibility it was case-related, but it was unlikely anyone would yet know of her new case. He jotted down a note to call Jeb about it.

SHELBY WALKED INTO her office to find Kris already seated at one of the computers, typing in commands. "Hi."

Kris diverted her eyes from the screen momentarily and nodded. Shelby crossed over to stand behind Kris, looking intently at the screen. "What are you working on?"

"I'm checking the location of each of the operatives."

"I already did that."

"I know. I'm checking it again." Kris turned around in her chair. "Do you have a problem with that?"

Suddenly uneasy, Shelby almost stepped back away from the cool blue eyes that were challenging her. "Just seems like a waste of time."

Kris hadn't intended, nor wanted, to scare Shelby, but she needed to keep the woman at arm's length for more reasons than one. *You might try doing it a little more nicely.* "Look, I'm not questioning your work. I'm checking how long each operative has been in place, and which ones are scheduled for recall or are close to completing their missions. It'll help to eliminate some of the names." *Don't ask how.*

"I..." Shelby bit off her words, clearly reading the silent message Kris was sending. *That doesn't make sense. The point is that they were in place when all three assassinations went down; it doesn't matter when they are scheduled for reassignment. But who am I to question her? She's the one with the experience. But we are supposed to be working on this together.* "How?"

The operative couldn't believe she hadn't intimidated Shelby into silence and tempered her response, knowing she couldn't take a chance on the analyst becoming suspicious. "If any more assassinations occur while we are investigating the case, we can automatically take them off the list."

Shelby decided that was a pretty big "if" because the assassinations had been spread out over six months, but decided not to voice that thought. "I'll work on the airlines some more."

She sat down, glancing over at the operative who was once again pulling up screens and scanning them. Kris had unnerved her. The look she'd been given was just a shade warmer than frosty, and for the first time Shelby wondered if her gut feeling about the woman had been wrong. *No, I was right, but I'd hate to have her for an enemy.* Disjointed images and thoughts from her trip to the mall began floating, unbidden, through her mind, and Shelby buried herself in her work, trying to forget the events of the previous evening.

Turning away from the monitor, Kris glanced at Shelby. She was talking on the phone to one of the airlines, but the operative knew her new partner had been watching her. What she couldn't figure out was why the other woman was so quiet. She'd learned the previous day that Shelby liked to talk. *I wasn't that hard on her, and I did explain what I was doing. So what gives? Is she suspicious?*

Kris glanced at the clock and grimaced; time just seemed to crawl in the small hole. When Shelby hung up, she walked over to her desk and said, "Let me have what you've got on the airlines so far."

Shelby handed the operative one of her legal tablets and immediately began dialing another number on her list. She looked back up when Kris remained in front of her desk, and was almost mesmerized by the blue eyes watching her before she hurriedly glanced away.

Something's definitely not right here. She doesn't know anything, yet she seems to have a major problem with me. I need to find out what's going on in her head. "Want to go get some coffee?"

She wants to get coffee? Shelby looked back up, surprised. Kris was patiently waiting for her answer with a half smile on her face and a raised eyebrow that disappeared beneath her bangs.

"Sure. There's a little canteen over by Dennis' office. Want to go there?"

"Sounds good." Kris had been watching Shelby intently and was relieved when she agreed.

A short time later, they were both sitting in the rear booth sipping their coffee. Kris wanted to come right out and ask what the problem was, but decided a subtler approach would be better. Before she could begin, Shelby spoke up.

"What'd you do last night?"

Interesting question. "Not much. Just rented a car and drove around."

"Drove around?"

"Been a long time since I've been here. Thought I'd take some time to get used to driving here again."

"Oh." *What did you expect? Think she's gonna tell you where she was? Get real.* "I thought I saw you at Fair Oaks last night." Shelby hadn't intended to mention that and was upset with herself for still harboring suspicions when her gut was telling her that Kris had nothing to do with it.

"Nope. Wasn't anywhere near there." *Well, this conversation is going nowhere fast. Guess it's up to me.* "How'd your shopping go?"

"Could've been better."

Kris could have sworn Shelby paled at her question, and she was obviously uneasy. She took a sip of coffee and asked nonchalantly, "Why? Didn't find what you were looking for?"

Relaxing a little, Shelby answered, "Matter of fact, they had a good sale at Hecht's. I got a couple of pairs of slacks, three skirts, and five blouses."

Kris smiled and teased, "Remind me never to go shopping with you."

"Well, they had a big sale. I got seventy-five percent off almost everything I bought. Never could turn down a good deal."

Choosing to end the bantering, Kris asked, "So, what wasn't good about it?" She didn't understand the reticence Shelby had initially displayed and was determined to get to the bottom of it.

"I found a little kitten in the parking lot. I bet she's not more than three months old. She's really adorable. Poor thing was starved. I'm gonna put an ad in the *Post* today to try and find her a good home. I need to make a vet appointment, too."

Kris had always loved animals, but her lifestyle didn't allow her to be able to provide a good home. On the few occasions she had seen an animal being mistreated, the perpetrator had learned a quick and painful lesson and wasn't likely to repeat the offense by the time she finished her on-the-spot training session. "She's a lot better off with you than whatever asshole turned her loose. You probably saved her life."

"Maybe I did, but she saved mine, too." Shelby hadn't intended to voice her thoughts aloud and abruptly stood up. "We better head on back. I'm expecting a lot of return phone calls."

"Wait a minute," Kris began, but Shelby was already halfway to the door. Kris quickly caught up with the shorter woman, listened as Shelby greeted the Marine, then followed her into the office and closed the door. "So, what happened?"

"Someone shot at me in the mall parking lot. The only reason they missed was because I bent down to pick up the kitten."

Suddenly all the pieces started falling into place for Kris, and Shelby's actions that morning began to make sense. "You think I had something to do with it?"

"No. Like I said, I thought I saw you, but no." Shelby saw a quick flicker of emotions cross the operative's face before Kris turned away, and she searched for something more to say.

Staring at the wall, Kris fought an emotion with which she was unfamiliar—hurt. It was clear to her that Shelby had at least considered her being the shooter, and she wasn't sure whom she was more annoyed with—Shelby for her suspicion, or herself for caring what the other woman thought.. She unconsciously donned her most intimidating persona. It was Blue who turned back, and in a steely voice growled, "I don't miss." Then she stalked out of the office.

Shelby sank into her chair, trying to slow her racing heart. Last night's fear paled in comparison to her current feelings, sparked by the angry blue-eyed woman who'd just left.. *You wanted to know what a wet operative looks like. You may have just seen one.* "I really blew that." *I owe her an apology.*

KRIS IGNORED THE secretary and knocked on Earl's door before opening it and entering. "You need to assign someone to protect Shelby, immediately."

Earl felt his guts tighten at the sight of Blue, but calmly asked, "Why?"

"She was shot at in the Fair Oaks Mall parking lot last night. Seems to me someone here should've known about that. Isn't it routine procedure for the police to report any incidents involving a CIA employee?"

"Yes, it is. How is she?"

"How would anyone be? She's scared."

"Do we know it's related?"

Kris smiled sardonically. "You want to take the chance that it's not?"

Earl pressed the intercom. "Cathy, get Jeb on the phone." After talking to Jeb and learning he knew nothing of the incident, he procured Dennis' number from his secretary and called him. Cutting off the director's greeting, he asked, "Do you know anything about a shooting incident involving Shelby Carson last night?"

Dennis' stomach sank. He'd gotten busy and hadn't yet notified his boss. "Yes, I do. I was going to contact Jeb..."

"You were going to? When? Tomorrow? Next week?"

"I had to take care of some priority—"

"What could be a bigger priority than one of our staff operatives getting shot at? I want a copy of the police report, now!"

Kris listened to the one-sided conversation and narrowed her eyes. She hadn't liked Dennis when she met him, and liked him even less now.

Within minutes, the fax machine in Earl's office began to spew out the report. He read it, then handed it to the operative.

Kris decided the entire incident didn't make any sense. Shelby's car had been parked halfway down the lane. She would've been in clear view of anyone who chose to shoot at her long before she ever bent down to pick up the kitten. No professional would've missed such an easy shot. It was much more likely that someone had wanted to scare Shelby, and simply waited for the analyst to be close enough to a car to do just that. *But why?*

She didn't believe in coincidences, and her instincts earmarked the shooting as case-related. She was glad she'd decided to bring it to Earl's attention, because Shelby needed to be protected, and it was obvious Dennis was worthless. It never occurred to her to wonder why she felt so strongly about keeping Shelby safe.

Waiting for Kris to finish reading, Earl took a deep breath, knowing he was going to piss the operative off and wishing there was some way he could avoid it. "I agree that Shelby should be protected. You're it."

"The hell I am!"

His voice hard, Earl said, "I said you're it, and you are. If anything happens to her, I'm holding you personally responsible. I'll set you both up in a safe house."

"I can't do it."

"Why not?"

Kris forced herself to calm, and in the most reasonable tone she could muster said, "It'll never work. She doesn't trust me."

"I don't care if she trusts you or not, neither one of you has a choice. Deal with it."

"This is domestic."

Earl knew where Kris was going and stopped her cold. There was no way he was going to involve the FBI. "You want to be a desk jockey for the rest of your career?"

Kris sighed and stood up. She had wanted Shelby protected, but hadn't anticipated being the guardian of choice. "Who's going to tell her?"

"After I get a safe house set up, we'll meet in Jeb's office. She'll be told then."

Kris left Earl's office, her mood steadily deteriorating. *How in the hell am I going to able to take care of business if I'm busy playing bodyguard? From a safe house, yet.* Her inner voice argued back. *Why don't you just admit the real problem? You're afraid to be that close to her, aren't you?*

She shut out the words and began analyzing her diminishing options as she headed for the canteen, unwilling to return to the office yet. Shelby's suspicion had hurt, but she couldn't afford to become emotionally involved. Cynically, she thought, *So what if she doesn't trust me and is afraid of me? Probably better that way, anyway.*

Then what's the problem? Kris couldn't answer that question, so she ignored it.

SHELBY SAT LOOKING at the papers on her desk, her mind far away. *I like her. I like her and I hurt her feelings. I'd hate to know what she thinks of me right now.*

Standing up, Shelby paced around the small office. Yes, she did like Kris, and was also attracted to her, which made absolutely no sense. The woman was dangerous. She'd seen it with her own eyes that morning, yet it hadn't lessened her desire to befriend the aloof operative. Shelby relied heavily on her gut instinct, and it was telling her in no uncertain terms that she needed to find a way to breach the cool exterior Kris wore like armor. And the tiny doubt that had plagued her just might have done irreparable damage.

Pulled from her thoughts by the ringing of the phone, she watched Kris walk through the door as she answered, "Carson."

Dennis said crisply, "Earl's called a meeting in Jeb's office. He wants both of you there now."

Shelby's stomach fell. Something was definitely wrong if Jeb and Earl were involved, and Shelby worried that she was going to be taken off the case. "Okay. I'll tell Kris." She glanced at the operative, only to catch the woman watching her. "I'm sorry. I..."

"Forget it. It's no big deal."

"Yes, it is. To me, it is. I knew it wasn't you."

Kris' defenses cracked at the sincerity and trust shining from the depths of the soft green eyes. "It's okay," she said reassuringly, "I would've thought about it, too." And deep down, she knew it was true.

Shelby suddenly averted her eyes, the intensity of the moment jarring her. "Um, we've got a meeting in Jeb's office."

Kris just nodded and they walked out the door. Shelby didn't know what to expect and prepared for the worst. "I guess you know what it's about?"

"Yep. You."

"Oh." Shelby hesitated, then voiced her concern. "Did you ask to work with someone else?"

Kris looked down at the smaller woman in disbelief. *If I didn't know better, I'd think she wanted to work this case with me.* "You're not going to be rid of me that easily."

"You didn't ask to be reassigned?"

From playing bodyguard, yes. "Not from the case."

Shelby looked up at the cryptic answer, but before she could ask another question, they arrived at Jeb's office.

Kris moved her chair against the wall, settled her tall frame comfortably into it, and waited for Earl to begin.

Dennis glanced furtively at Blue. It was the first time he'd seen her without her sunglasses, and he'd wondered if the rumor floating around about how striking her eyes were was true. He found out sooner than he anticipated when icy blue eyes met his gaze, and he quickly looked away, totally unnerved by the cold look Blue had directed at him.

Jeb was sitting quietly behind his desk. He hadn't missed the exchange between Blue and Dennis, and just wished for the meeting to be over. Earl scared him, but the tall woman gave new meaning to the word. He would be very happy when they both left his office.

Earl waited until everyone was seated before beginning. "As you all know, there has been an attempt on Shelby's life. It may be completely unrelated to our work here, but I'm not willing to take that chance."

He directed his attention to Shelby. "Until the completion of this case, you're moving to a safe house, starting today. Kris is going with you. You don't go anywhere without her, not even just to answer the door. Is that clear?"

Shelby was annoyed that she'd had no input in this decision, and shook her head in simple disagreement. "No. I can't."

"That's not an option. This is for your own protection. You want someone else taking potshots at you?" Earl hadn't intended to be so harsh, but the analyst was an innocent, and she obviously had no idea just how dicey this case had the potential to become.

Kris glared at Earl when Shelby's face paled, and was pleased to see the woman recover quickly.

"No, I don't want to be shot at. But I don't want to live in some strange house for who knows how long, either. Besides, I have obligations at home." Shelby looked at Kris. "Does *she* want to?"

Smirking, Kris turned mirth-filled eyes toward Earl to see how he was going to handle that. She knew he'd never expected Shelby to say no, although Kris wondered if Shelby's reluctance was because she would have to spend the time with her.

Earl rose to his full height and glared at Shelby as his voice resonated throughout the room. "Neither of you has a choice. You signed a contract when you began working for the CIA. Have you forgotten about that?"

"No, I didn't." At that point, Shelby was beyond intimidation; besides, Earl couldn't touch the daunting level Kris had achieved earlier. "But I don't recall anything in it about having to live in a safe house."

"It does state that you will abide by the decisions of your superiors."

Shelby looked at Dennis, then down at the floor, marshalling her thoughts. She knew it was possible that her life *was* in danger, but it was just as possible that the incident at the mall had nothing to do with their case. The daily news was full of stories about crazies with guns.

She had to spend eight hours a day in a small office without any windows and a guard outside of the door. Cameras mounted in the hallways monitored her every move each time she left the office, and it was likely the safe house would be just as secure. Living in a house where her every move was being observed by people watching monitors was not something she wanted to do. Besides, she hadn't had a chance to find the kitten a home yet.

Shelby loved her job, but valued her personal freedom highly. She decided to up the stakes, hoping her outstanding track record as an analyst would enable her to pull it off. She doubted her gamble would backfire, but the worst-case scenario would be having to comply with Earl's order to stay in a Company safe house. And even though the idea of staying with Kris was very attractive, there was no doubt in her mind that the operative would clam up and never let her guard down while under constant scrutiny.

Her voice was quiet, but determined. "Then I quit."

Kris was the first to recover, and her low, rich chuckle floated across the silent room. She ignored the furious look Earl directed her way.

"Shelby, listen to me. This is for your own good. We're only trying to keep you safe."

"I know you are and I'm sorry, but I think you're over-reacting. Random acts of violence happen all the time."

Dennis couldn't afford to lose his top analyst and glanced at Jeb to get his attention. Once he had it, he whispered a suggestion into his superior's ear.

Jeb nodded. It was worth a shot. "Shelby, how about if Kris stays at your place until your involvement with the case is finished?"

Shelby was surprised by the offer. Her intent had been to get them to back off on the safe house and put surveillance on her apartment, but this was even better than she'd hoped for. Deep down, she really was concerned about her safety, and instinctively knew the operative would protect her from any harm. Of equal importance to her was the fact that it would allow her to get to know Kris outside of work, and she felt a surge of excitement at the prospect.

She glanced over at Kris, only to find her expression noncommittal. *No help there.* "Only if it's okay with her." And Shelby sent a silent prayer to anyone listening that it would be.

Kris felt four pairs of eyes on her. *Things are definitely looking up.* She was grudgingly impressed that Shelby had held her own with these guys. That was no small feat. "Fine."

Earl's eyes drilled into Shelby's. "You understand, the same rules apply? You don't go anywhere without her."

"I understand."

"Good." Earl turned to Kris. "Any questions?"

"I'll let you know."

Chapter Four

THE TWO WOMEN walked back to the office silently, each preoccupied with her own thoughts. Kris was sorting the things she needed to do in order of priority and allotting a certain amount of time for each item so that she could get everything done before quitting time. Shelby was nervously wondering what Kris would think of her apartment and what it would be like having her stay there. Then it suddenly occurred to her that she had been so busy playing with the kitten that she hadn't made her bed. *I didn't straighten up the bathroom, either. Oh great! She's going to think I'm a slob!* Her logical side disagreed. *Relax already. It's just a little cluttered.*

Kris followed Shelby into the office, noticing that she hadn't greeted the hallway guard and wondering what the analyst was thinking about. *I'll have plenty of time to find out later. I need to get going.* She glanced at her quiet companion. "I'll be back before five."

Shelby's brow furrowed slightly. "Okay." *She's probably just going to get her things.* "Do you want me to wait by the door near the north parking lot? That's where I parked."

"No. I'll come down here and pick you up. It's not a good idea to change your routine. Tomorrow we'll ride in together. Since we've been seen working together, no one will think anything of it."

"Okay." The reality of the potential danger in working this case suddenly enveloped Shelby and a worried expression crossed her face, but she was determined not to show any weakness to her confident partner. "Bye."

Kris hadn't missed the fleeting look of consternation and felt a pang of sympathy for her partner. She'd been so wrapped up in her own plight that she hadn't taken into consideration how uncomfortable the whole set-up must be for the younger woman. *So what do I care?* Kris smiled reassuringly and said, "Later," before walking out the door, her demeanor at odds with the unspoken thought.

Shelby sank into her chair, her heart racing. *She has the most beautiful smile.* Smiling ruefully to herself, she wondered what was wrong with her. She could be in danger; an operative she knew nothing about, and who could be an assassin, was going to be staying at her apartment; and all the woman had to do was smile and she melted.

As her pulse returned to normal, the analyst began doing what she excelled at—analyzing. Only this time, Shelby was doing some self-analysis, because it was becoming very apparent to that her interest in Kris had far surpassed normal curiosity. Telling herself that it didn't make sense hadn't helped; she could feel herself react every single time Kris looked at her. And when she gazed into the radiant blue eyes, Shelby felt like she was being pulled through a portal of discovery.

I don't remember ever being attracted to a woman before. How do I feel about that? Shelby stared unseeingly at the wall as she pondered that thought. *And does it matter how I feel? I think I need to get a grip and think about who she is. I know nothing about her. I don't even know which name she is on the list, and undoubtedly she can be very dangerous. I saw that for myself this morning. She was so distant and cold, she didn't even look like the same woman.* Shelby shuddered, remembering, but at the same time justified Kris' actions. *I did hurt her feelings. I never meant to do that, but I did. She does have feelings—she just keeps them hidden.*

Her interest in Kris extended way beyond a very real physical attraction. She wanted to know everything about her. How old was she? Where did she go to college? Where did she live when she wasn't on assignment? What did she like and dislike? She wondered if she would ever be able to get past the cool, confident demeanor and get to know her partner on a personal level. Would Kris even allow such a thing?

Shelby thought then of Brian, a man she had been dating on and off for the previous six months. He was a nice guy and she had fun with him, but her level of interest had never surpassed that of casual dating—going out to eat or seeing a movie. She'd told him that she wasn't interested in a relationship other than friendship, and encouraged him to date other women. He still called occasionally, though she had been pleased to find out he was following her advice. Now that she thought about it, none of the men she had ever dated had made her feel the way she did with just one look from Kris, nor had she ever been so intensely interested in everything about them either.

Shelby leaned back in her chair, folded her arms, and sighed with frustration. She knew she'd have to conceal her interest; she didn't want to alienate the operative. *The truth is—I'd like us to become friends, preferably, very good friends, but how do you develop any sort of relationshp with an enigma? She's so controlled and sophisticated,* and I can't even tell what she's thinking half the time. I know one thing, though—I'll be safe with her around.

The analyst ran a hand through her hair, and then leaned forward, resting her chin in her palm. *I need to get busy.* Shelby looked at the phone numbers remaining on her call list, but she remained distracted. *I wonder what she likes to eat? Maybe we'd better stop at the grocery store on the way home.* Shelby snorted at the ease with which "we" had overridden the normal "I." *Geez, I'm acting like I have a crush on her.* She shook her head wryly and challenged herself, *Don't you?* Struggling to do so, Shelby finally pushed her errant thoughts to the back of her mind, reached for the phone, and began dialing an airline.

QUICKLY PACKING ALL belongings, Kris left the hotel, planning on checking out later by phone. She had to make a drop before she picked up Shelby, and they weren't going to like what she had to tell them. With luck they would forget about her, permanently this time. *Fat chance of that.* The operative narrowed her eyes. *Great, be a cynic. That'll help a lot.*

Kris' thoughts turned to Shelby. She couldn't deny that she found her new partner interesting as well as attractive. Shelby had an innocent yet wise aura that Kris found very appealing. She was also impressed with her perception and intelligence. And that was part of the problem. If she allowed her to get close, the younger woman might start getting suspicious and it could only end in betrayal—her own.

*I wish...*Kris shut off the thought, not wanting to focus on her bleak life or on just how lonely she was. The only sign of her distress was the slow, tired gait with which she walked to her car. *It's going to be hard being around her all the time.*

As Kris approached her destination, she checked again for any sign of a tail and found none. For some reason, whoever was following her seemed to think it was only necessary after work hours. She smirked. *Really stupid move, guys.* She reviewed the message she was leaving:

> Will be out of the net until further notice. Any attempt to make contact could result in a security breach. Contact will be resumed at a later date.

Much, much later.

Kris seriously doubted they would honor her request, but she had to try. Her free time had just become non-existent, and even though Kris knew she could escape the scrutiny of Shelby's security team if necessary, her hope was that her control was not aware of that. *They seem to have a lot of inside information; my assignment as a bodyguard might not be news to them.*

Suddenly suspicious, Kris thought about the odd shooting incident and wondered if the whole chain of events wasn't a part of someone's master scenario. Shelby seemed to have unlimited access to all the Company's computerized information. What if they knew that? Perhaps she *was* a target. It was definitely something to think about.

She turned onto M Street and drove toward an emergency drop location in Georgetown. Kris figured that by leaving her information there, she would reinforce the seriousness of the message. Her biggest problem was that she didn't really know who she was dealing with. If her note didn't accomplish what she intended, it should at least provide her some insight on the reliability of their sources and whether they had infiltrated the Agency. She sighed, anxious to rid herself of this new complication in her life, if only temporarily.

It was likely that her tail would pick her up after work again, and it was going to be difficult shaking him without alerting Shelby to his presence. *And speaking of Shelby, I should do a drive by and check out her neighborhood.* Kris realized she had forgotten to ask the analyst her address, and cursed the omission. Knowing that even her specially modified cell phone was not totally secure, she left Georgetown and turned into a convenience store parking lot, steering her car toward a phone booth located at the far end of the structure. Kris dialed the office number and waited for Shelby to answer.

"Carson."

"Hi. What's your address?"

Shelby smiled at the sound of Kris' voice, even as her mind pondered why the operative wanted her address now.

"The Fairfax Gardens, 3857 Armstrong Street. I live in building two, apartment 203. What are you up to?"

Kris committed the address to memory. "I'm going to drive through the neighborhood and get a feel for it." *And plan escape routes, just in case.*

"Oh."

The operative was surprised that one word could convey so much and projected confidence in her voice to help set Shelby at ease. "It's just a routine precaution. Nothing to worry about." *Hopefully.*

Somewhat reassured, Shelby searched for a way to extend the conversation. "Do you need directions?"

Kris knew exactly where that apartment complex was, but she had finished her errands ahead of schedule and was in no hurry to hang up. "Sure." Her brow furrowed when it dawned on her that she was allowing her personal interest in the analyst to dictate her actions. When Shelby finished relaying the directions, she said, "Thanks," and immediately hung up the phone, angry for allowing herself to be drawn to the other woman.

Shelby just stared at the phone with its mocking disconnect buzz. *She did it again. We were having a perfectly normal conversation and she just withdrew. Why do you do that?* The analyst knew she might never discover the answer, but was determined to try.

She looked speculatively at the computer on her desk. She could access Kris' personnel file if Kris was actually her real name. *One way to find out.* Fingers poised above the keyboard, Shelby stopped, warring with her conscience. Her interest was strictly personal and had nothing to do with the case. She also knew Central Affairs monitored all computer activity, internal and external. That didn't really bother her, though, because she figured she could find some way to justify the query.

Shelby silently argued with herself. *What would she think of me if she thought I was nosing around in her file?*

How would she ever find out?

True.

How would you like it if she accessed your file?

I'd love it, because she wouldn't do it unless she was interested in me beyond the case.

You're just trying to justify it.

Shelby sighed. *Yes, I am.* She shoved her curiosity to the back of her mind and dialed the next telephone number on her list.

KRIS DROVE THROUGH the Fairfax Gardens apartment complex, noting nothing that distinguished it from the multitude of others with which she was familiar. There were four sand-colored brick buildings, each three stories high and accessed by outside steps. There was only a handful of cars in the parking lot that extended from the first building to the last. Security-wise, if there were a problem it would be a nightmare; there was no alternate escape route, such as a back stairway.

The operative drove around the bordering residential streets until she was completely familiar with the surrounding area. Glancing at her watch, she quickly accelerated toward the Beltway, not wanting to be late and cause Shelby to vary from her routine. *Is that the only reason?* Shoving down the anticipation she was feeling, Kris issued a stern warning to herself. *This is just a job. I can't afford to forget that.*

Shelby looked at the clock for what seemed like the tenth time in the last five minutes and felt a pang of disappointment. It was 4:59

and Kris still hadn't returned. It seemed fairly obvious that her interest in having the tall woman stay with her certainly wasn't reciprocated by her partner. *Did you really expect it to be?* Shelby shook her head. *No. But it would've been nice.*

Kris suddenly walked in, interrupting her thoughts; a warm smile lit Shelby's face. Finding herself tongue-tied, she simply said, "Hi." *Oh, that was real original.*

Kris was unable to suppress an answering smile. Shelby was just so sweet. "Hi yourself. Ready?"

Shelby nodded and quickly retrieved her purse. "Am I ever! It's been a long day."

"You drive a red Mercury Sable, right?"

Shelby blinked. "Uh, yeah. How did—"

Kris chuckled. "Read the police report after you told me about the incident. What row are you in?"

"C, about halfway down."

"I'm driving a blue Buick Regal. I found a place in A. Wait until you see me in your rearview before heading for the parkway." Kris knew her tail would most likely be on the job. "One more thing: if you don't see me, don't worry about it; I'll be around."

"Okay." Shelby was just about to walk out the door when she stopped and turned to face Kris. "Do we have time to stop at the grocery store? I need to pick up a few things, and also I don't know what you like to eat."

Although her face remained impassive, Kris' was unaccountably pleased by Shelby's thoughtfulness. "It's not a good idea to stop since we're not riding together. Whatever you have in the fridge is fine."

Shelby wanted Kris to feel comfortable, and that included having meals she liked. "How about tomorrow?"

Grinning inwardly at Shelby's tenacity, Kris agreed. "Sure." She was rewarded with a sunny smile before they split up for their respective parking lanes.

Kris' muscles tensed reflexively and she traversed the lot in a full state of alertness, her senses fully extended and her demeanor predatory. She surveyed the parking lot in a deceptively casual manner, never taking her eyes off Shelby until the analyst was settled in her car and had begun to back out of her parking place. Seeing nothing out of the ordinary, she quickly moved to her own car and pulled into position behind the red Sable.

Just as Kris had suspected he would, her tail picked her up on the parkway. She smiled grimly. *Soon, I'll either know who you are or you'll be dead.* Kris turned off on the same exit she had the previous evening and drove back to the Sheraton. After parking her car in the underground garage, she quickly made her way to her room and changed into the jeans and pullover top she'd purposely left behind.

Kris took the metal fire escape to the second floor and, rather than lowering it to the cement below, she grasped the metal rungs with her hands and swung herself down until she could easily jump to the ground. She cut through an adjoining building, exiting the rear door and casually walking up the side street to a dark green Lexus she had parked there earlier. Ten minutes later, the operative steered the Chevy into Shelby's apartment complex minus one tail.

Shelby knew Kris had turned off back on the parkway, but was surprised when she got to her apartment and the operative hadn't reappeared. She gave up trying to guess what Kris was doing, glad to have the opportunity to make her bed and pick up the bathroom, dismissing the inner voice that advised her to wait until the operative returned before crossing the parking lot and entering her apartment.

When she opened the door, the kitten came running and meowing. Shelby picked it up, smiling as she cuddled it. "Bet you're hungry." She carried her into the kitchen and set her down, opened a small can of kitten food and poured it into the refugee's dish before quickly making her way to the bedroom. Shelby hadn't had a chance to finish her tasks when a knock sounded at the door. "Just a minute." She quickly threw her towels in the hamper before opening the door in invitation. Then froze, staring at the visage in her doorway before retreating into the apartment.

"You didn't even look to see who it was!" Blue was in full intimidation mode; she knew she was scaring Shelby, but the analyst needed to be held to account on all security measures.

"I was expecting you."

Blue snapped, "Did you *know* it was me?"

"I made a mistake, okay?" Shelby was struggling with a combination of fear and anger. What she had done was careless, but she felt like Kris was overreacting, and the operative was downright scary. At the same time, she was crushed that she had appeared inept. "It won't happen again."

"Make sure it doesn't." Kris set down her overnight bag. She'd left the remainder of her clothes in the car, easily accessible if she needed them.

Shelby retreated to her bedroom and closed the door. Yes, what she had done was stupid, but it wasn't like she was used to living some cloak and dagger lifestyle, either. *And when in the heck did she have time to change into jeans? Well, I sure didn't make any points with her. But she didn't have to be such a bitch, either.* The analyst squared her shoulders. *I knew it wasn't going to be easy, so let me see if we can start all over again.*

Kris sank down onto the couch and lowered her head into her

hands. *Why did I do that? That was not necessary. I could have explained the danger to her nicely.* In a moment of total honesty, Kris acknowledged, *I did it to push her away. She doesn't deserve to be treated like that. I've always been able to maintain a professional distance when I needed to, but I'm having difficulty doing that with her. This is just a job; she shouldn't matter to me. But she does. And that's the problem. There's something about her...*

The operative heard the bedroom door open and quickly stood up. She gazed around the apartment, taking in the comfortable, homey décor. The carpet was buff and the overstuffed couch and matching chair were a blend of very light mauves, blues, and teals intricately woven into a beige background. Centered on small tables on either end of the couch, there was a pair of mauve tinted glass lamps with an attractive flower painted on the base. A matching heavy oak coffee table sat in front of the couch. Kris' perusal was interrupted by Shelby's voice.

"Want something to drink?"

Kris wanted to apologize, to say something light, anything, but the words weren't there. "Do you have any Coke?"

"Diet okay?" Shelby chuckled at the look on Kris' face. "Guess that's a no. How about ginger ale?"

"Sounds good."

When Shelby returned from the kitchen, Kris accepted the can she offered. "Do I get a tour?"

"Sure, but why don't you just sit down and relax for a few. I want to change clothes. You already did. How did you manage that, by the way?"

"Trick of the trade."

Shelby chuckled at the cryptic comment. "Uh huh. Be right back."

"Take your time." Kris leaned back against the couch and quirked a half-smile. "I'm not going anywhere." She grinned, listening to Shelby chuckle as she walked away.

She resumed her perusal of the small apartment, her eyes taking in an open laptop on one end of the dining room table with a few papers lying next to it and a vase of artificial flowers pushed off to the side. On one wall, there was a bookcase with glass doors, and on the opposite wall a patio door led to a large balcony. Kris crossed the room headed toward the balcony, when the bookcase caught her attention as she passed. Stopping, she gazed curiously at the contents.

It contained a small collection of mystical creatures. Leprechauns, fairies and elves danced around a family of unicorns. On the shelf below, a statue of Pegasus with his wings fully extended as he reared was facing an intricately painted dragon with fire spewing from its mouth. A few of the fairies and elves looked old, and Kris wondered how Shelby had come to develop an interest in the magical creatures of fairy tales and myths.

Her acute hearing picked up the sound of a footfall on carpet and she stepped away from the bookcase, not wanting to be caught studying the knickknacks. Continuing to the patio door, she slid it open. As she stepped out onto the balcony, Shelby joined her.

"I love sitting out here in the evening. It's so peaceful."

Kris glanced down at Shelby, taking in the tranquil look on her face, and nodded, hating that she was going to have to spoil it. "It is nice out here, but you should avoid doing that for a while."

Shelby sighed, knowing that what Kris said made sense. "Okay. What would you like for dinner?"

"Anything is fine. Do you have any TV dinners? I can just throw one in the microwave."

"No. I don't usually buy those. Do you like spaghetti? Or how about pork chops? I've got some chili I made in the freezer."

"Shelby, wait." Kris waited until she had her attention. "I'm not your guest. You don't have to cook for me. You didn't ask for this any more than I did. Just do what you usually do and pretend I'm not even here."

Yeah, right. As if I could, even if I wanted to. "No. I won't do that. You are here and you're stuck with me because I might be in danger. I'm glad you're here, and I'm not going to ignore you."

She's glad I'm here? Kris liked how that thought felt, but it troubled her, too. She knew she had to put a halt to anything other than a business association. "You might as well, because I'm here to do a job, that's it."

"Fine. But I'm still not ignoring you, and if I make something to eat, I'm making enough for both of us. I wouldn't want the person protecting me to be too weak to do her job effectively."

Kris had to smother a smile at Shelby's last comment. "I didn't mean to offend you. I just don't want you to go to any extra trouble on account of my staying here."

Shelby met Kris' eyes. "It's no trouble."

Kris had to force herself to look away from the dancing green pools brimming with sincerity. The operative realized she wasn't going to win this battle and strategically capitulated. "What do you want me to do?"

"Protect me, of course." Shelby grinned when a smile finally appeared on Kris' face.

"That I can do."

"Why don't you put your things in the bedroom? I'll change the bedding for you after dinner."

"I'm not taking your bed. I'll sleep on the couch."

Shelby looked at the couch and then looked up at Kris. "Just how do you think you're going to fit on it?"

"It'll be more comfortable than a lot of places I've slept."

Nodding her understanding, Shelby decided to make dinner. They could talk about it later. It didn't make any sense to her to have Kris sleep on the couch. She'd fallen asleep on it more than once and it was just big enough for her. Kris was more than half a foot taller than she was.

Shelby walked over to a closet in the alcove by the apartment door and pushed aside her winter coat and a couple of lighter jackets. "You can hang your clothes in here, if you want."

"Thanks." Kris grinned ruefully as she watched Shelby walk into the kitchen. Maintaining a professional distance was going to be even tougher than she had thought it would be.

An hour later, they finished eating the spaghetti dinner Shelby had prepared and Kris helped her clear the table, placing the dishes in the dishwasher. "That was delicious. You're a good cook."

A slight blush appeared on Shelby's face. "Thanks."

The remainder of the evening passed quickly with Shelby carrying most of the conversation, determined to get the tall woman to relax. As she listened to Shelby chatter, Kris felt some of her tension fade while she softly petted the kitten that had deserted Shelby's lap to curl up in hers.

At eleven, Shelby stood up. "I'm beat. I'm going to take a shower and go to bed. I'll put out some towels and a washcloth for you when I'm finished."

Kris nodded and turned on the mute button on the TV. She looked back at Shelby when the analyst called her name. "Yeah?"

"I want to sleep on the couch. There's a small TV in the bedroom you can watch."

"I thought we'd already settled where we were sleeping?"

"You're not gonna be comfortable on the couch. Why don't you take the bed?"

Kris found it hard to reject the sincere appeal that was evident both in Shelby's voice and on her face. "I won't be able to hear or see enough from the bedroom."

Shelby sighed. "Okay." She had enjoyed Kris's company so much she had almost forgotten why Kris was there.

"Shelby." Kris waited for the analyst to look at her. "Thanks for the offer." Kris was favored with a smile that warmed her heart. *Oh, am I in trouble.* "Night."

"Goodnight."

A short time later the lights in the apartment were extinguished and both women faded into their respective dreams.

Chapter Five

JEB LOOKED UP in surprise when the doorbell chimed. His wife Sharon had gone to bed before the late news started, so he hurried to the door, not wanting her to be awakened. When he saw his younger brother through the peephole, a smile spread across his face and he unlocked the door, pulling it open.

"Michael! When did you get back? Come on in." Jeb looked up at his brother, grinning. Michael was 6'3" with closely cropped, nearly black hair. Jeb ruefully acknowledged his brother had gotten the looks in the family. His wife had even commented that Michael could have been a model for the cover of Harlequin romances, had he chosen to.

"Hey, Jimbo. Just got back. I decided to take a few days of leave." Michael had actually been in town for two days, but his brother didn't need to know that. "I know it's late, but I couldn't wait to see you. It's been what, two years?"

"At least. You're staying here, aren't you?"

"I don't want to put you out..."

"You won't be. Hell, the spare bedroom hasn't been used since the last time you stayed here. You still on cold loan?"

Jeb had been secretly relieved when Michael had requested to be transferred from field operations to the much safer work of providing technical assistance to allies on their intelligence gathering operations.

"Yeah."

"Want something to drink?"

"How about some of that good Scotch you keep hidden." Michael watched his brother prepare their drinks, his thoughts far away. For two years, his life had been a living hell, but for the past six months he'd been laying the groundwork to change that. There were only a few more pieces to put into play, but he needed some information first, and his doting big brother would be a good source.

Jeb handed Michael a Scotch on the rocks. "It's more comfortable in the living room." A few hours and much catching up later, Jeb looked at the clock, surprised it was approaching 3:00. "I gotta get a few hours of sleep. You must be tired, too."

"Yeah, I am."

Michael followed his brother out of the living room, turning into the guestroom as Jeb continued on to the master bedroom.

KRIS ROUSED FOR the third time as her subconscious picked up on a barely discernable noise. Alert now, she listened intently in the dark, silent room, her eyes traversing shapes illuminated only by a sliver of light visible between the drawn drapes. Satisfied there was no cause for alarm, she decided to get up anyway. Her internal clock was uncannily accurate and Kris knew it was close to 05:00, her customary waking time.

The operative quietly made her way to the bathroom, but detoured toward a faint light coming from the bedroom farther down the hallway. She stopped in the doorway and gazed at Shelby, the nightlight in the globe of the lamp next to the bed casting a small beam of light across both the sleeping woman's face and the kitten sleeping next to her on the pillow.

Smiling at the wayward locks of blonde hair mussed by sleep and the sheet wrapped around Shelby's middle, Kris resisted the urge to straighten out the bedding and cover her up, not wanting to waken or frighten her. *You look so content. What are you dreaming about?* Kris was glad it apparently was more peaceful than the nightmare visions in *her* dreams.

She wondered briefly why the nightlight burned. Kris had studied people for years in order to better learn how to blend in with the local populace when on an assignment, and one thing she'd learned was that there was usually an underlying reason for each habit a person exhibited. The operative suddenly felt a surge of protectiveness toward this virtual stranger.

Kris backed out of the doorway, unsettled by the intensity of her reaction and struggling to bury the troubling emotion. She was finally able to do so only by forcing her true identity into her mind's eye, and along with it, the distancing she had developed in order to survive.

After a quick detour to the bathroom, Kris entered the kitchen and turned on an overhead light. She saw the tell-tale red light glowing on the coffee maker on the speckled beige Formica counter, and switched the timer off to start the coffee brewing as she studied the kitchen. The night before, her impressions of the apartment had been general assessments made primarily from a security standpoint. Alone now, she could study the decor unobserved and hopefully gain some insight into her new partner. Kris' analytic mind refuted the contention that her interest was solely professional. With steely resolve she quelled the doubts that plagued her, unwilling to admit to any personal curiosity.

With an eye trained to notice the smallest details, Kris scanned the tiny room. It was little more than a wide aisle between the dining room and hall, and she decided it would be a tight fit for more than one person at a time. A white refrigerator and stove were centered on one side, with a sink and dishwasher on the other, and cupboards surrounding all the appliances. Thinking of Shelby's short stature, Kris opened a cupboard over the refrigerator out of curiosity. She had expected it to be empty, but instead found a cache of cooking herbs and spices. *Makes sense. Stuff she probably doesn't use every day.*

She looked into the dining room, her eyes skimming the bookcase of figurines she had examined the previous night, then turned her attention to a matching bookcase that was filled with more traditional wares—hardback and paperback books. Kris' eyes skipped over the college textbooks and lingered on the other titles, which included quite a variety of reading material—ranging from sagas like *The Clan of the Cave Bear* to thrillers, most notably *Silence of the Lambs*. Finishing her perusal, the operative concluded that Shelby's favorite reading material was probably romance and mystery novels, but it was difficult to ascertain for sure because of the mishmash of other genres evidenced on the shelves.

The next thing to capture her attention was a picture on the wall. It was a still-life painting of a single pink rose, elegant in its simplicity and a sharp contrast to the magical creatures displayed in the bookcase. Kris glanced quickly at the papers spread over the table, discerning that Shelby was taking an online course in investigative techniques. She smiled, impressed. *You don't intend to be caught short, do you?*

Demanding, high-pitched mewing interrupted her thoughts. She looked down at the little beggar and grinned. "Come on. Your food is in the kitchen." Kris quickly opened a small can of food and dumped it into the dish Shelby had left on the floor. Watching the kitten bolt it down, her thoughts turned back in time.

Her mother came home from work carrying a covered basket. She set it on the floor and said, "Happy birthday, Natasha."

She frowned and looked up at her mother. Even at the tender age of five she knew they were very poor, and to receive a gift was incomprehensible to the young child.

"Go ahead and look," her mother encouraged.

Not needing a second invitation, she opened the lid of the basket and her eyes widened in surprise as she lifted out a tiny white kitten. She had asked her mother for a kitten many times, but had been steadfastly refused on the grounds that they could not afford to feed a cat. Gently holding the kitten close, she rubbed her cheek softly against its fur, smiling delightedly. "Thank you, Mama. I love it." She carefully set the kitten back in the basket and threw herself into her mother's embrace, her thin arms dwarfed by her mother's stature. She promised her mother, "I'll share my food with it."

Her mother had kissed her head. "Igor said that if you help him around the store each day after school, he will pay you with food for the kitten."

"I will, Mama. I'll help him every day!"

She had, too, until her life had spun irrevocably out of control. Kris deliberately cut off the recollection. It had been years since she had allowed that memory to surface, and she was angry that it had slipped past her defenses now. *What's wrong with me, anyway? It's gotta be this damn case.* Shaking her head, she resolutely ignored the inner voice that suggested, *More likely your new partner. She's getting to you.*

The operative stalked to the balcony door, threw aside the drapes, unlocked it and stepped outside. Dawn had barely begun to lighten the sky, and she stayed in the shadows while carefully scanning the parking lot for anything unusual. Kris relied heavily on a finely honed sixth sense that alerted her to danger, and her instincts corroborated her visual scan—there was nothing out of the ordinary.

Shelby was a problem, and Kris knew she needed to regain control of her emotions to avoid any more lapses. *Damn woman isn't making it any easier, either.* Discovering the relationship between operatives' locations and the assassinations required a very organized, intelligent approach. Then she worked relentlessly, even skipping lunch to prove herself. *Why? What does she care what I think? And she has to go and insist on cooking for both of us, and even tries to give me her bed. Why couldn't I have gotten some dull, boring analyst?*

SHELBY WOKE TO the smell of brewing coffee and glanced at her alarm clock, noting it was only 5:30. Much more interested in spending time with the enigmatic operative than staying in bed, she decided to forgo the extra hour of sleep and got up, donning her robe.

She was greeted by a gray furball sitting contentedly next to an empty dish, cleaning her face thoroughly with a paw. "You are too cute!" Shelby bent down and stroked the kitten a couple of times before standing up and letting the kitten resume her bath.

Kris must have gone back to bed. Walking quietly into the living room, she saw an empty couch and slightly separated drapes. Shelby moved so that she could see through the small opening, and gazed at the tall operative standing on the small balcony in just her long white nightshirt. A steady breeze was blowing wisps of hair across her face, but Shelby could see a far-away, troubled expression on the other woman's countenance. She wondered what demons haunted Kris, yet knew any attempt to find out would be rebuffed, so she returned to the kitchen with an alternative approach in mind.

Kris, who had been lost in her thoughts, whirled around when she felt a presence behind her. Her resolve to distance herself began to fade when she saw Shelby standing there in a pink cotton robe with locks of hair lying every which way, smiling warmly and holding out a cup of coffee.

"It was ready. Thought you might like a cup."

"Thanks." Kris raised an eyebrow. "Where's yours?"

"I left it inside. I didn't know if you wanted any company."

Kris smiled. "I don't want you out here. I'll join you inside."

Shelby couldn't keep her smile from widening and turned away, a little embarrassed that she was so pleased Kris was going to join her. *You'd think drinking coffee together was a big deal.*

The operative watched the analyst walk back inside before slowly following her. *It's only for coffee.*

Quickly gathering her papers and stacking them in a pile on a corner of the table, Shelby closed the laptop and set it on the floor next to the bookcase. She glanced up to find Kris watching her. "Thought I should make a little room."

Shelby waited for Kris to sit down and then joined her, searching for a neutral subject that wouldn't be too intrusive, but would allow her to learn more about her companion. She decided their jobs should be a safe topic. "Have you worked for the Company long?"

Kris looked intently at Shelby's open, friendly face and decided to answer. "Ever since I graduated from college." She almost chuckled at the expression on Shelby's face that clearly asked, 'and?' "Eight years. How 'bout you?"

"Not even a year yet. It wasn't my first job out of college. I kind of stumbled into it, answered an ad in the paper." Shelby knew they sometimes sent representatives to the various universities, and asked, "Did they recruit you out of college?"

"No. An aunt and uncle raised me. My uncle wanted me to follow in his footsteps and go to West Point. We compromised on the Company." That part was mostly true, except those two cold strangers had not been relatives. Kris had joined the CIA with a much different agenda than the one her "relatives" had planned for her, and she had successfully implemented it until her recent recall from the field had allowed the shadows of her past to once again materialize.

Shelby gazed at the contemplative expression on Kris' face, wishing she knew what the other woman was thinking about. Her thoughts were interrupted when the kitten jumped into her lap. "Oh no. Not at the table." She gently set the kitten on the floor and chuckled when it walked away, insulted at the rebuff.

"What did you name the kitten?"

"I haven't. I didn't want to name her because I'm not keeping her. I don't want her to be lonely when I go to work, so I'm going to try and find her a home where someone is home during the day."

"I don't think you're going to find her a better home than the one she has right now."

Shelby blushed at the unexpected compliment. "Thanks. I just don't want her to be lonely."

"She's not. Look at her."

Shelby watched the kitten chase around the room after one of the small balls she had bought for her.

"She probably sleeps all day when you're gone. I read once that cats sleep twenty hours a day. Anyway, you didn't put an ad in the paper yet, did you?"

Busted! Shelby had justified that by being too busy working on the new case, but she had found time to make a vet appointment for Saturday. "No."

Kris quirked a half-smile. "So, what're you gonna name her?"

"Maybe Angel." She laughed when Kris rolled her eyes. "Well, do you have any better suggestions?"

"How about Scruffy."

"I'm sure!" Shelby studied the frolicking kitten, trying to think of a fitting name. "Her fur is the color of clouds during a thunderstorm."

Kris turned mirth filled eyes on Shelby. "Don't tell me you're gonna name her Thunder."

Shelby chuckled, enjoying the exchange. "You're not being serious. I was thinking more along the lines of Stormy. I think it kind of fits her."

Glancing at the kitten, Kris agreed. "Yeah, it does."

"Glad you approve," Shelby teased, then smiled inwardly when a slight blush darkened Kris' cheeks. "What do you like for breakfast?"

"Coffee."

Shelby was not going to be deterred in her effort to make Kris more comfortable. "What else?"

"I don't usually eat breakfast."

Two can play this game. "When you do eat breakfast, what do you like?"

Kris hid a smile at Shelby's tenacity. It was apparent her that while she was determined not to burden her hostess, Shelby was just as determined to make her feel welcome. "Eggs, bacon, toast, juice, fruit..." She started laughing when her companion's forehead furrowed in concern. "I'm only kidding. An English muffin or bagel is usually all I have unless I eat a late breakfast on the weekend."

Shelby shook her head at the recalcitrant woman. *You just might have a surprise coming Saturday.* "I've got some plain bagels. Do you like orange juice?"

"Yeah, that sounds good." She watched Shelby gather their breakfast in the small kitchen and stood up to help her carry the glasses of juice.

A short time later, Shelby glanced at the clock. "I can't believe it's time to get ready for work already. Why don't you use the bathroom first?"

"Nah. You go ahead. It won't take me long."

"Okay."

Kris watched Shelby cut through the kitchen to the hallway then disappear from view before she got up to refill her coffee cup. The operative knew she was enjoying Shelby's company more than she should; she was drawn to her on some basic level she seemed unable to control, and that frightened her.

LATER THAT DAY, both women were ensconced in front of computers. Shelby had already silently chastised herself several times for not focusing, instead alternating between unobtrusively watching Kris and trying to figure out a way to draw out the investigation without offering the elusive assassin any more opportunities. She knew that the relationship between the locales of the operatives and the assassinations could be purely coincidental, too. Her evidence had merely exposed a potential connection that had to be evaluated and eliminated. *What I would give to know if it is anyone on the list.* Shelby sighed. *But I don't know, and I can't take a chance it's not.*

She had been distracted since they had arrived at Langley that morning, but had finally been able to concentrate on the airline manifests long enough to eliminate three names from the list. Unobserved, Shelby watched Kris a moment before speaking. "I've got three names we can eliminate."

Kris swiveled around in her chair. "Who?"

"Celt, Leopold, and Shain."

"How'd you eliminate them?"

"Weather. All three would have had to travel by air to be in the vicinity of the assassinations when they occurred. Those three were long shots anyway because they were the farthest away, and not close to any major transportation hubs. Each of them would have experienced long flight delays because of weather on one of the days the assassinations were committed. Since the m.o. is the same, I think it's safe to eliminate them, but I did request a list of satellite transmissions from their locations for each date of an assassination to include the day before and after. If there's any unusual activity or suspicious transmission we can bump that suspect up to the top of the list."

Kris grinned, impressed with Shelby's thorough research. "I've got a couple more: Justice and Kingpin. Kingpin was in the hospital undergoing an emergency appendectomy on the date of the second assassination. Local authorities detained Justice for spying the day the last assassination went down. He was just released yesterday, and arrived in Frankfurt this morning."

"I shouldn't have included hi.."

"Yes, you should've. The incident was kept secret, and was just entered into the computer this morning. Your list is solid."

Shelby warmed at the compliment. "Thanks."

"No thanks necessary, you're a good analyst."

Shelby blushed and started rifling through a stack of papers on her desk.

Kris watched her for a moment longer then returned her gaze to the monitor. *She's adorable when she blushes.*

GREGOR STOOD IN front of his superior officer in the Russian Federation Embassy, weathering the scorching verbal assault on his performance. He inwardly sighed with relief when Dimitri temporarily ran out of descriptive words.

His face still red with fury, Dimitri snapped, "You obviously did not impress the importance of this mission on your operative. These actions are not acceptable. We dictate to our subordinates; they do not dictate to us. If you had done your job properly, this would never have occurred."

Gregor resented his superior's castigation, but was glad Dimitri had calmed down. "I followed procedure. If there is any blame, place it on our superiors for not attempting contact before now."

"That is not your concern!"

Gregor feared he had gone too far, but felt it necessary to defend himself. He remembered clearly his meeting with the operative in question and how he had explained in excruciating detail that non-compliance with his directives was not an option. He also remembered that his graphic rendition of the repercussions for failure had not seemed to faze his contact.

"I did emphasize that failure to comply would result in grave consequences."

"Apparently, your cautions were ineffective. Re-establish contact; exert whatever pressure is necessary. If you are not successful, your usefulness here is at an end."

"As you wish." Gregor turned abruptly and left Dimitri's office. He was well aware of what would happen if he returned to the Motherland in disgrace. If he were lucky, he would be assigned to most desolate area of the Siberian tundra. If he were not, he would find himself in a shallow, unmarked grave.

SHELBY GLANCED UP at the clock, pleased that quitting time had finally arrived. She gathered up the sensitive information she had been working on. The fortified steel filing cabinet anchored to the floor against the wall was secure enough for her usual documents, but to a trained eye, the satellite transmissions would identify the locations of not only the field operatives they were investigating, but many others as well, so heightened security precautions were necessary. Taking her materials over to the wall safe, she asked, "You got anything that needs locking up?"

"Yeah." Kris handed Shelby a similar stack of printouts, more than ready to leave the confines of the suffocating office.

Shelby locked the safe, then gave the dial a couple of spins. "I thought we could stop at Giant Food on Main Street. That okay with you?"

Kris had forgotten she'd agreed to go grocery shopping and shrugged. "Sure."

Shelby had learned that morning to let Kris go out first, then wait until she'd finished her perusal of the parking lot before joining her. Receiving the all-clear, she slid into the driver's seat and waited for Kris to get settled and buckled up before exiting her parking place and getting in the line of cars waiting to merge with the traffic on the parkway. Shelby glanced at Kris and immediately picked up on an increase in tension and alertness that seemed second nature to the operative. She knew Kris was just doing her job, protecting her, but she wondered if the woman ever relaxed in public places.

Kris was studying the cars traveling along side of them, but was paying particular attention to those to their rear. She had considered insisting that she drive, but had sensed Shelby would balk at that, and she couldn't very well commandeer a private vehicle. The operative still didn't know what to make of the shooting incident in the mall parking lot. Something about it bothered her, but she couldn't bring the niggling thought to the forefront of her mind. Until she knew more, she would treat it as a failed attempt on the analyst's life.

A short time later, determined to shop for groceries Kris liked too, Shelby broke the silence. "What's your favorite food?" When no answer was forthcoming, she glanced over at Kris and reflexively tightened her hands nervously on the wheel. The operative had that hard, cold expression on her face, and she seemed coiled to strike out at a second's notice. "What's wrong?"

Kris debated whether or not to answer. They were being followed again, but this time it was not the black Honda Accord. It was a dark blue Ford Taurus, an excellent choice because of the popularity of the model. This tail was also much more skilled than the previous one had been, and using Shelby's car that morning had obviously proved no stumbling block. Kris was fairly certain the driver didn't know she'd picked him up and decided to proceed to the grocery store as planned and lose him afterwards. If he were well trained, he would remain in the car and wait for them. Her hope was that he would follow them inside so she could make a visual ID. All she could determine from her discreet observation in the side mirror was that the driver had a short haircut and therefore appeared to be a male.

Should I worry her now or wait until we leave the store? Kris made a quick decision and said, "Do not look in the rearview mirror. Keep looking straight ahead, just like you're doing. We have company."

Shelby kept her eyes glued to the road, ignoring the strong urge to look in her rearview mirror. "What should I do?"

"Nothing. We're going to go to the grocery store, just like we planned. When we leave, I'm gonna drive."

The analyst's stomach tightened nervously, and the fact that her life really could be in danger settled across her shoulders like a heavy yoke. Up until now, she had managed to force that reality to the back of her mind, preferring to think the shooting had been a random event.

Kris saw Shelby's face pale and fleetingly questioned her decision to tell her about their tail, but knew her companion needed to understand the seriousness of the situation. "Hey, just take it easy and try to relax."

Yeah, right. "What are you going to do?"

"Lose him and see if he shows up at your apartment."

"You think he might know where I live?" Shelby tensed again, her knuckles turning white from her tightened grip on the steering wheel.

"It's possible. Whoever is following us is a professional." Kris reached over and gently squeezed Shelby's arm. "It'll be okay. You're safe with me. I'm not going to let anything happen to you."

Shelby found the conviction in Kris' voice reassuring, and her tension began to diminish as she spared a quick look at the operative before turning her gaze back to the road. Kris' face reflected determination and confidence. Shelby acknowledged that if anyone could keep her safe, this woman could.

Chapter Six

AS THEY PULLED into the grocery store parking lot, Kris opened her jacket wider, allowing clear access to her gun. She saw their pursuer drive slowly past without turning in, and got a sense that he was strictly on an information-gathering mission. Glancing at Shelby when the car came to a stop in a parking place, Kris said, "Don't get out until I'm on your side of the car." Then she quickly exited the vehicle.

She had a hunch their being followed was related to the note she'd left at the drop in Georgetown the previous afternoon, and cursed Earl for putting Shelby at risk by consigning the analyst to her care. Kris grudgingly acknowledged that her boss couldn't have known the danger in that and vowed to keep her charge safe from the dark elements closing in on her.

Blue scanned the parking lot as she casually walked around the car, but the Ford Taurus hadn't returned. It was possible that they didn't know where Shelby lived, but she thought that unlikely. She briefly considered the most likely possibilities. If the tail was intended for her, there had to be a leak within the Agency for them to know she was riding with Shelby. Finding that leak might provide her with a valuable bargaining chip should one become necessary.

Second case scenario was that if the tail was related to the shooting incident at the mall, then someone was targeting Shelby, and she intended to find out who. It was also feasible that they were both being targeted, either because of the case or separately for unrelated reasons. This last scenario was potentially the most dangerous, because it would be the hardest to defend against. Regardless, her work was cut out for her.

Blue stood far enough away from the door to allow Shelby to exit the car, then remained between her and the street until they entered the store. Once they were inside, she glanced down at her companion to see how she was handling the situation.

Shelby hadn't been nearly as bothered at being followed by an unknown assailant as she was by the idea that he might know where she lived. In the last couple of days, her previously routine life had become a cloak and dagger affair. First she'd been shot at, and now someone was following them. She had come to the conclusion that it had to be work-related, because the entire sequence of events hadn't started until she had actually been assigned to the case. Shelby fleetingly wondered how Kris could live in a world of danger and deception, where events like these were commonplace.

No longer in the mood to shop, Shelby got a shopping cart anyway, deciding her activities were not going to be curtailed by some stranger in a car, but she acknowledged that her bravery stemmed in part from the comforting presence of the tall woman at her side. She glanced up to see concerned blue eyes regarding her. "Is he gone?"

"For now. He may be parked on the street to avoid being seen."

Oh great! "I wish I knew why he was following us."

Kris snorted. "You and me both."

Shelby decided she'd feel safer at home, even if he did know where she lived, and looked around the store trying to decide where to start. "So, what do you like?" When Kris didn't answer her, she glanced up to find the operative's eyes trained on the door.

After several minutes, Blue finally turned her attention back to Shelby. While it would have been a stupid move for the driver of the Taurus to follow them inside, she wasn't going to take any chances. Not missing the tight set to Shelby's shoulders as she began pushing the cart down the aisle, she decided to try and get her to relax a little. "I want to pick up a few TV dinners."

Her answer had the desired effect when Shelby turned to her indignantly. "You're not serious?"

Kris chuckled at Shelby's disbelieving expression and winked. "Just kidding. I like almost anything. Why don't we get a couple of steaks to broil tonight? With baked potatoes and salad. How's that sound?"

Shelby grinned. "Now you're talking." She decided to use her own judgment for the bulk of the groceries, since it was becoming apparent Kris wasn't going to be very forthcoming.

MARKOV CONTINUED DOWN down the street to the next light before turning around and pulling into a service station across from the grocery store. He pulled out his cellular phone and punched in the number of his immediate superior, puzzling over why some of the higher echelon seemed to be working independently in tracking this woman.

Gregor had been expecting the call and answered the phone immediately. He listened with satisfaction to Markov's report. He'd had little time to garner information from his contacts, but what they had provided him with was apparently accurate, because the woman who got out of the car matched the description he had passed on to Markov. "Break off contact. I ran the plates and have an address. I don't want to chance you being spotted."

Markov protested indignantly, "I will not be seen."

Ignoring his subordinate's response, Gregor ordered, "Return at once," and turned the phone off, frowning.

So, she was staying with another woman. It was an interesting development that didn't fit the profile they'd been developing on her over the years. She tended to be a loner. He needed to find out what the connection was—other than that they both worked for the Agency. That alone wouldn't be reason enough for the cohabitation, and he speculated on how it might be related to the cryptic message left at the emergency drop. He was going to have to make some further inquiries and find out who Shelby Carson was.

Gregor knew that the more information he had, the more pressure he could exert. Having minutely examined his contact's entire file that afternoon, he had found something he could use as leverage, sensing he might need every bit of ammunition he could muster.

SHELBY WALKED DOWN the last aisle, smiling inwardly. The operative had decided to help after all, and had casually added things they passed in the store including pepper cheese, cheddar cheese, wheat crackers, blueberry and cherry yogurt, lemon-flavored seasoning, crushed garlic, red pepper flakes, onions, a large bag of crunchy Cheetos, and microwave popcorn.

Noticing that most of the selections were either snack foods or seasonings, Shelby decided Kris probably didn't get to eat many things she liked while in the field. She had been tempted to comment on a few of the spicy items, but hadn't wanted to dissuade her tall companion from getting what she wanted. That was, until now. "You actually eat that stuff?"

Kris looked at the comical expression on Shelby's face, then to the roll of meat in her hand and shrugged. "Yeah. Makes a good sandwich with a nice thick slice of onion and spicy mustard."

Shelby nodded in mock understanding. "Oh, that's how you do it. You drown out the taste with the mustard and onion." She shuddered. "I can't stand that stuff. When we were kids and Mom made it for lunch, we called it liver the worst."

The twinkling was apparent in the green eyes regarding her, and Kris quirked a half-smile as she held out the package and pointed out, "This is braunschweiger, not liverwurst."

"They're all the same. Braunschweiger, liverwurst, goose liver.

Yuck!"

Kris just grinned and tossed the meat into the cart. "I didn't say anything about that weird cereal you got."

"What are you talking about, my Maypo? Maypo's not weird!"

"Whatever you say. I never even heard of it." The operative was enjoying the banter, and pleased that some of Shelby's tension had faded. As a rule, she was bored by shopping, but was finding she didn't mind it nearly as much tonight.

"It's really good. It's a maple-flavored oat cereal. Taste's great."

Kris raised an eyebrow in disbelief. "I think I'll pass. Sounds way too sweet."

"I happen to like sweet."

Oh, so do I. Kris put a halt to her unruly thoughts. "Nothing wrong with that. We done?"

"Yeah. Just have to get some milk."

Blue's eyes turned glacial. A guy in jeans and a blue polo shirt had mirrored their progress for just a little too long for it to be coincidence. She quickly assessed him in the mirror mounted at the end of the aisle. *Thank God for shoplifters.*

He was too far away for her to determine if he was carrying a weapon, and she needed to get Shelby out of the store safely. She briefly considered just ushering Shelby out to the car, but that would leave him to their rear and if he was good, it could be a fatal move. Blue decided that surprise was her best weapon, and if it turned out the guy hadn't been following them and was an innocent, no serious harm would be done.

She moved to Shelby's left and quietly said, "Let me push the cart. Stay between me and the freezer case."

Alarmed, Shelby bit off a question and moved to Kris' right. Her heart rate sped up until she could hear it pounding in her ears as she kept pace with the tall woman.

Blue was counting on the man to follow their progress in the mirror, so she traveled slowly up the aisle glancing at frozen selections as she passed. If he actually was following them, he should avoid eye contact, and the operative intended to use that to her advantage.

Rounding the corner, she quirked a tiny smile. As she had expected, the guy was gazing at a canned vegetable display. She ambled past him to make sure no one was paying attention before suddenly turning and ramming him with her shopping cart.

The unexpected attack carried Markov into the display shelves, and any hope of regaining his balance was lost when he felt his legs swept from beneath him. Biting off a curse, he landed on his stomach in the middle of the aisle, surrounded by rolling cans.

Shelby was momentarily stunned and stood there unmoving until Kris grabbed her arm, pulling her down the aisle. She heard several customers talking loudly and watched store employees run past them to the scene of the accident. When they finally exited the grocery store, she breathed a sigh of relief.

Blue escorted Shelby to the passenger seat, then jogged around the car and quickly settled herself into the driver's side. She knew the store would detain him until they were sure he was uninjured or he had signed a waiver releasing the store from any liability. In the meantime, she intended to search for a parked blue Taurus. Innocent civilians didn't carry guns, and she'd caught a glimpse of one when he fell. A feral grin flickered across Blue's face. The hunter had just become the hunted.

Markov assured the manager for the third time that he was fine as he silently cursed the tall woman. He could not allow knowledge of his disobedience to reach his superiors. If the police or medical personnel were called, he would have to force his way out of the store before they arrived, something he didn't want to do. His job entailed keeping a low profile, and he was already humiliated beyond belief.

Finally, after signing an alias to a form releasing the store from culpability, he departed, carefully scanning the parking lot to make sure the red car was gone. He continually surveyed his surroundings as he crossed first the parking lot and then the street to get to where his car was parked behind the service station.

He opened his car door and froze. The unmistakable sound of a round being chambered reached his ears as he simultaneously felt a hard object pressed firmly against his back.

Shelby was pressed against the entrance to the women's restroom, her eyes wide. She had known what Kris was going to do, but was still surprised when the operative had appeared behind the man. She watched Kris search the man, pocket the gun and wallet she found, then order him to get in the passenger side of the car, before climbing into the backseat behind him, her aim never wavering.

"Who are you?"

Markov maintained a stony silence. He would tell this woman nothing.

Blue softened her voice and purred into the Russian's ear, "It's simple, really. You tell me what I want to know, you live. You don't, you die. So, what'll it be?"

Markov was chilled and tantalized by the voice in his ear; instinctively, he knew this woman would do as she said. "I was paid to follow you." Intense pain filled his head as blue steel impacted with the back of his skull. His eyes watered and Russian curses filled the air.

Blue growled, "I'm losing my patience."

"I am Markov. I was sent by the Bear."

"Why?"

"He did not say."

Blue knew that was probably true, but decided to make sure. She pressed her gun into the base of Markov's neck. "I don't believe you."

"It is true! When you went into the store, he ordered me to return."

"Why didn't you?"

Markov hesitated, felt the pressure at the base of his neck increase. "I wanted to give him a description of your partner."

Blue felt her stomach tighten. "Why?"

"He was interested in her. I wanted to impress him."

Blue handed the man his wallet. "Hold that up where I can see. Now take out your ID." She looked at the diplomatic ID card issued to all embassy personnel by the State Department, and learned his full name was Boris Ivanovich Markov. The other information on the ID didn't interest her. "What else you got in there, Boris?"

Markov began removing each item from his wallet and held it up until she ordered, "Next."

Blue was looking for phone numbers or code names, and smiled when he tried to hide a small folded piece of paper from her sight. It never ceased to amaze her how stupid some operatives were.

She shoved the barrel of the gun against his head. "Hand me that piece of paper you're trying to hide. Try anything funny, you die and I get it anyway."

Markov tensed. That paper had Dimitri's personal phone number on it. He could not allow this woman to have it. He slowly moved the folded piece of paper from behind his international license and then suddenly thrust it to his mouth.

Blue had anticipated the move and slammed her left fist into the side of his head. Ignoring Markov's grunt of pain, she growled, "You don't get it yet, do you?" She pressed her weapon against Markov's head. "Now pick it up."

Markov shook his head to clear it, and slowly reached down to retrieve the piece of paper from his lap. Any thought of defying her again deserted him when he heard her chuckle softly in his ear.

"You try that again and your brain is gonna be splattered all over the inside of this car." Blue took it from him and slid it in her pocket. "That's a good boy. Now listen carefully. If I ever see you again, you're a dead man. That goes for annoying my partner, too. You got that?"

Markov nodded. "Yes."

"Good. I'm glad we understand each other." She got out of the car, keeping her gun hidden from view, not wanting to attract any curious eyes. "Get out of here."

Blue watched him drive away before turning her attention back to her companion. She would have to wait to see what was on the slip of paper that Markov risked his life to keep her from getting.

Shelby's face was pale. She had flinched when Kris belted the man with her gun, and again when she clobbered him on the side of his head. She hadn't been able to hear the conversation, but his curses had carried beyond the confines of the car. She wasn't positive, but the guttural tone had sounded like Russian. *What is going on?*

"Let's get out of here."

Nodding, Shelby stepped from the doorway and walked in front of Kris to her car. Once they were back on the road, Shelby asked, "Who was he?"

"Just someone following orders."

"That's all he told you? Is that why you hit him?"

Kris glanced at Shelby and suddenly realized how upset she was. "I hit him because he was lying. In this business, force is all some people understand." She purposely made no mention of why she hit him the second time.

"Do you know who sent him?"

"Yes." Kris briefly made eye contact with the other woman. "Don't worry about it. I'll handle it."

Yeah, right. Not much chance of her not worrying after what she'd just witnessed. She hoped Kris would take care of it, and that her life would return to some semblance of normal.

They arrived home a short time later. After thoroughly inspecting the apartment, Kris returned to the kitchen where Shelby had just fed the kitten. "Does she always gobble down her food like that?" Rather than arising from actual curiosity, her question was intended to divert Shelby's attention from the recent events.

"Yeah. I think she might stop doing it once she feels secure here and knows she'll always have food. Poor thing. How terrible for her to be abandoned like that."

Kris nodded in agreement, then decided she should change out of her work clothes. She would've preferred changing right in the living room, but decided that since it wasn't her apartment, the bathroom would be more appropriate. "I'm gonna change."

Shelby watched Kris walk to the bathroom, fully appreciating the natural grace with which the tall woman moved until she became aware of what she was doing and blushed furiously.

Locking the bathroom door, Kris pulled out the tattered piece of paper. It was blank except for a local telephone number she readily identified as embassy from the prefix. She folded it and put it in the pocket of the jeans she donned. Tomorrow, she would find out who was at the other end of that phone line. It would be interesting to see if the voice matched that of her contact.

Shelby went to her bedroom, changed, and took extra time to hang her clothes in their proper place, smiling as she did so.

Her amusement faded when she walked into the living room and saw Kris' gun lying on the end table next to the operative. She remembered how comfortable the operative had looked, standing with her gun pressed against that man's back. The sight of it now was a cold, harsh reminder of the seriousness of their situation. She glanced at Kris. "Everything okay?"

"Yeah." Kris followed Shelby's gaze to her weapon. "I need it close."

"I know. It just seems strange to have one in my apartment. I'll make us something to eat."

Kris was again reminded of what different worlds they lived in. "Need any help?"

"No. I've got some homemade spaghetti in the freezer. I'll just heat that up."

The operative's thoughts turned to her conversation with Markov, and she sighed. Kris knew she'd been taking a chance by blowing off her contact, but she had wanted to push the boundaries to find out how much leeway she had. *Guess I found out.*

Kris was also extremely concerned about their interest in Shelby and knew it had originated solely because of their working and living arrangement. Questions filled her mind. *How did they know I would be riding with Shelby? How did they find out what kind of car she drove so quickly?* Was someone leaking information? If so, *who?*

When they'd met, her contact had not indicated any knowledge of the case she was working. He had only been interested in the locations of field operatives. She snorted. It was always the same. *Spy on the spies.* Information was power, and the Russians would hold a huge advantage if they knew who their counterparts were and where they were located. The Wall coming down hadn't made any difference in this covert power quest. If anything, each country's interest in what the other was doing had increased. *Some things never change.*

Shelby walked into the living room and joined Kris on the couch. She wasn't satisfied with the answers the operative had given her in the car. "Was this case the reason that guy was following us?"

Kris looked at the earnest face and felt her stomach sink to new depths. Unable to bring herself to lie in the face of such honesty, Kris decided to share what she could. "They were following me. In my line of work you make a lot of enemies." *Except that now you are involved, but I see no point in worrying you any more than you already are.*

Musing aloud, Shelby said, "It sounded like that guy was speaking Russian."

Kris tensed but remained silent. *Damn it.* She had hoped Shelby hadn't heard the invectives Markov spouted.

"Are you going to tell Earl?"

The operative pinned Shelby with cool blue eyes. "I said I would handle it. How I do that is none of your concern." When the open expression on Shelby's face disappeared, Kris cursed herself, but didn't offer any further explanation.

Shelby was hurt by the rebuff, but if it was unrelated to the case it really wasn't any of her business. "Then the shooting in the mall was random?"

"I don't know. Let's wait and see what happens in the next few days."

Shelby nodded. Knowing there was no sense in questioning the unanswerable any further, she got up to check on dinner.

A short time later, after eating and clearing the table, the two women returned to the living room. Kris turned off the lamp and approached the balcony door. It was still dusk, but she didn't intend to give any adversary an advantage. Standing to the side, she gazed out across the parking lot for several minutes before joining Shelby on the couch.

At dinner the conversation had been practically nonexistent, and Shelby searched for a way to ease the tension between them. "Have you ever watched *Buffy*?"

Kris couldn't stop the amusement from appearing on her face. "As in *'The Vampire Slayer?'*"

"Yeah. Have you?"

"Nope. Never had any desire to."

"Do you mind if I turn it on?"

Kris shrugged. "Doesn't matter to me."

Slightly over an hour later, Shelby grinned, knowing Kris had enjoyed the program. "Not too bad, huh?"

Kris had found the program entertaining, but answered noncommittally. "It was okay."

Sure, it was just okay. That's why you were laughing at a couple of parts. "What do you want to watch now?"

Kris stood up. "I need to take a trip around the neighborhood. Make sure it's secure. I'll be back shortly."

Shelby watched the operative's retreat in silence. She might have expected her to check the area out later, but not now. It was almost if the tall woman was afraid to enjoy herself.

She got up and walked through the empty apartment. Shelby knew she should be relieved that Kris had identified the tail and that it had nothing to do with the case, but instead she was concerned for the operative's safety. She didn't understand why Kris wouldn't just tell Earl and be done with it instead of taking care of it alone. She had the support of the whole Company at her fingertips. Shelby decided to try and talk to her about it again the next day.

Blue surveyed the parking lot from the darker shadows near the side of the building and breathed deeply of the fresh air. She'd needed to get out of the apartment for a while—away from the comfortable, homey décor, and away from Shelby. She needed to rein in whatever force kept driving her towards the smaller woman, but was finding it increasingly difficult as they spent more time together.

She wished her contact would show up, longing for a diversion from the image of pain on Shelby's face that continued to play in slow motion through her mind, or from the troubling thoughts that plagued her.

Fate was not kind; no opportunity for action presented itself, and Kris returned to the apartment an hour later. Tomorrow was another day, and maybe when it dawned, so would a better course of action to divert the subversive elements in her life away from her new partner.

Chapter Seven

SHELBY WOKE TO the pleasant aroma of brewing coffee wafting through the air for the second time in as many days. She rolled onto her back, recalling her less than successful attempts at conversation the evening before when the operative had returned from her security check. Kris had been pleasant enough, just distant, and Shelby had found that she was doing most of the talking. *If that's what it takes, fine.* Donning her robe, she walked out to the kitchen and saw Kris kneeling on the dining room floor, petting Stormy. "Good morning."

Kris stood quickly. "Morning."

Stormy strolled over to Shelby, looked up and meowed loudly. Laughing, Shelby bent down to pet her. "She is just too cute! Did you feed her?"

"Yeah." Kris shrugged. "She was hungry."

Noting the slightly defensive answer, Shelby smiled warmly. "Thanks. Now that she's eaten, it's our turn. What do you want for breakfast?"

"Almost anything. Except your Maypo." Kris was almost as surprised as Shelby at the joking answer and half turned away to cover it.

Shelby playfully glared at Kris. "We could have bagels again."

"A bagel sounds good to me. Why don't you go ahead and have your cereal? Just because I don't want it, doesn't mean you shouldn't enjoy it."

"Yeah, I know. Okay, bagel for you and Maypo for me." Shelby busied herself getting out the cereal and was about to pull a bagel out of the bag when she felt Kris behind her.

"You don't have to get mine."

"I know I don't. But this kitchen is hardly big enough for two, and how much work is it to take a bagel out of the package, put it on a saucer and hand it to you? Now will you get out of my way?"

"Yes, ma'am."

Shelby laughed and handed her the bagel. "Here. Go ahead and get your own saucer if it makes you feel better."

Kris grinned and took a saucer from the cupboard before retreating into the dining room, still smiling. She sat at the table watching Shelby make her cereal.

Joining Kris at the table, Shelby asked, "Did you go out again last night?"

"Yeah. Around midnight. Everything was fine. No problems now, either."

"Oh good!"

Kris shrugged. "I didn't expect him to come back." And she hadn't, but it wouldn't have surprised her if he had, either. She was pulled from her musing when Shelby spoke again.

"So, what's up for today? More of the same?"

"Yeah. I figure by Friday, we should have the list narrowed down to about ten." Kris looked at Shelby speculatively. "How many names do you think will be left on the list when we're done?"

"I don't know." Shelby grinned mischievously. "I've got an idea. How about we both guess, and then the loser has to treat the winner to dinner."

Even though Kris had asked the question intending to find out if Shelby knew her code name, she found the idea of taking the analyst out to dinner was very attractive. *Quit thinking date. It'll be farewell.* Kris was unable to disagree with the logical assessment. *Yes, it will be, but it's better than nothing.* She smiled slightly as she settled the internal argument.

"You're on."

"Oh good! Let's see. I guess seven."

"Seven?" Why seven?"

"Because seven is a lucky number. Besides, there are five names on that list that I'll be really surprised if we eliminate."

"Why?" Kris knew her tone had been too curt when she saw a shadow cross the analyst's face.

"It's just a gut feeling based on some other information I've had access to over the last several months, but has nothing to do with this case." *That was really stupid, Shelby.*

Kris raised an eyebrow. "How about telling me which five names? Nothing classified about that."

Shelby acknowledged that was true and said, "Okay. You're right. I'm talking about Atlas, Blue, Jet, Roman, and Silver."

The operative smiled inwardly, having worked with the other four on various cases during her career. *Smart woman.* "Did Dennis tell you my code name?"

"No."

"Why not?"

"Probably because he figured I'd be more objective if I didn't know." Shelby met Blue's unwavering gaze. "Why? Are you one of those five?"

"Does is matter? What my code name is has nothing to do with solving this case."

Shelby pointedly remarked, "Which five operatives I think will not be eliminated didn't really have anything to do with the case, either."

When am I going to learn that this woman is no pushover? That's one of the things I really like about her. Kris nodded and thought quickly. "No, it didn't. I never should've asked."

So that's it? End of conversation? Shelby never spoke the words. Even though she was not surprised at the operative's evasiveness, she was disappointed. She turned her attention to her cereal and took a bite.

Two things were obvious to her. The first was that Kris didn't trust her to be objective. The second was that the operative was very likely one of those five names or she would've come right out and said she wasn't. *So which one? I think Blue fits, but that would be too obvious. Besides, if any of the stories in the rumor mill are true about Blue, it couldn't be Kris. Or could it?* After the events of the previous evening, Shelby wasn't nearly as certain.

She looked up from her cereal at the sound of her name and found herself gazing into serious blue eyes.

Shelby's silence bothered Kris and she felt the need to explain, which disconcerted her to no end. "Do you trust me?"

What a loaded question. Shelby smiled. "I guess I'd better. You're keeping me safe."

The corner of Kris' mouth turned up at the neutral answer. "I know trust is something earned, and you don't really know me. But trust me when I tell you that it's better for you not to know who I am."

Shelby wasn't quite sure what to make of the odd expression on Kris' face, but the intensity of the words washed over her and she suddenly realized the tall woman wasn't evading her question, but rather was answering it with total honestly. She gazed back into the operative's eyes and nodded. "Okay."

"Thanks." Kris searched for a way to dissipate the tension, and her eyes landed on the bookcase holding Shelby's knickknacks.

"That's a pretty interesting collection you have there. Some of the pieces look old. When did you start collecting them?"

Shelby's eyes took on a far away look as her thoughts turned to her childhood. "I've always loved to read. When I was ten, I started reading fantasy books. I became intrigued with unicorns first. They were so beautiful and magical. I used to imagine riding away on one them."

She laughed quietly. "It's kind of silly, really. The little people are to keep them company. I didn't want the unicorns to be lonely. The dragons came later when I learned they are supposed to bring good luck."

"I don't think it's silly. It's a nice collection." Kris sensed that Shelby had given her a very abbreviated version of the history behind the pieces. *And why did you want to ride away? What aren't you saying? Were you lonely, and that's why you didn't want them to be? I know about lonely.* "When did you—"

"It's 7:00. I gotta start getting ready."

Kris watched Shelby rise abruptly and quickly rinse out her bowl as she passed through the kitchen on the way to her bedroom. *I guess we all have secrets.*

Just leave it be.

I need to know.

She's my partner.

No you don't. You're already becoming emotionally involved.

Deciding to use the time to check out the parking lot, Kris donned her clothes, carefully locked the door, and then departed. As she performed her surveillance, she positioned herself so that the door was within her view the entire time she was out of the apartment and she could easily reach the stairs should it become necessary.

KRIS HAD SHOWN no previous interest in talking about personal things, and Shelby had been caught totally off guard by the question about her collection. Her childhood memories were not happy ones, and she seldom revisited them. She focused on pushing the thoughts from the forefront of her mind and concentrated on what else was bothering her. *I wanted to tell her what my childhood was like. And that doesn't make any sense. It's ancient history, and I don't even know her.*

She'd understand.

Shelby shook off the thought as she gazed into the closet, trying to decide what to wear. She heard the door close as Kris left the apartment. Turning her eyes toward the sound, she absently picked up Stormy and gently hugged the kitten. *I wonder what she's thinking.*

Kris returned a short time later. She stepped through the doorway and swallowed—hard.

Shelby was walking out of the bathroom, toweling her hair dry, her robe hanging open. When she saw the operative step into the apartment, she let the towel fall and hastily pulled her robe closed.

Cheeks blazing, Shelby mumbled, "Oh, you're back," and rapidly walked into her bedroom. *That was really dumb. I never even heard her. How embarrassing!*

Taking a deep breath, Kris closed the door. She had only caught a glimpse of the lovely body that the robe quickly covered, but her heart was still pounding wildly. As she attempted to regain control of her zealous libido, she tried to blow off her reaction as typical, but was unable to. None of her previous encounters with men or women had ever elicited such a visceral response. Kris didn't know if there was any truth to the proverbial value of a cold shower, but she intended to find out, and headed for the bathroom.

Kris returned to the kitchen after showering and reached for the cup of coffee Shelby was holding out to her. "Thanks."

"You're welcome." The analyst felt awkward and looked away.

Shelby's sudden shyness was endearing, and Kris wanted to hug her and tell her it was no big deal. Knowing that impulse was one she couldn't act on, she suddenly said, "Three."

"Three?" Shelby's brow furrowed. "What are you talking about?"

"Our bet. I think we'll get the list down to three."

After the tense conversation about her code name, Shelby had figured Kris was no longer interested. "It's still on?"

"Of course, but be prepared to lose."

"I don't think so!" She matched the smug grin on Kris' face with one of her own.

Chuckling, Kris looked at her watch. "'Bout time to go."

"You didn't see anyone?"

"No."

Shelby smiled and said emphatically, "Good."

The operative quirked a half smile as she shook her head, wondering where the analyst found her optimism. *Send some my way, woman. I could use it right about now.*

Totally unaware of the warm smile covering her face, Kris watched as Shelby bade the kitten farewell.

THE OPERATIVE WAITED until Shelby was thoroughly engrossed in her work, then pulled up the embassy file on the Russian Federation. She scrolled through the short list of names and their purported designations. Locating Markov, Kris found that he was officially assigned as a driver to both Gregor Mikhailovich Koslov and Dimitri Nekitych Pyetsky, who were both listed as political attachés. *Yeah, right.*

Not recognizing either name, she clicked on Koslov first, and a close-up photo opened on her screen. Her eyes narrowed as she recognized the man. She read all the biographical information available, then returned to the main screen and clicked on Pyetsky. Kris blanched as the familiar face appeared on the monitor before her.

Shelby glanced at her companion. "Are you okay? You look a little pale."

Quickly pressing the ALT and TAB key on her keyboard simultaneously, Kris nodded and smiled wanly. "Yeah. It's just a little warm in here today."

Shelby hadn't thought so, but Kris did look uncomfortable. "I was going to get something to drink. Want anything?"

Regaining her composure, Kris smiled. "What are the choices?"

"Cranberry or orange juice, Coke, Cherry Coke, Diet Coke, Ginger Ale, Sprite, and iced tea."

"Coke sounds good." Kris reached into her pocket, but Shelby waved her off. "I'll get it this time."

Kris watched her walk out of the office, then quickly switched the screen back to the man she knew as Sergei Pavlovich Yanov. *You rotten bastard. You've done pretty well, haven't you?* She read his biography noting that some key information had not been uncovered, which didn't really surprise her. If it had been, he would have been deported upon his arrival in the States.

The operative closed the screen and processed the information. She had a phone call to make before deciding on a specific course of action, and the stakes had just been raised.

"HEY, SHELBY."

The analyst secured the bottle of cranberry juice from the tray of the drink machine and smiled at the familiar voice. "Hi, Maggie. How's it going?"

"I was going to ask you the same thing. Rumor has it you're working on a really hot case."

Shelby shrugged. "Same ol'. How about you?"

"I'm stuck doing a records audit right now. Who's that woman you're working with? Is she new or a transferee?"

"She's just on loan for this case."

"So it *is* a hot case." Maggie grinned triumphantly. "I knew it!"

"Oh come on, Maggie. You know how the rumor mill is. Everything is so exaggerated. It's just a regular case, but it requires a lot of research so I got some help." Shelby smiled, very disturbed but determined not to show it. "Really."

"Okay." Maggie grinned conspiratorially. "So, heard any good gossip?"

"No. I've been kind of busy and haven't been to the cafeteria much lately. Seems like most of the rumors start there."

"I picked up something new there yesterday, besides lunch."

Shelby grinned. "Okay. I'll bite. What'd you hear?"

"You ever hear of Blue?"

Suddenly tense, Shelby said warily, "Yeah."

"Blue is here."

Shelby forced skepticism into her voice. "I'm sure. For what?"

"Who knows? Who knows why they do anything they do around here?"

"True. Let me know if you hear anything else."

"No problem. Gotta go."

"Me too. See you later."

Maggie watched Shelby walk down the hall before heading back to her own office.

Kris listened to Shelby greet the Marine as she walked into the office. "Took you long enough. I was going to send out a search party."

"Very funny! Had to catch up on the rumor mill."

"Anything interesting?"

Shelby gazed at the beautiful blue eyes regarding her curiously. "You know how the rumor mill is. You gotta take everything with a grain of salt."

You are avoiding my question. Why? What did you hear? Kris took the Coke Shelby handed her and smiled disarmingly. "I hear you. Funny thing is, though, most of the rumors have some truth to them. It's just usually distorted."

"Yep. That's why I don't pay much attention to them," Shelby responded dismissively. "Find anything interesting in the satellite transmissions?"

Looks like I'm going to have to do my own homework. "No."

"I can't believe we haven't eliminated even one name today." Shelby didn't particularly care that they hadn't narrowed the list down, but wanted to steer the conversation away from Kris' question.

"It's still early. I'm sure we'll find a couple more before we leave."

Kris was disappointed that Shelby appeared to be so driven to bring the case to a conclusion. She had no choice but to hurry the case along, but the analyst wasn't under the constraints she was. *Can you blame her? She's stuck with you twenty-four hours a day. Since she's been working on this case, she's been shot at and followed. Why wouldn't she want to hurry the case along?*

True. Kris silenced the discordant voices and returned her attention to the monitor.

KRIS STOOD UP at 11:30. "I need to take care of some personal business. Mind if I use your car?"

She's going out now? A crease appeared on Shelby's brow. "No."

Raising a questioning eyebrow, Kris smiled, "No, you don't mind, or no, I can't use your car?"

The analyst returned her smile. "No, I don't mind." She opened the desk drawer and pulled the keys from her purse, handing them to Kris. "Aren't you gonna wear your sunglasses?"

Kris cut wary eyes toward Shelby. "It was cloudy this morning and supposed to rain, remember? I thought I'd wait and see if I needed them."

"They look nice on you. You should put them on." *God, Shelby, couldn't you think of anything better than that? All you're gonna do is make her suspicious.*

"What gives?"

"Do you remember when you asked me to trust you this morning?" When Kris nodded, Shelby continued, "It's your turn to trust me. Please put your sunglasses on until you get in the car."

Swayed by the worry reflected on Shelby's countenance, Kris pulled the glasses from her jacket pocket and casually donned them. When she got back, she intended to find out what was going on. A barely audible, "Thanks," followed her through the door.

Shelby momentarily questioned her decision to lend the operative her car. She had no doubt that Kris was going to follow up on whatever information she'd obtained from the guy she'd questioned the evening before, and she wished the operative had taken some back-up, just in case. She also knew if she hadn't lent Kris her car, the agent would've just called a cab and retrieved her rental car from the apartment complex parking lot.

The analyst tried to figure out how an operative from another country could've found out who Kris was and tracked her to Virginia. None of what happened the previous evening made any sense. No closer to finding answers than she had been the night before, Shelby's thoughts turned to what she was going to tell Kris when she got back.

She knew the operative was going to ask her why she had insisted she wear her sunglasses. *What do I tell her?* There was no evidence that Kris was Blue, yet she'd felt the need to protect her from the prying eyes in the building just in case.

Shelby was barely able to stifle a snort at that thought. *Protect Blue? Protect an operative with a reputation for deadly ruthlessness and success? What's gotten into me?* Kris hadn't looked like she needed any help at all the previous night. In fact, she had been coolly efficient. Logically, it was unlikely that Blue or Kris would ever need her help. *So, what do I tell her?*

'Well, uh, you see, I heard this rumor about Blue being at headquarters so I thought you should put your sunglasses on.' Yeah, right! Maybe it would be best to just tell Kris about the rumor and let the operative draw her own conclusions. *She's gonna know I think she could be Blue, and what if I'm wrong? What will she think of me?* Shelby decided the only option she had was to play it by ear, and she turned her attention back to the documents spread across her desk.

KRIS MADE SURE she wasn't being tailed and then pulled into a service station that had a public telephone. She dialed the number she had already memorized.

"General Pyetsky."

She had expected the voice of her contact, not *him*. She slowly hung up the phone and walked back to Shelby's car. Mechanically climbing into the driver's seat, she tried not to think, but the memories evoked by that voice wouldn't be held at bay.

It was a cold, overcast winter morning. She was eight years old, watching out the window as a car pulled up in front of their apartment. She turned to her mother. "He is here."

"This is an honor, Natasha. You are going to a school for gifted children. I am so proud of you."

But she had heard her mother softly crying every night that week and she didn't want to go. She didn't want to be gifted. She wanted to be normal and live with her mother and her cat, Sasha.

Tears rolled down her face. "I don't want to leave, Mama. Please don't make me."

Her mother hugged her. "I will write you a letter every day. And you get to come home for every holiday. I'll make your favorite dishes and invite all of our friends."

"What will happen to Sasha?"

"Don't you worry about Sasha. I'll take good care of her."

She watched out the window as the man walked up to their door and knocked.

"Mama, please don't open the door. I don't want to go."

"Natasha, it will be all right." *She opened the door.*

He walked in and asked, "Is this Natasha Lubinyenka?"

"Yes, this is my daughter."

She saw a tear in her mother's eye and glared at the man. "I am not going." *He laughed at her and tried to grab her arm. She jumped back.* "My mother needs me to help her. I am staying."

His smile faded and he suddenly had a grip on her arm. "You will learn obedience at the Institute." *His hand was steadily squeezing her arm tighter and tighter.*

She cried out, "Mama, he's hurting me."

"Let go of her. She will walk to the car with you."

The stranger hit her mother so hard, she stumbled back against the table. Then he half carried and half dragged her from the house. Her mother came running after them, begging the man to quit hurting her.

She grabbed hold of her mother and hung on for dear life. As she watched in horror, the man brutally punched her mother in the stomach. She was crying as he shoved her into the car. The last thing she saw as they drove away was her mother lying crumpled on the ground.

Chapter Eight

GREGOR CLOSED THE file one of his sources had provided on Shelby Carson and sat back in his chair, mentally reviewing the contents.

Shelby's father died when she was a toddler and her mother, Lisa, and stepfather, Jonathan Whiteman, had reared her. There was little information on her biological father, but there was a thick dossier on Whiteman, who had recently completed three years of parole after being convicted of domestic violence. Shelby's only sister had married and moved to Seattle, and two teenaged half-brothers lived with her mother in Arlington.

She had done well in college, graduating with a 3.6 grade point average, and had worked for two years as a computer analyst while concurrently obtaining a Master's degree in psychology before joining the CIA. It was after she joined the Agency that the file got interesting.

Her rise to a top-level analyst had been nothing short of meteoric. With her promotion had come the awarding of the highest security clearance the Agency granted, and the background search that usually took nine months to a year had been expedited and completed in only four months.

A slow smile warmed Gregor's face as he picked up the phone and began dialing.

SITTING ON ONE end of the couch after changing out of her work clothes, Kris tucked up a leg and shifted to face Shelby. Raising an eyebrow, she asked, "So, why the sudden interest in my wearing sunglasses?"

Shelby thought she'd gotten away with not offering an explanation. Kris had been unusually quiet since her return from lunch and had rebuffed her questions with noncommittal answers. Wanting to lighten the atmosphere, she quipped, "I already told you. They look good on you." Kris smiled, but her eyes remained serious and Shelby sighed at the inquiry in the unwavering blue gaze. "There's a rumor going around that one of the operatives on our list is at headquarters."

"And?"

"I don't know if they're talking about you, but I suspect they have no idea what the operative looks like, so just in case, I thought you should be more disguised."

Roiling inwardly, Kris took a deep breath. "Shelby. Who is the operative?"

"Blue."

"And you think that's who I am?"

Grinning, Shelby countered, "I don't know that it's not."

The corner of Kris' mouth turned up. *She was trying to protect me. Why should she care?* "Thanks for looking out for me."

Shelby smiled shyly and looked away. "You're welcome."

Kris searched for something light to say. She was usually adept at casual conversation when necessary, but Shelby's concern had touched her and she was still trying to come to grips with that.

"Do you see your aunt and uncle very often?"

Kris glanced at Shelby, surprised at the question. "No. You could say we're estranged."

"Oh."

The operative was curious about Shelby's family, and wanted the focus of the conversation off her own past, but understood that if she expected the analyst to be open with her, she had to be forthcoming as well. "What's your family like?"

"Pretty average, I guess. My sister Ann lives in Seattle, and my half-brothers, Jimmy and Jason, live with my mother in Arlington. What about you? Do you have any sisters or brothers?"

Well, that certainly was the short version. "No. I'm an only child. Remember I told you my aunt and uncle raised me?" Shelby nodded and Kris continued. "My father was in the Army and died on a training mission when I was a baby. I don't even remember him. Mom was killed by a car when I was ten."

"Oh, I'm so sorry."

Kris shrugged. "It's okay. It was a long time ago."

Shelby was pleased that Kris was finally sharing. "Did your aunt and uncle have any kids?"

"No."

"That must have been really hard for you. I'm glad I had a sister to grow up with. My two half-brothers are pretty good kids, but there's almost ten years between us, so I was more of a babysitter to them than anything else."

Kris stood up and walked over to a picture on top of one of the bookshelves, inclining her head towards it. The picture was of an attractive woman in her forties with golden brown, shoulder-length hair who was smiling at the camera, but Kris sensed the smile was forced. "This is your mom?"

Joining her, Shelby said, "Yeah. She had it taken last year. My sister and I have been asking her for an up-to-date picture for a while, so it was her Christmas present to us."

"Your mom's an attractive woman."

"I think so, too, but then I'm probably a little prejudiced."

Kris inclined her head to one side and studied Shelby. "You have her nose."

"Well now, that's different. I've been told I resemble her."

The operative looked at the picture again. While there was a family resemblance, she was put off by the woman in the picture. Kris was sure Shelby's mom did not possess the same sunny personality her daughter did. "A little. You're better looking, though."

Shelby could feel her cheeks warm and chuckled to cover her reaction to the compliment. "Thanks, but don't ever let her hear you say so."

"I don't think you have to worry about that. I'll be gone in a week or so."

The younger woman smiled sadly at the flippant comment. "I bet you'll be glad. No more sitting at a desk, looking at a monitor all day long."

Kris suddenly realized how her comment had sounded. "I'll be glad because I don't like being cooped up in an office." *And because I need to get away from the constant scrutiny and surveillance I'm under.* "I'll miss working with you, though." *What in the hell am I doing?*

When the two women sat back down on the couch, Stormy jumped between them, meowing plaintively, and both women automatically reached out to pet her. Kris pulled her hand back when her stroke landed on Shelby's hand rather than the kitten.

Laughing, Shelby said, "I guess we both had the same idea. Talk about a greedy kitten. Notice how she got right in the middle of us. Nothing stupid about this one."

"I hear you." Kris' attention was actually focused on how soft Shelby's hand had felt beneath her fingertips and, as her thoughts became heated, she suddenly stood up.

"What's wrong?"

"Um. Nothing. Just stretching my legs. Is there a public gym around here anywhere?"

"I have a membership at Theresa's Fitness Center."

"Want to go?" Kris was starting to feel caged in, and she knew it was time to find a physical outlet to control her excess energy and urges. She would've preferred running in the neighborhood, but couldn't guarantee Shelby's safety on the streets.

Shelby was more than ready to do something normal. "Sure. Let me get my things together."

Kris quickly changed into a pair of silky, dark blue jogging shorts and a matching tank top. After attaching a miniature cellular phone to the waistband and concealing her gun within the folds of a sweatshirt she was carrying, Kris went downstairs to check the area. Returning a short time later, she walked into the apartment and looked at Shelby admiringy. Her companion was wearing a stylishly cut teal workout suit, with close-fitting leggings emphasizing shapely legs and a white form-fitting top offset by a lightweight teal vest trimmed in black. "You look very nice. Ready?"

Shelby's could feel her cheeks warm, but the tingling feeling she was experiencing under the intensity of Kris' admiring gaze overshadowed that reaction. When she finally found her voice, she nodded and said, "You look pretty good yourself."

She silently cheered when the tips of Kris' ears reddened, knowing that her compliment had not been ignored. "Ready?" she mimicked.

Kris nodded. She was more than ready, and still wondering how a simple compliment could evoke the strong physical reaction it had. While she readily acknowledged an attraction to the younger woman, she had sought to limit their association to one of professional respect. Kris was finding it disconcerting that both her emotions and her body had shown a distinct proclivity to ignore the constraints she tried to place upon them and act of their accord. And for a woman who was used to being in complete control, it was a peculiarly vulnerable feeling.

As they started out the door, the phone rang. Shelby smiled apologetically and answered it. "Hello."

"Hi, Shelby. It's Mom. How come you haven't returned my phone calls? I've been worried sick about you."

"I was going to later. I've just been a little busy lately."

"Too busy for your own mother?"

Shelby silently sighed. "No, Mom." In an effort to change the focus of the conversation, she asked, "Did Jimmy and Jason both make the baseball team?"

"If you'd stop over more often, you could ask them yourself."

"Mom, what did you do, take a crabby pill before you called?"

Kris was barely able to stifle a snicker at the comment. She was standing in the doorway and hadn't intended to eavesdrop, but the apartment was too small to avoid hearing the conversation.

"I can't believe you are talking to your own mother like that. All the years I sacrificed and went through hell to give you things I never had, and you don't even appreciate it."

Shelby's face momentarily darkened. *You'll always be a victim, won't you, Mom? What about the hell Ann and I went through because you did nothing to stop it?* "Mom, what's wrong? You've been on my case since I picked up the phone."

"I had a busy day at work today and then had to come home and cook for the boys. Can I relax yet? No. Because you haven't called me all week, and I was worried about you. Do you appreciate my concern? Of course not. Instead you insult me."

Shelby rolled her eyes, strolled over to the couch and flopped down. "I shouldn't have said that. But I've been really busy with work stuff, too, and just haven't had much time to call. So can we call a truce?"

Somewhat mollified, Lisa said, "Yes, dear. I just miss you."

"I miss you, too. I'll stop over next weekend."

"Can't you stop over this weekend? I'll make dinner. I could really use some adult company."

Shelby sighed inwardly. "Let me see how things go at work and I'll get back to you, okay?"

"Just for a couple of hours, Shelby?"

"I've got to go. I'll call you later."

"Why? What's the big hurry? I haven't talked to you all week."

Kris had watched various emotions flicker across Shelby's face and had heard the frustration in her voice for long enough. She walked over to the apartment door and knocked loudly.

Shelby jumped at the noise, but seeing Kris at the door, she immediately understood that the other woman was giving her an out. "Mom, I gotta go. Someone's at the door."

"Well, okay, dear. Now don't forget to call me back."

"I won't. Bye, Mom."

Shelby shook her head, laid down the phone, and glanced at Kris. "Thanks."

"Didn't mean to butt in, but I figured you needed a break."

"Did I ever! She was really on a roll tonight."

Locking up, she followed Kris to the car. After the operative pulled out of the parking lot, Shelby turned curious green eyes on her companion. "What was your mother like? Do you remember?"

Kris was caught off guard by the question and torn about whether or not to answer. Her emotions were still raw from her recollections earlier that day, but she sensed Shelby needed to talk. She hadn't talked to anyone about her mother since she was a child. It had been forbidden at the Institute, so she had tucked all the memories of her mother into a safe, dark corner in her mind—separate from the brutal memories of their parting.

Almost before she was aware of having made a decision, Kris began speaking. "She was pretty cool for a mother. At least that's the way I remember her. She was tall, but I think I'm probably taller now, and had short, dark brown hair. Mom had a pretty smile and hazel eyes that changed colors depending on what she wore. She used to smile and laugh a lot."

Kris' eyes were unfocused as an image of her mother formed in her mind. "Mom raised me by herself and worked long hours at a factory to support us. It was hard for her with no one to help her, but she never complained or took it out on me. We didn't have fancy things, barely got by, but it didn't seem to matter."

Shelby saw a softness she had sensed but never witnessed on the operative's face as she spoke of her mother, and knew she was seeing a side of the woman that few had ever been privy to.

Kris shrugged. "That's about it."

"She sounds like she was a great mother."

"Yeah, she was." Kris looked away from Shelby, concerned about the comfort she felt in talking to her. She had chosen to share that memory and it had felt good to do so, and that worried her.

AFTER SIGNING IN as a guest, Kris glanced at Shelby. "Where to first?"

"I usually warm up, then work out on some of weight equipment. We can do whatever you want, though."

Kris smiled. "No, that sounds fine. Lead on."

Shelby inclined her head to the right. "Over this way." She led the way to a room in the back of the facility that had an assortment of stationary bicycles and rowing machines in the front of the room, and stair steppers in the rear. "I usually warm up on the bike for about twenty minutes."

Noting that all of the machines faced forward, Kris opted for the stair stepper. She wanted a vigorous workout, and it would allow her to keep an eye on Shelby at the same time. "I'm going to do the stair stepper."

"Okay." Shelby mounted one of the stationary bicycles and adjusted the tension as she began pedaling. She would rather have had Kris right next to her, but knew they would be able to work together on the remainder of the regimen.

Kris was lucky enough to find a vacant stair stepper just to the left and rear of Shelby's location and started moving the high steps in a steady, rhythmic pace, gradually increasing her speed to where it was comfortable yet taxing. She normally found this type of exercise incredibly boring, but watching Shelby's shapely legs smoothly work the bicycle in front of her was proving quite enjoyable. It wasn't until a salty drop of sweat blinded her in one eye that she realized her own speed had increased proportionally with her enjoyment, and she consciously slowed down. Stepping off the platform, she joined Shelby when she saw her begin to slow. "All warmed up?"

"Yeah. How about you?"

"Oh, absolutely."

Shelby noticed the drops of moisture that had escaped from the sweatband Kris wore around her head and the sheen of sweat apparent on her body, and chuckled. "You sure are. Don't you believe in starting slow and easy?"

Kris bit off a chuckle, knowing her mind had gone in a totally different direction than Shelby's. "Always."

Shelby shook her head, amused. "Well, your definition of slow and easy must be different than mine."

No. I don't think it is. Want to find out? Kris cut off her train of thought and issued a stern warning to herself. *Don't even go there!* She looked at Shelby and shrugged noncommittally, then followed her to the workout room.

The two women steadily progressed through the various pieces of equipment designed to tone different parts of the body. Kris limited her use of the apparatus to those in which her view wasn't obscured. They were currently at a machine that worked the muscles of the abdomen and shoulders. Kris noticed Shelby seemed to be straining as she operated the overhead bar, even though she hadn't said anything. She laid her hand on Shelby's arm. "Wait a minute. The tension is too tight for you."

Shelby had been so intent on watching the smooth rippling of Kris' sinewy muscles each time she leaned back and then slowly sat up drawing the bar over her head, she hadn't even thought about adjusting the tension when she sat down, and the feel of Kris' hand further distracted her. Once the setting was adjusted, she easily maneuvered the overhead bar. "Thanks."

Kris smiled. "Next time, say something, okay?"

Smiling, Shelby nodded as she positioned herself on the padded bench. Reaching up, she securely grasped the overhead bar in her hands before slowly pulling it forward, then letting it guide her back down until she had achieved a steady rhythmic motion.

Kris stood off to the side and suddenly found herself transfixed by the movement of Shelby's breasts and abdomen each time she laid back in the chair and brought the bar back over her head. Sucking in a deep breath, Kris tried to will her eyes away from the incredibly sensual movement, but couldn't summon the motivation to do so. When her companion released the bar, Kris finally quit staring and glanced away, sure that if she didn't Shelby would see the desire reflected in her eyes.

Shelby swung around on the bench only to find Kris gazing

around the room. Disappointed that the operative hadn't been watching her work out, she said, "We've been through all the ones I normally do. Anything else you want to try?"

Kris was still uncomfortably aroused. "No. I'd rather run for a while, stretch out my legs a bit."

"Okay." Shelby usually enjoyed a couple of nice leisurely laps jogging around the track, and was looking forward to running with the Kris. After five laps, Shelby had had enough. She sensed Kris had kept her pace slow for her benefit, but the heavy workout had taken a toll. She slowed to a walk. "That's it for me."

Kris slowed along with Shelby, and looked at the flushed, tired face. She had to restrain herself from brushing an errant lock of hair from Shelby's face. "Okay. Let's go."

When they arrived on the ground floor, Shelby headed towards the locker room.

"Where are you going?"

"To take a shower. I have clean towels in my locker."

"It would be better if we shower at your place."

"Oh yeah, right." Shelby couldn't believe she had actually momentarily forgotten about the danger they could be in.

Noticing the sudden worry reflected in her companion's face, Kris gazed into Shelby's eyes, losing herself in the soft green pools. "Don't worry. You're safe with me."

Shelby never hesitated. "I know."

Kris looked away first. *What are you doing?* "Ready?"

Shelby nodded, and they were walking toward the entrance when two smiling men stepped into their path, intercepting them.

The taller of the two said, "Hi, ladies. I'm Bob, and this is Greg. We were going to stop next door and get a sandwich. Would you care to join us?"

Kris quickly assessed the men. Bob sported a muscular physique. Boyishly handsome, his fashionably cut blonde hair fell over his forehead. His companion was a couple of inches shorter, with brown hair and a slighter build. He lacked the well-defined muscles of his companion, but appeared to be very fit. She dismissed them as potential threats, figuring them for regulars at the health club. "No thanks."

Bob turned his attention to Shelby. "What about you? It'd be fun."

Shelby smiled. "No thanks. We've gotta be going."

"Could I have your phone number, then? Maybe we could get together when you don't have," looking pointedly at Kris, he finished, "company."

Her eyes paling, Kris said pleasantly, "Would you mind getting out of our way? We said we weren't interested."

"How about letting your friend answer for herself."

Kris glanced at Shelby who said, "I don't give my phone number to strangers."

Greg looked at his friend. "Come on. We're wasting our time."

Bob wasn't used to being turned down. Most of the women at the gym welcomed his attention. He had been intrigued by the two strangers, but was angry with the tall woman, convinced the other one would've accepted his invitation had she not stepped in. His ego bruised by the rebuff, he glared at Kris. "What are you? A couple of dykes?"

Shelby met Bob's eyes. "Is that what you say to every woman who turns you down?"

Bob's face turned red. "You little bitch." Glaring, he took a step forward, only to find his progress halted abruptly when Blue stepped between him and Shelby.

"Get out of our way, now."

Intimidated by the cold eyes glaring at him, Bob stepped back.

Kris grasped Shelby's arm and began leading her around the men toward the door. "You were wasting your breath."

Bob watched the two women progress through the door, then jerked his head after them. "Come on."

Greg shook his head. "No. Just forget them."

Bob ignored him and walked outside. He stood near the door watching the women get into the car and drive away before walking back inside to join Greg.

Blue kept an eye on Bob until she merged with traffic on the street. She knew his ego had been injured, but considered him no threat.

"Why was he watching us?"

"Oh, he just wanted the last word."

Shelby chuckled. "I never thought of that." She gazed at Kris, thoughtfully. "I've never been called a dyke before."

"Does that bother you?"

"That someone thinks I'm a dyke? Not really. It's not something I ever thought about much." *Until lately.* "Did it bother you?"

Kris chuckled. "No. I don't have a problem with dykes, lesbians or gays."

"Oh, I don't either. I just never thought of myself as one." *But I am attracted to you, even though I haven't associated my interest in those terms.*

Nodding, Kris glanced at Shelby but remained silent, an inscrutable expression her face. A few minutes later, Shelby saw a convenience store. "Let's stop and pick up some lunch meat and bread." The drive home was quiet, with both women questioning their attraction to, and growing feelings for, the other.

Kris saw no sign of a tail, but as a precaution drove down the streets immediately bordering the complex. She scanned the parking lot as she drove in, noting it was empty except for parked vehicles. Exiting the car, she moved to the passenger side and waited as Shelby got out, closing the door behind her.

"We are going to have to go grocery shopping soon. Sandwiches are fine for tonight, but I'd like a little more choice." Shelby was walking slightly in front of Kris and when the tall woman didn't respond, added pointedly, "Since we ended up leaving all our groceries at the store last night."

Several things processed in Blue's mind concurrently, each impression separated only by nanoseconds—a silver Cavalier pulling in too slowly. A window rolling down. An object being extended from the driver's side.

She threw her body against Shelby's, wrapping her arms around the analyst in a tackling move. Her momentum carried them both to the ground, and their impact coincided with the unmistakable crack of a weapon being fired and shattering the relative silence of their surroundings.

Blue rolled them beneath the undercarriage of a nearby Jeep Cherokee before releasing Shelby and taking a covering position in front of her, weapon drawn and ready; but the Chevy accelerated out of the parking lot and into the street. Following procedure, she reached for the miniature cellular phone attached to her waistband, relieved that it hadn't become dislodged during their fall.

She quickly glanced at it and pressed one, the speed dial associated with Earl's private phone. When he answered, she simply stated, "Code 1, apartment complex," and disconnected.

Shelby was terrified and scooted further under the car until she heard Kris whisper, "Don't go any farther. We may have to move fast if he comes back."

Blue rose to her knees, and kept well below the windows of the car as she chanced a quick look around. The silver Cavalier had not returned, but, unwilling to take any chances, she remained in place, shielding Shelby's body with her own.

Fortunately, the shot hadn't attracted the attention of any of the apartment dwellers and Blue knew that was most likely because, to an untrained ear, a shot sounded remarkably similar to a car backfiring. She knew it would only be a matter of minutes before Earl's team arrived and she waited patiently for her associates, senses on full alert.

Shelby remained frozen in place, not uttering a word. She had no intention of doing anything to divert Kris' attention. Her arm was throbbing painfully, and her hip hurt, although not as badly. She could see blood dripping from a scrape extending the length of Kris' arm as she held her gun over them protectively.

Confusing questions tumbled through her numb mind. *Which one of us was shot at? Are these the guys that Kris said she'd take care of? What's really going on? Was this about the case, or only about Kris?*

A quarter of an hour later, which seemed like an eternity to Shelby, she watched Kris answer her cell phone. "Okay. Earl's here. Stay down until I make a visual ID."

The sounds of a couple cars and quiet voices filled the air. She watched Kris cautiously rise, and then stoop down.

"It's okay." She extended her arm to Shelby and helped her up. "You okay?"

Shelby stretched painfully, taking inventory. Noting Kris' concerned gaze, she said, "My hip's a little sore and my arm is killing me, but yeah, I think so."

Earl strode over to Kris and Shelby. "What in the hell happened?"

Blue shrugged. "Not much I can tell you. The shot was fired from a silver Cavalier, probably a '95 or '96. I didn't get much of a look and by the time I was in a position to see the license number, he was too far away."

"He's probably long gone."

Though Kris nodded in agreement, Earl quickly assigned search corridors to the six agents that had accompanied him. "Any idea who it might be?"

Kris shook her head. "None."

"What about you, Shelby? That's twice you've been shot at in a parking lot. Once could have been coincidence, but twice? Not likely, is it?"

"No."

Kris gazed at Shelby. Noting her pale, drawn face, she turned to Earl. "Any reason you can't direct the operation from inside?"

"No. Let's go." He moved behind Kris as she slowly walked next to the limping analyst. This was the strangest case he could remember working on since he'd retired from the field. More was going on than was apparent, but what that could be, he had no idea. He was going to have to devote some of his time to trying to find out. Earl also questioned the wisdom of leaving Shelby on the case. There was no proof that either shooting was case-related, yet it couldn't be ruled out either. He decided to see what Shelby wanted to do.

As they walked through the door, Kris reached down and picked up Stormy, then handed her to Shelby. She'd known that greeting the kitten would be her companion's first priority upon entering the apartment and, noticing how she was favoring her arm and trying to hide a slight limp, had wanted to save her any further discomfort. She was rewarded with a warm smile.

Once all three of them were seated in the living room, Earl opened the discussion. "Shelby, I'm thinking about taking you off this case. Do you have a problem with that?"

A quick influx of color suffused the pale face. "Yes, I do. I started it, and I want to see it through."

Earl had expected that answer. "Okay, how about moving to a safe house?"

Kris stood up. "I don't think that's a good idea. There is obviously a leak on this case and until you find it, she's safer with me."

"Hey look, I wasn't insinuating you can't handle the assignment. I'm just trying to look out for her welfare."

"How are you going to keep the location secret? She can be shot at just as easily going in and out of a safe house as here. Unless you intend to keep her locked up twenty-four hours a day, what are you going to do—surround her with operatives every time she moves? You could be exposing her to even more danger if the security breach includes one of the agents guarding her."

Shelby tried to think of something light to say to ease the tension between Earl and Kris. "You know, Kris, you must have really pissed Bob off."

As Shelby's words sank in, Kris grinned. "Nah. He was just an overgrown wus."

"What are you two talking about, and who is Bob?"

Smiling, Shelby said, "Oh, just a guy we met at the gym who wasn't too happy about taking no for an answer."

Earl looked at Kris, only to find her gazing at him, amused. He could just imagine what had transpired. "Any possibility?"

"No, Earl. Shelby was just tweaking you."

He turned toward Shelby. "Is there anyone that you can think of who might have a personal grudge against you—an old boyfriend, someone from your old job, anyone at all?"

"No." Shelby hesitated as an image appeared in her mind, but discarded it as paranoia. "I can't think of anyone who would shoot at me."

Kris watched Shelby closely. She instinctively felt there was something she wasn't sharing. The operative intended to pursue it later.

Earl mused aloud. "Then we're no closer to finding an answer than we were before."

Kris' voice turned serious. "No, but Earl, everything points to a leak. You need to find it." *But I'll probably beat you to it.*

Shelby lifted Stormy from her lap and stood up. "I need to use the bathroom. I'll be right back."

Once Blue heard the door close, she met Earl's direct gaze with her own. "Did you know the grapevine has Blue at Langley?

Thought you might find that interesting."

"Shit!"

"My thoughts exactly. Now tell me you don't have a leak."

Earl mused, "It would seem so. How'd you find out?"

"Shelby mentioned it earlier."

Raising an eyebrow, Earl looked at her in surprise. "You told her Blue was your code name?"

"Not hardly. She somehow pieced it together herself, but I don't think she's really made up her mind whether I am or not."

Shelby's eyes widened as she neared the living room. *So I was right!* She knew the evidence had pointed toward Kris being Blue, but even though she'd actively thought about it, deep down she really hadn't believed it, even going so far as to convince herself that an operative that valuable and deadly would not be brought in to work a desk case.

But this was cold, harsh reality. She could no longer hide behind the comfort of not knowing for certain. The woman she was growing increasingly fond of was the notorious Blue, whose reputation was whispered of with awe throughout the Company's corridors and was the beating pulse of the rumor mill. *But, does knowing for sure really make any difference? No. It doesn't.*

Shelby saw Kris staring at her. For one brief fleeting moment, haunted blue eyes met tumultuous green ones. Then Kris stalked past, and in a voice totally devoid of emotion, flatly stated, "Now you know," before walking out onto the balcony.

Earl answered his cell phone and after disconnecting followed Kris out onto the balcony. "Relax. She's on our side. It doesn't really matter."

Kris looked at her boss. *Not to you it doesn't. To Shelby, it might.* "Right."

"We're finished. The teams came up empty. I'm leaving two agents behind for the rest of the night. I'll be in touch."

The operative nodded and followed Earl back into the apartment, securing the door when he left. She turned around to find somber green eyes gazing at her.

Chapter Nine

KRIS MET SHELBY'S gaze. She would have had to have been blind to have missed the surprise in those gorgeous green eyes when the analyst overheard her conversation with Earl. At that instant she'd realized that Shelby had never really believed that she was Blue. *It's better this way. She'll be afraid of me and back off.*

Shelby was at a loss for words; Kris seemed more distant than ever. She wracked her brain for anything that might dispel the tension permeating the apartment, and then caught a glimpse of the underside of Kris' arm. "You're still bleeding." She headed for the kitchen, calling back over her shoulder, "I'll get some peroxide to clean that up."

Kris stared at Shelby's retreating figure, confused. She hadn't sensed the fear she'd expected to see. *Doesn't she get it? She should be afraid—very afraid. Why isn't she?* Irritably, she growled, "Surprised?"

Shelby sighed. Stopping, she turned to face the operative. "Surprised about what, Kris? That you bleed, just like I do? Or that you are Blue?"

Narrowing her eyes as she approached Shelby, Blue snorted, then drawled sardonically, "Both. I'm sure you've heard the rumors."

Nodding, Shelby ignored the derisive expression and met Blue's intense gaze. "Yes, I have. So, all of a sudden I'm supposed to think you're some invincible, cold-blooded machine? You're still human, Kris. You have feelings, no matter how deeply you bury them, and you can get hurt, too, even though you're loath to admit it; and yes, you bleed, just like I do. So, just what am I supposed to be so surprised about?"

Blue snapped. "Don't you get it? I am *not* like you. Think about who I am. You should be afraid of me."

Shelby stared at the intimidating woman glaring down at her. Kris did scare her when she was like this, but it was a fear of what the operative was capable of, not fear for her own safety. Shelby spoke with quiet certainty. "You wouldn't hurt me."

Kris' eyes widened in amazement and she looked away, biting off a scathing retort. The operative had faced down many powerful foes, yet this woman refused to be intimidated; she struggled to understand that. This was totally outside her realm of experience. She wanted to scream in frustration.

Blue was an expert at manipulation and could usually cajole the most unlikely people into doing whatever she wanted them to. As for those that didn't—well, there were other ways to get them to comply with her wishes. But the woman standing in front of her wasn't like those countless others. She didn't want to try to manipulate Shelby and wasn't sure she could anyway. Her interest in the analyst had long since surpassed anything she could rationalize. *Why is she different? And why am I letting her get to me?* Kris knew part of the answer. *Because she cares.*

Kris became angry. Angry because Shelby cared, and angry because she was glad that Shelby cared, and angry because she couldn't let Shelby know that she cared.

Shelby watched the naked emotions play across the usually unrevealing face as the operative's eyes turned distant and troubled. She wanted to say something, anything, to stop Kris from looking so unhappy and angry, but was leery of interrupting her thoughts, knowing she had very probably pushed her too far already. She turned around, reaching into the cupboard for the bottle of peroxide.

"How's your arm?"

Surprised, Shelby plucked the bottle from the shelf and turned around. "It's a little sore."

"Mind if I check it out?"

"Uh, sure." Shelby held out her left arm and the tall woman grasped it, gently probing the bruised area around the analyst's wrist with a deft touch.

Kris looked up. "I wanted to make sure we didn't need to get it X-rayed. It feels okay, but it's going to be sore for a few days. You were limping?"

"I landed on my hip." Shelby smiled wanly. "I have more padding there." She handed Kris the peroxide. "Need some help?"

Kris shook her head. "Why don't you go ahead and shower? Then I'll take mine and clean this up."

The operative watched Shelby slowly make her way down the hall before returning to the door to retrieve the bag of lunch meat one of Earl's men had recovered from the parking lot. She put the perishables in the refrigerator, laid the partly squashed loaf of bread on the counter, and walked into the living room.

Shelby returned to the kitchen a short time later, smiling when she saw the bread. It would make some interesting looking sandwiches. She saw Kris looking out the balcony door. "Your turn."

She opened the refrigerator, retrieving the braunschweiger, sliced turkey, spicy mustard, and a small jar of Miracle Whip. Taking out an onion, she set it on the counter with the rest of the food and reached into the cupboard for a couple of saucers before remembering she had used the last of the napkins. She pulled the step stool over and climbed on it to reach the extra package stored in one of the high cupboards.

Kris rounded the doorway into the kitchen only to bump solidly into Shelby, who was stepping off the stool. Her surprise gave way to a plethora of fleeting impressions as her body reacted to the contact. She steadied Shelby and stepped away. "You okay? I didn't hurt you, did I?"

No. No, I'm not okay. Shelby tried to slow her racing heart and had trouble finding her voice. "Yeah. Sorry."

"My fault. I didn't want you to go to any trouble on my account." *She even remembered how I like my sandwich.* "You go ahead and make yours. I'll make mine when I get out of the shower."

"I have a better idea. Why don't you go take your shower, and I'll fix both sandwiches. I really don't mind." She smiled winningly. "Okay?"

Gazing at Shelby, Kris nodded slowly. "Thank you. I'd like that."

Shelby smiled at the small victory, turning her attention back to the sandwiches as Kris left. She was still wired from the energy rolling off the operative in waves a few moments earlier, and her body instinctively reveled in the sensation.

Her thoughts turned reflective. She had given up trying to justify her feelings for Kris. For the first time in her life, Shelby thought she understood what her sister, Ann, had said two years before about her decision to marry Steven and move to Seattle.

"Shelby, have you ever met anyone that just took your breath away and you didn't know why, but they did? Such a strong attraction that you couldn't ignore it, and you just knew you had to know more about that person? That's how I feel about Steve. I was lucky; he feels the same way."

Now Shelby knew. Kris had never encouraged her interest in any way; and to the best of her knowledge, the operative had no interest in her. Yet her burning desire to know all about the enigmatic woman increased with each passing day. She smiled ruefully. *Hey, Ann, what would you think if I told you I know what you mean now? What would you think if I told you I have that feeling for another woman? What would you think if I told you she was an assassin, on a list of suspects for a series of unsanctioned hits?*

The internal conversation ended as Shelby acknowledged that it didn't matter what her sister, or anyone else, thought. It didn't matter to her that Kris was a woman; what mattered was what she felt. She really didn't think her partner was the killer they were looking for—so she dismissed that part of the equation.

If the rumors were to be believed, Kris was indeed a very deadly operative. On a logical level, she understood the operative's activities were government-sanctioned, but she wondered how Kris could've become hard and calloused enough to kill without remorse. *Or did she?* Shelby suddenly realized she didn't know the answer to that.

She briefly pondered why she didn't have more of a problem dealing with her feelings for a woman. Her mother and stepfather had both preached about the sins of society and in their minds, homosexuality was one of them. Her face darkened momentarily. *Like he had the right to talk about anyone else.*

Shelby's mind shied away from thoughts of her stepfather. Her background in psychology had demanded much self-analysis. She genuinely enjoyed interacting with others, but trust was something she guarded zealously. *Do I trust Kris? Beyond the surface? I want to. Do I dare?*

She sadly acknowledged that she was unlikely to ever find out because she was trapped in a no-win situation. Her feelings weren't something that were going to go away when Kris left, and the chance of them being reciprocated was infinitesimally small.

Kris took her time in the shower. Shelby had thrown her for a loop, and she needed some time to try and get a handle on her feelings. She grinned ruefully. Even though she had mentally prepared to face a different reaction from Shelby, her body had obviously not listened to her mind and she had to physically refrain from just wrapping the small woman into a hug when they had collided. She snorted. *Don't think that would've gone over very well.* An image of Shelby's flushed face appeared in her mind. *Or would it have? It was an accident, why was she embarrassed? Maybe she wasn't.*

She cares about me. Kris savored that thought as it caressed her mind, liking the way it felt. *She wouldn't if she knew who and what you really are.* The cold, stark reality of the logical observation quickly extinguished her pleasure at Shelby's concern, and she turned her attention back to showering.

The operative had just finished donning a pair of shorts and a T-shirt when a quiet rap sounded on the door. Kris opened it to find Shelby standing there, holding out the bottle of peroxide.

"You forgot this."

Kris smiled at the thoughtfulness. "Thanks." She opened the bottle, held her arm over the sink and began pouring the disinfectant over the painfully scraped flesh.

Shelby stared at Kris, grabbed the bottle from her hand, and set it down. "I can't believe you did that." She reached around Kris, removed a large cotton ball from a container on the shelf over the toilet, and began gently dabbing the excess moisture from Kris' arm.

Resisting the instant urge to pull her arm away when Shelby grasped it, Kris watched her, and when the other woman finally seemed satisfied, she asked dryly, "Finished?"

"No. I'm going to put some antibiotic ointment on it. It would be easier if you sat down."

Kris dropped to the toilet seat, shaking her head, but actually enjoying the attention. She appreciated Shelby's feather light touch and smiled. "Thanks." The answering smile warmed her heart.

"You're all set. Let's go eat."

Kris trailed Shelby to the dining room and sat down at the table. "Looks good."

Shelby chuckled. "Whatever you say." She picked up her sandwich and took a bite, realizing suddenly that she was starved. She quipped, "Hey, next time you decide to tackle me, could you pick a softer landing spot?"

Kris had just taken a drink of Coke and fought to keep it from going down the wrong way. *How about your bed?* Stilling the inner voice, she commented wryly, "I'll be sure and keep that in mind."

A short time later, their sandwiches eaten, the two women remained sitting across from each other at the table. Shelby decided to bring up what had been bothering her most about the shooting. "How come we were shot at? You said the guy following us at the grocery store had nothing to do with the case. Then how come they came here? You said you would take care of it. I thought that's why you left work earlier today."

"We weren't shot at by the guy following me."

"Then who?"

"I was going to ask you the same question. You hesitated when Earl asked you if you had any enemies. Why?"

Shelby answered evasively. "I was just considering, that's all."

Kris met Shelby's eyes. "If you don't have any enemies, you wouldn't have to think about it. Who came to mind?"

"No one that would shoot at me, okay?" Shelby shoved her chair back, standing.

The operative stood with her. "Do you want to bet your life on that? *You* are the one being shot at. Whoever it is might get lucky next time. Damn it, talk to me."

Shelby walked over to the bookcase and stared blindly at her collection. "My stepfather threatened me when I testified against him in court for domestic violence against my mother. She refused to testify, but I did, so he was convicted. Since he was such a fine upstanding citizen, all he got was three years probation. I haven't seen him since I got a restraining order against him, but that's probably expired by now."

Sighing, she turned to face Kris. "I don't know why he came to mind today. He's a despicable excuse for a man, but I really don't think he's capable of murder."

Kris looked into the guarded eyes and instinctively knew there was more. "He hurt you, too, didn't he?"

Shelby turned back to the bookcase. "It doesn't matter. It was a long time ago."

Kris moved behind her and laid a hand on her shoulder, squeezing it gently. "It matters to me, Shelby."

Looking at Kris' reflection in the glass, Shelby asked, "Why?"

"Because you're a wonderful, delightful woman I've been lucky enough to get to know, and I care about you." Kris hadn't intended to voice her thoughts, but had no regrets about doing so.

Shelby's brow furrowed as she regarded the woman behind her. This was what she had wanted and part of her was elated. But this meant sharing on a deeply personal level. Would the operative think less of her? Could she trust Kris not to pity her? "You care about me?"

Kris nodded her answer, knowing Shelby was watching her in the glass.

Making her decision, Shelby opened the bookcase door and pulled out a white horse with sparkling pink wings. She stared at the statue of Pegasus. "When I was a child, I used to believe in magic. I knew that one day the real Pegasus would come and take me away from the pain and the hurt to a magical kingdom full of love. He never did, so I quit believing, but I loved the magical creatures anyway because I could escape into their world through books. They kept me from being lonely when I was locked in my room or spending hours in a corner. I prayed to God a lot, promising him I would be good, asking him to help me be the perfect little girl my stepfather wanted me to be so he wouldn't hurt me any more. All that praying— it never did any good."

Taking a deep breath, Shelby began speaking in a voice totally devoid of emotion. "There's not much to tell. My father died when I was two. Mom worked for a couple of years, supporting me and my sister by herself, then married Jonathan Whiteman. He seemed like a dream come true. He took us to amusement parks, picnics, Sunday afternoon drives, and when the circus came to town, he took us there. He bought us dolls and stuffed animals, always smiling and playing with us. He asked us to call him daddy and told everyone we were his girls and how much he loved us. We grew to love him and thought we were the luckiest kids in the world to get such a nice, new daddy."

Kris, disturbed by the matter-of-fact monologue, began moving her hand in a soothing, circular motion over Shelby's back, hoping to offer the smaller woman comfort through the contact.

"Slowly, things began to change. He started punishing us by making us stand in the corner for hours. We were just little kids. Each minute seemed like an eternity, and he would hit us if we sat down. As we got older, the punishments started getting really physical. A lot of times, Ann and I never even did what we were accused of."

When Shelby paused, Kris gently asked, "What about your mother? Didn't she do anything?"

Shelby sighed loudly. "She said he was only doing it because he loved us, and if we were good it wouldn't happen."

Kris could feel the white hot threads of anger course through her. "That's not love!"

"No. It's not. But we didn't know that, and I didn't find out until a few years ago that she did try to stop it. We just figured we were really bad kids and were too ashamed and embarrassed to tell anyone. I thought things would get better when my first half-brother was born. It didn't. It got even worse. He got a perverse pleasure out of beating us with the buckle end of his belt until we bled." Shelby shuddered at the memory.

Kris moved behind her, gently massaging her shoulders, trying to work some of the tension out of them. She said softly, "You don't have to continue. I get the picture." *What I'd give to have fifteen minutes with that fucker.*

But a dam had broken, and Shelby couldn't stop the litany. "I used to change for gym in the toilet stalls and afterwards wait until all the other girls finished showering before I took mine. The bruises that showed, like when he hit us in the face, we always explained away as a fall or some other accident we made up. One day when I was fourteen, he hit me for the last time. Something just snapped. I told him if he ever laid a hand on me or Ann again, I'd call the cops. He just laughed until I told him we'd taken pictures of the bruises and bloody welts from the beatings with our Polaroid camera and had them hidden at school." Shelby chuckled mirthlessly. "We hadn't, but the threat worked. I didn't find out until four years ago that he'd been beating my mother all those years, too. She finally told me she had tried to stop him from beating us, but he'd just get mad and beat us even worse, so she quit saying anything, hoping things would improve."

She turned to face Kris. "You know what hurt the most? He shattered our love and trust. God, I hate him. I know I shouldn't after all this time, but I still do."

Kris struggled to contain the anger that was now burning hotly within her. In what she hoped was a soothing voice, she said, "You have every right to hate him."

"I used to blame myself, knowing I must have done something terrible to make him beat us so much."

"No! Don't ever think that."

"I don't anymore. It took me a while to get there, though. Now I understand he was just sick." She shrugged. "Bet you're sorry you asked."

"No, I'm not. I understand only too well."

"What do you mean?"

"Before I moved in with my aunt and uncle, I spent two years in...a boarding school. The headmaster was an expert at emotional and mental abuse to ensure blind obedience. His favorite tactic was complete isolation. After a while I'd have done anything to stay out of that room. He occasionally engaged in corporal punishment, too, but preferred to mess with our heads. I've never quit hating him either, Shelby. So, I do understand."

The two women looked at each other awkwardly. Shelby put the statue back in the cupboard and closed the door. She blurted out, "I care about you, too," before abruptly turning away and glancing at the table. "I'll clean up out here."

I know you do. "I'm glad you do. Now, how about getting off of your leg and letting me take care of the k.p.?"

Shelby smiled. "Thanks."

At 10:30, Kris rose from where she'd joined Shelby in front of the TV. "I'm going outside for a few minutes. I'll be right back."

"How come? I thought Earl said he was going have a couple of agents on surveillance outside for the rest of tonight."

"They are. I'm just gonna go check on them and make sure they're doing their job."

Shelby grinned. "Don't scare them off, okay?"

Kris chuckled. "Would I do something like that?" She was amused by Shelby's insight and chuckled when an emphatic, "Yes," followed her out the door.

When the phone rang, Shelby debated whether to answer it. Because Kim was out of town on a business trip, she knew it was probably her mother wanting to know about dinner.

"Hi, dear. It's Mom. Are you coming over Sunday?"

"I'd love to, but I really can't this weekend."

Disbelief colored Lisa's tone. "Why not?"

"Remember? I told you I'm working overtime on a case right now." *Well, that's not really a lie. I am tied up because of the case.*

"No one works twenty-four hours a day, Shelby. I'm sure you can fit a couple of hours for your family into your busy schedule."

Shelby sighed inwardly at the harsh voice. "Look, Mom, I'm working with someone who just transferred in, and she is staying here until the case is over. You yourself taught me how rude it is to ignore company."

Lisa couldn't argue that point and, suddenly curious about the spies she was sure her daughter worked with, said, "Bring her along."

"I can ask her, but I really don't think she would be comfortable in a house full of strangers."

"Well, ask her anyway. Tell her I am making my special fried chicken."

"Okay, I'll ask her, but don't count on it."

"You could try being a little more positive, dear. I'm sure you could convince her to come if you really wanted to. Bye bye."

Shelby refrained from slamming the phone down. Her mother never failed to get in a dig of some kind, and she'd done it again. She knew her mother was unhappy with her because she had been steadily decreasing the frequency of her visits.

She had hoped by doing that, her mother might get a hint and figure out that her constant criticism and complaining wasn't appreciated. So far it hadn't worked, and Shelby wondered if her mother even realized that she was doing it. Maybe she should be more direct and talk with her about it.

She stifled a chuckle as she thought about asking Kris if she would mind accompanying her to dinner at her mother's house. Now that she knew who she was, it seemed even more unlikely that the operative would accept. *I'm not being fair. She's still a woman, just like I am, and has feelings, too. She has no real family. When's the last time she got invited to someone's house for dinner?* Shelby snorted. *Let's be realistic here. With her looks, she probably gets invitations all the time. But does she go? Mom can be great when she isn't in her whiny, critical mode. I think Kris would really like Jimmy and Jason. Maybe I will mention it and see what her reaction is.*

Kris returned a short time later, and the two women retired for the night soon thereafter. Shelby had expected to be too wired to sleep, but quickly entered the dreamscape.

The operative stayed awake a little longer, her thoughts focused on one Jonathan Whiteman. She finally fell asleep after vowing to discover his whereabouts and find out just what he'd been doing for the past few years.

BLUE WAS OFF the couch, gun in hand, before she was even sure what had awakened her. She was running toward Shelby's room as the sounds of a faint struggle consciously registered, and she entered the room in a crouch, presenting the smallest possible target.

Her heart slowed when she realized the room was empty except for Shelby, who appeared to be in the throes of a nightmare. She was still asleep, but her bedcovers were tangled and twisted as though she'd been battling demons, and Kris realized she probably had been. She silently cursed herself for asking the younger woman to recall the horrors of her childhood.

She quickly approached the bed, laid her gun on the nightstand, and knelt beside the bed. "Shelby, it's okay. Wake up."

"No!" Shelby thrashed, fighting the bedcovers, and when Kris laid a hand on her shoulder trying to wake her, she jerked away, the nightlight illuminating tears on her face.

Kris wrapped her arms around Shelby, moved onto the edge of the bed, and lifted the smaller woman into a half-sitting position, tucking her firmly against her own body. "Shelby, wake up. You're safe. I've got you."

As Shelby started to calm in her arms, she continued her quiet assurances. "It's okay. You're safe. I won't let anyone hurt you."

Jonathan's enraged face began fading as Shelby drifted toward consciousness, her fear replaced by a strong feeling of comfort and safety. Her eyes fluttered open and she realized Kris was sitting on the bed gently rocking her back and forth.

Kris looked into the puzzled emerald eyes gazing at up at her. "You were having a nightmare."

Shelby nodded. "I haven't had one of those for years. Thanks for waking me up."

"It's the least I could do. I'm sorry, Shelby. I had no business asking you what I did today."

"It's not your fault. I think with everything that has been happening, my defenses were down."

Kris released Shelby. "You should get some sleep."

Shelby grasped her arm. "Wait. Would you stay in here? Just for a little while. I know I'm just being a baby, but please?"

"Sure." Kris thought of her own all-too-frequent nightmares. "You're not being a baby. Nightmares are hell."

Kris sat on the bed next to Shelby until the faint light of dawn appeared in the sky, ready to vanquish her demons should they reappear. Then she silently moved back to the couch in the living room, lying down to catch a quick hour of sleep.

SITTING AT HER desk the next morning, Shelby decided to broach the subject of her mother's invitation. "Hey, Kris." When the operative looked at her, she asked, "My mother invited us to dinner

Sunday. Want to go?"

Even though she hadn't met Shelby's mother, she already strongly disliked her. In her mind, any mother who allowed her children to be abused should be dealt with in the same manner as the actual abuser. Kris raised an eyebrow until it disappeared behind a thick covering of bangs. "Us?"

"Yeah. I told her you had transferred in to work on a case with me and were staying at my house. I figured she'd just forget about dinner until after you left. Wrong. I think she's curious about who I work with."

Kris nodded. "Okay." It would be interesting to meet Shelby's mother. She also knew her options would have been limited if the analyst had insisted on going, and was glad that she'd been given a choice.

Shelby smiled broadly. "Oh good! Thanks!"

Kris grinned at Shelby's enthusiasm and turned back to her monitor, just biding her time until lunch. She wanted to meet with her contact immediately, but had no means of relaying a message except through one of the drops. The quickest way, short of using the telephone number she'd gotten from Markov, would be using the emergency drop in Georgetown and leaving her cell phone number.

Her priority right now was to get the Russians to quit following her. The chance to deal with Sergei a.k.a. Dimitri would come soon enough. She also wanted to eliminate the slight possibility that Markov had acted independently of his superiors and shot at them, but that didn't feel right. She was convinced someone else was targeting Shelby.

Kris thought about her meeting with Earl that morning. They had found the bullet, but when they finished digging it out of the blacktop it was unrecognizable. It would take a couple of days for their lab to determine what type of weapon it was fired from. She and Earl had jointly decided not to continue the additional surveillance because of the lack of CIA jurisdiction domestically. Kris had been secretly relieved, because she had no choice but to set up a meeting with her contact on the apartment grounds. Her only other option, one that she refused to entertain, would have been to leave Shelby alone.

"I'm going to lunch. I'll be back shortly."

"Want some company?"

Another time, another place, yes. Not here and not now. "If I wasn't going to take care of some business, I'd love it. How about Monday?"

"Okay." Shelby hadn't expected to be invited along, but Kris' words warmed the cool office air even as she speculated where the operative was going this time.

Chapter Ten

HE PRESSED A memory button on his cell phone as he drove toward Arlington, and waited for it to be answered. "Did you get it?"

"No. And I don't know if I'm going to be able to."

"Why not? It's not like I asked you to do anything difficult."

"I can't find out without being obvious. Come on. I've already told you everything I know. I don't want to raise any suspicions. It might jeopardize what I'm doing for both of us."

"That has nothing to do with this."

"I know, but you worry me when you get so obsessed. Are you coming over tonight?"

"Maybe."

"Maybe? What's that supposed to mean?"

"I'll call you later." Disgusted, the tall man broke the connection, tossing his cellular phone onto the passenger seat.

KRIS HELPED SHELBY unpack the groceries, following her instructions on where to put the things that had to be placed in the upper row of cupboards. "Think you got enough food?" she asked facetiously.

Grinning, Shelby said, "Well, I wanted to make sure we didn't run out of anything. It's not like my life has been very routine lately. Who knows when I'll get another chance to go shopping?"

Kris laughed. "I don't think you'll have to worry about it for a long time now."

"You helped pay, so that makes you an accomplice."

Quirking a half smile, Kris said, "Couldn't see myself letting you spend a month's salary on groceries."

"Very funny!"

"Just calling it the way I see it."

The rest of the evening passed comfortably, the two women

spending it enjoying each other's company. The conversation was easy and relaxed as they watched TV and explored their mutual interests. Boundaries were unconsciously disregarded, with both of them relishing each tidbit of information the other chose to share, and committing even the smallest morsels to memory.

RIGHT ON SCHEDULE, Shelby woke from her sleep and sat up, the darkness of her bedroom broken only by the light of the bedside lamp. She'd been determined to wake up before Kris, and fell asleep the previous night while silently chanting, 'Wake up at 05:00,' over and over again. Although she rarely used it, her internal alarm clock never failed her.

Postponing all but the essentials of her wake-up routine in the bathroom, she continued silently to the kitchen. It was going to be hard enough not to wake Kris, and Shelby didn't intend to make any unnecessary noise.

She knew the operative was always up by 05:30, so her timing should be just about right. Fifteen minutes later, finished with her advance preparations, Shelby put the bacon in the microwave, set the timer and took one last look at the table to make sure she hadn't forgotten anything. Satisfied, she tiptoed into the living room and gazed at Kris.

The tall woman was sleeping all scrunched up on her side, the pillow and her feet pressed against opposite ends of the couch. *How can you sleep like that?* Shelby was startled when alert blue eyes opened, meeting her own gaze. "How'd you do that?"

"Do what?"

"I thought you were sleeping."

"I was." Kris smiled. "It smells good in here."

"Thanks." Shelby was still trying to figure out how anyone could be totally alert when they woke up. "But you woke up, awake."

"Tool of the trade. Allowing myself the luxury of waking up slowly could cost me my life."

"Oh." *I never even thought of that.* Shelby smiled. "Good morning."

Kris sat up and returned the smile. "G'morning."

"How do you like your eggs?"

"Over medium. What's the special occasion?"

"Well, I just thought—I have what I like for breakfast every day, but you don't, so I thought today we could have what you like." At the puzzled look on Kris' face, Shelby added, "Remember, you said you liked eggs, bacon, toast, juice, fruit..."

"I was only kidding."

A blonde eyebrow rose in question. "You don't like that?"

"No. I mean, yes, I do. But you didn't have to—"

"I wanted to. It'll be ready in about five minutes." Shelby gazed warmly at Kris, who appeared somewhat stunned. "Think you'll be ready to eat then?"

Kris slowly nodded. "Count on it."

A short time later both women were thoroughly enjoying the hearty breakfast and conversing easily. Kris took a bite of her egg as she listened to Shelby talk about a movie she had recently seen.

She felt a slight vibration at her waist and silently cursed. Kris had modified her cell phone to include a vibrate setting, and she had no doubt as to the identity of the caller. *Bastard. Couldn't even wait for the sun to rise, could you? What in the hell am I going to tell Shelby?*

Kris didn't want Shelby to think she didn't fully appreciate all the trouble she'd gone to, and leaving the table in the middle of the meal could certainly imply that. Besides, she was thoroughly enjoying the company and didn't want to leave the table. *As if I have a choice.*

When Shelby finished speaking, Kris abruptly stood up. "Excuse me, but nature calls." Kris immediately left the table and quickly made her way down the hall, shutting and locking the bathroom door behind her. She turned the tap water on full force and waited for the phone to ring again.

IGNORING THE EARLY hour, Gregor punched in the numbers from the note on his cell phone, allowing it to ring the requested three times and then hanging up. He looked at the tersely worded note again. While he was pleased that she had reestablished contact, he wondered why she had done so.

He had a few other questions he intended to ask as well, beginning with what had happened the evening before at the apartment complex. It would not do for one of their special contacts to be killed before she had provided any information of value. Gregor intended to have both the information he needed and the answers to his questions before another day dawned.

Five minutes later, he redialed the telephone number, this time waiting for it to be answered.

WHEN HER CELL phone lit up, Kris quelled her anger, and her tone was sharp, but quiet. "Yes?"

"I will be at the apartment complex tonight at 10:30."

"Fine." Kris clicked off and reattached the small phone to the waistband of the shorts she had donned earlier.

Shelby had watched Kris depart the dining room, puzzled. Had something she'd prepared upset the tall woman's system in some way? *My cooking couldn't be that bad, could it?* The food seemed fine to her and the operative had looked more irritated than sick, but, irrationally, she continued to worry. Moments later, she watched Kris return from what had to be the shortest bathroom break on record.

"Didn't mean to be rude."

Shelby smiled. "No problem. Are you okay?"

"Yeah. I'm fine, and breakfast is delicious!"

"You already told me that, but thanks again."

"I just wanted to make sure you hadn't forgotten. So, what are we going to do today?"

"We could go to Teresa's."

Chuckling, Kris quipped, "To work off our breakfast?"

"Well, it was kind of big."

"I thought it was just right."

"Good." She smiled to herself. *I actually got up at 05:00 a.m. on a Saturday just to surprise Kris with breakfast. It was worth it, though.* Shelby knew she would be hard-pressed to explain the elaborate breakfast without divulging the extent of her real feelings. *You've no idea how important you've become to me, and I wanted to do something just for you.*

Kris still couldn't believe all the trouble Shelby had gone to on her behalf and gazed into the warm green eyes. "Thank you."

"You're welcome." Shelby was immersed in a warm glow as she gazed into the beautiful blue eyes shining with gratitude, and she began to lose herself in their depths.

Kris leaned forward, her thoughts totally focused on the woman across from her until the table stopped her forward progress. She silently cursed the barrier between them until she realized what she'd been about to do. *I can't believe I almost kissed her.* But Kris was having trouble conjuring up all the reasons why she shouldn't have, and inwardly regretted the lost opportunity, even as she questioned her loss of control.

As Kris leaned back in her chair, so did Shelby, her heart still fluttering wildly as sexual tension charged the air. She could almost feel those full sensuous lips on her own, and at the thought, her body shivered in anticipation.

The silence lengthened. Both women's faces were flushed as each tried to come to grips with what had almost happened and their own reaction to it, and they carefully searched the eyes of the other to verify their feelings weren't one-sided. They both almost sighed in relief when a very loud "meow" drew them from their introspections.

Shelby smiled down at Stormy. "It's not my fault you stayed on the bed." She glanced at Kris. "I'm gonna go ahead and feed her."

Kris nodded, her eyes following the blonde into the kitchen as she dodged the kitten that was winding between her legs. The operative listened to the steady stream of softly spoken words directed at the kitten as she appreciatively assessed and admired each movement and expression, every attribute of the attractive woman moving around the kitchen preparing the little feline's food.

Sitting back down at the table, Shelby said, "I can't believe she didn't complain before now. Guess I threw her schedule off by getting up so early."

That wasn't the only thing you threw off. Kris smiled. "She told you about it, too."

Shelby chuckled. "In no uncertain terms." She took a sip of coffee and made a face. "I'm going to warm this up. You ready for more?"

Kris handed her cup to Shelby. "Thanks."

Shelby took the cup, smiling inwardly. Kris hadn't even protested. *Things are definitely looking up.*

They finished their coffee and Kris stood up. "I'm going to take a quick look around. Be back in a few."

As Shelby began clearing the breakfast dishes, she looked forward to another day with the enigmatic woman, even as she regretfully acknowledged that their remaining time together was dwindling.

The events at the table played themselves over and over again in her mind. She had seen her own desire reflected in Kris' eyes, and the feeling had been electric. *But what now? Damn table.* Shelby chuckled at the thought. Cursing the table wasn't going to accomplish anything. Dare she talk to Kris about how she felt, or would that create a chasm in the closeness they were beginning to share? Shelby searched for a plausible way to maintain contact with the operative after the case was completed. Failing to come up with any innovative ideas, she wished for more time—anything to delay the inevitable.

Shelby sighed and decided to put off thinking about that until later. It was Saturday, and she had Kris all to herself. She intended to make the most of the day and relish every single second of the time they spent together. *Like you haven't been doing that already?* She rolled her eyes at the inner voice. *So what if I have?*

Kris finished checking the area and leaned against the cement wall beneath the steps. *What would it be like to have someone to come home to?* The thought was foreign to her, something she had never allowed herself to consider. *If that someone were Shelby, it would be great. It's obvious we both want more. Is that the closest we're ever going to get?*

The operative didn't have any illusions about the likelihood of living a normal life. Quite frankly, there was absolutely nothing normal about hers. Could that ever change? Kris focused on that question as she explored her options for doing just that. It would be almost impossible unless she had help. Unbidden, a certainty rose in her mind: *Shelby would help.* She immediately discarded that notion. If she asked Shelby, the details she would have to reveal might cause her to lose the very person for whom she was willing to risk everything. It might also put Shelby in even more danger. *Unacceptable.* Kris shook her head in frustration. *If not Shelby, then who?* She returned to the apartment without an answer. There wasn't one.

AFTER SPENDING AN enjoyable day together, the two women were relaxing on the couch, watching TV and talking. Now that she had forgiven them for taking her to the vet, their feline companion was content to alternately grace each lap with her presence.

Kris stood up. "I'm going outside for a while."

Shelby nodded. Kris had already been out once that evening and she'd expected her to leave again, but not quite so early.

Standing there gazing at Shelby, Kris made a decision. "I'm going out the back way."

"What back way? The balcony?"

"Your bedroom window."

Shelby became uneasy. "Why? You've never gone out that way before. Besides, we're on the second floor and there's no fire escape in the back. Is someone out there?"

"Not that I know of." Kris hoped that was true. She was going out over an hour early to prevent being caught unawares.

"So why?"

Kris had known Shelby would question the sudden change in her routine and had an answer prepared. "In my line of work, it's dangerous to establish patterns. I think it's time to vary it. It'll be safer."

Although Kris' reasoning made sense, Shelby was still uneasy. She decided not to push it. The most important thing was the operative's safety, and if Kris felt it was safer to leave from the window, Shelby didn't want to dissuade her from doing so. "Makes sense."

"Would you mind closing the window and screen after me?"

"No problem."

Blue pinned Shelby with her eyes. "And stay away from the window after I leave."

A chill made its way down Shelby's spine. *Something is going on.* She began worrying about Kris, but she nodded. "Be careful."

Kris smiled reassuringly. "I always am."

Following the operative to the bedroom, she watched Kris open the window, slide the screen to the side, and maneuver her tall form through the opening until all that was visible were her hands. She stepped up to the opening and watched as Kris dropped from the window and landed in a roll on the grass below, then quickly disappeared into the darkness.

Waiting in the shadows until Shelby closed the screen and window, Kris turned her attention to the situation at hand. Fading into the darkness, Blue began hunting.

GREGOR HAD MARKOV drive by the apartment complex several times before instructing him to park out of sight on a side street. He got out and approached the structure from the rear, arriving early to conceal himself in the dark area behind the building. The element of surprise was always an advantage when dealing with subordinates.

Gregor stayed in the shadows as he slowly crept along the rear of the building until he had a good vantage point. He'd considered hiding among the trees, but discarded that as too obvious. Reaching his selected spot, he melted into the darkness, his hand on his gun. He planned to interrogate Blue back in the car and didn't expect her to accompany him without a show of force. He intended to drive home the seriousness of her situation, no matter what it took.

Having waited for twenty minutes, Gregor was quickly losing patience. The time set for their meeting was almost upon them, and he was surprised that she hadn't yet made an appearance to reconnoiter. Maybe the reports in their files exaggerated her abilities.

He jumped when he heard a low voice say, "Looking for me?"

Drawing his gun as he turned around, he growled, "Too many stunts like that will get you killed."

"Not likely, unless the person who does it is someone more skilled than you."

Gregor grunted in pain as his gun fell soundlessly to the ground and he straightened up to find the operative's gun trained on his chest. "What are you doing?" he hissed.

"You might try answering the same question. You pulled your weapon first."

"You startled me." Gregor met Blue's intense gaze. "I have to protect myself."

Blue smiled sardonically. "You don't lie very well. You knew who I was when you drew it."

"We can talk in the car." Gregor bent down to pick up his weapon, then froze when he heard a round being chambered.

"I wouldn't." Seeing that she had his attention, she directed, "Pick it up by the barrel and stand up."

Slowly rising, Gregor's stomach tightened in fear. "Are you crazy? When my superiors hear of this—"

Blue interrupted. "Hear what? That you drew on me and I acted defensively? They would expect no less."

Gregor narrowed his eyes. What she said was true. If Dimitri found out she'd gotten the drop on him, he was finished as a controller. "What do you want?"

"Hand me your gun. Nice and easy."

Blue took the weapon, and then ordered Gregor to place his hands on the wall as she expertly searched him, removing a small .38 special from his waistband. She removed the ammunition from both guns. "You can turn around now."

Handing both weapons back to Gregor, she unchambered the round in her own weapon and secured it at the small of her back. "Now we can talk."

Gregor tried desperately to think of a way to regain control of the meeting and cursed his lack of foresight in not bringing Markov with him. "It's not secure here. We can talk in the car."

Blue nodded at the wooded area. "We can talk there." She had no doubt that he had pulled his gun to ensure that she would accompany him to the car and knew that the ensuing talk wouldn't have been a very pleasant experience.

Cursing inwardly, Gregor decided his only option was to do as she suggested. Once they were out of sight, he demanded, "Where is the information I requested?"

Kris handed him a folded piece of paper which he took and opened. "There are only three names here."

"Patience, Gregor, patience. These things take time."

Startled at her use of his real name, he growled, "I expect you to have more on Monday."

"I'll do what I can."

"You will do what I say."

Blue subdued the urge to just kill him and be done with it. "I said I would do what I can."

Gregor's stomach tightened. This woman was dangerous and unpredictable. Once he got what he needed, he was going to recommend to Dimitri that she be eliminated. "Make sure you do." Blue smiled coldly at him and Gregor turned away, anxious to be done with the meeting.

"Not so fast." Blue smiled humorlessly. "Know of any reason why someone is shooting at me?"

Gregor couldn't believe he'd forgotten to ask her that himself and realized he was more shaken by her actions then he had thought.

Turning around, he met her gaze steadily. "No. I was going to ask you the same question."

Blue keyed in on his words. "Oh?"

"Since you didn't see fit to keep in contact, I came here yesterday to pay you a visit." He smiled coldly, knowing he finally had the advantage. "I had no reason to kill you."

Blue didn't miss the past tense and glared at Gregor. "What about now?"

"You are still more valuable to me alive than dead. My superiors are very interested in knowing what is going on. We don't take kindly to one of our own being fired upon. I'm sure you must have some idea."

One of your own? When hell freezes over. Blue didn't like Gregor's attitude, but she needed information. "I don't know yet. I'm working on it. What did you see?"

Gregor divulged what little information he had. "Very little. I was parked on a side street waiting for your partner's car to return. I saw you both get out and walk toward the building. A silver Chevrolet Cavalier pulled into the parking lot, and at the same time a shot was fired. There appeared to be only one occupant. Knowing that the gunfire would bring the authorities, I could not stay. I saw you cover the blonde woman as I was leaving."

Blue nodded. She didn't know any more now than she had before, except that Gregor was bolder than she'd thought. She hadn't expected him to show up at the apartment complex unannounced.

Gregor ordered, "I expect to be kept informed of any new developments." Blue met his eyes noncommittally until he broke contact and walked away.

She tracked him until he disappeared, then blended back into the shadows to ensure he didn't return. She hadn't been surprised that he had pulled his weapon, but he had to have been desperate to come to the apartment complex unannounced the previous evening, and that made her distinctly uneasy.

Blue began to feel suffocated by the forces surrounding her. Time was growing very short, and her options even more limited. There were only fourteen names left on the list, but it was no longer just a matter of completing the case. She needed to find a way to break free of the past, but her first priority, regardless of any danger to herself, was to find out who was targeting Shelby. For the first time, Blue wondered if she would live long enough to do either. *I have to.* An hour after Gregor left, Kris climbed the wrought iron stairs and slid her key into the lock.

Shelby paced worriedly through the apartment. Kris had been gone for more than two hours, and with each passing minute she became increasingly concerned. Standing out of sight near the balcony door, Shelby searched the parking lot, illuminated by yellow gaslights, but saw nothing except for the usual Friday night traffic arriving and departing. *What if something happened to her?*

She can take care of herself. Shelby nodded acknowledgement to herself, but was still troubled. *She's not perfect. No one is. What if that guy following her was out there waiting and surprised her?* Shelby jumped when she saw the door begin to open. She hadn't even heard the key in the lock. "Thank God you're back! I was worried about you."

"No need."

Shelby turned away and walked into the kitchen muttering, "Easy for you to say."

Kris didn't know what to say to that. "I didn't mean to worry you."

"Well, you did. You've never been gone longer than an hour. I didn't know if I should come looking for you or call Earl, except that I don't have his number."

"Shelby. Don't ever leave the apartment when I'm gone."

"What if something happens to you?"

"It won't."

Shelby heard the confidence in Kris' voice and wished she could be so sure. "I hope you're right. I would still appreciate you letting me know next time you decide to take your time."

Kris nodded. "Okay." She was still having trouble coming to grips with the fact that Shelby genuinely cared about her. When she allowed herself to explore the feeling, it felt really good and warm, and she wanted to embrace it even as she backed away.

Shelby turned around and met Kris' gaze. "What's really going on? I know something is; I can feel it." When the operative remained silent, Shelby sighed. "I wish you would trust me."

"It's not about that. There are things about me that it's better for you not to know."

"How can you be so sure? Why don't you let me be the judge of that?" She walked over to the couch, waiting for Kris to join her.

She had spent the last two hours reflecting on her feelings for Kris and becoming almost frantic with worry. No longer willing to ignore the tentative connection between them, Shelby threw caution to the wind and spoke from her heart.

"I haven't known you very long, but you've become very important to me. I don't know why, and it doesn't make sense, but you have. Nothing you can say will change that. I know you'll be gone in a week, but at least let me in until you leave. Then you can walk out the door and forget you ever met me."

A myriad of emotions crossed Kris' face as she looked deeply into the warm green eyes. She shook her head. "I can't."

Shelby looked down, hurt. She knew Kris cared, but obviously not enough to trust her.

Kris reached over and squeezed Shelby's hand. "I can't ever forget I met you," she clarified softly.

When Kris released her hand, Shelby grasped it in her own, not wanting to relinquish the contact. "Do you trust me?"

"More than I've ever trusted anyone."

"Then, please, Kris, share with me?"

The operative gazed into the concerned face of her companion and deliberately ignored the cold, logical warnings sounding in her mind. What could it hurt to share the bare minimums? The analyst already knew she had some personal business she'd been attending to. "I'll tell you what I can, but I can't tell you everything. Deal?"

Shelby nodded and Kris continued. "Tonight I had to the meet the man who's been having me followed. That's why I was gone so long. I needed to be out there before he arrived to circumvent any unpleasant surprises he might have had planned. He made a couple of mistakes; that's all the help I needed."

"Will he leave you alone now?"

Kris sighed inwardly. "He won't have anyone follow us again, and he had nothing to do with the shooting, but I already knew that."

"But it's not over, is it?"

Knowing it wasn't safe to divulge any more information, Kris said, "It will be, soon." *One way or another.*

"You can't tell me what's going on?"

"No. It's a personal matter that I have to deal with."

"Is there anything I can do to help?"

Kris thought about the time she'd spent with Shelby and how, when she was in her company, her problems faded into the background. She thought about the shared laughter, sometimes at television shows and sometimes just plain silliness. She thought about how Shelby always put her first, as she tried to do the same. "You already are helping."

Shelby produced a good facsimile of Kris' glare. "Did I ever mention that I hate cryptic answers?"

Chuckling, Kris said, "Okay. I'll try to keep them to a minimum." Her hand was still firmly held by Shelby's smaller one, and she no longer felt the need to break the contact, allowing herself to relax and enjoy it until her companion chose to relinquish her grasp.

"Do you like your job?"

Kris glanced at Shelby, carefully choosing her words. "I like working on my own, being my own, boss, yes."

"What about the rest? Always living in the field, being on guard all the time, and, um..."

"You want to know if I like killing people?"

"Well, no. I mean, I don't think you would..."

"No, Shelby, I don't. I hate it. I have to put my mind in a special place to do it."

"Why do you do it, then?"

"Because someone has to do it; because that someone has to be me."

"No, it doesn't. You could request out of wet ops."

"No, I can't." *Yet.*

About to dispute that further, Shelby looked at the strained look on her companion's face and closed her mouth. The last thing she wanted to do was push Kris away when she'd finally opened up a little.

"You look tired. Why don't you sleep in my bed? You looked so uncomfortable this morning, all squashed on the couch."

Kris shook her head and smiled. "Thanks for offering again, but I can't protect you from in there."

Shelby considered that irrefutable logic, then smiled shyly. "You could if we shared the bed. There's plenty of room, and you'd be a lot more comfortable." Before Kris could offer any protest, she hurried on. "And if you're more comfortable, you'll sleep better. And if you sleep better, you'll be more rested and alert so you can protect me even better."

No, no, no. Well, actually, I'd love to share your bed with you. "I'm going to be up and down a lot tonight. I want to make sure my visitors don't return. It'll be better for me to sleep on the couch." *Well, maybe not better, but a lot less tempting.*

"Okay." Shelby intended to extend the invitation again the following night. It made no sense for Kris to be so uncomfortable, and she'd feel a lot better with the tall woman right next to her. *A lot better in what way?* She smiled inwardly. *Both.*

GREGOR RETURNED TO the embassy and, after sending word of his arrival, waited for Dimitri to summon him. The call came and he left his quarters, en route to his superior's office. "Comrade."

"Well?"

Gregor hand over the small piece of paper, preparing for the explosion that was sure to come.

"This is all!"

"Yes, but she will provide more on Monday."

Dimitri narrowed his eyes. "See that she does. You're dismissed."

"Comrade Petrov."

"What is it?"

"I would like to recommend elimination once we get the remainder of the names." Gregor actually planned on getting a little more from her than just the names, but his superior didn't need to know that yet.

Dimitri looked at his subordinate shrewdly. He knew something had precipitated this request, and speculated that Gregor had been outwitted. Considering whom he'd gone up against, it wasn't surprising. "Why?"

"She is insane, and unpredictable. She doesn't follow orders. She mocks us by providing such a short list of names. She shows no loyalty. She's—"

"Enough! Do you have specific examples of the malfeasance you mention?" Dimitri smiled coldly. "Well?"

Gregor had no intentions of incriminating himself. "No, Comrade."

"I didn't think so. You're dismissed." Dimitri smiled inwardly. Gregor was right. She was dangerous, but he still had a use for her.

When the door closed, he encrypted the three names, adding a personal request at the bottom of the list. Dimitri assigned it the highest priority before sending it to his superiors in Moscow. He expected to hear something within forty-eight hours, if not sooner. Then he would decide if he needed to get personally involved in handling Natasha Lubinyenka.

Chapter Eleven

SHELBY WATCHED KRIS, something she never tired of doing, as her companion drove them toward her mother's house in Arlington. She found her beauty simply breathtaking, and the energy that rolled off the operative in waves, tantalizing. When she was with Kris, nothing else mattered.

The driver glanced at her unusually silent companion. "You're awfully quiet. What're you thinking about?"

You. "Just about how nice this weekend has been."

Kris shot Shelby a quick smile. "Yeah, it has been." With the exception of her unpleasant meeting with Gregor, it had. Today they hadn't even had a tail to shake.

"I think you're gonna like Jimmy and Jason. Don't be surprised at anything they ask you, though. Mom probably told them I was bringing a spy to dinner."

"You are kidding, right?"

"Nope. She thinks everyone who works for the Company is a spy. She's not very thrilled about where I work."

"How come?"

"She thinks it's too dangerous. I've told her it's not. That was pretty much true, until lately." Shelby grinned ruefully. "I'm glad I don't have to explain away the stuff that's happened this past week."

Kris said vehemently, "It'll be over soon. That I can promise you."

Concerned, Shelby looked at Kris. "Hey, it's not your fault."

I wish I were absolutely positive of that. Smiling appreciatively, Kris uttered a heartfelt, "Thanks."

"There it is. It's the house right just past the stop sign with the black Tempo in the driveway."

Kris pulled into the driveway of a white ranch-style house with green shutters. She rounded the car and waited for Shelby to get out, then accompanied her to the side door where she positioned herself slightly to the rear as Shelby knocked on the door, opened it and walked in. A woman of medium stature resembling the picture Kris had examined approached them with a strained smile on her face.

"Hi, Mom. This is Kris." Shelby glanced at Kris. "This is my mother, Lisa."

Lisa looked at the tall woman standing in her doorway, casually dressed in jeans and a blue polo shirt that seemed custom made to fit her body. She was beautiful, but Lisa found herself taken aback by the woman's commanding presence and the intense blue eyes that met hers unwaveringly. *So this is the woman.* "Nice to meet you, Kris."

She then hugged her daughter tightly for several moments before releasing her. She ignored the puzzled look Shelby gave her and said, "Why don't you both go into the living room. I'll get you something to drink."

Shelby smiled. "I'll get our drinks, Mom." Turning to Kris, she asked, "Coffee or Coke?"

"Coffee."

Shelby got two mugs from the cupboard and filled them from the coffeemaker sitting on the counter. She handed one to Kris and led her companion into the living room.

Lisa watched them, anger and concern warring for control of her emotions.

"Shelby!" Jimmy jumped up and hugged his older sister.

Jason watched the show of affection with amusement. "Hey, sis." His attention turned to the tall woman. "Are you a spy, too?"

Shelby started laughing. "Jason, how many times do I have to tell you I am not a spy?"

"I know. I know." He looked at Kris curiously. "Are you?"

Kris quirked a half-smile and decided to play along. "I'm a field operative."

Jimmy piped up, "What do you do?"

"Whatever they need me to do." Kris grinned when Jimmy rolled his eyes.

Shelby said, "Hey, you two! Where are your manners?"

Jason and Jimmy both stood up, towering over Shelby. Jason was the taller of the two, and both had unruly dark brown hair and hazel eyes. Jimmy had a smattering of freckles across his nose and Jason a more mature face, but except for those small distinctions, they could have been twins.

Jason extended his hand, "Hi, I'm Jason."

Kris took the proffered hand gravely. "Kris." She repeated the exercise with Jimmy, then joined Shelby on the couch. Glancing at the baseball game on the television, she asked, "Who's playing?"

"Baltimore and Cleveland."

Kris winked at Shelby and engaged the teenagers in a lively conversation about the finer points of the game.

Lisa waited a few minutes to allow Shelby to greet her brothers before making her way to the living room doorway. "Shelby, could you help me for a few minutes?"

"Sure." Looking at her half-brothers, Shelby said, "Hey, come on you guys. Give Kris a break, would ya?" Trailing her mother into the kitchen, Shelby watched as she closed the door. Her brow furrowed. "Why did you do that?"

"Because I want to talk to you privately. Jonathan was here earlier." Lisa raised a hand and said, "Wait a minute. Let me finish. Then you can go off, if you still think it's necessary. Those are his sons. He has every right to visit them. He said he stayed away while he was on probation because he realized how wrong he'd been for all those years and wanted to find some way to make it up to us."

"Yeah, right, Mom. And how many times did he tell you that while you were married to him? A hundred? A thousand?"

"People change. I think he deserves another chance." When Shelby did not respond, she continued justifying her feelings. "The boys have really missed him. They were so happy to see him." She looked at her daughter's disbelieving face and mumbled, "He wants to see you, too."

Exploding, Shelby said, "It'll be a cold day in hell before I let that bastard near me!"

"You watch your mouth in this house!"

Shelby's eyes were flashing as she looked at her mother angrily. "He couldn't change in all the years he was married to you, yet all of a sudden, you think he's seen the light? I can't believe you. That is so naïve."

"God is the only one who judges, not us. Our responsibility is to forgive and help those who need our help. If I can forgive him, why can't you?"

"He is a control freak, Mom. And he's sick. He'll never change."

Lisa's hazel eyes stared pointedly into Shelby's green ones. "I thought you told me your job was safe."

Puzzled at the abrupt change of subject, Shelby said, "It pretty much is."

"Pretty much? What does that mean? It is or it isn't."

Shelby felt her stomach tighten. "Why are you asking about my job?"

Lisa looked at her daughter accusingly. "Because you lied to me. You said it was safe, and it's not. Why didn't you tell me you were shot at on Thursday?"

Because I knew this would happen. Shelby said defensively, "Who told you that?"

Tears began tracking down Lisa's face. "Jonathan went to visit you Thursday. He wanted to apologize for his past behaviors and ask your forgiveness. He pulled into the parking lot just as someone shot at you. He said a tall woman knocked you down. Once he saw you were safe, he left, because he just got off probation and didn't want to be there when the police arrived."

Shelby struggled with anger and fear. Jonathan had been at her apartment complex. He knew where she lived. That in itself was frightening, but that he had been there the evening she was shot at was even more so.

She took a deep breath, and hugged her mother. "Mom, don't cry."

"I'm so worried about you. I want you to quit that job. I've been worried sick ever since he told me this morning."

Shelby released the older woman, watching her intently. "He told you this morning? Why didn't he tell you before now? If he was there, why didn't he call you right away, Mom?"

"He naturally assumed you'd tell me. When he asked me about it, I had no idea what he was talking about." The accusation was evident.

"I suppose you told him I was coming over today?"

Lisa nodded. "That's when he told me what happened."

"What kind of car does he drive?"

"What's that got to do with anything?"

"A lot."

"A silver Cavalier. But I don't see..."

"The driver of a silver Cavalier is currently the primary suspect in the shooting, Mom," Shelby informed her flatly.

Deeply ingrained defense mechanisms kicked in. "He would never hurt you."

Shelby raised her voice angrily. "What in hell did he do for years, Mom? Did you forget about that already? Did you forget he threatened me at the trial? How do you know he's not just covering his ass by telling you I was shot at? There weren't any other cars around."

"Are you sure you didn't misunderstand him at the trial?"

Pursing her lips, Shelby shook her head, struggling to control her anger. "Why don't you ask Jonathan?"

"I did. He said he was angry with you, but didn't threaten you. Wait!" Lisa beseeched as her daughter opened her mouth to protest. "He said he's glad you testified against him, that he was sick and now realizes that. Couldn't you please just give him a chance?"

Shelby momentarily closed her eyes; she couldn't believe what she was hearing. It wasn't that she didn't think someone could change, but she'd never forget the hatred in her stepfather's eyes coupled with the malevolent look on his face that day.

"Shelby? Are you okay?"

Shaking her head, Shelby said, "No, Mom. I'm not. He's still lying."

KRIS SAT IN the living room listening to the murmur of angry voices through the door, but the words were indistinguishable. She glanced at the two boys and found Jimmy looking at her.

"Don't worry." Jimmy smiled weakly. "They're probably just arguing about Dad. Shelby doesn't like our dad."

Jason said, "Yeah. He used to do some really mean things to Mom. He came over this morning and said he saw a doctor that helped him. Brought Mom some flowers, too. Said he had a lotta things to make up for. He's gonna take us to the game next Saturday. Mom's probably telling Shelby that he's better now. That's probably what's goin' on in the kitchen."

Kris tensed. Shelby didn't need the added stress, but her hands were tied. She couldn't very well go barging into the kitchen and rescue Shelby from her own mother; even if she made the attempt, the analyst would resent it. Her partner had proven on more than one occasion that she could handle herself in stressful situations. And Kris very much respected that.

"CAN'T YOU LET God into your heart and forgive him for the past? He's changed. You wouldn't believe how good he looks."

Calming down, Shelby studied her mother's face. "I don't give a damn how good he looks. How good is he inside? He's not. He's rotten to the core. I can't believe you're falling for his looks again. Do you want to end up back in the hospital? What about the boys?"

"You know he never touched the boys."

"No, he didn't. But do you really think, the next time he hurts you, they'll believe that you just happened to fall? Do you want them exposed to that?"

"They won't be. He's changed. I thought you would be more understanding and forgiving. Have you forgotten everything you were taught?"

Shelby met her mother's eyes. "No, Mom. I haven't forgotten anything at all. I especially remember the lesson *he* taught me. I'm not looking at the world through rose colored glasses like you are right now."

Lisa's disappointment was evident. "Well, I can see this conversation is going nowhere."

"You're right, it's not." Shelby thought of Kris and resisted the urge to forget about dinner and just leave. Determined to salvage what she could of the afternoon for the agent's sake, Shelby resolved to ignore her aggravation and resolutely set it aside. "Want me to set the table?"

Lisa nodded. She watched her daughter gather up the plates and silverware and wondered how she could convince her to quit her job. *I don't know what I'd do if anything happened to her.*

She wasn't really surprised Shelby was so adamant about Jonathan, but she would keep working on her. Jonathan had stressed how important it was for him to make a clean start with each one of them. She would do her part to help him.

Kris looked up when Shelby returned to the living room and joined her on the couch. Noting the strain on the younger woman's face, her concern grew. "You okay?"

Shelby smiled, but the smile didn't reach her eyes. "Yeah."

Jason looked at his sister. "Mom tell you Dad was here?" When Shelby nodded, he shrugged. "He's been seeing a doctor. He's not sick anymore, Shelby. He even apologized to me and Jimmy for not visiting."

Shelby was spared having to formulate a suitable answer when Lisa summoned them to the table. The two boys jumped up enthusiastically and hurried out to the dining room.

Kris looked at Shelby. "You sure you're okay?"

"Yeah. Just worried, that's all. I'll tell you about it later."

Distressed at how upset Shelby was, Kris could only nod.

They joined the others at the table. Kris looked at the feast set out—fried chicken, mashed potatoes and gravy, corn, salad, and dinner rolls. She followed Shelby's lead and sat next to her across from the two boys. Kris covertly watched Shelby as her mother sat down at the head of the table, then glanced up to find Lisa regarding her gravely.

"Thank you."

Kris raised an eyebrow. "Excuse me?"

"Thank you for protecting my daughter."

She took in the worried look and red eyes. The operative could see the woman loved her daughter, yet she hadn't taken steps to protect her children when they were unable to protect themselves. She couldn't respect that no matter how much Lisa loved Shelby.

Kris nodded. "Any time."

Jason and Jimmy looked up, their attention piqued. "What're you talking about, Mom?"

Lisa hedged. She didn't want to tell the boys yet. She'd only found out herself shortly before Shelby arrived and wanted to wait for the right moment. "I'll tell you about it later. How about passing the chicken?" She forced a smile as she took the platter from Jason and began passing the food around the table.

Kris could feel the tension emanating from Shelby and moved her leg sideways, bumping the shorter one next to hers. When Shelby looked at her, Kris quirked a half-smile. The answering smile caused her heart to skip a beat.

It was just the briefest contact, but Shelby felt her world begin to right itself. Some of her tension faded and she could sense Kris' diminish in concert.

Jason and Jimmy chattered excitedly about their upcoming baseball trip and when that didn't elicit anything except monosyllabic responses from the others, they began telling spy stories.

Shelby tried to introduce a neutral subject a number of times, but her heart wasn't in it and she was unsuccessful. Lisa and Kris' contributions were perfunctory, and the analyst found it increasingly difficult to carry on the conversation with the boys by herself.

Tiring of the lack of response, the teenagers eventually fell silent until the only sounds in the large room were those of silverware scraping against plates. After demolishing their food, both boys asked to be excused, wanting to leave the tension behind. Lisa sent them on their way, promising to bring dessert into the living room.

Shelby and Kris remained at the table with the older woman, drinking coffee.

"So, what are you, Kris—a bodyguard?"

Shelby started laughing at the look of shock that flitted across Kris' face before she quickly recovered.

"No. I'm a field operative. Once the case I'm working on with Shelby is completed, I'll be reassigned."

"Well, I'm really glad you are staying with Shelby. Jonathan said it was amazing how quickly you knocked her down and made sure she was safe."

Kris played along, even as she tensed. "And Jonathan knew this how?"

"He was there; he saw what you did. He said it was nothing short of amazing."

"So why'd he leave?" she challenged.

Lisa toyed nervously with her coffee cup, looking for an answer that would excuse his actions. "Shelby and her stepfather aren't on the best of terms right now."

Kris raised an eyebrow. "So he left while she was possibly still in danger?"

Lisa suddenly felt like she was being interrogated and didn't want to tell this intimidating woman that her ex-husband had been on parole, so she stood up and changed the subject. "How about some dessert?"

Kris seethed inwardly. She couldn't say what she wanted to

because to do so would betray Shelby's trust.

Shelby smiled. "I'll have some, Mom." She glanced at Kris. "Mom makes the best apple pie around. Why don't you try a piece?"

The operative inwardly shook her head. Shelby was upset, yet she was still trying to ease the sudden escalation of tension. For her benefit only, Kris smiled at Lisa. "Thanks. It sounds delicious."

Kris and Shelby departed an hour later, after thanking Lisa for the delicious dinner and bidding her and the two teenagers farewell. Within five minutes of their departure, a silver Cavalier pulled into the driveway they had vacated.

"WHAT'D YOU THINK of my mother?"

"Um, she seems nice. So, how'd she know?"

"My stepfather. You know the car that Earl is looking for? It was him. He told Mom he was just coming to see me, to try and make amends."

Kris glanced at Shelby. "Do you believe that?"

"I don't know what to believe, but I do know that he's still lying. He insists he didn't threaten me at the trial, but it's something I'll never forget. You had to see his face, how much he hated me. He said, 'You bitch, you'll pay. I'll see you in hell even if I have to join you there.'"

Kris reached over and grasped Shelby's hand. "Hey, I'm not gonna let anything happen to you. I promise."

Shelby turned to face the operative, holding tightly to her hand. "Thanks, but you're only gonna be here another week at most. This is something I have to take care of myself."

The taller woman briefly scanned Shelby's pale face. Mind made up, she said flatly, "I'm going to pay Jonathan a visit."

"Kris!"

Kris smiled grimly. "I'm not going to hurt him." *Unless he gives me a reason.* "Just talk to him." *And let the bastard knows that if he ever harms you in any way, he'll be begging to die before I'm finished with him.*

Shelby looked at Kris and shuddered. But this was her battle. Squaring her shoulders, she spoke with conviction. "I think I should be the one to talk to him."

Kris quickly searched Shelby's eyes before turning her attention back to the road, nodding at the determination and strength she'd seen. "When do you want to go?"

"Not today. I've had enough unpleasantness for one day. Besides, I need to find out where he lives and works, so we're likely to catch him at home. I don't want to have to go back more than once."

"I requested his FBI file. I should have it Monday."
"Why did you request it?"
Kris shrugged. "You mentioned his name, even if he was only a remote possibility. He needs to be ruled out as a suspect."
"Okay, after we review it, we'll decide when to go see him. I don't think he had anything to do with the shooting, though I wish I knew the real reason he was at my place." Shelby stared out the window for a few minutes, then turned troubled eyes to Kris. "I don't know what to do about my mother. She has all the classic symptoms of an abused woman. I really thought she was okay now. She'd never indicated any desire to see Jonathan again. I wish I could find a way to convince her to seek professional counseling. I can't help her. She thinks I'm too biased."
"Any possibility of getting her to go to a support group?"
"Not if she knew what it was. Maybe if I talk to one of the women's shelters, they might let me bring her to visit, just to remind her of what it was like. I think she's forgotten. She wouldn't go if she knew where we were going, though. I'd have to fabricate something, and I hate doing that."
"You don't know anyone who does any counseling?"
Shelby thought for just an instant. "Duh! A good friend of mine travels around the country giving seminars to abused women. Geesh! I can't believe I didn't think of her! She's been out of town, but I think she gets back on Wednesday."
Pleased to hear the obvious relief in Shelby's voice, Kris smiled. "Sounds like a plan."
Shelby suddenly said, "Let's go someplace and do something fun."
Nodding, Kris grinned. "Okay. Your wish is my command."
Shelby looked away to hide the flush that crept up on her face. *Don't even go there.* "We could see a movie, or visit the monuments, or go to Baltimore."
"Baltimore's almost an hour away. Why there?"
"To see the ocean. It's really nice off the harbor."
Kris glanced at the clock on the dashboard. It was only 3:00, so they had plenty of time. She smiled. "Sounds good," and she started maneuvering her way to US-50.

DIMITRI READ THE priority encrypted message for the third time. Two of the three names Natasha had provided were agents that were no longer in place, having been reassigned only days before. It couldn't be coincidence. She was obviously playing games. He would know with absolute certainty when information on the third name was returned.

He forced himself to remain calm. Anger was nonproductive. He'd actually been very lucky. Normally, it would've taken several days to get operatives in position to verify the information she'd passed over, but they'd had men already close to two of the target locations, and headquarters had indicated information on the third name would be forthcoming within hours.

To achieve an invaluable advantage, his agency needed to know where their counterparts were. Then it was just a matter of observing them. He was in a position to obtain that information, but this prime opportunity—that could be an information coup and mean a promotion for him—was quickly disintegrating into a waste of time and money, which he could not allow.

It was time for him to get personally involved. Obviously, Gregor hadn't done his job, but right now, he still needed him. It would take too long to train a replacement. He smiled cruelly. It was time to remind Natasha just who she was and what her job was. Knowing better than to underestimate her, he decided to be certain his ace in the hole was in place.

Dimitri leaned back in his chair, musing on his subordinate's actions. Gregor thought he was so clever in not sharing all the information he had obtained on Lubinyenka. Specifically, keeping her partner's high security clearance and level of access to himself. He looked up as the encryption machine came to life and waited until it stopped before retrieving the paper it had spewed forth. He read it and slammed his fist on the desk. *Damn it! Does she take us for fools?*

He began typing:

> Priority one. Implement Plan G. Extract Masha. Next available flight. Attendants—three class A operatives. Inform K1 AXIS will be terminated after information extraction.

After encrypting the message and sending it, Dimitri summoned Gregor. When his subordinate arrived, he began issuing orders. "Prepare the interrogation room."

"It is already..."

"Not the one here, you fool! The other location. And have our visitors' quarters readied. Someone else will be joining us for the session." Dimitri smiled to himself. It would be most interesting to see the expression on Gregor's face when he learned who the visitor was to be.

"Put ten of our people on standby to move at my command. Make sure each is intimately familiar with the apartment layout and the location where they are to be positioned around the building. I want every window and door covered. It has to be quick and quiet.

You know what to do."

Dimitri stood suddenly and walked up to Gregor. "Once she is down, you will not touch her. Is that clear?" He knew the man had a personal grudge since she'd obviously outwitted him on their last meeting, but this was his game.

"Yes, Comrade."

"Good. I'm glad we understand each other. Have you found out who else has an interest in her?"

"No. All my contacts have come up empty. Perhaps the shot was intended for the analyst."

"Perhaps. Have two men remain on location to guard her."

Gregor was relieved, but suspicious. Because of his own agenda, he didn't want anything to happen to Shelby, but why was Dimitri protecting her? "Why, Comrade? She is not our responsibility."

Dimitri had expected the question. "If she turns up dead, Natasha will be reassigned before we have the names we need." Sarcastically, he continued, "Now if you are done questioning my decisions, you are dismissed."

Bowing his head slightly, Gregor held his anger in check as he exited the room.

The Russian eyed the departing man contemptuously. *You will not enjoy Siberia, Gregor, but there you will learn discipline and compliance.*

KRIS GRINNED, GENUINELY happy as Shelby's delighted laughter rang through the air, the look of joy on her face warming the deepest recesses of her heart.

"Oh, I love it! Thank you! You shouldn't have. I love it!" She gripped the large, white plush unicorn with both arms, hugging it close to her. Her eyes were shining as she bumped Kris with its horn.

Laughing, Kris said, "You're welcome. You want me to carry it for you?" It had been a stroke of luck to find a unicorn in one of the shops they had visited.

"No. I've got it." Shelby had no intentions of letting go of her gift, even though it was almost four feet long and a foot and a half wide. She held it against her, securely wrapped in her arms, her face resting against its head.

An hour later they arrived home. Kris unlocked the door and picked up Stormy while Shelby deposited her unicorn in the middle of the couch. She took the kitten from Kris and set her next to the stuffed animal. The little feline hissed and backed up, her fur standing on end.

The two women laughed at the kitten's antics. Kris teased, "I don't know; maybe we should get rid of it. She doesn't seem to like it."

Shelby turned and wrapped both arms around Kris. With heartfelt conviction, she said, "No way. That's the best gift I've ever gotten."

Kris suddenly swallowed hard and momentarily struggled with her emotions as she hugged Shelby back. "I'm glad. Because you're very special." She was reluctant to let go of the smaller woman who fit so comfortably against her, so she rested her chin on the blonde head lying against her breasts.

The moment extended into minutes when Shelby made no move to extricate herself from the comfortable arms in which she was enfolded. Kris' breasts were so soft, and the touch of the lean body against her own felt electrifying.

Kris barely grazed the top of Shelby's head with her lips and then released her. She needed some space, quickly. Her body was aching with desire, and her control was rapidly diminishing. *I am so far gone. What am I going to do?*

Shelby sighed inwardly, but didn't want to push Kris. "Want something to drink?"

Smiling appreciatively, Kris said, "A Coke would taste great right about now. How about if I take the unicorn to your bedroom so we have somewhere to sit down?"

"Well, okay, if you must."

A couple of hours later, after Kris returned from her final security check, Shelby stood up. "It's late. Time to say goodnight." She paused, then added, "I really think you'd be more comfortable if you'd share the bed."

"I'm sure I would be." *I know I would be.* "But..."

"I know. Just remember, you're welcome to change your mind." Shelby walked over to Kris, hugged her, quickly released her and walked down the hall to the bedroom.

Kris had to use every ounce of her considerable self-control to keep from following Shelby down the hallway. Her sleep that night was even more fitful than usual. During one of her many waking moments, Kris walked down to the bedroom door and glanced in. What she saw there brought a smile to her face. Shelby was sleeping with Stormy next to her on the pillow and her arm thrown over the unicorn. *Lucky stuffed animal.* Kris walked back to the living room and sat down on the couch. *There has got to be a way...*

Chapter Twelve

IT WAS NEARLY lunchtime when Shelby paused and focused her attention on Kris. The woman had been feverishly working at the computer all morning and had only grunted answers or scant acknowledgements of her comments. This time she was determined to get a full sentence in response. "Are we still going to lunch?"

Kris swiveled her chair around to face the analyst. She couldn't believe she'd forgotten they'd planned to lunch together today. "Yep. Where are we going?"

Shelby laughed. *Well, it was full sentence, but not by much.* "The cafeteria's the only place close enough to eat and be back in an hour." She didn't care where they ate. It was free time with Kris, and she lived for it.

"Okay. Give me ten minutes."

Happy their plans were still on, Shelby teased, "All right! But that's the limit. I'm really hungry."

Kris chuckled as she turned back to the monitor. All morning she'd been trying to dig up virtually useless information that she could provide to her control. However, her search to find more operatives who had recently departed their stations had proved fruitless. She was going to have to manufacture some data to leave at the drop. The operative hoped it would take them several days to check out the names she had already provided, because she needed to buy a little more time to explore all her options.

She sighed inwardly. *What the heck am I going to tell Shelby when I leave in the middle of the afternoon?* But, she was between a rock and hard place—it was either go, or have them show up at the complex again, something Kris definitely did not want to risk.

AFTER LUNCH, KRIS accompanied Shelby back to the office, then said she had to leave for an hour and made an abrupt departure. The operative had been gone forty-five minutes when Shelby answered the ringing phone. She fleetingly wished it were Kris, even though she was due back any time, and grinned to herself as she picked it up. *You are so hopeless.*

"Hey, Shelby, how ya doing? Dennis told me to call and let you know that you can come and pick up the file you guys requested on Jonathan Whiteman. Earl and his secretary had to attend a meeting outside the building, so they dropped it off here."

"Great, Joanne. I'll be right there." Shelby hung up the phone and wrote a quick note to Kris to let her know where she was in the event that her partner returned in her absence.

Retrieving the file and anxious to see what was in it, Shelby hurried back toward her office. As she rounded the corner into the hallway near the drink machine, she stopped abruptly to avoid running into a tall, attractive man with dark hair.

"Sorry. Guess I should slow down." Having apologized, Shelby was puzzled by the odd way the stranger was looking at her. She could have sworn there was recognition in his eyes, but couldn't recall having seen him before.

Shelby glanced at his badge, but the name didn't spark any recognition, then she shifted her gaze back to his face before spotting Kris approaching their office from the opposite end of the hall. The man was still standing directly in front of her, blocking her passage. "Um. Excuse me," she said pointedly, anxious to join Kris and take a look at the file.

Michael never said a word. He merely moved around her and turned the corner, heading for his brother's office.

The warm smile on Shelby's face faded as she neared Kris. The operative was glaring down the hallway in full intimidation mode. Shelby quickly glanced behind her, but the corridor was empty. "What's wrong?"

"Who were you talking to?"

Shelby blanched at the cold, dangerous tone. "No one I know. I almost ran into him coming around the corner. Why?"

"Looks like someone I once worked with. Bad news all around. Just wondered if you knew him."

Shelby shook her head. "Nope, never saw him before. He did look at me kinda strange, like he knew me or something, but I didn't recognize his name."

"You saw his ID?"

"Yeah. His name's Michael Benton."

Taut with tension, Blue walked into the office with her blonde partner. *So it was him. What is he doing here, now?* Temporarily setting her concerns aside, Kris glanced at the file Shelby was carrying. "What have you got there?"

Shelby glanced at the forgotten folder in her hand. "Jonathan's file. Dennis' secretary called while you were gone."

"Let's take a look." She smiled for Shelby's benefit, was all the while trying to figure out why Michael just happened to be there at headquarters when she was, and also just happened to be in the same hallway as Shelby's office.

Kris pulled her chair over to Shelby's desk and sat down, keeping a careful eye on the analyst as they began perusing the file. The operative could understand Shelby's desire to confront her stepfather, and respected her for it, but worried about it, too. Neither she nor Shelby thought his motives for contacting his stepdaughter again were nearly as altruistic as those Lisa had indicated.

The women skimmed the record together. His file was unremarkable until he was charged with domestic violence. Kris read the abbreviated version of the trial transcript, taking special note of Shelby's testimony. Looking at the pictures of Lisa taken at the hospital, she winced. Aside from the apparent cuts and contusions, she had suffered three broken ribs.

She glanced at Shelby out of the corner of her eye, seeing anger and pain reflected on her face. She wondered if it had been a good idea to disclose that she had requested the file, but quickly discarded the notion. "You okay?"

"Yeah. This just reminds me how important it is to get Mom to see the light. He's such a bastard!"

"I hear you." Kris had little patience for women like Lisa, who not only subjected themselves to repeated abuse, but allowed their children to be victimized as well. However, she had zero tolerance for brutes like Jonathan, male or female.

Shelby turned her attention back to the file, taking comfort in Kris' presence at her side. After the trial, Jonathan had requested and been granted permission to move to Maryland and had resided in a trailer park there. He had met all the requirements of his probation, including completing six sessions with a psychologist. She noted he'd been working at a service station for the previous six months. That was a far cry from his previous job as a bailiff at the county courthouse. After his conviction but prior to his current job, he had worked at two other service stations, as a cook in a local burger joint, and as a parking garage attendant. His probation officer had documented his complaints of the prejudice he was encountering because of the felony conviction.

"I doubt he's accepting responsibility for any prejudice he's encountered, so you can bet that was just more ammunition to fuel his hatred. Knowing that sure doesn't make me feel any better. And from the looks of it, he hasn't been able to get any kind of decent work."

"He brought it on himself," Kris commented with a distinct lack of sympathy.

Shelby sighed. "Yeah, but I know he still blames me for losing his court job. He always had such a superiority complex. Working at gas stations must be a real insult to him."

"Do you care?"

"Not really, other than that I wouldn't put it past him to try and get even. I still wish I knew for certain why he was at the apartment the other night."

The operative didn't bother answering. She intended to find out one way or another. If Shelby's visit to her stepfather didn't yield satisfactory answers, she would pay him a return visit and convince the bastard that Shelby didn't exist in his world.

Kris studied the picture included in the file, committing it to memory. It was a mug shot, but it didn't diminish the obvious attractiveness of the man staring at the camera. He had dark hair, blue eyes, was 6'1" and weighed 220 pounds. Shelby jotted down his address and phone number, and Kris closed the file and rose from her chair. "I'll return it."

Shelby watched her partner leave. She always seemed to be working several angles at once. *She's been acting distant ever since she saw that guy in the hallway. Wonder what that was all about?*

The operative ignored Shelby's questioning look as she left the office. She wanted to pay Earl a visit and find out if he knew what Michael was doing at headquarters. Her mission proved unsuccessful when she discovered her boss and his secretary were both out of the office until the next day.

She returned the file to Dennis' secretary, Joanne, and began making her way back to the office, before suddenly detouring to the canteen to pick up coffee for both of them.

Kris placed her order, then stood in front of the counter automatically scanning the occupants of the room. Her eyes traveled quickly past employees sitting at small tables along the wall, before focusing on the table furthest from the door. Michael was sitting with his back to her, talking to a short, attractive woman who had eyes only for her table partner. Kris took the two coffees and left unobserved.

Walking down the hall, her thoughts drifted back to the last time she'd seen Michael and her jaw tightened as the memories came flooding back.

After three months of painstakingly laying the groundwork, they had finally been given the go-ahead to bring in the Iranian operative who had requested political asylum. Her higher ups had delayed the decision, wanting to make absolutely certain that the foreign agent was not merely a plant to disseminate disinformation.

Blue smiled in satisfaction when she finally received the order. Everything the Iranian had given them had proven valuable, and her superiors now wanted him badly. Unfortunately, their stalling proved costly. Before he could be extracted, their contact was taken into custody, held in the paramilitary headquarters of a small Middle Eastern town until he could be transferred to the Iranian capital.

Frustrated, the American operative considered ambushing the vehicle en route to its destination, but discarded that option because it was unclear which route would be taken. An inside source advised them when the informant was to be moved from the detaining cell to Tehran, indicating his escort would consist of only two guards.

Blue knew that the element of surprise was their biggest advantage and hoped to be able to extract their target safely without any Iranian casualties. And so in the predawn darkness, she had directed her team of four, disguised in the garb of the local populace, to strategic locations near the headquarters.

The door to the building opened, and three men emerged—one shackled in chains between the other two. Blue spoke quietly into the tiny microphone clipped to her aba. "Go."

She had just reached the street when a short, three-shot burst rang out. Reflexes guided her actions even as the scene seemed to unfold in slow motion. She moved back under cover, noted the direction from which the shots were fired, and watched in horror as the remaining guard—his AK-47 on full automatic—sprayed the area around him as he fell to the ground, mortally wounded. The image of their target falling to the ground in a growing pool of blood was overshadowed by the screams of wounded and dying innocent bystanders—many of them women and children—and it burned itself into her mind. "Abort!"

Blue made her way to the rendezvous, cold fury burning slowly like a coal partially ignited. Michael Benton was what had gone wrong. The shots had come from his location, but she couldn't understand why he had opened fire.

Long before this fatal miscue, she'd asked to have Benton reassigned, complaining that he wasn't a team player; her request had been denied. He had an outstanding record and was considered a rising star. Her handler had dismissed her concerns as a personality conflict and told her to deal with it.

So she had. And now children and other innocent civilians were dead. Their target was dead. Three months of hard work down the drain, and what could have been the biggest information coup in recent history was now a mere memory.

Her team began arriving, and it soon became apparent to Blue as she questioned the others that they had been moving and had not seen the direction from which the shots were fired. As she waited for Michael, the scene of the carnage playing repeatedly through her mind. She wondered *how he could ever hope to justify his actions, and vowed to do her best to terminate his career.*

Michael presented some convincing arguments during the investigation, stating that one of the guards had turned his weapon on their target and he had acted to ensure the Iranian's safety. It was total bullshit, but in the end, it was her word against his, and all her evidence only resulted in him being taken out of the field and reassigned. She had since harbored a suspicion that he had been protected by someone higher up, but couldn't substantiate it.

She was leaving headquarters following the conclusion of the hearing when he approached her in the parking lot. "You won't get away with this. I'll destroy your career just like you destroyed mine." She just laughed. "If you think you're good enough, go ahead and try." His face reddened in anger, but he turned and walked away.

That was the last time she'd seen him, until today.

As Kris entered the office, Shelby smiled and accepted the coffee. "Thanks."

"My pleasure. How many names have we got left?"

"Nine, but I might be able to eliminate one more today."

"Good." Kris sat down, uncapped her coffee and took a sip. Turning her attention to the monitor, she called up the file on Michael, only to find she didn't have access. Cursing silently, she swung her chair around and faced Shelby.

Sensing she was being watched, Shelby looked up. "What?"

"How about pulling up Michael Benton's file?"

Surprised by the request, but pleased to be included, Shelby quickly thought it over. She was still curious about Kris' reaction to the man, but needed some sort of justification in her own mind to access his record and decided to be direct. "Who is Michael, Kris?"

The operative hesitated only briefly. "I worked with him once a couple of years ago. Because of him, a lot of people died that day, many of them innocent bystanders. He blew our operation by using poor judgment and disregarding orders. It was my word against his before the Oversight Committee because no one else saw what happened. I took it to the top, but since there were no other witnesses, he was retained and just transferred to advisor status instead of being terminated. Always felt like a cover-up to me."

"But he's history, right? What's he got to do with here and now?"

"Last time I saw him, he threatened me. I'd like to know what he's doing here."

After the events of the past week, that was all the justification Shelby needed. Maybe Michael was there because he knew Kris was. Maybe someone wasn't shooting at her at all, but was shooting at her partner. She scooted her chair over making room for Kris and grinned. "Ready?"

Pushing her own chair across the room, Kris settled behind the desk next to Shelby and watched her work the keyboard until Michael's ID photo appeared on the screen.

Shelby advanced to Michael's history and scanned the information, knowing Kris was doing the same. "Did you know he's Jeb's brother?"

"No. But Jeb's a nobody. Whoever protected him before had a lot more power."

Snickering, Shelby said, "Jeb'd have a fit if he ever heard you say that. Doesn't matter that it's true."

Kris winked. "Just calling it the way I see it."

Shelby finished reading and looked at the screen in front of her. "He's currently assigned to Israel. He must be on leave or something. I'm surprised he didn't show up on the list. No, wait! I know why. The search only included regular field agents, not advisors. Maybe we should add him."

Kris nodded. "Good idea." She quickly wrote down his home of record in Maryland, but as a precaution asked Shelby pull up Jeb's file to get his address, too. It didn't hurt to cover all the bases. Given the events of the past week, it was disturbing enough that he was in town.

SHELBY LAUGHED AS she won the battle for the remote. "Uh uh. We are not watching *Cops* again."

"Why not?"

"Come on! It's been on for an hour already. Let's watch *Miracle Pets*."

Kris grinned and raised an eyebrow dubiously. "Sure. Whatever you want."

"Oh ye of little faith. I think you'll like it. It features stories about pets that saved their owners. Some of the stories are really incredible. It makes you stop and think." Shelby reached over to Kris' lap and stroked Stormy. "Our little furry friends are pretty special."

So are you. Kris nodded, watching as Shelby raised her shoulders, rolling her neck before relaxing again. Sympathetically, she asked, "Neck stiff?"

"Kinda. Sitting hunched over the monitor all day takes a toll sometimes."

"I hear you. I don't know how you do that all the time."

"You sorta get used to it."

Kris had her doubts about that. "If you say so."

Shelby chuckled when Stormy scampered off of her partner's lap to chase a shadow across the room. "It's not like I have much choice."

Casually Kris suggested, "How about scooting over here and letting me see what I can do?"

The analyst barely hesitated before sliding across the couch and turning her back to Kris. Shelby sighed deeply and let her head drop forward as her partner's strong fingers began manipulating the tight muscles.

After a few moments, Kris took a pillow and dropped it on the floor between her feet. "Why don't you move down there? It'll be more comfortable." Once Shelby was sitting between her legs, she picked up where she'd left off, letting her fingers expertly probe and stroke her companion's neck and shoulders.

Shelby was in her own personal paradise, enjoying the feel of Kris' long legs bracketing and supporting her body almost as much as the fingers working their magic. She was much too content to move when the hands slowed, instead leaning back and settling herself comfortably against the operative.

Unable to resist, Kris began to lightly stroke the golden hair that was resting on her thigh, entranced by the silky feel as she drew her fingers lightly through the blonde locks.

Time ceased to have meaning as they sat there in silence, enjoying the closeness. When she could no longer delay a visit to the bathroom, Shelby sighed inwardly, wishing she hadn't had two glasses of iced tea earlier. Regretfully, she stood up and smiled. "Be right back."

Watching her walk out of the room, Kris sighed contentedly. The evening had been perfect. Everything felt so right with the smaller woman at her side. She found herself more and more often finding a reason to touch Shelby, and her overtures were always met with a smile. *I could get used to this.*

She started thinking about what she liked about Shelby and suddenly realized that it wasn't one thing, it was everything. Her laugh, her way of expressing herself, the sweet sound of her voice, the way she walked, her intelligence, her consideration and warmth, the way her eyes flashed when she was angry and danced when she was happy. *Everything.*

Kris had spent a considerable amount of time debating the wisdom of telling Shelby everything and asking for her help. She envisioned every possible scenario she could, from the younger woman hating her to the one she hoped for, in which Shelby agreed to help her. Logically, Kris knew she had to be demented to even consider revealing her secrets, but the idea of returning to the only adult life she'd known had become intolerable because one thing was becoming increasingly apparent to her—before Shelby, she hadn't been living, she'd merely been existing.

The operative also faced another certainty. She would not go back to that life. She would risk it all for the chance to share a future with Shelby. *If she wants me.*

Shelby returned and sat down on the couch. She leaned over her taller companion and picked up the remote. "What're you thinking about? You looked a million miles away."

Kris breathed in her partner's unique scent, fighting off the urge to pull Shelby into her lap. *No, not a million miles away; I was with you every minute you were gone.*

Instead, she took a steadying breath and stood up. "I need to go out one more time." She leaned down and brushed a lock of hair away from Shelby's eyes, her decision made. She wasn't sure what she was going to say or how she was going to say it, but the trip outside would give her time to formulate her thoughts. "You'll still be up when I get back, won't you? I want to talk to you about something."

Blue eyes intent with emotion made Shelby's heart begin fluttering. She smiled warmly, allowing her eyes to convey her response. "I'll be waiting up, just like I always am."

Kris grasped Shelby's hand and squeezed it, releasing it reluctantly. "I'll be back soon."

Shelby nodded in anticipation. *We're going to talk, really talk. I never thought I'd see this day.* She accompanied Kris to the door and locked it behind her. *Yes!*

Kris took the steps two at time, her Blue persona in place by the time she reached ground level. Instincts honed by years of living on the edge suddenly screamed out a warning and she quickly pulled her weapon and faded into the darkness behind the building, searching the shadows for the slightest movement or sound.

Hearing nothing, she kept her back to the cement wall and soundlessly worked her way along the length of the building. She cursed silently when she felt something impact against her shoulder and felt a burning sensation travel down her arm. Immediately dropping into a defensive crouch, Kris began edging her way back around the building. *I have to get back to Shelby.*

A sound focused her attention in the direction from which it had come, but she suddenly found it hard to concentrate. Kris watched in disbelief as the gun fell from her hand to the ground only a moment before she toppled over next to it. Her mind screamed out a warning. *Shelby!*

Speed was of the essence. The tranquilizer was fast-acting, but they only had thirty minutes before the target would begin to wake. Not only was it vital that they not be spotted, Dimitri had stressed the importance of minimizing the length of time the operative would be absent. Nevertheless, not taking any chances, Gregor waited for a full two minutes and then waited until his men had converged and were present before approaching the fallen operative.

He knelt down next to her and roughly shoved her from her side onto her stomach. Removing a pair of handcuffs from his pocket, he snapped them in place, tightening them brutally. This woman had caused him considerable grief and he intended to exact what little revenge he could, knowing that once he turned her over to Dimitri he would be summarily dismissed.

He glanced at two of his men. "Get her to the car." The operatives flanked her, each grabbing an arm and pulling her along.

Gregor would have preferred to let them continue dragging her, letting the movement take its toll on her wrists, but knew better than to leave evidence of their presence. "Pick her up. Hurry up!"

Within minutes, she was stuffed into the back of a blue Ford Taurus and the vehicle set off for an unknown destination.

SHELBY PICKED UP Stormy and sat where Kris had been sitting a short time before. She listened to the contented purring of the small kitten and allowed her thoughts to roam freely. She had asked herself over and over again why she was so attracted to Kris, but knew the answer was the unfathomable magic between them. Everything seemed so right when they were together. Kris was beautiful, yes, but there was so much more about her that Shelby loved. *Like how she always puts me first, the way she looks at me when she thinks I'm not looking, and how she makes me feel with just the slightest touch.*

Shelby also felt an intense protectiveness towards Kris. She chuckled. *Not that she'd ever need my protection, at least physically.* Shelby had noticed an emotional vulnerability in the woman at the oddest times that was very appealing. Every once in a while when she was able to covertly watch Kris, Shelby had seen a sad, lost look in those beautiful blue eyes that broke her heart. She knew the operative was unaware of displaying what she would certainly consider a weakness, but it woke a fierce desire within her to prevent anyone from ever hurting the woman who had claimed her heart.

Shelby smiled happily. *She's so cute when her mouth curls up into that little smile she shares only with me, and I love her dry sense of humor. She is really protective, but I like that.*

Silly, she is supposed to be protective, she's your bodyguard. Shelby answered her inner voice. *No. It goes way beyond a job. I can feel it.*

Suddenly uneasy, Shelby lifted the kitten from her lap and stood up. Kris had been gone only a matter of minutes, but out of nowhere had come a strong feeling that something was very wrong. She dismissed the idea as ridiculous; Kris was undoubtedly fine. But her uneasiness continued to grow. *She's in trouble.*

Shelby usually trusted her instincts, but worried that her overactive imagination and emotional attachment might have conjured up the feeling rather than it arising from any inner sense. Trying to ignore the feeling, she discovered that it nonetheless persisted and grew. *Should I go and look for her?* She clearly remembered Kris' admonition to stay inside no matter what. She'd agreed at the time, but that was before she'd felt like this.

She picked up the phone, only to set it back down. Whom could she call and what could she say? 'Um, you see, Kris went outside and she's been gone twenty minutes and I'm worried about her.' *Yeah, right!*

Forcing herself to remain calm, Shelby sat down on the couch and flicked through the channels, finally tossing the remote on the end table in disgust. It was no use. She couldn't concentrate on anything except the clock, and it seemed like only a minute had passed since she'd looked at it last. She decided to wait another half hour before doing something. Just exactly what form that action would take, she wasn't sure, but Shelby figured she had an interminable half hour to try and figure out what she would do if Kris still hadn't returned.

BLUE WAS SLOWLY regaining consciousness, but deliberately hid her growing awareness of her surroundings. She was lying on what felt like a cement floor with her hands and legs secured. Tensing her muscles slightly, she could feel the steel vises on her wrists tighte,n and relaxed to relieve some of the pressure.

Sensing that she was alone, Blue opened her eyes and looked around. The room was barren except for two chairs, a table, and some leather restraints attached to chains hanging from the ceiling in the center of the room. She grimaced, all too familiar with the uses for the device. She hoped this strike was directed only at her and that Shelby was safe, but her stomach tightened in worry.

She lay unmoving, watching as the door opened and five men walked in, only one of whom she recognized. Her eyes narrowed at the sight of Sergei, and suddenly she knew what had prompted her abduction. Somehow they must have already found out the information she gave them was bogus. *Shit!* She'd known the risks, but had expected that maneuver to buy more time. Not bothering to ponder how they'd discovered her deception so quickly, Blue focused her energy on preparing herself both mentally and physically for the punishment she was sure was to come.

"Put her in the restraints."

The four burly men approached, two observing while two roughly grabbed her and dragged her across the room. Not willing to cooperate with her adversaries in any way, Kris kept her body limp, forcing two to hold her erect while her wrists and ankles were secured by the leather bands, then tightened.

"Nice to see you again, Natasha."

Blue glared at Sergei but remained quiet.

"Not happy to see me? That wouldn't be because of the useless information you gave us, now would it?"

"I don't know what you're talking about."

Sergei crossed the room and backhanded Blue viciously across the face. "You will answer honestly when I talk to you. Did you really think you'd get away with that?"

Blue could feel the blood trickling from her mouth as she stared back at Sergei. "Get away with what?"

At a look from the Russian, one of the men delivered a solid blow to Blue's midsection. "You disgust me." Sergei knew there was a remote chance that she could be telling the truth and the computers just hadn't been updated, but he felt it unlikely. "I should kill you now, but I have another job for you. If you do it well, I might spare your life."

Blue tried to keep the pain at bay. She had no intention of doing anything he wished, but she would have to play the game in order to leave the room alive.

The Russian agent paced back and forth in front of her. "The woman you're staying with is a highly regarded analyst with access to very sensitive information. Such access would be of great value to us. I want her password, and you will obtain it without arousing suspicion."

"That's...impossible," Blue managed to spit out.

"For someone less skilled than you, perhaps. But I'm sure you can find a way." Sergei smiled cruelly. "Just in case you doubt my resolve," he nodded to two of the men and watched as they approached the woman.

Blue knew what was coming and began focusing her mind to ignore the pain to come.

Sergei had picked the two men because they were interrogation experts, trained to deliver the maximum amount of punishment without doing any major bodily damage. He had already told them that they were to leave no marks on any part of her body that would normally be exposed, not wanting to arouse the suspicions of anyone at the Company. The bruise he'd left on her cheek could easily be covered.

The Russian officer stood back with his arms crossed in front of his chest, observing the punishment being meted out. He always enjoyed this part of an interrogation and smiled with satisfaction at the grunts of pain that followed the blows. He allowed the brutalization to continue for several minutes after she'd passed out before calling a halt. He hadn't forgotten her stubbornness as a child and wanted to make sure she understood his message. Sergei knew that every time she moved for the next week, she would be reminded of his lesson.

The fact that she would be terminated once they had the password was of no consequence at the moment. He walked over and began slapping her face lightly. "Wake up. I have another surprise for you."

Blue had allowed herself to sink into blackness instead of fighting it. Her slow return to consciousness was suddenly accelerated when she was drenched with cold water. Her eyes opened as she spat out water, gritting her teeth as pain rolled over her. She wanted to double over in agony, but her bonds denied her even that luxury.

"Oh, good, you're back with us. You had me worried for a while. Are you ready to see your mother now?"

Blue remained silent, her mind disbelieving. Her mother was dead. She'd been dead for almost twenty years. Obviously, Sergei wasn't done torturing her yet, but she'd buried her mother long ago. "She's dead."

"No, Natasha, she isn't dead, but that isn't what we wanted you to think. You had no reason to doubt us. You were but a child. It suited our purposes for you to believe that." He looked at one of the men. "Release her." To her, smiling, "It wouldn't do for your mother to see you all trussed up, now would it?"

Blue didn't know what to believe as she fell to the ground in a heap, her arms wrapped around her throbbing midsection. She tried to hold the pain at bay, but the men had been experts, and it was unrelenting in its intensity.

"I'll be back after your reunion," Sergei promised as he left.

A few minutes later the door to the interrogation room opened. A tall, thin woman with gray hair walked in and looked curiously at the female lying curled up on the floor. The last twenty-four hours had been so confusing. Twenty years before, Masha was told her little girl had died in a fire at the school. Then yesterday, she was rushed from her home and flown to America to meet with her miraculously resurrected daughter. Masha hadn't seen Sergei since the day he'd informed her of Natasha's death, and she hadn't been pleased to see him again. She didn't know what he was up to, but she didn't trust him.

Masha approached the figure on the floor. She didn't believe this was her daughter, but the poor woman had obviously been beaten and she would try to help her. Kneeling down, she gazed into the pain-filled eyes regarding her and rocked back on her heels. *Those eyes! Can it be?* She extended trembling fingers and tentatively brushed the woman's cheek.

Blue stared in disbelief. This elderly woman could be her mother's twin, albeit aged. Her hazel eyes reflected kindness, and her face mirrored the character and strength she remembered seeing as a child. She shut her eyes, refusing to be taken in by the cruel ruse. It had to be some kind of trick, a look-alike actress hired to fool her.

Masha let her fingertips rest against the injured woman's cheek and spoke hesitantly in Russian. "They told me you were my daughter. I didn't believe them. Now, I'm not so sure. You have her eyes. Let me help you sit up."

Wracked with excruciating pain, Kris shook her head. "No." She needed more time to divert her senses away from the damage that had been inflicted and the agony she was experiencing. Trying to concentrate on the woman at her side, Kris chose the one thing that only her mother would know about because she had never mentioned it to anyone at the school. "How's Sasha?"

Masha's mouth dropped open and her hand clutched at her chest. "It can't be!" She softly stroked Kris' cheek. "You really are alive! All these years I have mourned you, and you are alive." Tears rolled down the older woman's face. "Sasha lived for fifteen years after you left. Every time I petted her, I remembered how happy you were when you got her."

A myriad of emotions flickered through the operative's mind, but she was still not totally convinced. "Is Leonard still around?"

Masha looked puzzled. "Maybe I was wrong. My daughter would know that Leonard died when she was five." Disappointment flooded the older woman's features and she sighed heavily. "I knew it was too good to be true."

"Mother?" Kris' voice was barely audible as she tried to come to terms with the fact that this most probably *was* her mother. It was an odd feeling. She'd buried her in her mind so long ago.

"You were testing me," the older woman stated knowingly.

Kris smiled weakly. "Yeah."

"I should've guessed. You always were suspicious. Oh, what have they done to you? What's going on?"

Trying to ignore the red-hot waves of pain, Kris concentrated on the conversation and spoke quietly. "There's no time for that. Do you have any idea where we are?"

"No. When we left the airport, we drove around the city for a long time. I tried to see the address, but they ushered me in the back way. I think this street is Georgia; that's all I saw."

"Are they treating you okay?"

"Yes. They left me in a room with a bed and bathroom all day. They brought me food a few hours ago. But enough of that; how can I help you?"

"You can't. Do just as they say. I need to get you out of here—"

She heard footsteps outside the doorway and clamped her mouth shut, then watched in silence as her mother obeyed an order to accompany one of the guards and departed.

Sergei walked into the room and smiled. "Have a nice visit?"

"I don't believe that is my mother."

"Oh, I think you do. As a child you didn't care about the program. You did nothing but count down days until you could go home. We needed your full attention, so we killed her. " Sergei smiled coldly. "Isn't it ironic that you now hold her fate in your hands. She was dead to you once. Are you going to be responsible for her real death? If I do not have that password within a week, you will watch her die a slow and painful death, followed closely by your own."

"Boris!" When his subordinate arrived, Sergei ordered, "Get her prepared for the return trip." He walked out of the room, ignoring the eyes that tracked him.

After a weak struggle, Blue was subdued and given a dose of sedative large enough to ensure she would remain unconsciousness for at least a couple of hours.

Sergei intended to be absolutely certain that she had no recollection of the whereabouts of the safe house. He glanced at his watch, satisfied. Her total absence would not exceed the hour and a half he'd allowed for. He dictated a short note to one of the guards and pinned it to her T-shirt. It wouldn't do for her partner to get excited and notify the Company when she was returned unconscious. He handed her unloaded weapon to one of the guards, and sent for Gregor.

"Deliver her to the door of her apartment and ring the doorbell. Make sure you are not seen." Sergei walked over to Gregor and stopped, his face only inches from his subordinate's. "She will remain unrestrained and you will make sure that she is handled carefully. Is that clear?"

"Yes, Comrade."

"Return her now!"

Gregor bowed his head slightly, turned to the guards and began issuing orders.

SHELBY WAS GROWING frantic. She knew Kris wouldn't worry her unnecessarily again and looked at the phone but dismissed the thought of using it, trying to decide on a course of action. Walking to her bedroom, Shelby donned a light jacket. It had been almost an hour since the operative had left; she wasn't waiting any longer. What if Kris was lying hurt out on the grounds? If the woman wanted to be mad later, fine, but she wasn't willing to ignore her instincts any longer. She picked up a can of pepper spray and put it in her pocket. *Doesn't hurt to be prepared.*

She went to the door, unlocked it, and carefully looked out. Waving to her neighbors who were just arriving home, she locked the door behind her and began the descent to the first floor. Listening and looking for anything out of the ordinary, Shelby reached the ground level and began walking toward the front.

She knew Kris always checked out the parking lot and decided to check there first, just to rule out the easiest places. Walking around the backs of the buildings would be a bit scarier. It was totally dark back there, with clusters of trees on the property and a lightly wooded area just beyond.

Two pairs of eyes watched her every move—one through the windshield of a car parked on the side street bordering the parking lot, and the other from a cluster of trees just beyond the apartment property. Neither man made any move to intercept her, not wanting to reveal their presence unless she tried to leave the grounds or was endangered in some way.

After traversing the entire parking lot, Shelby headed for the large grassy area behind the buildings. A couple of times, the hairs on the nape of her neck stood up, but when she looked around, she didn't see anyone. She decided to start behind her own building and work her way to the perimeter. Slowly walking along, her eyes flickered over the area, looking for anything that might provide a clue to Kris' whereabouts.

Deep down, she already knew the operative wasn't around unless she was lying injured somewhere, because Kris would've already intercepted her—upset that she'd left the apartment. She pulled her keys out of her pocket and turned on the small flashlight on the keypad that doubled as a panic alarm. She aimed it at the ground and suddenly stopped.

Just to her left, the longish grass was flattened, a sharp contrast against the undisturbed growth. She approached the area, blocking the dim light with her body as she followed the trail until it suddenly ended. Frustrated, she walked a little further hoping to pick up the track again, but the rest of the grass was undisturbed.

Just as she was about to turn away, her light touched on a dark object. She redirected the narrow beam, and her heart momentarily stopped when she recognized what she was looking at. Shelby bent down and picked up Kris' cellular phone. Her fear for Kris intensifying, she quickly but thoroughly searched the remainder of the yard, and finding nothing else ran back to her apartment.

After locking the door, she sank down onto the couch studying the cell phone. Shelby didn't know Earl's number, but remembered Kris had pushed only one of the buttons to summon him the night they were shot at. Hesitating only briefly, she pressed the number 1 and waited for it to be answered.

Chapter Thirteen

STARTLED WHEN THE doorbell chimed, Shelby looked up and automatically pressed the off button on the cellular phone before quickly making her way to the door. She'd heard quiet footfalls in the stairwell, but had disregarded them because Kris never made a sound when she climbed the steps.

With her eye at the peephole Shelby gazed out, seeing nothing. She carefully surveyed the area again. Directing her gaze downward, her heart began pounding in fear. The angle of the peephole and the scant light limited visibility, but Shelby could make out a long, jean-clad leg and an arm, the bicep covered by a light blue sleeve.

Oh my God, that's what Kris was wearing! She was barely cognizant of the thought, or of the potential danger, as she unlocked the deadbolt and pulled the door open until the chain stopped it. The fear she'd managed to hold at bay escalated at the sight of Kris lying unmoving on the ground outside her door. Driven by fear for her partner, she fumbled with releasing the chain, uttering an uncharacteristic curse at her awkwardness.

Pulling the door wide open, Shelby knelt down, immediately noticing the dried blood on Kris' mouth and then registering that her clothes and hair were wet. She laid two fingers gently against the operative's neck, searching for a pulse, and sighed in relief at the steady, regular rhythm. Her eyes cut to a folded piece of paper pinned to Kris' collar, then to the gun lying on the ground between her body and the door. Tearing the paper slightly in her haste to remove it, Shelby opened the note, resting her hand on Kris' arm as she read the neat script.

> She is just sleeping off a sedative and should awaken within two hours. Do not call anyone. To do so would greatly endanger both of your lives.

Quickly pocketing the note, Shelby swallowed her fear, unwilling to devote any time to deciphering the cryptic, threatening message. Her first priority was to get Kris inside, but that wasn't going to be easy—the tall woman outweighed her by at least thirty pounds. She picked up the gun and put it in her jacket pocket. *All I need is for someone to see that.*

Positioning herself at Kris' head, she placed her hands under the operative's shoulders, but quickly realized she was not going to be able to drag her partner inside by herself. Shelby gently squeezed Kris' arm, reluctant to break contact. "Don't worry; I'll be right back."

Barely aware of having spoken aloud, Shelby stood up and began to step over Kris. Her movement caused the gun to bump against her hip, and she realized the weapon was protruding from her pocket. Backing into the apartment, she laid it on the floor in the foyer closet, then shooed Stormy away from the front door before pulling it closed and stepping carefully over Kris. She hurriedly walked the several paces to her closest neighbor and knocked, beginning her entreaty as soon as Bill answered the door.

"Hi, my friend got a little inebriated and passed out. I was wondering if you'd mind helping me get her into the apartment."

Bill laughed. "Hey, no problem. Been there, done that." He followed Shelby to her fallen friend. Looking at the small streak of blood on Kris' chin, he commented, "She run into the door or something?" When Shelby nodded, he asked curiously, "What did you do, try to wake her up with water?"

Shelby forced a laugh. "Didn't work. You know how drunks are."

"Right." Bill eyed the attractive woman lying on the ground. "Boy, is she going to feel like hell in the morning."

"I hear you." Shelby helped Bill raise Kris up to a sitting position, then watched as he hefted her over his shoulder in a fireman's carry and slowly stood up.

"Where do you want her?"

"In my bedroom. She needs the bed worse than I do tonight."

"You ain't lying. She's really out."

Shelby grabbed two sheets and a couple of towels out of the linen closet on the way down the hallway. Once she got Kris' wet clothes off, she didn't want her lying on a wet sheet. Preparing the bed, she quickly pulled down the covers, leaving the sheets folded in half and spreading them on one side of the bed before laying a large towel on the other side.

She stood aside as Bill deposited the operative on the bed, then accompanied him out of the apartment, thanking him profusely. After securing the door, she practically ran back to the bedroom, her convivial mask replaced with worry. She turned on the light and leaned over Kris, gently brushed her wet bangs aside and laid a hand lightly on her forehead. It was cool, but not alarmingly so.

Wryly aware it was mostly for her own benefit, she nervously began talking to the sleeping woman. "Don't worry; I'll take care of stuff tonight. You have no idea how worried I was about you. I'm just so glad you're okay." Shelby continued stroking the operative's cheek and muttering soothing words as her mind sorted out the best way to remove Kris' wet clothes. Her heart tightened at the red mark on Kris' face and the dried blood on her mouth, and she left to get a washcloth, also grabbing Kris' sleeping shirt from the hook next to her own on the bathroom door.

Shelby returned to the bedroom, slipped her jacket off and tossed it on a chair. She picked up the washcloth and tenderly wiped the blood from Kris' mouth, noting it had apparently come from a cut on the inside of her cheek. Next, she untied the operative's shoes and tugged them off. Shaking her head as she decided on her quickest option, she muttered apologetically, "I've gotta get you out of those wet clothes."

A quick trip to the kitchen and she returned with a large pair of scissors, lifted the bottom of Kris' shirt and began cutting it up the middle. She gently chastised Kris as she worked. "I don't want to hear any complaints about your clothes, either. You got that? You're the one who turns up wet and unconscious at the door, scaring me half to death." Shelby's voice changed from scolding to concerned. "Who did this to you? And why are you soaking wet?"

As she cut through the fabric, the shirt fell to the sides and Shelby suddenly froze, gasping in horror, "Oh, Kris!"

Angry red and purple bruises covered every inch of the exposed skin. Holding her breath, Shelby finished splitting the shirt, noting that the damage seemed concentrated beneath her friend's bra line – from her lower ribs down. Wanting to assess all injuries, Shelby gingerly approached the lower body. She had difficulty unfastening the tall woman's wet jeans, but finally got the zipper down after a struggle. Fearful of what she might find, Shelby gently pulled down the waistband of Kris' underwear, sighing with relief when she saw the bruising didn't extend much lower.

Unaware of tears tracking down her face, Shelby went back to removing the shirt, cutting a path from the center of the garment to each arm until it fell away. "Why couldn't you just talk to me? What's so hard about that? Maybe I could've helped before...before..." Her voice broke as her fingers hovered just above the bruised skin, never quite touching while she studied the jeans. They were going to be harder, and Shelby settled on just splitting them at the outside seam, thankful that they weren't overly snug.

Finally finished, she set the scissors down, ignoring the blister that had formed on her thumb. Freeing Kris from the jeans, she tossed them on the floor, followed a few minutes later by the remnants of the shirt. In the best business-like manner she could muster under the circumstances, Shelby picked up the scissors again. "Sorry, but this is all your own fault." Slightly embarrassed, she cut the bra in front, snipped the straps, then slit the blue-stained underwear at the sides, adding both to the pile of wet clothes on the floor. Shelby gazed at the beautiful body, marred only by the mottled color of Kris' abdomen, before averting her eyes, chastising herself for having indulged in the guilty pleasure.

She gently laid her hand on the mass of bruises, alarmed at the warmth of the angry skin. Wiping the tears from her face, she began working the damp sheets and towel free. "Your sleeping shirt's gonna have to wait until you wake up."

Quickly making her way to the kitchen, she grabbed a universal cold/hot pack out of the freezer. Returning to the agent's side, she opened the cold compress and covered the worst of the bruises, laying a comforting hand on Kris' arm when her patient stirred uneasily. Pulling the covers over her, Shelby said sympathetically, "I know it hurts. This'll help."

Her distress over Kris' injuries was compounded by a myriad of fragmented questions crowding her thoughts, though she had temporarily managed to ignore the clamor in her mind by focusing on Kris' care. After toweling the dark hair dry and placing another pillow beneath the operative's head, she couldn't think of anything else to do for her.

Sitting gingerly on the edge of the bed, Shelby took one of Kris' hands into her own. "You are going to have to talk to me when you wake up. No more of this 'it's better if you don't know' stuff. Do you hear me? Don't you know I love you?" Shelby squeezed Kris' hand reassuringly when she stirred. "I don't know what I'll do if something happens to you." Looking at the now-still, silent woman, tears welled up again. "Oh, Kris, what have you gotten into?"

The last question reverberated chillingly through her mind. Shelby knew only highly trained experts would have been able to overcome Kris and beat her so brutally. She still questioned the wisdom of not calling an ambulance, but nothing appeared to be broken, and each time she checked Kris' pulse, it was strong and regular. *You should call someone.* She tried to ignore the voice of reason. *I know, but I can't. Not yet. Not until I talk to her. If I do, they'll hurt her. And if you don't, both of you are going to end up dead.* Shelby sighed, and leaned against the headboard, still holding Kris' hand. *Not yet.*

Even as she made the decision, she was haunted by doubts.

What possible justification could she give for not calling Dennis or Earl? *I will, just not yet. I need to talk to Kris first, to get all the facts.* She removed the cold pack after twenty minutes, her uncertainty continuing to torment her. Her eyes finally closed in exhaustion, the emotional events of the evening taking their toll.

Shelby's eyes snapped open and turned to Kris. She heard a moan and immediately knew that was what had awakened her. Glancing at the clock, she noted it was nearly 01:00, so she'd only been asleep for half an hour. If the note were to be believed, Kris should be waking up at any time. Shelby returned her attention to her companion, watching as Kris continued to shift restlessly. When her eyes fluttered open, Shelby squeezed her hand. Her heart cried out in sympathy when pain-filled blue eyes met her gaze.

Her mind still groggy, Kris tried with little success to ignore the throbbing. As she gazed at Shelby, she tried to connect the pain she felt wracking her body with the sight of her partner regarding her with such loving concern. Gradually, the pieces began to fall into place. An image of her mother filled her mind. *I am so screwed.* She closed her eyes tightly, half-expecting Shelby to start grilling her with questions. Instead, a soft voice asked, "How about some Alleve?"

Her mouth dry, Kris rasped, "Thanks."

"Be right back."

Kris' mind reviewed the events of the evening and she sighed in frustration. *What the hell am I going to do? What is Shelby thinking?* The effects of the sedative had just about completely worn off, and it even hurt to take deep breaths. Attempting to assess the extent of her injuries, she began moving her legs and quickly discovered she was naked. This was even worse than she'd thought. Shelby had seen the damage, and there was no way she was going to let Kris brush it off as a simple mugging.

Shelby returned a couple of minutes later with two pills and a large glass of water.

"Let me help you sit up."

"Wait." Kris knew she had to sit up to drink, but the idea of moving was abhorrent. She also knew it would be much worse for her not to move, and the idea of having to accept help for such a basic movement increased her feeling of helplessness.

Shelby watched the conflicting emotions flicker across the tall woman's face and suddenly realized the reason. "If you'd rather do it yourself, it's okay." She held her breath as she waited for Kris to respond. If the woman couldn't accept her help for something so simple, they had no future.

Kris gazed into the sympathetic, green eyes regarding her gravely. She nodded. "Thanks, I'd appreciate a hand. I'm a little sore."

Relieved, Shelby looked at Kris pointedly and managed a wry smile. "I would imagine you are." She slid an arm beneath the tall woman's shoulders, helping her up until Kris was supporting herself on an elbow.

Kris took the two pills and swallowed them with water. After drinking deeply, she handed the glass to Shelby and broached the obvious. "You saw."

"Kinda hard to miss."

Nodding, Kris decided to take care of immediate needs first. "I've got to use the bathroom." She focused on getting out of the bed with a minimum of movement.

"Need some help?"

Kris knew she could manage by herself, but was unwilling to turn down the compassionate offer, knowing it could be one of the last she'd receive. "Yes, but let me get my feet on the floor first."

Nodding, Shelby waited at the side of the bed. She watched as Kris gingerly brought her legs around until her feet reached the floor. Holding out an arm, she said, "Take hold. I'll help you stand up."

Kris grasped Shelby's arm and began to stand, surprised at the strength of the smaller woman even as her body protested every movement. She leaned heavily on Shelby for several moments until a wave of dizziness passed and the pain became more manageable. Shifting her weight to her own legs, Kris began shuffling slowly to the bathroom with Shelby at her side. At the bathroom door, her companion handed over the sleeping shirt she had grabbed earlier.

Shelby had already tried to think of all the likely scenarios, and some of the possibilities were frightening. There was no doubt in her mind that Kris was involved in something illegal. *But what?* And she had obviously displeased some highly trained people; tonight had proven that. Her thoughts turned briefly to the note, the threat it had contained. Shelby sighed. She could speculate all night, but only Kris held all the answers.

Even though she was burning with a desire to know just what was going on, Shelby was more concerned about how Kris felt, and it was obvious to her that the operative was still very groggy and desperately in need of healing sleep. She decided to put her questions on hold until later.

Left alone, Kris examined her body, unsurprised at the damage. She was lucky, really. None of her ribs appeared to be broken, even though it hurt to breathe deeply. She carefully donned the shirt and opened the bathroom door to look for Shelby. Seeing her standing in the bedroom doorway, she asked, "Did you happen to see my gun?" She hoped it had been returned with her.

"Yeah. I put it in the closet. I'll go get it."

Kris knew it wouldn't have been returned loaded. "Would you bring the box of ammo on the top shelf, too?"

"Okay. Go on into the bedroom and I'll bring it in there."

Kris eased down into the chair near the bed and waited for Shelby to return. She knew she had a lot of explaining to do, and wished the painkiller would kick in to alleviate some of her discomfort. On top of that, she was exhausted. She snorted derisively. *Just woke up and I'm still tired. Go figure.*

Shelby reentered the bedroom and handed Kris the gun and box of shells, watching as Kris reloaded. She noticed the operative's movements lacked their usual smoothness, and couldn't miss the signs of pain Kris was trying desperately to hide.

Looking up, the agent said, "I know you have a lot of questions. Make yourself comfortable, it's a long story."

Kris is finally willing to trust me with the truth! Our friendship just progressed light years from what it was a few hours ago. Shelby decided right then and there to show Kris that her trust wasn't misplaced, and fully extended her own trust, silently committed to helping the operative out of the mess she was in any way she could.

The analyst studied the woman sitting on the chair gazing at her. Kris' stoic act didn't fool Shelby; she knew the injuries were really hurting. Her face was pale and drawn, and fatigue lined her face. All her movements were guarded and goose bumps lined her arms. A few more hours wasn't really going to make any difference, and she couldn't stand the idea of being responsible for causing Kris to suffer any more than she already was.

"I don't have any questions that can't wait a few more hours. You look terrible. Why don't you get some sleep? We can talk in the morning."

Kris sighed in relief. "Thanks."

Shelby smiled. "You take the bed. You need it a lot more than I do. I'm sleeping on the couch tonight, so don't bother arguing about it."

"Please don't."

"The couch isn't big enough for you even when you're not hurt. You take the bed."

"Only if you sleep in here, too."

Shelby eyes reflected surprise. "I don't want to hurt you. If I move..."

Kris gazed at Shelby, her thoughts tormented. Even if it was to be for just one night, she wanted the comfort of having the smaller woman close. It might be the only chance she'd get, depending on how Shelby felt about her after they talked in the morning. "You won't hurt me."

Indecisive, Shelby paused, then slowly nodded her head. "Okay. I'm going to change." A couple of minutes later, Shelby slid carefully into the opposite side of the bed, taking care not to jar her companion, who was already lying down.

Kris reached over and took Shelby's hand. She found the simple comfort afforded by the contact relaxing, allowing her to put her troubles and concerns in a dark corner of her mind and fall back into the blackness from which she'd so recently emerged.

Her hand joined with her partner's, Shelby's mind began to quiet and she soon followed Kris into the realms of sleep.

KRIS SLEPT FITFULLY, waking before Shelby the following morning. She lay quietly, fully feeling the effects of the punishment inflicted on her body the night before. Her grimace turned into a smile at the sight of the woman sleeping next to her. Sometime during the night, they had both moved toward the center of the bed, driven by a need their waking minds hadn't allowed them to acknowledge.

Ignoring her discomfort, Kris gazed at her companion. The pain would still be there later, but whether or not Shelby would was something she could only hope for. Her blonde, sleep-tousled hair lay splayed across the pillow and her face was peaceful, bearing none of the worry and concern that had lined it the previous night. Kris stored away each and every detail her eyes recorded. *Please let this be the beginning, and not the end.*

Sighing silently, Kris knew there was no sense in denying it any longer: she had fallen totally in love with this woman. What she hadn't figured out was why Shelby seemed to care so much for her. *I tried to remain distant.* She directed her internal conversation to her partner. *But you wouldn't let me. You ignored the barriers I put up as if they didn't exist. Why? What did you see? Even when you found out I am an assassin, that didn't deter you. Will you hate me when I tell you who I really am? I'll understand if you do. No matter what you decide, I will always love you.*

Kris knew that after the confession she was going to make, Shelby would hold all the cards, and whatever actions she took would determine if they had any future or if they immediately parted ways. She continued to wonder if her decision to reveal everything was the best, after all. *What right do I have to involve her in this? She's already in much greater danger because of me. I don't know if I can protect her from any repercussions from the Company. Am I being fair to her?* Her thoughts tormented her, causing her to vacillate between hope and despair.

Slowly sitting up, Kris doubled over in agony at the effort; she had stiffened up overnight. Her breathing quick and shallow to lessen the toll on her body, the agent silently cursed, waiting for the pain to abate.

Shelby woke to see Kris sitting with her arms wrapped around her middle as she leaned forward across her legs, and she winced in sympathy. "Can I help?"

"I'm okay; just takes me a minute to get moving. But thanks." Kris managed to get out of bed and started down the hallway.

Shelby followed Kris out of the bedroom, then went to the foyer and rummaged through Kris' clothes bag. Pulling out a T-shirt and a pair of jogging shorts, she grabbed a clean pair of underwear and returned to the bathroom. Waiting until she heard the toilet flush, she knocked on the door. When Kris opened the door, she said, "Here you go. Hope these are all right."

Taking the clothes from Shelby, Kris smiled. "Thanks."

"You're welcome. I'll go start the coffee."

After a quick shower, Kris stepped out of the bath. Examining the bruises again, she cursed her bad luck. There was no doubt in her mind that Sergei had expedited the request for verification of the information she had provided. She couldn't ever remember being in a worse spot. In the past, only *her* life had been at risk. Now, because of her, her mother and Shelby had been drawn into this dangerous situation.

Her body protesting every movement, Kris slowly dressed and then looked in the medicine cabinet for the Alleve. She took two, then made her way to the kitchen, joining Shelby at the table.

Kris studied Shelby intently, trying to decide on where to start. She looked into the warm, curious eyes and started speaking in a low, even voice. "Some things in life we don't have any control over, like our parents, our economic status when we're children, where we're born, stuff like that."

Shelby nodded, surprised at the observation. She'd expected Kris to make some shocking revelation and had been prepared for that, not for hearing her share her views on life. "I hear you. I sure wouldn't have chosen Jonathan for a stepfather."

"That's exactly what I mean. As children, we don't have any control over our lives. Remember, I told you I attended a boarding school for a couple of years?"

"Yeah." Shelby smiled, wondering where this was going.

Kris looked into her coffee cup. *It's now or never.* Forgetting about her injury, she took a deep breath, narrowing her eyes momentarily against the discomfort until it abated. "Would you promise me something?"

"If I can. You gotta tell me what it is first."

"No matter what I tell you, will you promise to let me finish before forming any conclusions?"

Suddenly very uneasy, Shelby carefully searched Kris' face. "This is something really bad, isn't it?"

"Yeah, you could say that."

Shelby thought about the resolution she'd made to stand by Kris; that included trusting her. "Okay, I promise."

Kris took a sip of coffee, and plunged in. "That boarding school I went to—it wasn't a boarding school. It was a school for gifted Russian children who were hand-selected to be inserted in the United States as moles."

Shelby had prepared herself for almost anything, figuring that Kris was involved in something illegal, and had even allowed herself to admit the possibility that it could involve foreign agents. The idea that the operative could be such an agent, however, was one she'd never contemplated. Shelby shook her head, but the words lingered in her mind like a waking nightmare.

Her eyes widening in shock, Shelby blurted out in disbelief, "You're a Russian agent?" She shoved her chair back, rising abruptly, "I don't believe this!" She desperately needed some space and strode into the living room to harness her roiling emotions, running a hand through her hair as her head began throbbing. She had grown to know and love Kris—and to trust her. Now she questioned whether she'd ever truly known her at all, because essentially everything about the agent was a lie.

Kris' heart sank as Shelby turned and left the dining room. She didn't blame her. She had just dumped a load of bad news on the younger woman, and put her in a very compromising situation. She could clearly imagine the internal battle Shelby was waging, and as the silence lengthened, her thoughts became even more anguished. Far greater than any worries about her limited options if Shelby refused to help was her overwhelming fear of losing her friend. Kris could hardly bear to contemplate how empty her life would be again without her. The operative knew Shelby's initial reaction could've been a lot worse, and now Kris could only wait and see what her partner would decide to do.

Shelby gazed out the balcony door for an interminable time as she examined her choices. Logically, she knew that she shouldn't trust the operative, but there was one truth she clung tightly to: Kris was trustworthy. She'd sensed it from the time she'd met her. Yes, she might be a foreign agent, but did that fact change the basic makeup of the woman? Shelby made her decision. No it didn't, and no logic could offer an argument to dispel her belief in that. She made her way back to the kitchen.

Kris gazed at Shelby beseechingly as she returned to the kitchen, silently imploring her to hear her out. She was painfully aware of how much she was asking, and once again questioned her decision to involve Shelby.

The emotional pain in Kris' eyes was palpable, and sighing audibly, Shelby slid back down into her chair, asking rhetorically, "Why did it have to be this?"

"I've asked myself that same question for years." Her thoughts tumultuous, Kris felt the weight of the yoke she'd carried most of her life resting heavily on her shoulders.

I trust you. Now convince me I made the right decision. Trying to quell the doubts raging in her mind, Shelby asked quietly, "When did they activate you?"

"The day I arrived back in the States."

Shelby felt a flicker of hope. "You've never heard from them before now?"

Kris shook her head. "No."

"Talk to me, Kris. And don't leave anything out."

Inwardly sighing with relief, Kris began relating her past. "At the school, I was subjected to brainwashing techniques to ensure complete compliance with the program. I resisted for two years, until they told me my mother had died. Determined to get out of there, I started playing the game, and within six months I was given a complete set of documents and placed with two Russian spies already here. They were the aunt and uncle I told you about."

Shelby found herself drawn into the story. "You said you didn't like them."

"I hated them *and* the headmaster at the school. They constantly preached the sins of capitalism, but the more I interacted in school and at college, the more I realized my views of this country were very different from theirs." Kris met Shelby's eyes and held them. "I began to love this country and the opportunities available here, and I spent every waking moment trying to find a way out."

"If you weren't going to help them, why'd you join the Company?"

Kris told Shelby what she could. "I knew if I proved myself the best of the best, I would remain in the field and be inaccessible to the Russians. In any other job, they could've kept tabs on me a lot more easily. When the USSR collapsed and the Russian Federation was formed, I began to hope I never would be contacted. Many moles never are."

"Why didn't you just tell the CIA and offer to double?"

The operative sighed inwardly. Shelby really cut to the chase, and she still had to be careful what she revealed. "I really didn't want to double. I love this country, and it has my loyalty, but I am still Russian. That complicates things."

Shelby nodded. *What a horrid way to live. To always wonder if you'd be called upon and staying on the move to prevent that from happening.* "Is that why you said you had to stay in wet ops?"

Kris nodded. *Partly.* "I knew if I was ever contacted, it would end my career. I'm not sure I would've been contacted now except for that major leak in the Company."

Shelby got up and refilled both of their cups as she digested the information. "We've got a lot more to talk about."

Kris thanked Shelby for the coffee, then said, "Go ahead, ask whatever you want."

"I want to know what happened to you last night."

"When I went out, they were waiting. I don't know how many there were, but I never had a chance; they shot me with a tranquilizer gun. They took me to an interrogation site to teach me a lesson."

"To teach you a lesson! For God's sake, Kris, they beat the shit out of you. What did you do to them?"

"They were demanding some intelligence from me, then found out the information I turned over to them was useless." Kris sighed. "I'd hoped it would take them longer to check it out. Was I ever wrong."

"What did they want?"

"To know where our operatives are. Somehow they knew I had access to some of that information, so I gave them the names of three agents that had just finished their mission and been reassigned." Kris chuckled mirthlessly. "Don't think they appreciated it very much."

Shelby nodded, suddenly understanding. "So that's why you were checking on assignment completion dates."

"Yep."

"Are those the guys that have been following us?"

"Yes, though I think I was followed by someone else when I first got into town. Haven't seen that tail again, though, so I don't know for sure."

"How'd you get wet last night?"

Of all the questions she could have asked... Kris mustered a wry grin. "I passed out during the beating. They turned a hose on me to wake me up. Crude, but effective."

Shelby's heart went out to Kris. "Did they make you talk?"

"No. They were just making a point. They've come up with something more interesting they want me to get for them. I have a week to get it. They have...unexpected leverage for their demands."

"What?"

Kris sighed audibly. "They've got my mother."

Confused, Shelby exclaimed, "You said she was dead!"

"All these years, I thought she was. After they worked me over, they sent her in. I thought it was just a trick, didn't want to believe it was her." Kris turned tormented eyes to Shelby. "But it was. She's alive! And she is their ace in the hole. If I don't give them what they want, they kill her first." Kris lowered her head to her hands, suddenly overwhelmed by the complexity of the situation.

Shelby thought over what Kris had said, instinctively knowing the operative was telling the truth. She had done nothing wrong except conceal her origins, but how would Kris ever convince the Company of that? *What a mess!* She reached across the table, laying her hand on top of Kris'. "Hey." When the agent looked up, she continued, "You must have a plan. How can I help?"

Kris couldn't believe her ears. "You'd help me, after everything I've told you? You don't hate me?"

Shelby smiled ruefully. "I could never hate you. Don't you think I know the chance you are taking telling me this? I could turn you in, and I know you've thought of that. Yet, you told me anyway. Why?"

"I felt I could trust you, and," she paused, once again considering the danger to Shelby, but knowing she had passed the point of no return. "And, I need your help. I was going to tell you last night, even before I found out they had my mother." Kris gazed into the emerald eyes, clearly conveying the depth of her feelings. "I wanted there to be a chance for more for us, but first I had to find a way out."

Shelby couldn't believe what she was hearing; her heart skipped a beat even as she was struggling to come to grips with the past Kris had revealed. "You wanted more for us?"

Kris reached across the table, taking hold of Shelby's hands as she gazed deeply into her eyes. "I love you. I'd give anything for the chance of a future with you."

Shelby found herself drawn into the intense blue eyes that brimmed with emotion. She'd known Kris cared about her, but to know that her own dreams were mirrored in the tall woman was more than she'd ever hoped for. "I love you, too." Her eyes moist with tears of joy, she pressed Kris' hands to her lips, softly kissing each one.

A wave of exhilaration swept through Kris, momentarily pushing aside her fears and concerns. She knew that Shelby could have just walked away yet, incredibly, she had opened her heart instead. *She loves me!* The three words caressed her, chasing away the loneliness and despair. Whatever was to come, she would bear it – because of this woman's love. She knew that, together, they would find a way out. "Will you help me?"

"In any way I can. But, Kris, I won't compromise my country to do it."

Kris nodded in understanding.

"You said they gave you another assignment. What do they

want?"

"Your password."

Her voice incredulous, the mood broken, Shelby exploded. "You've got to be kidding. No way in hell—"

"Shelby, I know that; I'd never ask you for it. But I've only got a week to locate the safe house where they have my mother. We've got to find the leak in this case. If we can, I should be able to find out where my mother's being held."

Calming down, Shelby agreed. "Makes sense. It would also give us something to give the Company."

"Yep. One of Russia's top spies is here under an alias. I'm going to serve him up on a silver platter, but I want to find the leak in the Company, too."

"Isn't that sort of doing the same thing you would have done if you'd doubled?"

"No. This is personal. Remember how you said you still hated your stepfather?" Shelby nodded and Kris continued. "Well, I hate this guy. When he took me to the Institute, he punched my mother and left her lying on the ground. He took a personal interest in my progress there and wouldn't let me go home for visits, citing fabricated violations of the Institute's rules. Then he told me she was dead. Now he's threatening to kill her. Besides, he's doing damage to this country, and I have to stop that if I can. I'd turn him over in a heartbeat."

Shelby shuddered at the venom in Kris' voice. "What can I do to help?"

"You can help me find the leak. Someone close to the case is providing information and has been since day one. We've got to find out who."

"Kris, I think we need to involve the Company now. What about talking to Earl?"

"We don't know where the leak is. What if he detains me? My mother would be as good as dead. I can't take that chance."

Shelby thought about the risks. "I could get burned for concealing information."

Kris sighed. "And I don't have the right to ask you to do that. Can't you give me just a few days to find my mother? Then if you feel you must turn me in, go ahead."

"You don't get it, do you? I am not going to turn you in. I'm trying to find a way to help you so there won't be any repercussions for either one of us. I just hate leaving the Company out of it."

"I hear you. But if I tell the wrong person, or they don't believe me, I'll be leaving Langley under lock and key."

Shelby felt her heart tighten painfully, knowing what Kris said was true. "How high up do you think the leak is?"

"Hard to say, but it has to be someone who has total access, and that's limited to deputy directors and above."

"Mostly. I have a lot of access; so do some of the other analysts and auditors."

"True. Are you up to it?"

"For you, yes."

Kris smiled warmly, her discomfort temporarily forgotten. "Thank you for trusting me. I won't let you down."

"I'm going to hold you to that. Have you told me everything?"

Kris was torn. She couldn't share the only omitted piece of information, even with Shelby. Not yet. But she was unwilling to lie to her either, so she remained silent.

Watching her, Shelby sighed. "I'm going to help you anyway. I don't know why, since you're still holding back, but I'm going to." She gazed deeply into the intense blue eyes regarding her gravely. "Please don't make me regret it."

Reaching across the table, and laying her hand on Shelby's cheek, Kris gently stroked it. "You won't. I promise."

Chapter Fourteen

"HOW ARE YOU feeling?" Shelby set her coffee mug down on the dining room table. She knew time was of the essence, but she also thought it might be best if Kris called in sick to allow her some time to recover.

"Sore."

"I think we should stay home today."

"No. We have to go to work."

"Are you sure? I think you need time to recuperate."

"I have to move around. If I don't, I'll stiffen up. The more I move, the quicker I heal." Kris ran a hand through her hair. "Besides, we've only got a week. I need to talk to Earl and find out who knows about this case. Dennis, Jeb, and Earl are givens. The director of operations would know because he's Earl's boss. But who else? And I want to ask him if he knows why Michael is hanging around."

What Kris said made sense, but Shelby could still vividly visualize the discoloration of her partner's abdomen and she wondered how Kris expected to be able to move around without showing the effects of her injuries.

"Okay, but it's going to be a short day. We find out what we can, then we leave."

Kris nodded. "Fine. Because I want to stake out the emergency drop in Georgetown."

Shelby wondered at the wisdom of them hanging around that location. "You've got to be kidding!"

"Don't worry, no one will see us. It may be our only hope of finding out who's relaying information. I don't think Earl's gonna have any answers. He knows there's a leak, and if he found out anything, I think he would've told us."

"Any possibility that Earl –"

"I don't think so. He trained me, and I just don't see him working for the other side, but anything is possible. Do you have any idea of how many staff people have the same access to information that you do? Even a rough guess?"

"No, but everyone in my hallway has a high level clearance. I think mine might be a little higher than most, because the Marine usually stands outside my door." Shelby abruptly changed the subject, asking something that had been bothering her. "Kris, didn't the Russians think I would be suspicious when they returned you to the door all beat up and soaked?"

Kris smiled grimly. "Sergei knew I would make up some story to cover. I'm just surprised I was out for so long. He took a real risk, not knowing if you'd call the Company or the police. That doesn't make sense to me."

"Be right back." Shelby quickly retrieved the note from her jacket in the bedroom and returned to the kitchen. "This was pinned to your clothes."

Reading the note, Kris narrowed her eyes. *That bastard.* He had tried to cover all the bases. Not only had he used her mother against her, he had threatened Shelby. The operative directed her thoughts to the Russian spymaster. *You're going down, you son of a bitch.*

Shelby inwardly shuddered as the agent changed right before her eyes; even though she'd witnessed the transformation several times, it still unnerved her. She laid her hand on Kris' arm. "Hey."

The analyst's touch had a calming effect, and Kris could feel her tension begin to fade. She gazed into the concerned green eyes regarding her somberly. "I want him badly."

"I know you do, and we're gonna make it happen."

Kris smiled at her partner's determination. *Who could ask for more than that?* "I hear you."

"If we're gonna get to work on time, I need to get in the shower."

Want any company? Kris grinned at the thought and nodded. "I'm going outside. I won't be gone long."

Shelby stopped and turned around. "Can't you just wait until we leave?"

"No. The Russians aren't going to bother with me now. They don't need to; they're in the driver's seat and they know it. But it wasn't them that shot at us in the parking lot; that was someone else. And it's been just a little too quiet lately."

Shelby asked incredulously, "You call last night quiet? I don't." The emotional roller coaster she'd been riding suddenly came to a screeching halt and tears threatened to spill. "I was so worried about you. You have no idea..."

Kris rose from her chair and crossed the room, determinedly ignoring the pain caused by the sudden movement. She wrapped her arms around Shelby, pulling the smaller woman close. Rubbing her hand soothingly on the tense back, she murmured, "I'm sorry I put you through that. I should've told you before now, but I was afraid to."

Returning the hug gently, not wanting to hurt Kris, Shelby calmed. "Sorry. There's just so much going on."

"You've got nothing to be sorry for." Kris drew her head back and looked deeply into Shelby's eyes. "I never thanked you for last night." She gently stroked her partner's face. "Thank you. Thank you for taking care of me last night, and for giving me a chance."

Comforted by the gentle fingers caressing her face, Shelby relaxed and a warm glow enveloped her. "It's the only thing I could do. I love you."

Overwhelmed by newly awakened feelings, Kris lowered her mouth, meeting Shelby's lips for a fleeting kiss, unprepared for the intensity of her reaction to the brief contact. Her voice raw with emotion, she said, "I love you so much." She released Shelby, focusing on controlling her libido, which, Kris wryly acknowledged, was still active despite the horrific events of the previous evening.

Shelby took a deep breath, trying to slow her racing heart. Her face flushed, she reveled in the pleasant sensations washing over her body and managed to croak, "Gotta take a shower," then turned, heading for the bathroom.

Kris watched until the blonde was out of sight before she was finally able to rein in her own emotions. She picked up her gun, clipped on her cell phone, and left the apartment. The operative walked gingerly down the stairs, her slightly narrowed eyes the only outward sign of any discomfort. She carefully checked the parking lot before making her way around the building, returning to the apartment a short time later. She was standing at the bathroom door when Shelby opened it. "I'm gonna take my shower now."

Shelby grinned, trying hard not to laugh. "I thought you already took one."

Kris cheeks reddened. "Um, well, it's therapeutic."

Shelby broke out laughing. "Okaaay."

Kris grinned and shrugged. "What can I say?"

"Nothing. You just said everything." Shelby was still chuckling as she walked away, very happy that her reaction to the fleeting kiss was not one-sided.

WHEN THEY ARRIVED in the office, Kris pushed her chair next to Shelby's behind the desk. "Okay, first go to the Russian Embassy."

The analyst brought up the screen. "Okay, now what? Embassy personnel?"

"Yeah. See that guy, Gregor Koslov? He's the second in charge. Remember the night I told you I was outside talking to the guy following us?" When her partner nodded, Kris said, "It was him."

Shelby pointed to a picture. "That guy looks like the man from the grocery store."

"It is. He's officially a driver, but probably does some of their dirty work. He wasn't supposed to follow us into the store. Found that out when I questioned him."

"Then why did he?"

"Wanted some glory."

Kris pointed to Dimitri Pyetsky. "This is the guy I'm gonna bring down. His name is really Sergei Pavlovich Yanov. If the Company had any idea he was in the country, they'd probably grab him and charge him with spying. They'd be right, too."

"When did you find out he was here?"

"I checked this file last week. I wanted to see who was running the show. Never expected to see Sergei."

Shelby nodded and read the short biography on each of the Russians assigned to the embassy. "Now go to Sergei?

"Yeah. You need to understand just how ruthless this guy is. He's very bad news."

Shelby quickly located his file, opened it, and looked at his picture. "He dyed his hair and grew a beard. No wonder no one made the connection."

"He's a master of disguise. This isn't anything compared to what he can do."

Shelby and Kris both began reading. During their reorganization, Sergei had distanced himself from the KGB to allow himself more flexibility in accomplishing the goals of the new Russian Federation. He was an expert sniper, highly skilled with knives, and had a black belt in karate.

He was known to be responsible for the deaths of three operatives, and was suspected of killing at least ten others. The Russian used any means at his disposal to extract information from captured agents, his favorite method being electrical shock, as evidenced by burns on the bodies of the operatives whose bodies had been found. One agent had managed to survive the torture session, but had been mentally devastated.

It was suspected that Sergei ran the Russian spy network in America, but he'd never been spotted in the States. He was also credited with the largest information coup in Russian history when he'd turned a high level CIA operative.

The full impact of what she'd read hit Shelby, and she realized just how dangerous their foe was. "You weren't kidding."

"No. I want you to understand what this guy is like, and go into this with open eyes. I can't sit here and lie to you and say, 'Don't worry.' This is going to be really dangerous, and if you want to change your mind about helping, I'll understand."

Shelby met Kris' eyes and held them. "I'm with you on this."

"There's one other thing I need to talk to you about." Kris looked away for a moment, trying to figure out the best way to explain her own limitations. "Shelby, I will protect you in any way I can, and would give my life for yours in a minute. But there is always the possibility that something could happen that I have no control over, like the other night. If a trained assassin targets someone and is persistent enough, eventually he or she could get lucky no matter how much protection you have. What I'm trying to say is –"

Shelby linked her fingers with the operative's. "Kris, it's okay. I know what you're saying. I would never hold you responsible if anything happened to me. I trust you to do your best. I know it's dangerous, so relax, okay?"

"Okay." Kris silently vowed to be extra vigilant in the coming days. There were too many unknown elements in the picture. "I'm gonna go see Earl. I'll bring us back some coffee."

"Sounds good. It's my turn to buy." Shelby pulled out a five and handed it to Kris. "I want the house blend."

Kris nodded and accepted the money. "I won't be gone long."

Shelby winked. "Good."

The operative walked out the door grinning, but the smile faded as she progressed down the hallway. Inwardly sighing, Kris was careful not to take too deep a breath. The Alleve had taken the edge off the pain, but every time she stood up or moved suddenly, it hurt. She had tried to hide her discomfort from Shelby, but had seen the sympathy clearly reflected in her partner's eyes and knew the analyst wasn't fooled.

She smiled grimly. The beating had just been business as usual, but Sergei had made a huge mistake by turning it personal. Most operatives had a code of honor that wouldn't allow the targeting of innocents. The Russian had broken that code, and Blue intended to make him pay.

Earl glanced up when Kris walked in. "What's up?"

"Uncover the leak yet?"

"No. Not even a whisper. I've got ears everywhere, and no one's heard a thing."

"That's what I figured. How many people know about the case?"

"Hell, I don't know offhand. You two, me, Jeb, Dennis, his boss—the director of ops." Earl paused, thinking. "That should be it."

"And secretaries?"

"Not the details, but they know you're here working on a case." Earl leaned back in his chair. "Have a seat. I was going to call you later anyway."

"I'd rather stand. I get enough sitting time on this case."

Grinning, Earl said, "Hey, how do you think I feel? We got the ballistics report back this morning. The bullet was too damaged to determine much except that it was fired from a rifle."

Kris raised an eyebrow. "Interesting."

"Care to tell me why?"

"You have to be good to fire a rifle from a moving car unless you have a driver. That bullet just missed. The silver Cavalier might've been coincidental. I could be wrong, but I got the impression there was only one person in the front seat."

"You ruling it out?"

Kris shook her head. "I'm not ruling out anything yet." Switching subjects, she asked, "You remember Michael Benton?"

"How could I forget that bastard?"

"I saw him in the canteen yesterday. Know what he's doing here?"

"No idea. Probably visiting his brother. You knew he was Jeb's brother, right?"

"I'd heard that. Jeb know why Michael was pulled from the field?"

"No, and he'll never know. That whole operation and the ensuing board inquiry have been sealed."

Kris nodded. "Why am I not surprised? I always thought he had friends in high places."

"I've wondered about that, too. Not much I can do about him being here; he is one of ours. How's the case coming? You going to be able to wrap it up by the end of the week?"

"Maybe. We've got nine names left. Just depends on how much time it takes to check out each one."

"Okay. Anything else? I've got a meeting with the director."

"No, that was it."

Kris turned and left the office. She hadn't expected Earl to provide any answers, but found it interesting that the recovered bullet had been fired from a rifle. A short time later, she returned to the office carrying two cups of coffee.

Shelby took the coffee cup and change Kris handed her, setting both down on her desk. "Thanks. Find out anything?"

"Not about the leak or Michael, but the ballistics report came back on the bullet that was recovered in your parking lot. It was a round from a rifle."

Surprise covered Shelby's face. "I didn't think...I just thought..."

Kris nodded in agreement. "Does your stepfather have a rifle?"

"Not that I know of. He used to go hunting, but I think he borrowed a rifle, or else he kept it at someone else's house."

Musing out loud, Kris said, "He spent four years in the Army."

"Yeah. He met Mom a couple of years after he got out."

Kris sat down at her PC and looked at Shelby. "I didn't get a good look inside the car that night, but all I saw was a driver. It's pretty hard to shoot a rifle while steering a car, though it can be done, and he was barely moving."

"I still don't think Jonathan did it."

"I know, but we can't rule him out until we find out why he was there in the first place." Unbidden, an image of Michael appeared in her mind. *I'm going to have to pay him a visit.* "When do you want to go see your stepfather?"

"Well, since we're going spying tonight..." Shelby laughed at the look on Kris' face. "Okay, so we're doing surveillance; how about tomorrow after work?"

"Sounds good. Oh, and Shelby? We'll probably be doing surveillance for the next several nights. Hopefully some time this week, we'll spot a suspect."

Shelby nodded. Normally the idea of sitting in a car for hours on end watching a building or whatever it was they were going to watch would've bored her to tears, but for time with Kris, she'd watch the grass grow.

LISA SMILED AT the tall, handsome man standing in the doorway. "Hi. Come on in."

Jonathan walked over and hugged her. "Hey, babe. What'd you make for lunch?" He pulled out the kitchen chair and sat down, slouching comfortably as he looked at Lisa expectantly.

"I made spaghetti." Lisa knew how much Jonathan had always liked her spaghetti. "How's that sound?"

"Great. When do the boys get home from school?"

"Around four." After serving her guest, Lisa sat down. She would wait for the boys to arrive before eating. "They're really going to be excited."

"This is good, babe. You're still the best cook in the county."

Lisa flushed with pleasure. "I'm so glad you're moving in; I've really missed you. Did you hear on any of those jobs you were checking out?"

Jonathan spoke around bites. "Nope. It's only been a week. If my record gets expunged, I can quit being a common laborer. But don't you worry—no matter what, I'll be working and helping support my beautiful wife and kids."

Smiling, Lisa nodded. She could only imagine how degrading it must be to a man like Jonathan to pump gas. She'd supported his decision to quit his gas station job and try to find something better. Her thoughts were interrupted when he spoke.

"Did you tell Shelby?"

"No. I want to wait until I see her again. I thought it would be a good idea to give her a little time to get used to the idea that you're back in our lives first."

Jonathan looked up sharply, but kept his voice calm. "What if she comes over before you tell her? I was planning on moving in this weekend."

"I wanted to talk to you about that. Another week won't make any difference. Let me talk to her first. She really does mean well."

"Lisa, I don't believe you!" Jonathan bit off the barrage of words threatening to erupt from his mouth, silently cursing himself for his stupidity.

As Lisa recoiled at Jonathan's harsh words, memories flooded her mind.

Reaching across the table, Jonathan took Lisa's hand into his own. His voice cajoling, he asked, "Are you going to let your daughter rule your life? I know you love her, and so do I, but this is our life. She doesn't live here. Would you allow her to deny us the happiness that we deserve? I know she would want you to be happy. I love you, Lisa. I thought you loved me, too."

Lisa relaxed. She really couldn't blame Jonathan for being upset. He'd so been looking forward to moving in. "I do love you. Tell you what. I'll call her tonight and tell her. I don't want to alienate her, or she'll never accept you again."

Somewhat mollified, Jonathan said, "Okay, babe, whatever you want to do is fine with me. Are we still going to tell the boys today?"

Smiling, Lisa said, "Oh yes. I've been looking forward to that, too." She glanced at his empty plate. "Want some more?"

"Yeah. Thanks."

Lisa served up a second plate of spaghetti and joined her ex-husband in waiting for Jason and Jimmy to arrive.

SHELBY WATCHED THE cars drive by, alert for anyone she recognized. It had been a whirlwind afternoon and evening. After leaving work, they'd gone back to the apartment, dropped off her car, and set out in the vehicle Kris had rented. They'd returned it to the depot Kris where had rented it, then taken a cab to a different rental car agency, filled out the necessary paperwork and departed in a green Ford Taurus. The two women were now parked between several other cars on a side street, and had been for the previous four hours.

The time had passed quickly for Shelby. She and Kris had discussed each person with knowledge of the case and speculated on who could be leaking information. She'd listened, spellbound, as Kris recalled the events leading to Michael's removal from the field, and then they'd just chatted. Well, actually, she'd done most of the talking, but Kris had contributed too.

She'd finally gotten the operative to agree to leave at 10:30, arguing that anyone going to the drop would be most likely to go early, while the street was well populated. She glanced at Kris, noting the tension reflected in the beautiful countenance. Shelby knew her partner was hurting and wished she could do something to ease her pain, but she didn't know what that would be. "Kris?"

"Hm?"

Shelby gazed at Kris. "How does it feel to know that your mother's alive?"

The operative had asked herself that very same thing. She mulled the question over in her mind, trying to figure out how to verbalize her feelings. Fearful that her brief glimpse of her mother would be her last, she had resisted fully embracing the joy of their reunion.

As the silence lengthened, Shelby wondered if she should've saved her question until after they'd rescued Kris' mother. She reached over and laid her hand on Kris' thigh, just feeling the need to touch her.

Kris covered Shelby's hand with her own and smiled, before turning her attention back to the building they were watching. "It feels strange. I'd gotten used to her being dead. Now I find out she's alive, but it's like talking to a stranger. I don't even know her anymore. I don't know what she does, or what she likes, or even if I'll ever see her again."

Shelby could feel the fear and confusion Kris was experiencing, and her heart tightened painfully. She reached over and linked her fingers with her companion's, lending quiet support. "We'll find her in time; I know we will."

Pushing her doubts back into the dark crevices whence they'd arisen, Kris took comfort in the staunch support of her partner and gently squeezed her hand. "Yeah, we will." And suddenly, she believed it. "They're holding her some place on Georgia Ave. That's all Mom saw before they took her inside," Kris reported. "Gotta give her a lot of credit for noticing that."

"She speaks English?"

"Not well, but she does understand it."

"Well, if she's anything like you, the men holding her are gonna have their hands full."

"Is that right? I'm not even gonna ask you what you mean by that." Kris winked at Shelby. "But she is feisty." Turning to her partner, she smiled warmly, and it hit her again, how lucky she was to have Shelby in her life. She glanced at her watch. "Ready to take off?"

"You gotta be kidding!"

Grinning, Kris started the car and headed for the apartment.

Shelby went through her greeting ritual with Stormy as Kris watched, amused. Seeing the mirth on her partner's face, she handed the kitten to Kris. "Your turn to say hello."

Kris rolled her eyes, but was actually quite fond of the little feline and gave her a quick hug before placing the refugee back in Shelby's arms.

Over the previous several hours, Shelby noticed that Kris' movements had become more stiff and deliberate. She set Stormy down and walked into the bathroom to get some painkiller. Returning to the living room where Kris was sitting on the couch, she handed her the tablets and a glass of water.

Kris gratefully accepted the pills and water from Shelby. "Thanks."

"Do you want an ice pack? That might help."

"Thanks, but I'll pass. I'm gonna take a shower instead."

A short time later, Kris entered the bedroom in her sleeping shirt. Shelby was already in bed, with the covers pulled down for Kris, Stormy lying down by her feet.

She settled carefully into the bed and looked pointedly at Shelby who was lying on her side facing her. "Why don't you move over this way a little?"

"I didn't want to—"

Kris placed a finger gently on Shelby's lips. "I'd feel a lot better if you were next to me."

Shelby moved over until her body was touching the taller form of her companion. "How do you feel?"

"Better than I did." Kris turned her head, gazing lovingly into warm emerald eyes. Tentatively, she reached out and brushed the back of her hand over Shelby's soft cheek and watched a flush appear on the analyst's fair skin. Knowing they needed to talk about what was escalating between them, Kris whispered, "Shelby?"

"Mmmm?"

Kris struggled to maintain her composure with the small, warm body pressed against hers. "I...we really should wait." It wasn't the articulate, rational appeal to reason she'd intended, nor did her husky voice carry quite the firmness she'd wanted to convey, but she did make Shelby smile.

"I know. You're not in any shape."

"That's not exactly what I meant," she protested mildly, even as the small hand that had wrapped around her arm distracted her. Covering the warm fingers, she squeezed slightly. "Our first time, I want it to be special. I want to give you everything I have to give. Right now, with everything that's going on..."

Shelby smiled gently and rested her head against a strong shoulder.

"Well," she teased, "I always heard you should make love before going into battle. You know, just in case."

Kris groaned, and the analyst laughed at the frustrated sound. "I'm just kidding, sweetheart." Shelby smiled as a blush crept over Kris' features, knowing her endearment had caused it. "Of course we'll wait. I want our first time to be perfect for you, too."

Blue eyes locked with green. "To be with you—it couldn't be anything but perfect."

Shelby blushed and buried her face against Kris' broad shoulder. A strong hand gently eased her back, and she rose up enough to lower her head over her partner's and meet her lips.

Long moments later, both women pulled back, eyes full of promises and bodies warmed by the contact. Settling against each other with their hands entwined, they drifted off to sleep, both dreaming of their future together.

SHELBY HAD NOTICED the answering machine light blinking when she'd gotten up that morning, and had listened to the message from her mother. It had been too early to call her back, so she'd decided to contact her from work. Dialing her mother's telephone number, she waited for the familiar voice to answer. "Hi, Mom. You called?"

"Hi, honey. How's work going?"

Shelby raised an eyebrow. Whenever her mother asked her about work, she was up to something. "Fine."

"I wanted to talk to you about Jonathan."

Shelby could feel herself tense, even though she tried to fight it and struggled to keep her voice reasonable. "What about Jonathan?"

Lisa wished she knew an easy way to break her news, but couldn't think of one. Without preamble, she blurted out, "Jonathan's going to be moving in." The silence extended for so long, she wondered if Shelby had heard her. "Did you hear what I said?"

I heard you, Mom. Loud and clear. Shelby sighed audibly. "Mom, please think about what you're doing."

"I have. He's changed, Shelby. Give him a chance, honey. For me."

Shelby shook her head, distressed. "Mom, the man is bad news. You're making a big mistake."

Lisa patiently explained, "I'm happy when I'm with him. It'll be better for the boys to have their father back. They need a male influence."

"A good male influence, Mom, and he isn't one." Shelby realized she was squeezing the phone and consciously relaxed her hand.

"Shelby, I'm trying to include you in the family decisions, but you aren't making it easy. You aren't the one trying to make ends meet and raise two boys alone."

Pursing her lips, Shelby spoke in a very controlled voice, "I give you money every month, Mom, so don't lay that on me. I could give you more..."

"No, honey. I feel bad enough about taking your money. When Jonathan moves in, I won't need it any more; we'll have two incomes. He's trying to get his record expunged. Isn't that great?"

Kris watched with concern as a myriad of emotions flickering across Shelby's face. She had to restrain herself from taking the phone and telling Lisa to go to hell. Instead, she walked over to her partner, and laid a supportive hand on Shelby's shoulder.

Shelby reached up with her free hand, making contact with Kris' fingers. "I'll stop over after work and we can talk about it then."

"Honey, I've already made up my mind. I just want you to be okay with it."

"Mom, I'm not okay with it. I'm against it. At least hear me out tonight."

Lisa sighed, but then brightened. Maybe she would be more persuasive in person when Shelby saw how excited Jason and Jimmy were. "Okay, honey. What time are you planning on coming over?"

Shelby turned her head and looked up at Kris mouthing, '5:30?'

Kris nodded. Whatever Shelby wanted to do was fine with her. They would just grab something to eat on the way to the surveillance site.

"5:30."

"Okay, dear, see you then." Lisa hung up the phone and started preparing the arguments she knew she'd need to convince Shelby.

Shelby turned tormented eyes to Kris. "She wants Jonathan to move back in. What's wrong with her?"

Kris just shook her head. It didn't make any sense to her, but she knew it was a common pattern with battered wives. She also knew Shelby knew that.

Standing up, the blonde smiled wanly. "I'm going to get some cranberry juice. Want anything?"

"A Coke would be great." She watched her partner walk out the door and sighed. Shelby wasn't getting any breaks, and she was just as responsible for her partner's stress as Lisa was.

"Hey, Shelby, I was just getting ready to come down to your office. Some of us are getting together after work and going to The Pub. How about you and your new partner coming along. It'll be fun."

Glancing away from the pop machine, Shelby looked at Maggie, surprise evident on her face. "Is this a first or something?"

"Sorta. Just thought it would be fun. Are you game?"

"Sorry, I can't. I'm going to my mother's right after work. Maybe some other time?"

Maggie grinned. "Sure, if we ever do it again."

Laughing, Shelby commented, "True. Have fun."

"But of course!" Maggie watched Shelby return to her office, then inserted her money into the vending machine and selected a bag of trail mix.

"HI, BABE. DID you talk to Shelby?"

"Yeah, but she's totally against the idea. She's going to stop over at 5:30. I think she's going to try and convince me not to let you move in."

Pleading, Jonathan said, "Lisa, please..."

"Don't worry. I'm going to work just as hard to win her acceptance. When she sees how enthusiastic the boys are, I think she'll change her mind."

Jonathan deliberately kept his calm. "What if you can't convince her? What happens then?"

"That shouldn't be a problem. If it is, we may want to wait just a little longer." When Lisa heard Jonathan sigh, she added, "It wouldn't be for long."

"Okay, babe. Whatever you want. I only want to make you happy."

Lisa smiled warmly. "I know you do. Love you."

"Love you, babe."

Jonathan waited for Lisa to hang up before viciously throwing his cell phone against the trailer wall. He stalked around the apartment, the familiar rage beginning to build. *That fucking little bitch. She is going to ruin my life forever.* He was living like some lowlife in a filthy trailer park because of her. If he didn't get his record expunged, all he had to look forward to were more minimum wage jobs. *I want my family back, and I am not going to let Shelby stand in my way. Too bad that shot missed her last week.*

He glanced at the rifle leaning in the corner of the living room, then crossed the room and picked it up. Pressing the stock against his shoulder, he pictured Shelby standing directly in his line of fire and carefully aligned the sight between her eyes, gently squeezing the trigger. A smile covered his face as he watched her head explode.

SHELBY LOOKED AT Kris and shook her head ruefully. "Here goes nothing." She waited for the operative to round the car, then accompanied her to the door. Knocking twice, she walked in, Kris following.

"Hi, Mom." She walked over and hugged her mother.

"Hi, honey. Would you and Kris like some spaghetti? I've got plenty left."

Shelby hesitated, but decided it might ease some of the tension. She glanced at her companion and smiled. "Mom makes great spaghetti."

Kris nodded. "Thanks, Lisa. That sounds great."

Lisa quickly served her guests and sat down to join them at the table. She had warned her sons to stay in the living room, promising that Shelby's spy friend would come and visit them after they were done talking.

The conversation was trivial, with Lisa talking about her flower garden and the boys' exploits at school. Kris excused herself when she finished eating, making her way to the living room and silently wishing her partner success.

Shelby smiled at her mother. "I love you, Mom, and I want you to be happy."

A warm smile covered Lisa's face. "I know you do, honey. I love you, too."

"What makes you think Jonathan has changed?"

Having been prepared for a heated debate, Lisa was encouraged by Shelby's calm demeanor. "Because he saw a psychologist. That was a big step for him. You know how proud he is. And each time he calls or visits, he makes me feel so special. He's attentive to both the boys and me. He's trying so hard to do everything right."

"You do know that seeing the psychologist was court-ordered, part of his sentence, right?"

"Yes, but he talks so positively about his visits to the doctor. He admits he was wrong. It's not easy for someone to face their mistakes, yet he has."

Shelby nodded. "Does he still see a psychologist?"

"No. The doctor told him he was a success story, and he didn't need to schedule any more sessions."

He is such a liar! "Have you been seeing Jonathan very often?"

Lisa looked away as she nodded. "He's been coming around for about a month now."

Shelby sighed inwardly. Her mother had kept her contact with him well hidden. "Mom, I want you to be totally honest with me. Has he ever done or said anything at all that reminded you of before? You know—raised his voice, clenched his fists, all the things he used to do before he lost his temper."

Lisa's thoughts returned to his visit earlier in the day. For a minute, she'd been scared, but she could understand why he was upset. He wanted them to be a family again.

"Mom? He has, hasn't he?"

"Oh, it was nothing. He just raised his voice a little. He was just a little upset you didn't want to give him a chance. I told him you needed some time."

Shelby's worst fears were confirmed. She'd known he was incapable of changing, but her mother had just verified it. "You remember my friend Kim?"

"How could I forget her? I can't ever remember laughing so hard as I did the last time she came over with you. Why?"

"Would you do me a favor?"

"What? I thought we were talking about Jonathan moving in."

"We are." Shelby paused, hoping her mother wouldn't explode. "Kim counsels abused women. I'd like you to talk to her."

"That's your answer!" Lisa stood up angrily. "You think *I* should see a psychiatrist?"

"No, Mom. She's a counselor. You've never talked to anyone about what you went through. If you agree to talk to her, I'll promise to try to be more impartial about Jonathan."

Pacing around the kitchen, Lisa said pointedly, "I really don't think I need to talk to a counselor."

"It wouldn't hurt to talk to her just once, Mom."

Lisa wasn't the least bit happy that her daughter thought she needed to talk to a professional, but Shelby had made the deal very sweet. "And if I do, you promise to be impartial about Jonathan?"

Shelby nodded. "Only one thing."

"What else?"

"You delay Jonathan's moving in until after you talk to her."

Lisa had been prepared to delay a week anyway and, wanting to keep the peace with Shelby, she capitulated. "Okay." She smiled at her daughter and held out her hand. "Deal."

Chuckling, Shelby sealed their deal with a handshake. "I'd better go rescue Kris."

All of a sudden, they heard Jimmy and Jason explode with laughter. She grinned at her mother. "I think she's holding her own."

A short time later the two women bid Lisa and the boys farewell. Kris waited until Shelby was in before making her way around the car to the driver's side. Settling into the seat, she asked, "How'd it go?"

"Better than I could've ever hoped for. She agreed to talk to Kim before letting Jonathan move in."

Kris smiled at the obvious relief in her partner's voice. "How'd you manage that?"

"I promised her I would be impartial about Jonathan. And I will be. But that includes looking at the bad as well as the good. I'm not sure she was thinking of that."

"As long as it worked."

"I hear you." Shelby watched Kris and sighed contentedly. They were headed to the apartment to change clothes, switch cars, and gather up some drinks and snacks before staking out the drop again. It would be another long night, but the payoff would be well worth it.

Kris suddenly yelled, "Hold on!" She slammed on the brakes, swerved to the right, and thrust her right hand out in a protective measure to keep Shelby from falling forward before her seat belt had a chance to tighten, grimacing in pain at the sudden movement. She had barely registered that she'd managed to miss the little boy who had darted out in front of the car chasing a ball when she heard a loud crack and saw the windshield fragment into a spider web.

Her movements fueled by adrenaline, Kris slammed the car into park and released her seat belt, simultaneously releasing her partner's restraining device, then threw her body on top of Shelby's. She could barely breathe as a vise tightened painfully around her chest at the glimpse she'd caught of the red splattering the windshield.

Chapter Fifteen

AFTER CAREFULLY SECURING the rifle with a bungee cord on a branch well hidden by foliage, the tall, dark-haired man quickly climbed down from his perch. He discreetly surveyed the area before getting on the bicycle leaning against the tree trunk and casually riding through the backyard of the vacant house to an adjoining side street, en route to his vehicle parked nearby.

He knew he'd missed his primary target—her head—but given the abrupt loss of velocity and swerving of the Sable, he felt very satisfied to have connected at all. With luck, the wound would be debilitating, but whether it was or not, it would still serve his purpose up to a point. Fear was always an effective tactic, and he was an expert at utilizing it.

SECONDS SEEMED LIKE an eternity, even though less than a minute had passed since the shot had resounded through the quiet neighborhood. Experience told Kris that the shooter was most likely gone, and she heard a tentative knock on the driver's side window simultaneously with the softly spoken words from beneath her.

"You're squishing me."

Kris breathed a sigh of relief at the welcome sound of Shelby's voice. "Sorry." She straightened up, her eyes watering in pain, quickly scanning the surrounding area. She ignored the woman who was tapping on the window, the mother of the child she had narrowly avoided hitting, immediately turning her attention back to Shelby once she was sure the pedestrians were safe.

Her partner was still leaning against the door where she'd been pushed when Kris fell on top of her, and she was now holding her upper left arm with her right hand. A red smudge stood out starkly against her pale face, and blood smeared from her saturated sleeve created a macabre design on her blouse. Exhibiting a measured calmness she didn't feel, Kris gently touched Shelby's hand and said, "Let me see that, okay?"

Shelby remained silent, but removed her hand and let Kris examine the wound. The operative noted that the bullet had passed through the fleshy part of her partner's upper arm, which accounted for the large volume of blood, and Kris worried about the very real threat of shock. Somewhat relieved that the shot had missed the bone, she gently lifted Shelby's hand and placed it back over the injury. "Press against that for a minute. I'm going to find something to make a compress with, then we'll get you to the hospital."

Nodding, Shelby applied pressure, surprised that her arm didn't really hurt. It was a surreal experience; she objectively noted that both her and Kris' tops were amply stained with red and the coppery odor of blood permeated the air. Perfectly content to remain where she was with her head resting against the door jamb, Shelby watched Kris stretch over the front seat to reach the gym bag on the rear floor. She was glad she'd just cleaned it out and replaced the dirty linen with clean, and then smiled at the mundane thought.

Kris ignored the pain that the stretching engendered and removed a towel, folding it into thirds. She carefully wrapped it snugly around her partner's arm, holding it in place with one hand while she gently helped Shelby right herself in the passenger seat. "Here, hold this in place. We've got to get you to the emergency room." The operative knew time was of the essence because shock was still a very real danger.

Quickly rolling down the window, she met the concerned gaze of the woman holding her toddler. "He okay?"

"Yes. I don't know how to thank you."

"No thanks needed."

The woman stared at Kris' red stained shirt. "You're hurt. I'll call an ambulance."

"No, I'm not, but my friend is; I really need to get her to the emergency room. It'll be quicker if I take her."

"Yes, of course." The woman retreated back to the small group of bystanders that had gathered once word had spread that the supposed backfire had actually been a gunshot.

Kris put the car in gear and sped off toward Arlington Memorial Hospital. She looked over at Shelby anxiously. "How're you doing?"

Shelby took a deep breath, exhaling slowly. Her arm had started to throb, setting her teeth on edge. "Okay."

The beating of the agent's heart had finally slowed to a normal rate, and she spared a quick glance at her passenger, worriedly taking in the pale face and tight set of her mouth. "I'm sorry."

The analyst looked at Kris, puzzled. "Why? You didn't do anything."

Kris pursed her lips grimly. "I know. That's the whole problem."

Shelby sighed. "Don't do this. Don't try to take responsibility for something you had no control over. Please?"

Kris cut her eyes sharply toward her companion. "I just feel like I should have sensed something."

Shifting in her seat to face the guilt-ridden woman, Shelby argued, "No one could have prevented that, not even you." Green eyes flickered over Kris' shoulder. "My God! There it is!"

Surprised at the abrupt change of subject, Kris asked, "There what is?"

"The bullet hole. It's in your neck rest. You could've been killed."

Kris shook her head at the shock in her partner's voice. Shelby was sitting next to her bleeding from a bullet hole in her arm, and she was worried that the shot had come close to hitting her bodyguard. At a loss for words, she reached over and placed her hand on Shelby's thigh, squeezing it gently. Parking the car in front of the emergency room, Kris quickly exited and made her way around the car to the passenger door, pulling it open. "Here we are. Wait here. I'll get a wheelchair."

Shelby smiled wanly. "Oh no you don't. I can walk." She swung her legs out of the car and got to her feet, grabbing on to Kris when she suddenly became light-headed.

Kris immediately wrapped the blonde in her arms, needing the brief moment of contact to reaffirm that she was, in fact, going to be okay, and thanking whatever powers guided the universe for saving the woman she loved. She steadied Shelby, then placed an arm around her waist, carefully avoiding the injury. "I've got you." She slowly guided Shelby toward the entrance, a squinting of her eyes the only indication of the extra strain being placed on her bruised muscles.

"I need some help here." Kris' voice rang out sharply over the noise in the busy emergency room, attracting the attention of a nurse, who immediately summoned one of the house officers.

Shelby was assisted into a wheelchair, and as she was abruptly pushed away, she looked over her shoulder to make sure Kris was behind her. The tall woman followed the green eyes tracking her, only to find her progress stopped by one of the nurses.

"Are you a family member?"

"No, but I'm responsible for her." She pulled out her CIA identification badge and showed it to the woman blocking her passage.

"If you're not family, you wait out here. Her injury doesn't appear to be life-threatening. I'll let you know her status after the doctor sees her."

Blue narrowed her eyes and growled, "She is a CIA employee. She was shot. I don't know that there won't be another attempt made while she's here. I am empowered by the government of this country to protect her. Now, you either move out of my way, or I'll move you. It's your choice."

In the face of the tirade from the intimidating woman, the nurse backed up. "It's against hospital rules. You can talk to the supervisor."

Noticing the confrontation, a woman in her forties approached. "What's the problem here?"

Emboldened by the appearance of her supervisor, the nurse said, "She thinks that just because she works for the CIA, we can bend the rules and let her in the treatment room."

If Blue hadn't been so concerned about Shelby, she would've laughed at the nurse's sudden courage in the wake of reinforcements. She focused on the newcomer. "We're working on a case. My partner was shot. She could still be in danger. It is my responsibility to protect her." Inclining her head toward the nurse, she added, "She refuses to let me pass."

The supervisor looked at her subordinate and said, "They need you over in trauma three." Once the woman had left the area, she turned her attention to Blue. "It is against hospital policy to allow anyone but family in with the patient. However, because of the possible further threat to her life, you can wait right outside the treatment room doors."

Blue nodded, preferring not to delay the care to her partner by insisting she be at her side, and followed the supervisor to the door through which Shelby had disappeared. The door didn't have a window and no one had entered or departed since Shelby had been taken inside. At least she could control who had access to the room; that would have to do, for now.

Standing on guard with her arms folded, Blue looked around the area for a pay phone, locating one within a few feet of her position. She wanted to call Lisa and Earl, but had seen signs forbidding the use of a cell phone inside the hospital. Keeping her attention focused on the door, Kris dialed Lisa's number.

"Hello."

"This is Kris. Shelby was injured shortly after we left your house. We're at Arlington Memorial."

"What do you mean, she was injured? What happened? Is she okay?"

"She's being seen right now. She'll be okay."

In a calmer voice, Lisa said, "I'll be right there."

Kris hoped Shelby wouldn't be upset because she'd notified her mother. She knew the emergency room personnel would do so anyway, but had felt obligated to make the call herself.

Severing the connection, she inserted more coins and punched in Earl's number. After a concise report, Kris returned to her post outside the treatment room, anticipating the arrival of the agents Earl was going to dispatch to ensure their safe exit from the hospital and return home, while a second team went to secure the apartment complex.

She was going to have to talk to Shelby about moving into a safe house. From the angle the bullet had entered the car, there was no doubt in her mind that Shelby was the intended victim. It was becoming increasingly clear that someone was targeting her partner.

Until she had evidence to refute it, Kris considered Jonathan the top suspect in the latest attack against Shelby. The shooting had occurred only one street away from Lisa's house, and Kris intended to ask Shelby's mother if her ex-husband knew that Shelby was planning on stopping by after work. She had a strong suspicion that he'd had prior knowledge.

The longer the door remained closed, the more Kris' worry increased. What if there was nerve damage, or something else she couldn't have ascertained with her quick assessment? Shelby had looked so pale, and she'd been quiet for most of the trip, except when she was trying to make Kris feel better. The agent began pacing back and forth in front of the door, ignoring the glances cast in her direction by the staff. The fury in her steps matched her self-indictment. *You should have sensed something. You were too complacent. You should have been more alert...*

SHELBY LAY ON the gurney watching a doctor and nurse clean her wound and prepare to suture it closed. She was still dizzy, but the fast-acting painkiller they'd given her had relieved the throbbing. She watched the fluid from the IV dripping slowly through the needle into her hand. The doctors had explained that she needed fluids because of the blood loss, and they were also giving her intravenous antibiotics which would be followed up with a prescription when she went home.

Shelby thought about the attack, awareness suddenly sinking in of just how close one of them had come to being killed. She shuddered as she realized if that little boy hadn't run in front of the car, causing Kris to slam on the brakes, one of them would surely be dead.

"Hold still."

She rolled her eyes at the doctor's unemotional tone, then glanced at the nurse, who'd started chuckling. When the woman winked at her, she smiled. Returning to her musings, Shelby wondered how Kris was holding up. The stark fear in her partner's eyes had been evident, but that had not slowed her movements as Kris covered her in the car. She clearly remembered the feel of Kris' body lying over her own as their hearts beat rapidly in tandem.

She had wondered if Kris could possibly be experiencing the same depth of feeling for her that she did for the enigmatic woman, but her question had been unequivocally answered in that nanosecond. She wasn't surprised that her partner was blaming herself. She was going to have to work on that. There was nothing Kris could have done any differently. She knew that. Now all she had to do was get Kris to believe it.

KRIS SAW LISA come charging down the corridor, heading straight for her.

Lisa stopped, breathing deeply from her run from the car to the hospital entrance. "Is she in there?"

As soon as Kris nodded, Lisa pushed past her and barged into the room, only to be ushered right back out by one of the nurses. "You've got to wait out here."

"I'm her mother."

Kindly but firmly, the nurse said, "She's going to be fine. She's very lucky; the bullet passed straight through her arm."

Lisa felt faint. "Bullet?"

Suddenly realizing the woman didn't have any idea of what had happened to her daughter, she said, "The doctor will be out to talk to you once he finishes. Just have a seat in the waiting room. It shouldn't be long." She turned around and went back into the room.

Lisa' fear turned to anger and she stalked over to Kris. "You were supposed to be protecting her. How did she get shot?"

Understanding Lisa's need to vent her emotions, Kris spoke calmly. "Someone obviously knew she was going to be at your house, and also knew the route we'd most likely take when we left. There was no way I could have foreseen that." Even as she uttered the words, Kris was haunted by doubts, searching for anything at all that she could have done differently.

"Well, you should have. That is your job, isn't it?"

Kris had had enough. She already felt totally responsible for dragging Shelby deeper into danger, beyond the limits of the case, and then not even being able to protect her. She didn't need a poor excuse for a mother telling her what she already knew. Blue met Lisa's eyes icily, watching dispassionately as the older woman retreated. "Did you tell Jonathan that Shelby was stopping over after work?"

"That is none of your business. It has nothing to do with this."

Blue smiled coldly. "It *is* my business, and it has *everything* to do with this. Jonathan threatened your daughter, or have you managed to forget that little detail?"

Lisa answered defensively, "I never heard him threaten her, and he said he didn't."

"So you'd take his word over Shelby's?" Blue closed the distance between them, never giving Lisa a chance to answer, fully intending to make her point up close and personal. "You know what, Lisa? I do take responsibility for not being able to protect Shelby. I have to live with that. But I think the shooter had some help. I don't know if it's Jonathan, but he is definitely a suspect. And I think you told him Shelby was coming over after work. Am I right?"

Lisa stared up at the intimidating woman. "Yes, I told him. He was supposed to come over, and I didn't think it would be a good idea for him to show up until after Shelby left. But he had nothing to do with this. You're just grasping at straws."

"Maybe so. But someone needs to be thinking of Shelby's best interests. You can rest assured that I will find out who shot your daughter, and they will pay."

Lisa felt a shiver of fear tingle down her spine. She'd seriously underestimated this woman, but anger guided her words. "How dare you accuse me of not looking out for my daughter! I can't begin to count the number of times I've tried to get her to quit that job."

Blue shook her head in disgust. "I'm not talking about her job. You knew she had been shot at once already. Jonathan told you. You knew he was there when the shot was fired. You knew he left and did nothing to help her. You knew Shelby was suspicious of his motives for being at her apartment. Yet, you still told him what your daughter's plans were tonight, without any regard for her feelings about him. No matter how you cut the deck, you did not think of her first."

Lisa stared at the operative, speechless, unable to believe the blatant contempt on her face. She couldn't envision Jonathan harming Shelby after all the treatment he'd received, and felt Kris was wrong to consider him a suspect. And now the bodyguard was just trying to cover for her own inadequacy by blaming her for revealing that Shelby was going to be at the house. She was drawn from her resentful thoughts by the sound of the door opening. She whirled around and followed a nurse who was indicating she could go in.

Kris watched Lisa enter, trying to get a peek at Shelby, but her view was blocked by the medical personnel. She knew she'd been hard on Lisa, but the woman was living in a fantasy world. Jonathan was dangerous, whether or not he was involved in the most recent attack, yet Lisa seemed blind to that fact. The operative paced restlessly back and forth, longing to see Shelby. Just for a minute. Just to make sure she really was okay. Just because she needed to see her really badly just then.

She cursed the hospital regulations that forbade her to go to Shelby, remembering a program she'd seen on HBO called *If These Walls Could Talk 2*. The movie had been divided into three different stories. The first account had detailed the heart-wrenching story of a couple that had been together for years. When one suddenly became gravely ill, her partner was not allowed to see her, and she'd died alone without the loving support of her soulmate. Kris could still clearly remember the frustration and anguish to which the surviving woman had been subjected—both by her partner's death and by unfeeling family members—all because their partnership was not legally recognized.

Kris shook the images from her mind. *That was different. But is it really? Isn't a lifelong relationship with Shelby what you really want?* Kris nodded. *Yes, I do want that. And we will have it, if Shelby wants it. But we'll never be in the position of that unfortunate couple, no matter where we have to live.*

She tried to assuage her concern with logic. Shelby was going to be fine. Her wound wasn't serious. Kris finally gave up her rational assessment when it failed to dispel her frustration at not being allowed at her partner's side. She continued to pace, stopping suddenly when the door opened again. She looked at the nurse. "Can I go back there yet?"

"Yes, we're making an exception for you because of the circumstances. Dr. Kowalski is writing Shelby's discharge orders now." The nurse glanced up at the operative. "You have a very persuasive friend."

Kris grinned. "That she is."

Sitting on the gurney with a large bandage around her bicep, Shelby was arguing with her mother. "I am not quitting my job. I already told you, I don't think this had anything to do with where I work."

"I suppose you think Jonathan did it, just like that bodyguard of yours."

Shelby couldn't stop a snort of amusement from escaping her mouth, even though she was tired and her arm hurt. It tickled her that her mother insisted on referring to Kris as her bodyguard. While technically she was, bodyguard was such an inadequate description of the agent's extensive capabilities, and of their relationship.

"I think it's possible. You admit you told him I was coming over." Shelby looked directly into her mother's eyes, her expression serious. "If he did it, Mom, would you still protect him?"

Lisa's mouth dropped open. She could understand the bodyguard trying to shift the blame to her, but how could her own daughter think such a thing? "Of course not!" Tears began to fall. "I can't believe you even asked me that."

Shelby shook her head. "Sorry, Mom. But you believed Jonathan when he told you he didn't threaten me at the trial, so I had to ask."

The older woman looked at her daughter, biting off a defense of her actions. Shelby was right. She had chosen to believe her ex-husband instead of her daughter. Doubts previously kept tightly under control began escaping, and Lisa knew she had a lot of thinking to do. "I didn't know what to believe. I thought you might have just read more into what he was saying than he actually said."

"I know." Shelby suddenly looked past her mother and smiled warmly.

Lisa's gaze followed her daughter's, and she snorted derisively. "Don't know why you're so happy to see her. You wouldn't be here if she'd done her job, no matter who did the shooting."

Shelby turned to her mother pointedly, her eyes flashing as her temper flared. "Don't you ever criticize Kris again. I would be dead if not for her. Did you already forget that she saved my life in the parking lot? You yourself thanked her for that, and now all of a sudden, she's at fault because she can't see through trees and houses? I can't believe you said that. I trust her, and that's all that matters!"

Kris listened in silence. She'd briefly seen Shelby's temper before, but had never witnessed her anger to the extent her partner was now displaying. And it was on her behalf. It was a strange but welcome feeling. She stood behind Lisa and winked at Shelby, hoping to calm her down. She quirked a half-smile when the corners of Shelby's mouth turned up.

Kris stepped next to Lisa, looking at the large bandage Shelby was sporting. "How's your arm?"

"It hurts a little, but they gave me something to help with the pain and the doctor's writing a prescription for Tylenol III."

Lisa stood there, puzzled. Her daughter could have died. She couldn't understand how Shelby could defend a woman who had failed at her job, and then sit there talking to her like they were best friends. "I'm not criticizing, but maybe you should get a male bodyguard." When twin glares met her gaze, she added uncomfortably, "It was just an idea."

A few minutes later, Shelby was given a prescription and a set of instructions for caring for the wound. Kris helped her down from the gurney. The three left the trauma room and began walking through the lobby.

"I want you to stay with me. Kris can stay at the house, too."

Shelby shook her head. "Thanks, Mom, but I'll be more comfortable in my own apartment."

"Just until you're able to go back to work. I'd feel a lot better if I knew you were safe."

Shelby understood her mother's concern, but had no intentions of staying any place that Jonathan frequented. "I won't be taking time off. The doctor said not to use my arm for heavy lifting or anything strenuous, but other than keeping the wound clean, that's the only restriction. I'll be fine, really."

Kris opened the door and carefully eyed the parking lot, locating the team of agents before nodding to Shelby to follow her.

Lisa didn't want to upset Shelby by insisting. "Okay, honey. Whatever you think is best. You be sure and call me if you need anything." Lisa hugged Shelby, carefully avoiding her injured arm. "Bye."

"Bye. I'll call you tomorrow."

Lisa smiled briefly before turning away, her thoughts troubled. She was going to call Jonathan the moment she arrived home.

THE DRIVE HOME was quiet. Shelby glanced over at Kris ruefully. "So much for surveillance tonight."

"Hey, don't worry about it." Kris flicked on the left turn signal and pulled into the apartment complex parking lot. She'd been in cell phone contact with the agents that Earl had assigned, and the parking lot and apartment were secure. "I do need to go tomorrow night, though. I'll ask Earl to send someone over to stay with you while I'm gone."

"Oh no, you won't!"

Kris had just switched off the ignition and quickly glanced at Shelby, startled at the vehemence in her voice. She felt the full fury of her partner's anger leaping out at her from the swirling emerald eyes. "It would only be for about four hours or so. I'm not going to leave you alone."

"That's right, you're not. And I'm not leaving you alone, either. I'm going!"

"Come on, be reasonable, Shelby. You were just shot. You don't need to be sitting in a car on a side street when you could be taking it easy at home."

Shelby met the concerned blue eyes pointedly. "And you were just beat up."

"That was different." One look at Shelby's face and Kris hurriedly said, "Wait, let me finish."

"No, Kris, let me finish. I'm not going to go through what I did Monday night again, wondering if you're okay and worrying something might have happened if you're late getting back. You asked me to help. I agreed. We're in this together, sweetheart." Shelby smiled as the tips of her partner's ears reddened.

The operative opened her mouth and closed it again. She'd actually feel a lot better if Shelby was with her rather than with another agent. Kris knew she couldn't expect anyone else to protect Shelby with their life, while she intended to do just that. "Okay. But tonight you let me take care of you. Deal?"

"Okay, but I think it's going to be an early night for me. That painkiller is really making me sleepy."

"Let's get you upstairs."

Kris exited the vehicle and moved around to the passenger side of the car. She extended her hand for Shelby to grab on to. Her partner grasped her hand, but exited the car under her own power without really taking advantage of the leverage she offered, and it suddenly occurred to Kris that even though Shelby had to feel like hell, she was worried about hurting her. Her heart ached with the depth of emotion washing over her. She shook her head, amazed that love could be so physically palpable.

LISA PULLED INTO her driveway, surprised to see Jonathan's car already there. She walked through the house, headed for the living room, knowing that was where she would likely find Jonathan and their sons. All three were engrossed in a baseball game. "Jonathan? Could I see you for a minute?"

"Oh, hi, babe. Just a minute, okay?"

"No. It's not okay. I'd like to talk to you now."

Jonathan looked up, surprised at Lisa's sharp tone. "Sure, babe." He looked at Jimmy. "I'll be right back. Let me know what happens."

Jason glanced at his mother uneasily. She never talked to his dad that way. The more time he spent with them, the less certain the teenager was becoming that his father had changed. There had been little things, like when his father had arrived an hour earlier, he'd gotten very upset because Jason was watching a scifi movie. Jonathan had told him to grow up, and then changed the channel to the baseball game. His father had apologized right afterward, but had sounded insincere.

The young man knew his father had put his mother in the hospital, and though he really wanted to believe the man was cured, he was beginning to get very worried, worried enough to say something to his mother even if she did get mad at him, or at least to call Shelby. She would know what he should do. Feeling better now that he'd made a decision, Jason picked up the remote and changed the channel, over the protests of Jimmy who insisted, "Dad wants the game on."

JONATHAN FOLLOWED LISA out to the kitchen, angry but wary. She had no business belittling him in front of Jason and Jimmy by demanding he accompany her anywhere. Jason was turning out to be a challenge anyway. He couldn't read the kid, and that bothered him. When Lisa closed the kitchen door, he walked over and hugged her, only to find his overture rebuffed. "What's wrong, babe?"

"When did you get here?"

Jonathan hid his irritation at her tone of voice. "About an hour ago. I was really surprised you weren't home. The boys said you practically ran out the door, telling them you were going to the hospital and would call from there. Are you okay?"

"I'm fine." Lisa looked at Jonathan pointedly. "I thought you were going to wait until I called you to come over."

"I had some errands to run, so I came by when I was done. Since I didn't see Shelby's car in the driveway, I didn't think you'd mind." He shrugged. "So, what's the problem? Why are you giving me the third degree? And why were you at the hospital?"

"Where'd you go shopping?"

"What does that have to do with anything? Now quit playing games and tell me what this is all about."

Lisa looked determinedly at her ex-husband. "Shortly after she left here this evening, Shelby was shot. You knew she was coming over."

Jonathan's face reflected his surprise. "What? That's terrible!" His brow furrowed at the implication of her words. "Surely you don't think... It's that damn job of hers. Lisa, I would never hurt our daughter."

Torn, wanting to believe him and not quite able to, Lisa just gazed at him, but she wanted to make one thing crystal clear. "Shelby is not your daughter. I turned a blind eye to your brutality once; it'll never happen again."

"Lisa, please," Jonathan begged. "I hate myself for what I did to her and Ann. I don't blame you for being dubious." He dropped his head, gazing at the floor. "I know I was wrong. How can I convince you that I've changed? I'll do whatever you want."

Looking at his forlorn expression, Lisa's heart softened. She wanted to believe him, but did she dare? Shelby insisted he'd threatened her at the trial, yet he'd never admitted to that. Could she trust Jonathan now? She needed some time.

"I don't know what to think, but I do know that I'd like a little breathing space right now. I think we should wait a while longer before you move in here."

Jonathan's voice choked. "I love you, Lisa. I would never hurt Shelby. Please believe me."

It took every bit of Lisa's rapidly diminishing resolve to stick to her decided course of action. "I love you, too. And I want you to know that I don't think you were responsible for Shelby getting shot. There's just so much going on right now, I need a few days to make sure we're making the right decision for the right reasons."

Lisa's words rocked Jonathan. He'd never expected her to resist his deliberately charming advances, and felt his anger begin to build. That damn little bitch had been lucky again and it was costing him dearly. His countenance, however, reflected a profound sadness. "Whatever you want, babe. All I care about is making you happy. I'll be sitting by my phone, waiting to hear from you." He moved to the door with slumped shoulders. "Bye, babe."

Lisa walked over and gave him a fleeting kiss. "I'll call you in a couple of days, okay?"

Nodding, Jonathan departed. Lisa tracked his progress to his car and watched as he drove away until she could no longer see the car. She sank into one of the kitchen chairs and sighed audibly. *I don't know what to do.* Lisa's eyes widened. Jonathan had never even asked how Shelby was.

SHELBY CHUCKLED AND patted the couch next to her. "Would you please sit down? You're making me crazy."

"You sure you don't need anything else? Want some more iced tea?" The younger woman started to rise, and Kris moved to her side. "What do you need? I'll get it."

Shelby grasped the operative's forearm with her right hand and said, "You—next to me."

Kris smiled. "Sounds good to me."

"Well, what are you waiting for, then?" Shelby was touched by the manic attentiveness Kris had shown since they'd arrived back at the apartment. The bodyguard had made them turkey breast sandwiches served with potato chips and iced tea, cleaned up their mess, arranged the couch so that Shelby could rest her arm on the pillows, and for the last several minutes had been hovering over her, not knowing what else to do.

Searching for an answer, Kris muttered, "Um, I just..."

Shelby smiled warmly. "I know, sweetheart. You've been wonderful about pampering me, but you need to take a break."

Once the analyst had reseated herself, Kris carefully lowered herself next to Shelby, not wanting to jar her.

"Will you relax? I won't break." Placing her hand gently on Kris' stomach, she asked, "How are you doing?"

"Fine." Kris quirked a half-smile at the disbelieving look on her partner's face. "Well, it is a little sore."

"Somehow, I have a feeling it's more than a little sore. Did you take some Alleve?"

"Yeah, last time I went into the bathroom."

"Good. Now let's talk."

Kris gazed into the somber green eyes, puzzled. "Okay."

"You're still blaming yourself."

The operative looked away. She felt so damned guilty. Why couldn't she have been the one shot? Shelby didn't deserve that. She didn't belong in the dark world of subterfuge and double-crosses, where every shadow held a new threat.

Shelby laid her hand on Kris' thigh. "I don't blame you."

Kris' eyes were haunted. "I still feel I should've sensed something, been more observant, just something—"

"You love me, right?"

Blue eyes looked gravely into green ones, willing Shelby to see the truth written there. "More than anything."

Shelby reached for Kris' hand and gripped it firmly. "Please stop beating yourself up over this. Promise me you'll let it go. Would you do that for me?"

Kris glanced around the room, vaguely aware of the TV droning in the background and Stormy sleeping on the back of the couch. What Shelby was asking seemed so simple on the surface, but it required her to forgive herself. "I'd do anything for you, but..."

"No buts. Okay?" Shelby released Kris' hand and shifted so she was directly facing her. She brushed the operative's longish bangs to the side, gazing into the vivid blue eyes. "It would really make me happy."

Enveloped in the love emanating from her partner, Kris slowly nodded, understanding that her self-condemnation was hurting Shelby. "Okay. I'll try."

The analyst grinned. "Great. Could we seal the deal with a kiss?"

Smiling, the tall woman shifted sideways and bent down, meeting Shelby's soft lips with her own. It was a sweet, lingering kiss, full of promises yet to be fulfilled.

SHORTLY AFTER THEIR arrival the following morning, Earl summoned Kris and Shelby into his office, along with Jeb and Dennis. The director of covert operations listened intently as Kris provided a detailed run down of the events prior to and following the attack. He directed his remarks toward Shelby. "You've been lucky so far; you might not be so fortunate the next time. I want you to move to a safe house until we figure out who is behind the attacks."

Shelby shook her head. "I don't think the shootings are related to my job. I wouldn't feel right about using taxpayers' money for a personal matter."

"How about letting me be the judge of that?"

The analyst looked at Kris for help, only to find her looking down at the floor. She narrowed her eyes and her demeanor changed subtly. *She's going to hear about this later.* "I don't want to move into a safe house. I think my stepfather could be responsible, and that is not Company business. If you feel I need more protection than Kris alone, then assign some agents for outside surveillance."

Earl clearly read the body language and remembered her threat the last time they had tried to coerce her into complying with their wishes. "At least think about it." When Shelby nodded, he continued, "I've notified the local police, and they're sending two officers out to question Whiteman. I'll call you when I get their report."

Accepting that as a dismissal, the two women stood and took their leave. Shelby walked alongside of Kris, trying to contain her anger. "I can't believe you; you didn't even support me in there. What's with that?" Shelby spoke quietly, but her words were fraught with frustration.

Kris sighed. The last thing she wanted was for Shelby to be angry with her, but safety had to be her number one concern. "I wish you would reconsider. If it is Jonathan, you'd be a lot more secure in a safe house."

Shelby glanced at Kris. "And what if it isn't? You said yourself there was a leak in the Agency. So now all of a sudden you're on their side. What about you, Kris? You don't need my help anymore?"

Kris' stomach dropped at the hurt in her partner's voice. "Yes, I do, but your safety is the most important thing to me. If anything happened to you, I don't know what I'd do. I shouldn't have dragged you into this."

Shelby shook her head. "Well, I am in it, and I plan to see it through. And next time you have a brainstorm like trying to coop me up, how about talking to me first? Or don't my feelings matter?"

"Of course they do!" Kris said vehemently. "I've just been thinking that whoever fired that shot has to be damn good. Spending a few years in the military or going hunting are very different from targeting a moving vehicle."

Shelby turned the corner and they entered the corridor her office was in. "Deer don't stand still and wait for you to shoot them."

"Well, yes, they do, sort of. It's only when you don't get a clean shot that you end up chasing through the woods after them. I don't know what it is yet, but something just doesn't feel right about this whole thing."

"Why didn't you say something before now?" Shelby slowed her step, watching Kris intently.

Matching her partner's stride, Kris admitted, "I'm just speculating, and if you'd agreed to move into a safe house..."

Shelby stopped in the hallway and faced her partner. "If I agreed to move into a safe house, Earl would've insisted you do, too, and your mother would be as good as dead."

Kris glanced at the barren institutional walls, their bleakness matching her mood as she realized what a huge error it had been not to include Shelby in her planning. "I thought about that, but I figured I could convince Earl to allow me to come and go as necessary. I would have found some pretext."

Crossing her arms, Shelby shook her head. "Didn't you once try to convince him you didn't want to work this case, too?"

Kris sighed at the relentless logic. *I screwed this up royally.* "Touché. I'm sorry. Forgive me?"

The analyst looked away. She understood that Kris was just being overprotective, which she really didn't mind as long as the agent included her in the operation. Shelby returned her gaze to Kris, nodding. "Yes. If you remember that we're in this together, no matter what happens."

"I won't forget." Kris had to refrain from hugging Shelby right there in the hallway. They began walking again, and turned into Shelby's office. Curious, Kris asked, "Do you think Jonathan shot you?"

Shelby's brow furrowed. "I don't know. Part of me insists there is no way he would cross the line from abuse to murder. Rationally, I know men like him do it all the time, but it usually takes something to trigger the escalation. I haven't done anything to him."

Kris mulled that over. "Does he know about the agreement you made with your mother, about him not moving in until she talks to Kim?"

The analyst's face paled. "I never thought of that. If she changes her mind about letting him move back in, I could be in trouble."

"I think you already might be." The words hung like a black cloud in the small room.

Chapter Sixteen

AS KRIS DROVE through the small trailer park, Shelby looked out the window. Most of the dwellings were singlewide structures in varying states of disrepair. Shutters hung haphazardly, and the few awnings still existing were rusty and dented. Dilapidated cars sat up on blocks, their tires long since removed, adding to the sense of entropy and decay. Litter fluttered across the ground, its movement directed by the gentle breeze, and a couple of resident cats picked at the sparse offerings in the uncovered garbage cans.

Kris commented dryly, "Not exactly a trailer park I would want to live in."

"Tell me about it. This place should be condemned. No wonder he wants to move back in with Mom so badly." Trying to ignore her growing uneasiness, Shelby pointed off to the left. "There's his car."

Glancing in the direction that Shelby had indicated, Kris pulled to the side of the road in front of a small, dingy white trailer, and turned off the ignition. The operative half-turned in her seat. "I'm going in with you."

Surprised at the change in plan, Shelby said, "I thought we agreed that you'd wait outside."

The operative wanted to meet Jonathan and assure herself that she wasn't letting Shelby walk into a lion's den alone. "We did. But I want to get a feel for him."

Shelby thought it over for a moment, actually happy that her partner was going to accompany her at the onset. "Okay, but then I need to talk to him alone. He won't give anything away in front of you."

Kris nodded her agreement then, sensing Shelby's discomfort, reached over and squeezed her hand. "Fine. But I'll be waiting right outside, and if I even hear him raise his voice, I'm coming in."

Resenting the tendril of fear she felt at the prospect of facing her stepfather, Shelby nevertheless forced a smile and gave Kris' hand an answering squeeze. "Well, it's now or never."

THE INSISTENT KNOCKING finally filtered through Jonothan's beer-induced sleep. Dragging himself up to a sitting position on the couch, he shook the cobwebs from his mind. He'd been furious when the cops had rousted him from bed that morning, asking him to provide proof of his whereabouts the previous evening, and when they'd departed, he'd sought solace in a six-pack of Budweiser.

He stalked angrily to the door, prepared to threaten the officers with harassment charges, knowing they had absolutely no evidence to tie him to the shooting. Totally unmindful of his appearance, Jonathan pulled open the door, his glare turning to a look of surprise at the sight of his stepdaughter and her bodyguard.

Shelby looked at the stubble covering Jonathan's face and the red-rimmed eyes squinting against the sunlight before taking in the grayish T-shirt and boxer shorts he was wearing. She suddenly wondered why she'd never been able to fully escape from her childhood fear of this pathetic man. The last time she'd seen him was in the courtroom. He'd been in complete control then, particularly when he'd uttered his threat against her, making certain he wasn't overheard. Now she was seeing the unvarnished version, and it finally sank in just how weak he was without anyone to bully or abuse.

Knowing her stepfather was still very dangerous, especially since his plans to move in with Lisa were being threatened, Shelby had no intention of letting her guard down. However, any lingering fear faded as she looked at him objectively, and she found herself feeling only contempt and revulsion. Shelby glanced quickly at Kris, but was unable to read any expression on her enigmatic companion's face. Keeping her voice neutral, she asked, "Aren't you going to invite us in?"

Jonathan swallowed uneasily at the surprising visit from his stepdaughter, and began backing out of the doorway. "Yeah, come on in. I'll be right back."

Kris tensed, watching the door down the narrow hallway through which Jonathan had disappeared. Even as her peripheral vision scanned the interior of the trailer, she was disgusted by the rank smell of garbage left sitting too long. Beer cans squashed to a fraction of their size lay scattered on the floor around the couch and end table. Some guests on the Jerry Springer show were screaming their hatred for each other from a small television set, and she smiled her appreciation when her partner turned it off.

Her eyes lighted on the barrel of a rifle, barely visible in a corner behind the entry door. Still watching the hallway, she moved toward the weapon and spared it a quick glance. It was a 20-gauge shotgun, and Kris immediately eliminated it as the weapon used in either shooting. Widening her focus to once again include the entire area, Kris could see Shelby still standing in the middle of the living room, shaking her head, a look of disgust on her face. That pretty much mirrored her own thoughts.

Shelby spoke quietly, not wanting her voice to carry beyond the room. "He never used to be like this."

Drolly, Kris commented, "He never had to clean up after himself before. He thrives on manipulation and control. Without anyone to bully, he's lost. Power is the whole focus of his life."

Jonathan reappeared a few moments later, clean-shaven and wearing jeans. He smiled with practiced ease. "Sorry for the mess; it's been a rough day." Looking at the large bandage on Shelby's arm, he added, "I'm glad you're okay. You really should get a less dangerous job."

Shelby rolled her eyes at Jonathan's feigned concern and glanced at her tall companion.

Kris nodded imperceptibly. "I'll be waiting outside." She stared at Jonathan, delivering an unspoken warning and smiling inwardly at the flicker of apprehension that appeared in his pale blue eyes.

When the tall woman had left, Jonathan crossed his arms, his smile disappearing. "I'm surprised you sent your bodyguard outside. Aren't you afraid of me?" His voice took on a derisive tone. "You must be, since you sicced the cops on me." He sighed in mock injury. "You never give up, do you?"

Shelby shook her head incredulously. "*I* never give up? *You're* the one that keeps pressuring Mom to take you back. You might have her fooled, but you don't fool me."

"It's not an act. I love your mother."

"You love to manipulate and bully her." Shelby gazed deeply into her stepfather's eyes. "It's only me and you now, no witnesses, so how about telling the truth? Did you shoot at me last night?"

"No, I didn't." Jonathan grinned malevolently, deciding to have a little fun since they were alone. "It's too bad that guy missed, though. It would've been satisfying to have witnessed your death."

Shelby was chilled by the words, but refused to show any fear. And he had piqued her curiosity. "You saw the guy that did it?"

Jonathan grinned cruelly and assumed the intimidating posture that had so cowed Shelby as a child   Enunciating each word, he spoke slowly and clearly. "Yeah. Seems I'm not the only one who would like you gone permanently. Great minds think alike."

Refusing to allow her stepfather control of the conversation, Shelby calmly asked, "What did the guy look like?"

Jonathan smiled smugly. "You really think I'm going to tell you? Maybe he'll be luckier next time."

Keeping her irritation hidden, Shelby returned his smile. "I'm sure Mom will be interested to hear that you witnessed the shooting.

I don't think you'll be moving in anytime soon."

Angry that the fear he'd expected to see in her eyes was absent, Jonathan decided to give his stepdaughter a physical reminder of whom she was dealing with. In two quick steps, he closed the distance between them and grabbed Shelby's injured arm, squeezing cruelly. "You little bitch, it's your word against mine. I'm warning you now, keep your mouth shut about me to your mother or there will be two of us after you, and both of us aren't going to miss."

When her former stepfather squeezed her wounded arm, Shelby's face paled and she gasped in pain, reflexively pulling away and holding her arm protectively with her other hand, tears welling in her eyes. Very pleased he'd gotten the response he wanted, Jonathan brutally shoved her.

Angered by the triumph visible on her stepfather's face, Shelby grabbed the doorframe, refusing to allow him to physically dismiss her. Her eyes started flashing as she launched a verbal counterattack. "Feel better now? You really get off on attacking women and children, don't you? You're pathetic. You had a real opportunity to get help, and just went through the motions. And I do plan on filing assault charges against you." Keeping her eyes on her stepfather, Shelby called out, "Hey, Kris, how about joining us?"

Jonathan's eyes widened at her verbal assault, and he stood there momentarily speechless in the face of Shelby's ire.

The door slammed open and Blue strode in, her anger barely under control. The only open window had been on the far side of the trailer, and the agent cursed the extra seconds it had taken her to reach the door after hearing Shelby's gasp of pain. She'd been following the discussion intently, not wanting to invade her partner's privacy but also not willing to leave Shelby totally at the mercy of her stepfather, should he try something.

Glancing at Shelby and witnessing the pain her partner was experiencing, Blue narrowed her eyes and focused on Jonathan, even though the analyst looked like she had the situation well in hand. She bore down on Jonathan as he backed away, trapping him against the far wall of the trailer. "You bastard!"

Jonathan met the operative's glare and snarled. "You move out of my way, or I'll move you."

Blue smiled coldly, her voice low and calm, belying the tension surging through her muscles. "What are you waiting for?"

Jonathan saw red. *Who is this bitch to challenge me? She has to be stupid, but she asked for it.* He viciously kicked his leg forward and simultaneously threw a left jab, only to find himself off balance as neither blow landed. A moment later he was doubled over, grunting in pain and coughing, trying to catch his breath after the sharp blow to his solar plexus. Unprepared, he never saw the fist that connected with his chin, and he sank to the floor, dazed.

Blue looked on dispassionately, struggling to control the throbbing her quick movement had wrought in her own bruised muscles. She cursed her weakness, and hoped Jonathan had had enough. Having no illusions about maintaining a sustained assault in her condition, she backed out of reach and quickly glanced at Shelby. "Are you okay?" she asked, before turning her attention back to her adversary.

"Yeah, but I'm going to call the police and file assault charges."

The operative nodded. If Shelby wanted to file charges, that was fine with her. Unfortunately, it would only be Jonathan's word against her partner's because she hadn't witnessed the incident, but Kris figured Shelby knew that.

"No."

Blue glanced at Jonathan, who was struggling to rise to his feet. "Why not, sleezeball? Afraid you might go back to jail this time? Couldn't happen to a nicer guy."

Jonathan sensed there was no dealing with the tall woman facing him, and turned his attention to Shelby. He'd never get his record expunged with a new assault charge pending, even if she couldn't prove it. "I'll make you a deal. You know I have something you want."

Shelby glanced at Kris, and then assumed a good approximation of her partner's stoic façade. She returned her attention to Jonathan, shrugging disinterestedly. "Maybe. What's the deal?"

Sensing an opportunity to regain the upper hand, Jonathan pressed his advantage. "If you don't press charges, I'll tell you what I saw yesterday when you were shot at."

Smiling inwardly, his reaction exactly what she'd been hoping for, Shelby shrugged. "How do I know you'll be telling the truth? You've lied before."

"If I'm lying, you can always press charges."

Shelby nodded. "Okay, deal. I find out you lied, and the deal is off."

Suppressing her own smirk of satisfaction, Kris observed the interaction between her partner and Jonathan, once again surprised by Shelby's comprehensive understanding of the human mind. She had played her stepfather like a well-tuned piano, and he'd totally fallen for it.

"Well?"

"The guy was tall, with dark hair. I didn't get a good look at him because he was concealed pretty well in a tree a couple of houses up from where your car ended up."

"That's all you know? Forget it. That could be anyone." Shelby looked at Kris. "Let me borrow your cell phone; I left mine in the car."

Seeing the resolute expression on Shelby's face as she accepted the phone from her partner, Jonathan interrupted, "Wait. There's more." Pulling out his wallet, he retrieved a small piece of paper and handed it to his stepdaughter. "I got his license number."

Kris asked a question that had been bothering her since she'd overheard the conversation earlier. "How was it that you were in the area and just happened to notice which car was his?"

The tall man shifted uncomfortably. He'd had plans for Shelby himself, but had been saved the trouble by the appearance of the other man. "I was just hanging around waiting for you and Shelby to leave so I could go visit Lisa when I saw him take a bicycle out of his car. He was carrying a small black gym bag."

Kris' disbelief was clearly evident. "You were just hanging around?"

"It's the truth."

Kris glanced at Shelby. Truth or not, her partner was obviously satisfied with the information Jonathan had given them, so it was time to end the visit. She smiled at Shelby. "Would you mind waiting for me outside? I want to talk to Jonathan alone for a minute." She winked to assure her partner that she really was only going to talk to him.

Once the analyst left, Blue glared at the tall man who was watching her cautiously. Knowing words alone would be ineffective, she removed her gun from the holster at the small of her back, holding it casually as she released the cylinder and made a point of checking to see that all the chambers contained rounds. Then she smiled, and in a voice few had heard and lived, purred, "If you come near Shelby, or make any attempt to harm her, ever, you're a dead man." Blue clicked the cylinder back in place to emphasize her words. "Is that clear?"

Jonathan looked into the ice-cold eyes and tried to back away, but was already trapped in place by the wall. He had no doubt that she meant exactly what she'd said, and for the first time in his life he felt a bone-chilling fear. Finding his voice, he muttered, "Yes."

Blue growled, "Good. I'm glad we understand each other."

Watching her leave, Jonathan wiped the perspiration from his brow, bewildered by the depth of his fear.

TURNING IN THE passenger seat to face Kris as they departed the trailer park, Shelby asked, "What'd you say to him?"

"I just told him to stay away from you."

Shelby raised an eyebrow. "That's it? Why do I get this feeling you're leaving something out?"

Kris grinned. "Or face the consequences."

"I don't think I even want to know," Shelby joked, but was secretly pleased that Kris had cared enough to warn her stepfather off. She had a feeling the operative's message would be much more effective than any peace bond or court order could ever be. Jonathan only understood power, and her partner was more than his match.

Shelby glanced out the window, her mind replaying the confrontation. She was pleased that she'd managed to stand up to her stepfather and outmaneuver him. The look of shock on his face had been priceless. She wondered if her bravery had been fueled by the operative's close presence and decided that, while that might have been a factor, the primary element was that she hadn't felt like a victim any longer. Shelby smiled, satisfied with the personal victory. When the car began to slow, she glanced over at her partner.

Kris pulled off the road a mile beyond the trailer park, put the car in park, and turned to face Shelby. She reached over, gently touching the bandage covering her partner's upper arm before dropping her hand. "I know he hurt you. Are you okay?"

"Yeah. It doesn't hurt as much now." Shelby sighed. "I just can't believe he did that. I expected more from him. Shows what I know."

"I didn't think he'd do anything either, and if he hadn't had any alcohol in him, he probably wouldn't have." Kris looked out the window, wishing she hadn't left Shelby alone with Jonathan but knowing she'd had little choice in the matter.

"Kris?" When her partner met her gaze, Shelby continued. "It was my decision to talk to him alone, so no second guessing, okay?" She reached for the operative's hand and stopped. "You hurt your hand."

Shrugging, Kris glanced at slightly swollen knuckles and quirked a half-smile. "Nah. It's fine."

"We could stop and get some ice..." Shelby trailed off when Kris raised an eyebrow, gazing at her pointedly. "It was just an idea."

The operative shifted the car into gear. "I want to stop and check out that tree Jonathan said the guy used as his stand. If he was a professional, he probably just left the weapon. There won't be any way to trace it if he did, but I'd like to get a feel for who we're dealing with."

"Okay. Want to stop and eat after that?"

Kris grinned and kidded, "You're not hungry, are you?"

"Oh, like you aren't? We never finished our sandwiches last night and we got up too late for breakfast—"

"I'm kidding. I'm hungry, too. Where to?"

"I'm kinda tired of sandwiches. There's a little spaghetti place near Mom's house. Want to go there?"

"Sounds good."

They quickly located the tree Jonathan had described as the hiding place for the shooter, and Kris parked on the street in front of the yard. She spent a few minutes surveying the tree, trying to decide the best way to reach the lowest branch without taxing her aching muscles any more than necessary.

Focusing, Kris crouched slightly before jumping up and grabbing onto the high branch, grimacing but holding on, and eventually swinging her body onto the tree limb. The next branches were comparatively easy, and she found the rifle a little higher in the tree, well hidden in foliage and secured by bungee cords.

Kris glanced around and silently commended the shooter on the excellent vantage point. She dropped to the ground a few minutes later, carefully holding the rifle by the trigger guard, aware that there was a remote possibility the sniper had been careless and not worn gloves or wiped the weapon clean after firing it.

"Jonathan was telling the truth. This is a professional sniper's rifle. I'll turn it over to Earl, but there won't be anything on it to identify the shooter or where the weapon was purchased. Anyone can get one through mail order catalogues if you know where to look."

Shelby glanced at the weapon, but her concern was for Kris. "Are you okay?"

The operative smiled wanly. "I'm fine, just a little sore still."

"Uh huh." Shelby knew 'a little sore' really meant Kris was in a good deal of pain. "I hope we see someone on tonight's surveillance. We really need a break."

"I hear you." Kris closed the car door behind Shelby, secured the rifle in the trunk, and slid into the driver's seat. Doubts began to plague Kris as she searched her mind for any way to expedite the searches for her mother's location and the leak in the case. Troubled, she began to wonder if they had any chance of success in either pursuit.

A small hand came to rest on her thigh and softly spoken words broke through her dark musings. "We're going to find her in time."

The operative glanced at the unshakable optimism on her partner's face. After all she'd been through the last week, that Shelby could be so positive amazed her. She cast her doubts aside, determined to prove the analyst right.

KRIS TOOK A sip of her Coke, her eyes steadily tracking the people walking along the Georgetown sidewalk, oblivious to her scrutiny. Shelby had grown quiet the last half hour and the operative suspected that her arm was probably bothering her, although her partner had insisted it was fine and had taken a pain killer in the restaurant.

While they were eating, her concern for her partner's welfare had overridden her logic and she'd suggested they cancel surveillance that night, but Shelby had pointedly vetoed the idea. Kris marveled at the iron will and quiet strength of the woman she loved, and vowed to do everything within her power to ensure they shared a future together.

The operative's thoughts turned to Dimitri. She wasn't surprised that the Russians were maintaining a low profile by leaving her alone; she'd expected that. But, it was going on 9:00 p.m. and no one had shown the slightest interest in the drop yet.

She glanced frequently in their rearview mirror, habit dictating her action, head swiveling back when she heard Shelby suck in a breath and whisper, "Maggie."

Taking in the wide eyed astonishment on her partner's face, she looked in the direction Shelby was gazing. Kris recognized the woman she had seen sitting in the canteen across from Michael earlier in the week. Her eyes riveted on the woman clad casually in jeans, and she watched her nonchalantly put something in the basket of the "blind" man sitting there begging for change. "You know her?"

Shelby nodded, stunned. "Yeah. She works down my hallway. She invited us out for a get-together last night, but I told her I was stopping over at my mother's..."

As the realization of what she'd said impacted her, Shelby turned and faced Kris, who was tracking Maggie down the street. "I forgot all about that. She knew too." The analyst fell silent, wondering how she could have misjudged her co-worker so badly, and then realized she'd never talked to her enough to really develop any kind of rapport with her. She glanced up as Kris started the car.

"That's her in the blue Mercedes," Kris said. "Let's see where she's going."

Shelby watched Kris expertly blend into the traffic behind the Mercedes, always keeping two or three cars between them and their target. She was glad Washington had a thriving nightlife, knowing they could easily keep Maggie in sight without being obvious until she'd reached her destination. Disappointment coloring her words, Shelby looked at her partner glumly. "I never even suspected her."

Kris reached over and linked her fingers with Shelby's. "You probably never had any reason to. Did she ever act suspiciously or do anything out of the ordinary?"

"No. But she was always big in the rumor mill. She's the one who told me she heard Blue was in town, and she asked a few questions about you when you first started working on the case. I never thought anything of that because she was always talking about some rumor she'd heard."

"Sounds to me like there was no reason for you to be suspicious. I wonder what her tie-in with Michael is."

Puzzled, Shelby asked, "What're you talking about?"

"I saw her in the canteen with Michael on Monday. I didn't know her identity at the time, but now it is evident that she's probably the one that passed him the information that you were headed to your mother's house after work yesterday. He fits Jonathan's description, meager as it was. We can run that license plate number tomorrow, but if it is Michael's, I doubt he registered it in his real name."

"Yeah, but I have access to each of the agent's various identities, unless he got one off the black market. I doubt he expected anyone to see him, so he might have just used whatever ID he had on him to obtain the car."

"True. Let's hope he did; I'd like to nail him. What I can't figure is why he would be shooting at you." Kris didn't expect Shelby to have an answer, and mulled the idea over in her mind. *It has to be to get to me. But why not just target me? Why Shelby?* The answer came unbidden. *To discredit me. That would be just like him. Killing me wouldn't give him any satisfaction unless he'd managed to destroy my career first. Well, two can play that game. He wants a war, he'll get it.*

"Kris? You okay?"

The operative nodded. "Just planning my next move."

"You mean *our* next move?"

Kris chuckled ruefully at having been caught thinking in the singular. "Yes. That's exactly what I meant."

Shelby returned the smile and said sweetly, "Just checking."

Glad for the cover of darkness, Kris cut the headlights when Maggie turned into an apartment complex, staying well back until the Mercedes was driven into a parking space in front of one of the garden apartments. The two women watched Maggie exit the vehicle and ascend the steps to a second-floor apartment, which she entered.

Kris glanced at Shelby's face, momentarily visible in the car headlights of a departing tenant. Her expression was strained and she looked tired. Her partner had had very little time to relax since the shooting, and that, combined with her confrontation with Jonathan, was taking a toll. The operative had intended to continue surveillance for a while to see if Maggie had any nocturnal visitors, but she was loath to do it at Shelby's expense. "How're you feeling?"

Shelby was touched by the worry in Kris' voice and smiled reassuringly. "Fairly well now. Those pills are pretty potent." She studied her companion in the dim light. "How about you? Climbing that tree had to hurt."

Kris reached over, pushing a wayward lock of hair from Shelby's face, drinking in the love she could feel emanating from the blonde woman. "It did for a while, but it's not too bad now. Aren't we a pair? I never meant for you to be hurt. I'd give anything if I could change that."

Shelby spoke softly, but with heartfelt sincerity. "I know you would, but you can't, and I'm doing just fine. So don't worry about it, okay? We've got too many other things to do right now."

Kris nodded. "Are you up to hanging out here for a little while? Maybe an hour or so, just to see if she has any visitors? It's okay if you don't want to."

"I want to." She held her wrist up until her watch was visible in the dim light. "Besides it's still early—only 9:30." Shelby privately felt as though it was midnight and she was exhausted, but she wasn't about to let Kris know that.

Still visualizing the earlier strain she'd seen on her partner's face, and feeling guilty about asking her to stay, Kris asked, "Are you sure?"

"Yes, I'm sure!" Shelby snapped. Her stomach tightened when she saw a fleeting look of hurt cross her partner's face. She laid a hand on Kris' thigh and smiled. "Thanks for caring. Now will you quit being such a worry wart?"

Kris knew she was being overprotective and chuckled at Shelby's description. "Worry wart?"

Shelby teased, "If the shoe fits..."

Kris muttered, "Go ahead, tease; paybacks are a bitch," grinning when she heard Shelby's answering chuckle.

The time passed slowly, both women tired but still hopeful of learning something new. Shelby caught herself dozing off, and broke the lengthy silence. "Do you think anyone will show up?"

Kris considered the question a moment. "Not really. But we might get lucky."

Shelby's expression turned pensive as she turned to face Kris. "Have you figured out why Michael is after me?"

"I think it's to discredit me. He blames me for him getting pulled from the field and reassigned as a technical advisor. It was his own actions that got him pulled, not my testimony. And if he's tied in with the Russians, in hindsight the incident that disgraced him makes a lot more sense. He may have had an entirely different agenda than the rest of the team. I never bought his excuses or the board's finding that he had just used poor judgment. Michael was too controlled for that."

The analyst mulled that over for a few moments. "You said that happened almost three years ago. Why did he wait so long? Why didn't he do something before now?"

Kris shrugged, speculating. "We're pretty inaccessible in the field. He'd have had no way of finding me to try and pay be back. Even those with top access don't necessarily know where we are all the time." She glanced in the side view mirror, tracking a tenant's progress to his vehicle. "Someone told him I was here, probably Maggie. We don't know what her relationship with Michael is, but she was totally focused on him that day in the canteen. I suspect they're more than casual friends."

Shelby searched her memory for what seemed liked the hundredth time for any clue she might have overlooked about Maggie's apparent disloyalty. "I wonder how long she's been providing the Russians with information."

"I don't know, but probably for a while now." Kris shifted, trying to get comfortable in the cramped confines of the car. "She seemed perfectly at ease making that drop. It would also explain how the Russians found out so quickly that I was in town."

"Yeah, that makes sense." A thought suddenly occurred to her, and she asked, "Do you think she knows you're a mole?"

Her senses fully extended, the operative's eyes never stopped perusing their surroundings as she considered Shelby's question. "No. But her handlers would want to know of any field agents at headquarters. It probably made Dimitri's day when he found out I was here."

Shelby nodded in agreement, watching a car drive past on a side street. "Once we get your mother out, he'll get what he has coming to him. It's only a matter of time."

Kris smiled at her partner's steadfast belief they would be successful, and knew Shelby's optimism was helping to fuel her own hope for her mother's safe rescue. "Have I told you lately that I love you?"

The blonde looked up at the ceiling of the car. "Lemme think: not more than twice today. Personally, I think that at least once an hour would be much more appropriate." Shelby smiled, loving the sound of Kris' laughter as it quietly surrounded her.

"Is that right? I'll be sure and keep that in mind."

"I'm gonna hold you to that." Shelby's smile faded, a serious expression replacing it. "I love you, too, Kris. Every second, every minute, every hour of every day, I wonder how I got so lucky."

Overwhelmed by Shelby's declaration, Kris swallowed, her reply trapped in her throat. Every time she looked into her partner's eyes, she was again reminded that love really did exist. It wasn't just an illusion, as she'd always believed. "I'm the one who's lucky."

They sat beside each other in the car, watching their surroundings in comfortable silence, their bond drawing them inexorably closer. Kris was first to spot the tall, dark-haired man walking up the sidewalk. "Here comes some guy. I never saw any headlights, so I doubt he lives here. He probably parked on a side street nearby."

As the figure drew closer, Shelby asked, "Is that Michael?" and glanced over at Kris, only to find her partner's eyes riveted on the newcomer.

Kris' words were laden with tension. "That's him. Now let's see if he goes to Maggie's apartment."

They followed his progress down the sidewalk and up the steps until he stopped in front of Maggie's apartment and knocked. The door opened immediately, and he disappeared inside.

Kris could see little point to remaining in the parking lot. While it would be interesting to follow Michael when he left, given the growing lateness of the evening it would be difficult to do so without alerting him to their presence. She also knew it was possible he might not leave the apartment until morning. She glanced over at Shelby. "You ready to call it a night?"

"Yeah, if you are."

The operative started the car, leaving the headlights off until they were out of sight of the apartment building. "I want to see if we can find his car."

"Good idea. It'd be nice to have proof it was Michael that shot me." Shelby began scanning the cars parked along the street, searching for a black Lincoln with a license plate matching the one Jonathan had given her earlier. Her efforts were rewarded minutes later when they located the car on a neighboring side street.

Not wanting to appear suspicious in the residential neighborhood, Kris drove past the car and headed for Shelby's apartment. "Guess that answers that."

"So, now that we know it's him, what do we do?" Shelby raised her hand to her mouth, trying to hide a yawn that wouldn't be denied.

Kris knew just how she felt, and was glad they were finally heading for the apartment. "Right now, nothing. If he knew of my connection to the Russians, he'd have already used it against me. It helps that we know who is behind the attacks and where he's been getting his information."

Shelby glanced at Kris curiously. "Aren't you going to turn them in?"

"Yeah, after we set them up so the Company can move in." Barely audibly, she added, "But not yet."

Shelby scarcely heard the whispered words, immediately understanding Kris' trepidation. If the Russians suspected the operative of setting up two of their agents, her mother would never survive long enough for them to locate her. Unable to think of anything to ease Kris' worry, she remained silent.

GREGOR HEADED THROUGH the hallways of the embassy toward Dimitri's office. He'd intended to best his superior and had failed. The Russian knew he was treading a thin line, and he considered himself very lucky not to have been sent back to the Motherland in disgrace. He'd never expected Dimitri to learn of Shelby's value on his own and then flaunt his knowledge. Now he had to convince Dimitri that he was still valuable. He had to find a way back into his superior's good graces and was willing to do anything, including grovel, to accomplish that goal.

As he neared the door, he heard Dimitri call out, "Wait, one more thing." He saw Markov re-enter the room, leaving the door ajar. "You will report any orders you receive from Gregor. Should you fail to do so, you'll end up beside him in an unmarked grave. Any questions?"

"No, Comrade."

"You are dismissed."

The cold words washed over Gregor and he quickly retreated through an open door in the hallway to prevent Markov from seeing him. He rested his head against a cool wall in the farthest corner of his hiding place, realizing it would be futile to try and reason with Dimitri. The die had been cast: he was a walking dead man.

STORMY DIDN'T GREET them at the door when they entered the apartment, and failed to appear when Kris shook the box of treats the little feline loved. "I think she's mad at us."

Shelby nodded. "Can't blame her, we've been gone so long."

After they showered, Kris helped Shelby apply a new dressing to her arm, then the two women returned to the living room to unwind before retiring. Stormy stood up on the couch, meowing loudly.

Shelby chuckled. "I think she's telling us she forgives us this time. Guess we'd better try and make it up to her."

Kris rolled her eyes, but was no less enthusiastic in greeting the ragamuffin who purred contentedly, rising up to meet the soft strokes being lavished upon her.

They had just decided to go to bed when the phone rang. Shelby glanced at the instrument, surprised. Late phone calls were always bad news, but she hesitated only momentarily before answering it. "Hello." Listening intently, she waited for a pause in the caller's stream of words and then handed the phone to Kris. "I think it's your mother."

Watching the brief play of emotions that flickered across Kris' countenance, Shelby marveled at the ease with which the operative switched to her native tongue, the guttural sounds rolling freely from her throat. While on a logical level she knew Kris wasn't an American as she'd originally thought, that knowledge didn't diminish the strangeness of hearing her converse with her mother in Russian. She welcomed the opportunity to observe a facet of her partner that hadn't been previously displayed, reminded once again of just how little they really knew about each other, and treasuring what she did.

A few short minutes later, Kris hung up the phone. She gazed at Shelby, her eyes worried. "Dimitri just wanted to remind me I've only got a couple more days to deliver your password. Very effective way to go about it."

"How's your mother holding up?"

"She's doing fine. Her only contact with anyone is when her meals are served. The hardest part for her is being so isolated, with nothing to do." Kris looked down at the floor. "She told me not to worry about her, she's not afraid of dying. Just to take care of myself. Then Dimitri took the phone from her."

Shelby put her arm around Kris, hugging her. "At least we know she's still okay."

Returning the hug, Kris said, "Yeah, you're right. Guess we'd better get some sleep."

Kris lay awake in the darkness, desperately seeking a viable plan to find her mother, and continuing to draw a blank. Short of kidnapping Markov or Gregor, she had no idea of how to locate her mother in the short amount of time left to them. If either of them disappeared, she would be the primary suspect, and Kris had no doubt Dimitri would immediately retaliate by killing her mother. Frustrated, she continued to search for a solution until her thoughts were interrupted by the quiet voice of her partner.

"Kris?"

"Hmm?"

Shelby nestled closer, concerned about the tension radiating from her bedmate. "You need to relax. You're so tight, you'll never fall asleep. Let your subconscious do the work. In the morning we can figure out a plan."

Kris sighed. "I just keep coming up empty."

"I know, sweetheart. I do too. I think we both need a good night's sleep. We'll figure out something tomorrow."

Knowing she was keeping Shelby awake, Kris focused on clearing her mind and relaxing. She leaned over and met her partner's lips for a sweet, lingering kiss, then hugged Shelby tightly, carefully staying clear of her injured arm, her own soreness overshadowed by the comforting feel of the small body tucked against her own.

She smiled when Shelby returned the hug with her good arm, each relishing the contact and drawing strength from the other.

Long moments later, their arms relaxed, but even as they fell asleep, their bodies remained in close contact.

Chapter Seventeen

ON THE ROOFTOP of a building across the street from the apartment complex, Michael relaxed for an hour before deciding it was safe enough to venture down to the parking lot he had under observation. He would've preferred to continue discrediting Blue by waging further attacks against the woman she was protecting, but he was running out of time.

In his mind, he'd already disgraced her with the shooting earlier in the week, and now he was going to execute a *coup de grâce*. Both women would die, and his goal would be achieved because Blue's reputation would be forever sullied—both by the successful earlier attack, and also by her ultimate failure to protect either of them against a car explosion.

The operative ran through his plan one last time. Knowing that the CIA would quickly cover up any incident on their own grounds, he'd discarded the idea of setting the bomb to detonate when the car was started at Shelby's workplace. Having seen a dark car drive through the parking lot several times that night, he suspected that Company agents were keeping an eye on the building, so it stood to reason that any mishap at this site would be covered up as well.

Michael knew his window of opportunity was rapidly disappearing, but he was unwilling to give the Company a chance to conceal his handiwork, so he'd broadened the focus of his attack. He grinned coldly, thinking about the modifications he'd made to the device while waiting on the roof. Their demise would be dramatic, public, and newsworthy. Knowing the women had to travel the Beltway to get to and from work, the agent had reset the detonator to explode at 53 mph. Michael felt no guilt over the innumerable accidents that were likely to occur as a result of the fiery explosion. When burning metal peppered the Beltway, the accident would become a headliner, and Blue's failure would be spectacularly demonstrated.

Staying in the darkest of the shadows, he approached their

rented green Ford Taurus and knelt down between it and the vehicle parked in the adjoining space. He removed his backpack, unzipped it, and carefully took out the small explosive device along with the tools he would need to reach the speedometer cable. Lying down on the blacktop, he scooted under the car, installed the bomb, and armed it, smiling when the tiny red light came on. He slid back out from under the car, satisfied that although the device was small, the devastating power of C4 would create an explosion equivalent to a half dozen sticks of dynamite and turn the car into a fireball. Shortly after they merged with traffic on the Beltway, the two women would be dead.

When finished, he glanced at his watch. It was 3:45 a.m. It had only taken him twenty minutes. Michael's smile widened as carefully checked the parking lot before rising to his full height and casually walking away.

KRIS AWOKE INSTANTLY, alert, as she did every morning. The primary difference in her waking routine now was that she no longer got out of bed immediately, much preferring to enjoy the precious time she got to spend lying next to the woman she loved more than life itself. Kris snuggled closer, relishing the feel of Shelby's soft skin against her own. It was such a heady feeling to wake up each morning with the smaller woman tucked against her, and to know that even in sleep their bodies remained connected, comforted by the contact.

She smiled, as the blonde, tousled head shifted on the pillow they shared. The worry lines that had marked her partner's face were absent, leaving an almost childlike innocence on her features. Kris frowned at the dark smudges showing beneath the chestnut-colored lashes, and hoped she'd still be around when they faded, not locked in some interrogation room in the stark, cold bowels of Langley. Refusing to give that very real fear a foothold, she raised her head and fleetingly kissed Shelby's cheek, surprised when the green eyes fluttered open.

"Mmm." Shelby smiled, stifling a yawn. "How about a real one, now that I'm awake."

Kris looked into the dancing green eyes and felt her heart begin thudding wildly against her chest, the way it did every single time Shelby looked at her that way. She lowered her mouth to the eagerly waiting lips and was lost in a flurry of sensations, ending the kiss breathlessly a few moments later. Her own voice sounding foreign to her ears, she croaked, "Soon." Kris' longing for the physical aspect of their relationship was reflected back at her by the passion in her partner's eyes.

Not trusting herself to speak, Shelby nodded and smiled. She was reveling in the warm glow that just a look from her partner elicited, and took a deep breath, trying to stem the desire rippling through her body. Shelby's tongue flickered over her lips, trying to recapture the feel of Kris' mouth on her own, amazed that there seemed to be so many nerve endings there that she'd never experienced before.

Kris murmured, "You're killing me," and met the moist lips for a long, lingering kiss. She broke away and suddenly sat up, the pain from her bruised muscles at the quick movement diminished by the feelings washing over her. Placing her feet on the floor, she stood up. "I gotta go take a shower."

Shelby laughed softly. "Need any help?"

Grinning wolfishly, Kris eyes slowly roamed down the blonde's body before returning to her partner's gaze and winking. "That might not be a good idea."

Flushed, Shelby watched Kris walk out of the room, buried her head in the pillow and moaned. She'd been shot, shot at, threatened, and her life was in danger, yet all of that faded into insignificance at just one look from the tall operative. She sent out a heartfelt plea to any higher entity that might be listening, to keep the two of them and Kris' mother safe, and to allow them a chance at a future together. The analyst didn't know if praying would do any good, but she decided it couldn't hurt.

A short time later, after Shelby took seconds in the shower, she joined Kris in the kitchen. She reached down and stroked Stormy, who was busy gobbling down her food. Looking up and seeing the worry in her partner's eyes, and knowing that today was likely to be another long day, she suggested, "Why don't we stop for breakfast on the way to work?"

Kris hesitated only a moment. She was anxious to put their plan into motion, but it was still early, and the idea of a little extra time with Shelby was very enticing. "Okay. Where do you want to go?"

A mischievous sparkle appeared in Shelby's eyes. "How about that little place we passed on the way to Georgetown last night?"

"Isn't that kind of out of the way? It's all stop-and-go city driving to get there."

Shelby grinned. "I know. Do you mind?"

Returning her partner's smile, Kris shook her head. "Nope. If that's where you want to go, that's where we're going."

SWIVELING IN HER office chair, Shelby glanced at Kris as she hung up the phone and grinned. "I think Jonathan's going to have a hard way to go with Mom."

Kris commented dryly, "'Bout time she listened to you for a change."

"Yeah, I know." Shelby winked at her partner. "But you know what they say—love is blind."

The simple, trite statement hit Kris like a ton of bricks. It was true. She honestly had no idea what the analyst had seen in her that was worth risking so much for.

Catching a glimpse of the vulnerability that fleetingly crossed Kris' face every now and then, Shelby stood up and crossed over to where her partner was sitting in front of her computer. Linking her fingers with the tall woman's, she spoke from her heart. "You are the best thing that ever happened to me. When you walked into Dennis' office that morning, I just knew I had to get to know you better. I'm so glad I did."

Kris gazed into the depths of the emotion-filled green eyes. "So am I." She stood up and hugged Shelby, savoring the few moments of contact before releasing her. "Did your mother agree to talk to Kim tomorrow?"

"Yeah. I think she's pretty confused right now. She really did want to believe Jonathan had changed. I feel bad for her, in a way."

Kris pursed her lips. "You're most likely saving her a lot of pain. Of both kinds."

"Yeah, you're right." Focusing on the task at hand, she asked, "What time are you leaving?"

The operative thought quickly. It would only take her a few minutes to get to her safe deposit box at the bank to pick up the bugs, tape recorder, and phone tap. Driving to Maggie's apartment would take the longest, but getting inside the apartment to install the bugs wouldn't be a problem. "I might as well go now and get it over with. I shouldn't be gone more than an hour."

"Okay. I'll keep checking the hall." Shelby shook her head, sighing. "I can't believe I've been out there four times already and haven't managed to catch her once."

Kris rolled her eyes. "Maybe you'll get lucky next time."

Shelby nodded. "I hope so, or there isn't going to be much sense in bugging her apartment." She wrapped her arms around Kris and laid her head against her chest. "Hurry back."

The tall woman smiled and returned the embrace. "Count on it."

TEN MINUTES AFTER Kris left, Shelby ventured out into the hallway again and headed for the vending machines. She grinned inwardly when she saw Maggie exit of her office, headed in the same direction.

"Hey, Maggie."

"Hi, Shelby. I haven't seen lately! Did the cops ever catch that guy that took a shot at you?"

The analyst paused, surprised that Maggie would even mention the incident. "You know about that?"

"Yeah." Maggie grinned conspiratorially and shrugged. "It's all over the grapevine."

Shelby knew that wasn't true, but played along. "I should've guessed. Heard anything good lately?"

"Not really. Oh wait, yes I did. Dennis is getting reassigned to Strategic Ops."

Snorting, Shelby said, "You've gotta be kidding me!"

Maggie grinned. "That's what I thought, too, but it's true."

Since Maggie was now in full gossip mode, Shelby decided it was the right time to plant her own bit of misinformation. "Hey, guess what I heard."

Looking at Shelby in surprise, Maggie asked, "What?"

"You remember when you told me Blue was at headquarters?" When Maggie nodded, Shelby continued. "Jet and Silver are here now, too."

Maggie sucked in a breath. "No kidding. Wonder why."

"I don't know, but it seems funny all three of those operatives would be here at the same time. Must be getting ready for something big to go down. We'll probably never know, though."

Trying not to appear too interested, Maggie nodded. "You're right, but I'm still going to put out some feelers. If I find out anything, I'll let you know."

Shelby smiled. "Thanks. You always hear a lot more than I do."

"That's because you hardly ever leave your office."

Shrugging, Shelby said, "I know, but Dennis has really been piling on the work."

Maggie nodded knowingly. "Well, I'm sure glad I don't work for him."

"You're lucky. Speaking of which, I'd better get back. See you later."

"Okay." Maggie watched Shelby walk back to her office, uneasy about the fact that three wet operatives had been recalled at the same time. She wouldn't be able to go straight home after work after all.

KRIS TOOK ONE last look around the apartment. It was apparent that Maggie was used to living luxuriously. All the furnishings and electronic equipment were top quality, and the computer sitting in the spare bedroom was a brand new Dell. The operative snorted derisively. The woman was obviously being well paid for her information, and yet she hadn't even bothered to have a security system installed. Not that it would have stopped any agent from getting in, but it would've been a deterrent.

Satisfied with the placement of the eavesdropping bugs, she glanced at her watch and hurriedly left the apartment. It had taken her longer to get to Maggie's than she'd intended because the traitor's apartment was not easily accessible from the Beltway, so she had taken the slower main thoroughfares and would be returning the same way. She had no intention of worrying her partner unnecessarily with a prolonged absence, and was going to have to hustle to get back within the hour she'd allotted.

THE OPERATIVE SAT in the car impatiently tapping her fingers on the wide bar across the center of the steering wheel. "At this rate, we'll never beat her to the drop."

Reaching over and laying her hand on the tall woman's leg, Shelby said, "Hey, relax a little. She probably has to come this way, too, and she doesn't even leave work for another half hour."

Kris forced herself to relax. Shelby was right. It just seemed that everything was working against them today. Normally, it only took twenty-five minutes to reach Georgetown on the Beltway, even in rush hour traffic, but today they hadn't crawled above 10 mph. Kris sighed inwardly. The traffic bulletin on the radio had indicated that the accident was just this side of their exit, so the gridlock wasn't likely to improve until they exited the highway. "The camera's all set?"

Shelby gently squeezed the leg her hand rested on. "Yep. New roll of film, and I've got such a high-powered lens, it should pick up her nose hairs. But you knew that already."

Kris quickly glanced at Shelby and found herself finally relaxing as she returned the warm grin directed at her. "Busted, huh?"

"Yep. Just think, by the end of the evening, we'll have everything we need on Maggie, and on Michael too, I bet."

"I hope so, because we're running out of time. I've got to contact Sergei and set up a meet. I'm just wondering what kind of double-cross he has set up. He's not going to just walk away happy."

A cold chill ran down Shelby's back. "Are you saying—"

"I'm just saying that I don't trust him. We've got to be prepared for anything."

Shelby glanced away, her thoughts turbulent. While she wanted an end to the danger and uncertainty, the possibility of disaster was all too real, and any resolution had the very real potential to separate her and Kris, perhaps forever. There were just so many chance variables. Sergei could kill Kris' mother, the operative could be arrested once she came clean with Earl, the meet could end up being a set-up, with Kris the target... Her thoughts trailed off, unwilling to process the last image. Not one of the scenarios was acceptable, some even less so than others. Shelby was finding it harder and harder to lend positive support in what seemed more and more like a no-win situation.

Wondering why her partner had become so quiet, Kris glanced at Shelby and was only able to see a side view of her face as she gazed out the window. What she saw hit her hard. The analyst's countenance was a mixture of worry, sadness and fear. The woman who had become her rock needed some support, and she'd been too immersed in the case to even see it. She finished formulating her strategy and decided to bounce it off Shelby, deciding that it might ease some of her concern. It was chock full of pitfalls, but it was the best she'd been able to come up with. "Shelby."

"Hmm?" Taking a moment to make sure her face didn't reflect her doubts, Shelby briefly met the blue eyes before they turned back to the road.

"You're worried, aren't you?"

Shelby rolled her eyes. "Uh, duh. Aren't you?"

"Yeah." Kris reached over and linked her fingers with Shelby's. "But I think we've got a good chance to pull this off. If we get everything we need tonight, I'm gonna call Sergei tomorrow and set up a meet on Sunday. Once that's firmed up, I'll call Earl and arrange for a team to be at whatever location Sergei names."

Shelby gazed at the now confident expression on her partner's face. "You make it sound so simple, but it's not. What if Sergei doesn't bring your mother along? And even if he does, how are you going to get her out of there without Earl knowing about her?"

Kris shrugged. "I'll tell Sergei there is no negotiating—I see my mother or he doesn't get the password. He'll go for it because he doesn't have a choice. Besides, he thinks he's in the driver's seat, and in a normal situation, he'd be right. Who could I turn to?" Squeezing, Shelby's hand, she continued, "He didn't count on you. And that's why we'll win."

The confident words and reassuring contact grounded Shelby, and she suddenly felt her confidence and optimism take a skyward leap. "What about your mother?"

"After I go inside, you bring the car around to the back of the house. Once I signal Earl's team, I'll get my mother to the rear of the house and once you and Mom are safe, I'll turn myself in."

"No!"

The operative's brow furrowed, surprised at the vehement response. "What do you mean, no?"

"That won't work. You've got to meet Earl ahead of time and

tell him the truth. We do it your way and you don't have anything left to bargain with; they'll already have Sergei."

"Yeah, but they can't prove he's Sergei. They need my testimony to do that."

Shelby shook her head in disagreement. "Maybe. But that's not good enough. What if they just haul in some of the men that he has with him? Wouldn't be the first time they ignored diplomatic immunity when they suspected someone of being a spy."

Kris considered Shelby's words carefully. She knew her plan wasn't perfect, and her partner's concern was valid. If the Company got what they needed at the time of the bust, she would lose any advantage in the bargaining process. And if she lost that, she could lose everything she was fighting for. The agent sighed and ran a hand through her hair, glad they'd finally inched their way to the exit. "You're right. I'll have to set up a time to meet with Earl and explain it all to him." Kris gazed at Shelby fleetingly before turning her attention back to the road. "You do know that he might ask me to surrender to him right then and there?"

"He could, but I don't think he will. You said you trusted Earl. I've got a feeling he trusts you, too. Even if he did want to take you into custody, all you'd have to do is tell him that my safety would be jeopardized." Shelby gazed into Kris' eyes. "And it would be, so you convince him, okay?"

Kris took a steadying breath at the implications of the frank statement. "He'll agree or he'll wake up with a terrible headache after I leave."

"I'm going with you and waiting in the car."

One look at the determined expression on her partner's face and Kris swallowed her protest. "Okay."

Shelby hid her surprise, pleased at the easy victory. "Good. Now let's go catch us some spies."

Kris raised her eyebrows and shook her head as she drove slowly through the congested Washington streets.

SHELBY COULD SEE her partner growing more restless with each passing minute. They'd been sitting in the car for more than an hour and a half, and still Maggie hadn't appeared. All talked out about the case and their plans, she searched for a light topic. "If you could live anywhere you wanted to, where would you go?"

Raising an eyebrow at the off the wall question, Kris quirked a half smile. "That's easy: wherever you were."

Though pleased by her partner's answer, Shelby protested, "I was being serious."

"So was I." Kris met Shelby's eyes and held them for a moment before returning her gaze to their surroundings. "I don't care where I live if I'm with you. If you're happy, I'll be happy. That's what's important to me, not where we are."

Shelby basked in the warmth generated by the words, and a silly grin appeared on her face. "I never knew you were such a romantic."

Kris could feel the blood rushing to her face and she glanced away. *A romantic? Me? No way! Let's be honest here—maybe a little where Shelby's concerned.*

The blonde woman cleared her throat, smiling warmly when Kris faced her. "That's not a bad thing. But don't worry, I won't tell anyone."

Kris shrugged, feigning indifference. "Wouldn't matter anyway. No one would believe you."

"Hmm. You don't think so?" Her eyes dancing mischievously, Shelby challenged, "Want to place a wager on that?"

"No!"

Shelby nodded. "Don't worry, sweetheart, your secret's safe with me." She chuckled when Kris' face reddened again, but her merriment died abruptly when Kris spoke.

"There she is." Kris inclined her head towards the right side of the street. "See the guy in the gray jogging suit? Right behind him."

The analyst already had the camera up and was snapping off shots as she tracked the woman's progress. Her photographic skill would be sorely tested because she had to have a shot of Maggie making the actual drop in the blind man's cauldron.

Kris listened to the whir of the camera as her partner fired off shot after shot until Maggie had made the drop and disappeared from sight. She waited for fifteen minutes to ensure Maggie had vacated the area, then turned to Shelby. "Come on. Let's go get it."

Stopping periodically along the street to gaze into shop windows, Shelby and Kris walked nonchalantly towards the drop point. Shelby was fully aware that the operative stayed between her and the street, protecting her each time they stopped at a storefront. It was a very comforting feeling.

Shelby circled behind him looking for the message container while Blue leaned over the blind man sitting on the ground. "Looks like you had a good day. People must be feeling generous."

The man nodded. "Perhaps you could spare a little something?"

"Sure," the agent said as she dropped some coins into the metal cup on the ground next to him.

In a lightning fast move, he grabbed Shelby's arm just as she retrieved the small microfiche container, but he froze when the cool, hard metal of a gun's bore pressed against his neck and the sound of a round being chambered registered.

Blue growled, "Let go of her arm." With her jacket loosely

draped over her arm and weapon, she was carefully shielding the gun from casual onlookers.

He wasted no time, immediately releasing the slender arm. "Please, they will kill me."

"No they won't. Because the only way they know there was a drop is if you tell them. But I would suggest you find another way to supplement your income."

The man's head bobbed up and down. "Yes, yes, I will do that."

Kris removed her weapon from his throat, glancing around to make sure no one was watching them. "Good. You'll live a lot longer if you do."

She nodded to Shelby and they began retracing their steps to the car. Once they departed the area, the analyst asked, "Now, on to Maggie's?"

"Yeah, but let's stop at the Burger King drive through along the way. You've gotta be hungry, I know I am."

Shelby was actually starved, but she didn't want Kris' concern for her to jeopardize getting the information they needed. "You sure we have time?"

Kris smiled reassuringly. "When the phone tap or bugs are activated, they automatically send signals to a remote tape recorder I hid outside her apartment. We won't miss anything. I just want to make sure we're there when Michael arrives. Pictures are worth a thousand words."

"So why did you bring that little tape recorder if it's already being recorded. In case someone finds the other one?"

"Partly, but also in case of a malfunction. I don't want to take any chances."

Shelby nodded in agreement and shifted in her seat. Lately, it seemed like she was spending a lot of hours in a car. She'd be glad when the repairs to her own were finished; it was a lot more comfortable than the rental was. She rewound the roll of film in the camera, then carefully removed it, secured it in the plastic container and placed it in her purse. She'd shot off twenty pictures, and needed a new roll with faster speed for the photos of Michael. It would most likely be at least dusk by the time he appeared, if he showed at all.

FOLLOWING A SHORTCUT Shelby suggested to bypass most of the busier thoroughfares, a short time later the two women parked in a congested area of the parking lot of Maggie apartment complex. Shelby was leaning against the car door, and straightened when the tape recorder came to life. Listening to it, she looked at Kris and gave her a thumbs up. "Bingo!"

The operative grinned at the happy smile on her partner's face.

Maggie had called Michael and he was due to arrive within half an hour. "Might be able to get an early night in after all. Once she tells him, we leave. No sense hanging around here and taking a chance on being spotted."

"Yes! Am I ever ready to get out of this car." Shelby raised up in her seat and murmured, "My poor butt!"

"Aw. You want me to kiss it and make it better." Kris laughed quietly at the startled expression on Shelby's face.

Recovering quickly, the analyst teased, "Well, I can think of places I'd rather have you kiss, but if that's what turns you on..."

Kris purred, "Oh, honey, everything about you turns me on."

The seductive tone of voice had its desired effect and Shelby flushed. "You are a tease!"

Kris' face was the epitome of innocence. *"Moi?"*

"Okay, Ms. Innocent; paybacks are a bitch."

The operative trapped a guffaw in her throat, but couldn't stop the snort accompanying it. *Ms. Innocent? Nothing could be further from the truth.*

Shelby chuckled. "Just wait, you'll see."

"I'm..." Kris stopped, suddenly all business. "He's here already. He's coming from the same direction he did last time. You ready?"

The analyst had automatically reached for the camera the moment her partner's expression changed, and it was now in position and focused on the tall man striding up the sidewalk. She snapped away, hoping to catch Maggie on film when the door opened.

After Michael entered the apartment and closed the door, Shelby set the camera down and glanced at Kris. "I got the apartment number and I might have gotten a clear shot of Maggie and Michael together. We'll have to wait and see."

Kris reached over and squeezed Shelby's hand. "Good job."

They didn't have long to wait before Maggie relayed the manufactured information Shelby had fed her. Kris started the car. "The other tape player will pick up anything else they talk about, but we've got them cold with what we've got right here."

Shelby nodded in agreement. "Too bad it's too late to take the film to the one hour developing at Wal-Mart. I don't want to take a chance on just dropping it off. I'm not letting it out of my sight."

"We can take it in tomorrow morning." Kris placed her hand on the smaller one resting on her thigh. "Thanks."

"You're welcome, but just remember—I've got a personal stake in this." Shelby glanced at Kris and smiled. "You."

Kris didn't answer but wrapped her hand around the one beneath hers, knowing Shelby would understand her unspoken feelings. "I'm going to call Earl when we get back to the apartment and set up a time to meet with him tomorrow. I'll wait to see how that goes before calling Sergei."

"Sounds good. I'll just be glad when this is all over."

Sighing, Kris said, "You and me both."

A short time later they were sitting on the couch, lavishing attention on Stormy and unwinding after the long day. Her eyes faraway and dreamy, Shelby glanced over at Kris. "I wonder what it would be like if we were just two normal people who met someplace and were attracted and fell in love. Like maybe while we were on vacation or something, and we got to do fun tourist things. And we moved in together, and there were no people shooting at us, or spies after us. If I didn't work for the CIA, and you didn't...you know..."

Kris raised an eyebrow, and smiled. "If everything works out, I won't be doing any more 'you know.'" Turning thoughtful, Kris said, "I guess I never thought of that, because nothing about my life has been normal for such a long time." *If we get out of this, I'll take you on that vacation.*

Shelby's expression turned puzzled. "What will you do? What do you want to do?"

Kris shrugged. "I don't know. I like electronics and computers, and I've always been amazed at how easy it is to crack any security system I've come up against. I've often entertained the idea of developing one that can't be easily breached and then marketing it. It would be a lucrative business because I know the weaknesses of most of the others on the market."

GREGOR SAT INDECISIVELY in the car, weighing the risks of his limited options. Sighing, he decided that although the odds with his selected course of action were not favorable, the only alternative was death. So, ignoring his apprehension, he opened the door and walked across the street to the apartment complex. He paused at the bottom of the steps, squared his shoulders, and began the short climb to the second floor, rehearsing his approach one final time. Rapping on the door, he waited impatiently for it to be answered, not wanting to remain exposed any longer than necessary.

Shelby stopped mid-sentence when the knocking sounded, and shook her head when Kris looked at her questioningly. Watching Kris stand and pick up her gun in one fluid movement, she was once again amazed at the vast differences in their world's. The analyst tracked her partner's movements to the door, curious about who could be visiting so late, but apprehensive, too.

Blue stood to one side of the door and raised her voice loudly enough to carry beyond the barrier. "Who is it?"

"Bear."

She narrowed her eyes at the familiar voice and glanced quickly through the peephole. "Why are you here?"

"Let me in. I can tell you where your mother is."

Blue thought rapidly, refusing to get her hopes up. She had no idea what Gregor was up to, but her time was running out, and she felt she had nothing to lose by listening to what he had to say. The operative unlocked the deadbolt, leaving the chain in place. Keeping her gun aimed at the opening, she ordered, "Throw your guns in here. Both of them."

She watched a .44 Magnum slide across the floor, followed by a .38 Special. Keeping her eyes trained on the opening, she waved to Shelby and pointed to the weapons, smiling her thanks when the woman picked up both guns and set them on the dining room table. She released the chain, kicked the door open, and aimed her gun at Gregor's chest. Once he crossed the threshold, she said, "Close and lock the door."

Gregor followed her instructions with slow deliberate movements. At her command, he faced the wall and placed his hands against it. The cold steel of her gun against his neck brought home the harsh reality of just how precarious his situation was.

When her frisk revealed no other weapons, Blue instructed, "Turn around and start talking."

"I want to make a deal. In exchange for political asylum, I will tell you where your mother is."

Blue snorted derisively. "Don't you think you're coming to the wrong person for that?"

"No. Your superiors do not know of our connection."

"Why now?"

The Russian thought over his words carefully. He hadn't expected instant cooperation, and what he related now would be the deciding factor. Knowing she hated the man he knew as Dimitri, he decided to be honest. "Once he has what he wants, Dimitri will kill you and your mother. He is also planning my termination at the end of this mission."

Blue wasn't surprised at Sergei's plans for her and her mother. She'd already figured their deaths were inevitable. What did surprise her was that Gregor had been included in the execution order. "Why has your death been ordered?"

The Russian looked at Shelby. "I knew how valuable she was. I failed to relay that information. Dimitri found out."

Blue laughed coldly as the puzzle pieces fell into place. "You're a fool. Thought you'd go over his head and it backfired." She knew Sergei would never tolerate disloyalty. "You tell me where my mother is, then I'll talk to my boss about your request."

Gregor looked at Blue angrily. "I am not stupid! I have no guarantee that you will help me once your mother is released."

"What about the risk I'm taking by approaching my superiors about you? You know who I am. The only risk you're taking is losing your bargaining chip for my help. If I arrange a meet between you and my superiors, I risk my life and freedom."

The Russian had not anticipated her coldly logical assessment. He shrugged his shoulders. "As you wish. I will contact the CIA directly."

Blue snorted. "And by the time you get through the layers of bureaucracy, Sergei's informants will have already notified him." She nodded towards the door, indicating the conversation was over.

Shelby sat on the couch, watching the exchange intently. Kris was playing a dangerous game by even considering the Russian's offer, but it was the closest they'd come to getting a lead on the whereabouts of her partner's mother's without contacting Sergei. It would greatly increase the chances of a safe rescue. Furthermore, Sergei was by far the best bargaining chip her partner had. If Gregor made good on his threat to contact the CIA, Kris' own plans could go up in smoke and she could lose her mother *and* her freedom.

The double agent's countenance revealed none of her qualms as she watched Gregor unlock and open the door. She breathed an inward sigh of relief when the Russian closed the door and turned back to face her.

Gregor cursed inwardly, hating the woman who had precipitated his fall from grace. "I agree to tell you where your mother is only if you arrange my transfer at the time of her rescue."

Blue nodded. "Deal."

MICHAEL WAITED UNTIL the parking lot was dark and quiet. He had no intention of sitting on the roof another night. It would only take him a few minutes to reset the detonator to go off at 35 mph. He cursed Blue's good luck at never having attained a speed of 53 mph that entire day, and decided to bring his plans to a head. He finished his adjustments to the explosive device a short time later and departed.

Gregor was in his car, ready to start it, when he saw the tall man stand up from his crouch next to the rental car Blue had been driving. There was something familiar about the man, but it was too dark for Gregor to see him clearly. Suspicious, he watched until the figure disappeared from sight.

Starting the car, he began driving around aimlessly, debating what to do. An hour later, he made his decision. He didn't care about what ultimately happened to Blue, but the fact remained that right now he needed her. Sighing, he picked up the phone and dialed her number.

The shrill ring of the cell phone woke both women. Kris reached over Shelby to the nightstand and grabbed it. "Yeah."

"Check your car very carefully in the morning."

Kris narrowed her eyes at the sound of Gregor's voice. "You want to explain that?"

"When I left, I saw someone suspicious near your car."

Kris snorted. "And you just realized you still needed me, right?"

"Something like that." Gregor disconnected.

Shelby turned tired eyes to Kris. "What's going on?"

"That was the guy who was here tonight. He thinks someone may have been tampering with the car. Someone just refuses to give up."

Shelby sighed audibly. "Great. At least he told us."

"Yeah, but only because he needs us." Kris returned to her warm spot next to Shelby and fleetingly kissed her partner. "Don't worry. I'll check it out in the morning. It's too dark to do anything about it now." Kissing Shelby again, she said, "We'd better get some sleep."

Shelby relaxed against her companion and fell asleep, the long day taking its toll. Her dreams were full of love and a lifetime of happiness with the woman at her side, where danger didn't lurk around every corner and no one was trying to kill them.

KRIS HUGGED SHELBY. "Would you quit worrying? I haven't yet come across a bomb I couldn't disarm."

"Yeah, because if you had, you wouldn't be here now." Shelby spoke the words lightly, but meant what she'd said.

"Oh, ye of little faith." Kris kissed Shelby, then released her and picked up the wire cutters, screwdriver, pliers and flashlight her partner had provided. "Be back in a few."

"Be careful."

Kris smiled reassuringly and left the apartment. She checked out the parking lot thoroughly before sliding under the car and shining the light upwards, almost immediately spotting the hole that had been drilled into the metal. Aiming the flashlight into the opening, she saw the telltale red blinking light and began the tedious job of disarming the explosive device.

Shelby stood out of sight at the balcony window, her eyes trained on the rental car. She couldn't see Kris, and her emotions fluctuated wildly between hope that any explosive would be easily disarmed and terror for her partner's safety.

When she finally saw Kris reappear next to the car, she sank down onto the couch, her knees weak with the visceral relief that washed over her. A few minutes later, she greeted Kris at the door with a bear hug, which her partner enthusiastically returned.

THE ANALYST SAT in the rental car across the street from the outdoor café, carefully studying Kris and Earl and trying to assess the director's reaction to her partner's revelations. Shelby sighed. She couldn't tell anything from either countenance, and wondered if all wet operatives protected themselves by remaining so outwardly unaffected.

She saw a sudden flicker of anger cross Kris' face but it was gone in a second, replaced by the stoic look that Kris donned when fully tense and alert. Frustrated that she couldn't hear the conversation, Shelby studied Earl's face carefully for any indication of what had caused her partner's anger.

EARL STARED AT, shocked and stunned by what he'd just heard, trying to maintain his composure and not allow the sudden anger of betrayal he felt to surface. This was one of the Company's top operatives. He'd trained her, mentored her and supported her, only to learn that she was a mole.

He tried to wrap his mind around the idea that she was a Russian, but was having difficulty doing so. Earl liked and respected Blue, making her revelation much harder to take; an enemy agent was an enemy agent, regardless of how he felt about her. He looked up when a low, bitter voice interrupted his tumultuous thoughts.

"Tell me this, Earl. What if you were stolen from your mother as a child, thrown into a training facility for double agents, sent to an enemy land, and then against all odds grew to love the country you were supposed to hate? How would you feel; what would you have done?"

The director gazed into the frustrated, angry blue eyes glaring at him. *What would I have done? She's in a no-win situation.* Blue had been a loyal operative for almost ten years, and she needed his support. The intuition he had depended on all his life was sure that she was telling the truth and could be trusted to deliver exactly what she'd promised. It was the fallout afterward that had him worried.

Making his decision to trust his instincts, Earl knew he would most likely face a board of inquiry for not forwarding this information to his superiors immediately. Although his heart wasn't in it, he made one last attempt to do it the Company way.

"I need to take you into custody." When he saw her eyes narrow, he quickly added, "You'll be in on the whole operation. I know we can't set it up without you. You will remain with me, directing the agents. Once we rescue your mother, we'll arrest Sergei and take Gregor into protective custody."

Irritated at Earl's suggested compromise, Kris leaned across the table. "No way! My mother is in there, and I'm going in. No disrespect intended, but I have a lot better chance of getting her out safely than your team would."

Earl eyed her impassively, giving no outward indication of what he was thinking.

Kris quietly reminded her boss what was at stake. "I'm giving you one of Russia's top spies, another that wants political asylum, plus a double agent and a traitor. In return, all I'm asking is to participate in the operation, and for you to request political asylum and immunity for me."

Earl sighed and, with a touch of acidity, asked, "Anything else?"

"You arrange for my mother to stay in the country and get a green card. Sergei has powerful friends, and she'd be dead within minutes of getting off the plane back in Russia. I want her dropped off at Shelby's apartment. She's agreed to let her stay there temporarily. Now that's the deal, or I'm outta here. Up to you."

Earl met Kris' steady gaze. "You don't want much, do you? Let's see if I've got this right." He ticked off each point on a finger as he enumerated. "You're a mole but you refuse to turn yourself in until your mother is rescued; you want a green card for your mother; you refuse to allow me to assign another operative to Shelby, who you've brainwashed into helping you..."

Kris let the comment about brainwashing Shelby slide. It would help protect her partner from any potential fallout. When she was debriefed, she intended to exonerate Shelby anyway. Interrupting Earl, she repeated, "You get Sergei, Gregor, Michael and Maggie. I think that should count for something. Besides, I know who we're up against. I have a lot better chance of protecting Shelby before the bust, and my mother during the rescue operation, than any of the other operatives. All I'm asking for is a deal for me and safety for my mother and Shelby."

"So I should risk my career by not taking you into custody now. I don't have the authority to agree to this deal, and you know it."

"You only have to wait until after my mother is safe and you have detained the others, then I'll turn myself in." Kris sighed. "If you had the authority, would you agree to the deal?"

Earl studied the woman sitting across from him and nodded his head. "Yes. I don't doubt your loyalty." He sat back, considering. "Okay. You call me with the time and place, and I'll have a team there."

Kris nodded and stood up, inwardly sighing with relief. She

paused when Earl spoke again.

"For whatever it's worth—I'll go to bat for you."

The operative watched in stunned disbelief as Earl rose and walked away. She'd known he didn't have the authority to grant her immunity, but he was willing to risk his reputation and his career on her, and that was more than she'd dared hope for.

Shelby waited impatiently for Kris to get in the car. "What did he say?"

"He agreed to send in a team with the understanding I turn myself in after the operation goes down." Kris glanced at Shelby, to gauge her reaction. "He said he'd go to bat for me when it was all over. I don't know how much good it'll do, but it was nice to hear."

Her face guarded, the analyst met Kris' eyes. "I knew he'd help you." However, Shelby was really worried about what would happen after Kris was taken into custody. What if Earl's support wasn't enough? What if they wouldn't let her go free, or put her in jail, or even sent her back to Russia?

Kris could see the worry in her partner's eyes; it mirrored her own doubts. There was nothing she could say to reassure Shelby, so she started the car and merged into the traffic.

WISHING THAT TIME could stand still, Shelby sat on the couch nestled against Kris and absorbing the feel and scent that was uniquely her partner's. Neither of them had talked much since they had returned to the apartment, and even Stormy purring on her lap didn't bring the analyst the pleasure that it usually did.

Kris had arranged the meet with Sergei for 8:00 p.m. that evening, and the point of no return was approaching way too quickly for Shelby. She wanted her partner's mother to be freed, but any sense of satisfaction that would be derived from a successful rescue operation was quelled by the thought of never seeing Kris again once she walked out the door.

Gregor had called and told Kris he would be picking her up at 7:30 p.m. and that Markov would be driving. Her emotions seesawing between despair and hope for the future, Shelby listened resolutely as Kris passed the information on to Earl. She had wanted to go along but Kris had begged her to remain behind, explaining that she couldn't protect both Shelby and her mother in what could become a shootout. Knowing what her partner said made sense, Shelby agreed, though sitting at the apartment just waiting would be unbearable.

The operative's mind was attuned to the smaller woman sitting against her, even as she ran various scenarios through her mind trying to mentally prepare herself for any surprises Sergei might have in store. Setting her thoughts of the meet aside, she tightened her hold on Shelby.

Kris thought about the two private messages she'd sent off – the last one on Thursday—neither of which had been acknowledged. There was one important thing from her past that she hadn't been able to share with Shelby, and was now glad she hadn't. What she'd hoped would be her ace in the hole had failed to materialize, and Kris was glad that she hadn't given her partner any false hope. She was on her own. Only fate knew what the future held. She picked up Shelby's hand in her lap and squeezed it.

Kris began speaking haltingly. "No matter what happens, remember that I love you. You are the most important thing in my life, and if—if I can't come back..." That train of thought was too dismal; her soul shriveled at the very notion of never returning to the woman she loved. Knowing she had to be strong for her partner, she struggled to hold the incipient depression at bay. "You will always be first in my heart, no matter where I am, or what I'm doing, whether we're together or apart. I just need you to know that."

A tear slid down Shelby's cheek. Kris had to be a lot more worried about the outcome than she'd been letting on, because that was as close to a farewell as she could get without actually mentioning those hated words: good bye. She tried to smile as Kris wiped the wetness from her face with a thumb. "I'm just worried."

"You've got good reason to be." Kris could feel her partner's pain. If only she could reassure her, say anything to alleviate Shelby's doubts and fears, but she couldn't lie to her. And it tore at the Russian's heart to see the sadness in those beautiful green eyes.

Shelby's troubled eyes gazed into vivid blue ones. "They owe you, Kris. You've been just as loyal as a native-born citizen, and risked your life time and again for this country. They've just got to take that into consideration."

Kris smiled ruefully. "Hopefully, they will." She was counting on the government of the country she had come to love as her own, and hoped that what she was offering would persuade even the most paranoid official of her fealty. She glanced at her watch; they only had minutes before the two agents arrived to take over guarding Shelby. She leaned down and placed her hand under Shelby's chin, urging it up, then brought her lips down to meet her partner's mouth—savoring the feel, memorizing each sensation, and wondering if it would be the last kiss they would ever share.

Shelby relished the feelings suffusing her body, and conveyed her own love for Kris through the simple contact that had started as a gentle kiss and became so much more. All of each woman's hopes and fears and doubts were conveyed to the other, neither wishing to relinquish the contact until taking a breath ceased to be a choice.

Kris rested her chin on Shelby's head, enjoying the feel of her partner's face resting against her breasts. She could feel their hearts beating in unison, and once their breathing slowed she greedily bent her head down, seeking the sensuous lips for another stolen moment. Parting at last, they gazed into each other's eyes. Words weren't necessary. Their body language spoke volumes as they leaned against each other.

When the doorbell sounded, Kris reluctantly released Shelby and admitted the two agents. The moment Shelby had been dreading had arrived. She tried unsuccessfully to stop the tears from filling her eyes and her voice from catching as she said, "Be careful."

Kris tried to quirk a half-smile, but failed miserably. Her own heart heavy, she just nodded and walked down the steps to whatever destiny fate had in store for her.

SERGEI SAT ON one of the comfortable couches in the living room of the safe house. Blue had called him late that morning and reported that she had the password, but she insisted on seeing her mother at the time of the exchange. The Russian had readily agreed to her condition, knowing that she'd get the added bonus of watching her mother die before she met the same fate. It would be a satisfying evening and a great victory for his homeland, because the password would allow them access to even the most sensitive information at the CIA.

Sergei thought back on the conversation. After some minor obligatory protests, he'd agreed to all of her terms and arranged for Markov and Gregor to pick her up and bring her to the safe house. He wanted to ensure that she came alone, warning Markov to be especially alert for any tails.

Fully respecting his opponent's skill, Sergei reviewed his defenses. He had six of his best men in place, only two of whom would be visible. The other four were hidden in the house—two assigned to windows on opposite sides of the house to watch for suspicious vehicles approaching from either direction, one guarding Blue's mother, and the other in the adjoining room. With her mother in the house, he didn't expect Blue to launch an attack, but Sergei knew that overconfidence was the most frequent cause of failure for people in his line of work and he didn't intend to be caught unprepared.

BLUE HAD RELAYED Gregor's report that beside himself and a driver, at least five more Russian agents and Sergei would be present at the safe house. Earl put two teams on alert, and they had been in place within thirty minutes of receiving the address. He lifted a pair of binoculars to his eyes, carefully searching the windows of the safe house for any activity. His vigilance paid off when a miniscule movement disturbed a curtain in an upstairs window.

Because he had to wait until Blue gave the signal, Earl's options were limited, but he had four agents out of sight on the roof of the target structure. When he gave the order, they would rappel through the upstairs windows and take out the guards on that level. Snipers would cover the windows while there was a simultaneous entry at both outside entrances.

Earl tensed as a blue Ford Taurus pulled into the driveway and the three passengers disembarked. Poised for action, he signaled their arrival to his team.

FLANKED BY GREGOR and Markov, Blue strode into the house where she found Sergei sitting on the couch, smiling.

"I'm so glad we've come to an understanding. I really didn't want to kill your mother so soon after such a warm reunion."

Keeping her voice expressionless, Blue asked, "Where is she?"

"She'll be joining us once you give me the password." Sergei smiled coldly, knowing the agent wouldn't agree, but having fun at her expense.

Refusing to be baited, Blue shrugged. "That isn't the deal."

Sergei eyes turned cold. "You still don't understand who's in charge here, do you?"

Meeting his gaze with a glare, she said, "What are you going to do, try and beat the password out of me? Have you forgotten the lessons you taught me?" Having made her point, Blue crossed her arms. "Let's cut the shit and get down to business."

The Russian smiled, imagining the slow, torturous death he had planned for his one-time protégée. He glanced at Markov and nodded. "Get her."

Blue's demeanor was calm but every muscle was tense, alerted by the adrenaline surging through her body. Her only weapon was a small .38 tucked into her waistband, just out of sight beneath her jacket; in order for their plan to succeed, she would have to get very close to her mother. When her mother appeared a short time later, she was flanked by Markov and another agent. Ignoring Sergei, she asked, "Are you okay?" and began walking toward the older woman.

Sergei moved to intercept her. "Oh no; first, the password."

The operative narrowed her eyes and spat, "Leprechaun." Pushing past the Russian, she approached her mother, drawing her into a hug while activating the transmitter she'd installed on her cell phone. Markov and the other agent glanced at their superior, awaiting orders.

Sergei watched the reunion with interest. It never failed to amaze him how a threat to a family member could render otherwise effective operatives helpless. This was going to be an enjoyable killing. Deciding the reunion had lasted long enough, he said, "One thing more." Waiting for Blue to turn around so he could see her face at the moment of her mother's death, he was pulling out his weapon as the front door crashed open.

Blue swept Masha's feet from beneath her and threw her weight against the older woman, drawing her weapon as they fell to the floor, ignoring her mother's grunt at the hard landing. The sounds of gunfire echoed through the room, and the operative targeted the Russian nearest her mother, inflicting a leg wound that dropped him to the floor.

Vaguely aware of shots being fired in the upper levels of the house, she quickly located Sergei behind the couch. Unwilling to leave her mother, she carefully aimed for the spymaster's arm, hoping to incapacitate him and end the gun battle. Before she could squeeze off a shot, Blue watched in horror as the Russian's head exploded, splattering the couch and floor around him with blood and gray matter.

She heard her mother gasp and felt the older woman's heart thundering at the sight of the carnage in front of them. Tracking the direction of the shot with her own weapon, she saw Gregor drop his gun as one of Earl's agents fired a round into his bicep. Her heart sank; she'd just lost her most valuable bargaining chip.

Chapter Eighteen

SHELBY ALMOST TRIPPED over Stormy on her way to the door. Glancing out the peephole, she opened the door to admit Earl and a statuesque woman who was obviously Kris' mother.

Entering the apartment, Earl turned to the woman standing next to him and said, "This is Shelby; you'll be staying here." He glanced at Shelby. "This is Masha, Kris' mother."

Shelby smiled briefly at the stranger before meeting Earl's eyes. "Kris?"

"She's on her way to Langley."

"Is she okay?"

Earl nodded. "She's fine. I've got to get down there for the debriefing." He nodded dismissively at the two agents that had been assigned to protect Shelby. "I've got a new team outside." Turning back to Shelby, he said, "You and Masha will be under constant surveillance." He handed her a cell phone. "Just press the number 1 if you need anything at all."

Shelby shook her head, sensing Earl was holding something back. "Wait! What's going to happen now?"

Meeting her worried eyes, Earl answered honestly, "I don't know." Shelby started to speak again when he raised a hand to forestall her. "I'm not at liberty to disclose any additional information."

Frustrated but understanding Earl's position, Shelby curtailed her questions. *At least Kris' request that Masha stay with me was honored.*

"I'll be in touch." Earl stood in the entranceway, hesitated a moment, then met the analyst's gaze. "Your debriefing will be at 10:00 tomorrow morning."

Shelby nodded, locked the door behind Earl, then turned her full attention to Masha, noting how tense and pale her face was. Knowing how traumatic the events of the last several days had to have been for the Russian, her heart went out to the older woman. Not sure how much English her guest could understand, she pointed to herself and said, "I'm Shelby." She then gestured toward the couch. "Let's go sit down."

Once Masha was seated, Shelby asked, "Can I get you something to drink?" She accompanied her words with hand gestures depicting pouring and drinking a beverage, and smiled when Masha nodded. She returned with two glasses of iced tea and handed one to Kris' mother. "Do you understand English?"

Masha gazed at the friendly woman addressing her. Her hostess was obviously worried. "Little." She raised her hand, pantomimed writing, and smiled when Shelby got up and returned a moment later with a tablet and pen. She began laboriously writing in English, struggling to use the foreign language to describe what had happened. A short time later, she handed the paper to Shelby.

"I was brought to where Natasha was waiting. We hugged. My daughter knocked me down. Many guns. Sergei is dead, shot in head by another Russian I saw before at the house. Natasha went with the Americans. I was brought here."

Shelby felt her stomach tighten as she read. Her voice sounding hollow, she asked in disbelief, "Sergei is dead?"

Masha nodded, instinctively reaching for the younger woman's hand. In halting English, she began, "Natasha—" then broke off in frustration when she couldn't find the words to assure her companion that her daughter hadn't been hurt.

Understanding what Masha was trying to say, Shelby said, "Natasha is okay." She was devastated by the news of Sergei's death. He had been Kris' ace in the hole and his murder threw her partner's deal into jeopardy. Her fears for her partner escalated, as did the throbbing in her head at all the unanswered questions that remained.

"Shelby?"

Her name sounded strange with the Russian inflection. Shelby squeezed Masha's hand, determined to be strong for Kris' mother's sake, even as she resolved to insist on some answers the next day when she met with Earl. Knowing there was nothing she could do before then, she gestured for Masha to follow her. She gave her a towel and washcloth and showed her where the bathroom was, then led her to the bedroom and gestured toward the bed.

Masha shook her head. "No." She pointed at Shelby, then at the bed.

Shelby couldn't bear the thought of sleeping in her bed alone and her voice was pleasant but firm as she insisted, "Masha."

The Russian didn't understand why the woman would give up her bed to a stranger, but she understood Shelby's message and nodded. She watched curiously as Shelby walked over and plucked a large unicorn from the bed, taking it with her when she left the room.

Shelby made up the couch and sat down, placing the unicorn on the floor nearby. She was too worried to fall asleep. When Shelby finally did doze, her rest was fitful, and she found herself pacing the floor long into the night, setting up a pattern that would become repetitious in the nights to follow. Even Stormy fled to the refuge of the bedroom, unwilling to share the couch with her unhappy, restless owner.

THE NEXT MORNING Shelby made breakfast for Masha and herself, but only picked at her own. Showing the Russian how to turn on the TV, she explained in writing that she had to go to work but would return in a few hours. After the morning's debriefing, she intended to take a few days off to get Kris' mother settled and into some sort of a routine before returning to work full time. Hopefully, her partner would be released shortly and could help with Masha's transition to American life.

Later that morning, Shelby walked out of Earl's office, still frustrated. The brief, superficial questions Earl had asked her about everything that had happened hadn't made sense. Of even more concern was his refusal to answer any of her questions about Kris.

On reflection, the cursory nature of the questioning became crystal clear. Shelby realized that when Kris had been debriefed, she must have protected her, making sure she wasn't considered culpable in any way. Unbidden tears came to her eyes as Shelby realized that though she couldn't do anything to help the woman she loved, Kris was still looking after her.

In the week that followed, neither Shelby nor Masha were allowed any contact with Kris. And somehow, the CIA had managed to keep the entire incident quiet. There had been absolutely no mention in the news media other than a small blurb about an accidental shooting at the Russian embassy resulting in the death of a high-ranking embassy official.

The only tangible evidence that a bargain had been struck was the postal arrival of an immigration packet addressed to Masha. Shelby explained each form to the Russian and helped her fill out the paperwork. The brief flare of hope that the packet engendered as a sign that maybe Kris' deal was being honored was eventually extinguished by the continuing silence about her partner's whereabouts or status.

As she drove to her mother's house, Shelby glanced over at the elderly Russian. Lisa and Masha planned to visit while Shelby went grocery shopping. The two older women had met earlier in the week when Shelby visited, and her mother had suggested she drop Masha off while she went to the store.

After Shelby left, Lisa smiled at Masha and invited her to sit at the table, fetching them both a cup of coffee. Shelby had been teaching Masha to speak English, and Lisa was amazed at how quickly the Russian was learning to speak the words she could write. "Have you heard from Natasha?" Lisa had learned that was Kris' real name, and Masha had spoken of their long-term separation when they'd first met.

Masha turned worried blue eyes toward Lisa. "No. I am worried for her."

Lisa said reassuringly, "She's just busy on a case. Sometimes I don't see Shelby for weeks at a time."

The Russian nodded. She understood that Lisa was trying to make her feel better, but she was distressed. It had already been over a week, and even though she'd written a letter that Shelby had taken to work to be delivered, her daughter had not responded.

When she and Shelby had visited Lisa earlier in the week, the discussion had turned to Jonathan, and Lisa's hope that he would not contact her again. Turning the conversation to her new friend, Masha asked, "Have you heard from Jonathan?" Lisa shook her head, then smiled when Masha said, "Good! He bad man."

"He needs help." Lisa shook her head. "I still can't believe he hurt Shelby."

"Shelby is good daughter. I like her."

The simple comment bought tears to Lisa's eyes. *Yes, Shelby is a good daughter. I wish I'd been a better mother.*

Lisa looked at Masha, and asked the question Shelby had refused to answer. "Is Natasha an American?" She was still trying to make sense of why Kris' mother was there and the operative wasn't.

Masha gazed into the kind eyes, sensing only friendliness. "Yes. But she Russian, too."

"Why did she change her name?"

"Kris spy. She do what she think good."

Lisa's eyes narrowed. "She's a Russian spy?"

Masha answered emphatically, "No. She American." Shelby had explained what Kris had done, and she was very proud of Natasha for standing up for what she believed was right.

"I'm sorry. I didn't mean—"

The Russian reached over and laid her hand on Lisa's, smiling. "Okay."

When Shelby returned to pick up Masha an hour later, the older women were deep in a cheerful, if slightly lop-sided conversation. As they left, she promised her mother they'd return for a visit over the weekend.

SHELBY WALKED ANXIOUSLY into Earl's office. He had called and requested her presence. "You asked to see me?"

"Yes. There have been some developments in the case, and we're pulling the agents off of you. We found out Michael was responsible for all the attacks, including the shooting at the mall. He's in custody now, and no longer a threat to you or Kris' mother."

"What about Kris? Where is she?"

Earl adopted an intimidating stance, looking pointedly into the worried green eyes. "That is not your concern. I want you to quit asking everyone up the chain of command about her. Just drop it."

Shelby stared at Earl. "What do you mean, drop it?" Knowing Earl was aware of just how close they'd become, she voiced a more business-like argument. "She was my partner. Her mother is staying with me. Surely her mother has a right to know."

Earl empathized with Shelby's concern. In truth, he didn't know the details of Kris' status or how long she would be held, but his superiors had insisted he put a stop to the analyst's queries. "You don't have a choice. We can always place Masha in our custody while her paperwork is processing."

Shelby pursed her lips, glaring at Earl and biting off a retort. She didn't want to do anything to jeopardize Kris' mother.

Trying to ease the tension, Earl said, "You did a good job on this case. Michael was the assassin you were looking for. It was your astute observation that detected the pattern and facilitated his capture. Congratulations."

Any other time, Shelby would've been thrilled to receive such high praise from a director, but it was meaningless now. Still angry, she said curtly, "Thank you."

Earl sighed; his hands were tied. "Do you have any other questions?"

Knowing they wouldn't be answered, Shelby said, "No," and left the office, unshed tears of frustration springing to her eyes. She knew she should feel some satisfaction that Michael had been apprehended, but it was diminished because her partner remained in custody as well.

IT WAS SATURDAY, a full two weeks since Shelby had last seen Kris, and her patience had run out. Silence was not helping her partner's cause. The analyst shuddered as she reflected that the CIA could just make her partner disappear. Reviewing her limited options, she'd decided to request a meeting with Earl and Dennis on Monday and threaten to leak the incident to the newspapers unless Kris was released. She'd searched for viable alternatives, but had been stymied at every turn. Shelby realized she had no other choice except to exploit the CIA paranoia about another public scandal and hope for the best. She had agonized over this long-shot plan to win Kris' freedom, well aware that it could mean the end of her career. But if the choice came down to Kris or her career, there was no contest. She could find a new line of work. She would never find another Kris, and her heart wouldn't allow her to give up until she'd exhausted every resource.

Irritated, she tossed down the newspaper. She stood up and started pacing, ending up in the dining room in front of her cabinet of mythical figures. She gazed absently at the knickknacks, wistfully longing for her childhood certitude in the power of magic. Kris' absence was a constant ache, a reminder that nothing could ever fill her heart and life as the operative had. Dark circles had formed beneath her eyes, the result of too many sleepless nights filled with unending tears rolling from anguished eyes.

Masha, who had been watching TV, studied the young woman gazing into the cabinet. During the two weeks they had shared the apartment, she had come to care deeply for Shelby. The American was a stranger, yet she had opened her home and shown her nothing but kindness. She knew Shelby had a deep bond with her daughter and had extended that friendship to include her. She'd had plenty of time to do little but wonder at the generosity shown her, even as she worried what the future held for both herself and her daughter. Would she ever see Natasha again or would she be sent back to Russia? If she did return to her homeland, would she be branded a traitor? Would she ever have the chance to establish a relationship with her only child? What kind of person had her daughter become; would she want her mother back in her life? Shelby seemed to think she would, but Masha needed to talk to Natasha and draw her own conclusions.

The questions were endless, and only time would provide the answers to them. As she gazed at Shelby, Masha knew her immediate priority was to try and raise the younger woman's spirits. She walked up behind Shelby, laid her hand on the blonde's shoulder, and spoke with conviction. "No be sad. Natasha good job."

Pulled from her reverie, Shelby nodded, then turned and hugged Masha, appreciating her unfailing support. "I know. I'm just worried."

They walked over to the couch and sat down. It was time for the news and Shelby watched it religiously each day, vacillating between the hope of hearing something that might signal Kris' release and the fear of what she might actually see. She reached over and gently squeezed the Russian's hand. "Maybe today."

When the news ended without any mention of Kris or the Russian embassy, Masha lifted Stormy from her lap and turned to face

Shelby. Even though she didn't understand all the words, she could see the resignation in the younger woman's face. "We go see Lisa?"

The analyst smiled and nodded. "Yes." She picked up the phone and punched in the numbers, waiting for her mother to answer. "Hi, Mom. Mind if Masha and I stop over a little later?"

Lisa laughed. "Of course not."

"Okay, we'll see you in a bit. Bye."

Shelby picked up the newspaper from its resting place on the coffee table and beckoned for Masha to move closer. In a combination of English, gestures, and recently learned Russian words, she painstakingly explained her plan to try and get Kris released.

Listening carefully, Masha nodded her understanding. When Shelby finished speaking, she said, "You make enemies."

Sighing, Shelby replied, "Yes, but—"

"I love Natasha," Masha interrupted gently.

Shelby smiled. "I know you do. She loves you, too."

Gesturing at Shelby, Masha stated, "You love her."

Momentarily caught off guard, Shelby agreed, "Yes, I do."

The Russian looked around the apartment. "She stay here with you?"

"Yes. She," Shelby searched for a simple word to explain that Kris had been protecting her, "guarded me."

"She sleep in your bed?"

Shelby was unable to stop a blush from creeping over her face as the kind, wise eyes gazed at her.

Masha smiled and displayed her new knowledge of casual English. "Okay."

"Okay?" Shelby wasn't quite sure how to take that.

Reaching for Shelby's hand, Masha nodded. "Okay."

She squeezed the older woman's hand, sharing their common love of the absent woman. Gathering their things, they departed for Lisa's house.

LISA PUT ON a pot of fresh coffee in anticipation of her guests. Her daughter and Kris' mother had visited several times during the past two weeks, but the profound sadness she could see on her daughter's face at each visit broke her heart. She'd asked about the case, but Shelby had told her it was over and that she couldn't discuss it. The biggest surprise had been when she'd first learned that Masha was staying with her daughter, but when she'd asked after Kris, Shelby would only say she was away. The only time Lisa had heard any enthusiasm in her daughter's voice was when she'd told Shelby that she was going to start attending a support group for battered wives.

Drawn to the immediate present by a knock on the front door, Lisa opened it, expecting to see Shelby, and took a step backward at the unexpected figure in her doorway.

Smiling, Jonathan said, "Hey, babe, I've missed you."

After meeting with Kim and then following up with phone conversations, Lisa was beginning to understand that she had been at fault in their unhealthy relationship, too, for not leaving Jonathan, and for allowing the abuse to continue against both herself and her children. "Jonathan, I told you I needed some time, and I would call you, so why are you here?"

His smiled faded. "You talked to Shelby, didn't you?"

Lisa crossed her arms, blocking the entrance. She did not doubt anything Shelby had told her, but she decided to let her former husband dig himself into a deeper hole. She had heard the full account from her daughter and wanted to see how closely the man would stick to the truth. "Do you mean about how you deliberately grabbed her arm where she'd been shot and threatened her again? Is that what you're talking about?"

Sorrowfully, he said, "Yes, I did do that, but please let me explain."

When Lisa remained silent, Jonathan pleaded, "Please, babe?"

"Okay, explain."

He edged into the doorway, hoping Lisa would invite him in. "I was minding my own business when there was a knock on the door. It was the cops. I knew I hadn't done anything, but they asked me all sorts of questions about where I was the night before. And then it hit me: Shelby must have turned me in to the cops for shooting her." He looked up at Lisa sadly. "I would never do anything like that. Can you imagine how I felt?"

Lisa stood impassively. "So, what happened when Shelby got there?"

Jonathan cleared his throat. "Um, well, I was so hurt at being falsely accused, I drank a six pack, then I needed to clear my head, so I laid down to take a nap. Couple of hours later, I got woken up again. It was Shelby and that tall bit–woman. Of course I let them in. The tall one eventually went back outside so we could talk."

Lisa waited patiently. So far, what Jonathan had related was accurate. She was curious as to how he was going to try and explain his hostile actions. "And?"

"Well, you gotta understand, I was a bit woozy from the beer, and Shelby ordered me to stay away from you and even threatened to tell you I shot her."

Lisa summoned every ounce of courage she possessed to confront her former husband for the very first time. "Stop right there. You are a liar. Shelby was right—you haven't changed at all, you've just become a better actor."

Jonathan dropped his eyes to the floor. "I knew you wouldn't believe me." He looked back up at Lisa beseechingly. "I swear I'm telling you the truth. If it had happened like whatever Shelby told you, why would I be here?"

Looking at her former husband, Lisa fought the urge to believe him. "You tell me."

"Babe, you know how stressed Shelby's been. I would be, too, if someone was shooting at me. I think she threatened to put the blame on me because she is so confused right now."

Lisa hated to admit it, but Jonathan was right about the pressure her daughter had been under. Nevertheless, she met his eyes resolutely. "She wouldn't lie, no matter how bad things were. You know that."

His frustration building, Jonathan pleaded, "Please believe me. I just got angry when she threatened me, I never meant her any harm."

"How come when Kris came in the trailer, you got into it with her?"

"That fucking bitch got right in my face and wouldn't move. She just got lucky."

Lisa retorted, "Well, that 'fucking bitch' was protecting Shelby from you."

Jonathan could see his plans to move back in crumbling to dust in front of him. Losing his calm demeanor, he glared at Lisa and snapped, "So, you still think I'm lying."

Trying to calm Jonathan in order to avoid a physical confrontation, Lisa suggested, "Maybe you misunderstood what she said."

Jonathan's face reddened. "Oh, so now I'm not only a liar but I'm stupid, too." He pushed Lisa into the house, following her menacingly. "Just who in the hell do you think you are?" He shoved her again. "All of a sudden my word isn't good enough for you." Spittle flew from his mouth, striking her face. "You stupid bitch!"

Backing away from Jonathan, Lisa shouted, "Get out of here now or I'm calling the cops."

Hearing his mother yell, Jason jumped up from in front of the TV and ran towards the kitchen, Jimmy following closely on his heels. The teenager had just cleared the doorway, when he saw his father brutally slap his mother, blood from a split lip dripping down her chin. He stepped in front of his mother and grabbed his father's arm, which was raised again. "Leave her alone, Dad."

Jonathan jerked his arm free of his son's grasp and glared at Jason. "Get out of here. *Now!*" He captured Jimmy with his gaze and added, "Both of you."

Jason shook his head and stood his ground, staring at a bulging vein in his father's forehead as the man's face reddened in anger. He felt his stomach tighten in fear and hoped his dad couldn't see how scared he was. He ignored his mother, who was trying to pull him back away from the angry man. "Dad, please leave."

Jonathan's open palm slammed against Jason's cheek. "You disrespectful brat, I told you to get out of here."

Gritting his teeth against the pain, Jason repeated, "Dad, just go. Please." He threw up an arm to block his father's next blow, further angering the bigger man.

When her attempts to remove her son from Jonathan's path were unsuccessful, Lisa moved to stand beside him, ignoring the boy when he said, "Mom, get out of here." There was no way she was leaving Jason alone at Jonathan's mercy.

Jonathan's last vestige of control slipped and his anger turned to fury. Not only had all his plans been thwarted, his wife and stepdaughter had poisoned his own sons' minds so that they stood against him, too. Outraged, he backhanded Lisa.

Jason thrust his weight against his father and attempted to push him out the door, hollering, "Jimmy, call 911!"

Watching in horror as his hero disintegrated before his eyes, his brother's frantic words spurred the youngster to action. Jimmy grabbed the phone from the counter and dialed the emergency number.

Determined to teach his son who was in control, Jonathan hit Jason, loosening the teen's hold on his arm. Suddenly realizing that Jimmy had called the police, a surge of adrenaline allowed him to toss his wife and older son away from him.

Devastated, Jimmy stared disbelievingly at his mother sprawled on the floor and his brother crumpled against the wall. Unable to move, his wide eyes tracked his father's furious approach. As the phone was wrenched out of his hands, the boy missed hearing the dispatcher come on the line.

The frightened look on his son's face disgusted Jonathan. His youngest son was nothing but a sissy. At least Jason had the balls to stand up to him. He heard the dispatcher's voice coming over the receiver and pressed the off button before tossing the phone back to Jimmy, sneering when the boy flinched.

Knowing the dispatcher had probably already summoned a unit to respond, he turned around and hurried out the door without a backward glance. He had no intention of ending up in jail again.

Jason reached his mother at the same time Jimmy did. They helped her to her feet. "You okay, Mom?"

"I'm okay." Lisa hugged her sons, horrified at the bruising on Jason's face. "I'm so sorry."

"It's okay, Mom," Jason assured her. "He's gone now."

Hearing a commotion out in the yard, all three hurried toward the door where they almost bumped into a policewoman who was just raising her hand to knock.

"Is everyone okay?"

Lisa nodded. "We're okay. How'd you get here so fast?"

"Just luck, really. My partner and I were only a street over. When the dispatcher lost contact, we got the call."

"Were you in time to catch him?"

"Yeah. He tried to run, though. My partner tackled him and the guy just about pulled Pete's arm of the socket trying to get away. He'll be charged with resisting arrest and assault on a police officer, as well as whatever charges you wish to press."

Lisa sighed. "He'll never learn."

"I have to get the camera. I'll need to take pictures for evidence in court. I'll be right back to take statements."

Taking a deep breath, Lisa nodded. This time she would see it through. "Okay."

Once the officer had gone to her car, Jimmy looked at his mother. "Mom, why?"

"He's sick, honey. He needs help."

"Dad already got treatment." Jimmy struggled to make sense of what had happened. "He said he was better."

Lisa gazed into her son's eyes. "I know. It might not be possible to cure him, but he needs to learn to be able to control himself."

Jimmy nodded as he wrapped his mind around that thought.

Lisa knew she hadn't protected her daughters and she couldn't undo that. And because she hadn't taken a stand sooner, her sons had suffered physical and emotional damage trying to defend her. The only thing she could do was make sure she didn't repeat the same mistakes she'd made so many years before.

She looked at the boys. "I'm filing charges against your father and testifying in court this time. He's going to jail."

Jason nodded. "Can I testify?"

Lisa started crying harder. Jason was only a teenager and he was already braver than she'd ever been. She managed to say, "I'm proud of you both."

"Mom, please don't cry," Jimmy said, his own tears very near the surface.

Lisa gave him a watery smile. "I'm fine, honey. I'm just glad you're both okay."

HAL AND RON sat on one side of the interrogation table, waiting for Blue to sit down on the other. They both knew it wasn't going to be a pleasant debriefing, because of the amount of time it had taken them to tie up all the loose ends.

Blue slid into a chair and glared at the two men sitting opposite her. "What do you want now? I kept my part of the bargain, and you still hung me out to dry."

The taller of the two men cleared his throat. "We didn't have a choice—"

Blue spat, "Bullshit! I could've been killed, my partner could've been killed, my mother could've been killed—and you didn't have a choice? Do you really expect me to believe that? And even supposing that's true, where in the hell have you been for the last two weeks."

Ron spoke quietly. "Michael was one of ours."

The operative's eyes widened briefly. "So you are the ones that protected him when he fucked up our extraction three years ago."

Hal nodded. "We've suspected him of working for the other side for quite some time, but we needed solid evidence to take him down. With the pictures and recordings your partner gave Earl, we have that."

Blue shook her head in disbelief. "You had no way of knowing we'd uncover anything on him, yet you still jeopardized innocent lives? Shelby and my mother could have been killed. I don't fucking believe this."

"Every time we made a move, the Russians knew about it. We had to find the leak. You were our best bet."

Suddenly some pieces began falling into place. "You let Michael know I was returning to headquarters and when I'd be arriving." Both men remained silent, and Blue continued her accusatory litany. "Our deal was that I notify you when I was activated, and I'd be granted immunity. I did as I'd promised. Instead of honoring your part of our agreement, you left me to catch Michael and fend off the Russians alone." She snorted and said sarcastically, "And we're supposed to be on the same side? Am I the only one who sees something wrong with this picture?"

"Our options were limited. We had to break Michael before we could fulfill our part of the agreement."

Kris crossed her arms and sat back in the chair. "Care to explain that? You were given pictures and recordings."

"Yes, we were, but he claimed he was just going along with Maggie, and was going to turn her in. Before we could turn him again, we had to break him. He's good; it took a while." Ron met Blue's eyes. "If we couldn't break him, we needed you around until we did."

Blue finally understood why she'd been held in total isolation after her initial debriefing. These guys had covered up who and what she was, but the operative wanted to hear them admit it. "How were you going to manage that? Earl knows the whole story."

"He's been sworn to secrecy." Ron smiled. "It didn't hurt that he was on your side anyway. Made our job really easy."

Blue commented acidly, "I assume you broke Michael. Mind telling me what you would have needed me for if you hadn't been able to?"

"To shadow him, report his every move and contact. You know the routine, you've done it before."

Blue shook her head in disgust.

Ron protested, "Just until he agreed to double."

Blue rose angrily to her feet and began pacing back and forth behind the table. "So he walks? He is responsible for several unsanctioned assassinations, he tried to kill Shelby, he tried to kill me, and he walks?" Her disbelief and outrage were apparent in her voice and in her stride.

Hal shrugged. "We need him. Gregor withdrew his request for political asylum, but he doesn't know about Michael. It could take us years to get another agent in place to provide information Michael is already in a position to get for us."

"And you trust him?"

"No. But it seems he was a little more attached to Maggie than we realized. In exchange for her complete cooperation, we plea-bargain to a lesser charge than treason and she gets probation. Michael knows if he reneges on any part of the deal, we'll throw the book at both of them."

Blue was irritated at having been used, but knew these agents were acting in what they felt were the best interests of the country.

She sighed. "So now what? Am I free to go, or do you have some other surprises in store for me?"

Accepting a folder from Ron, she pulled out a sheaf of papers and began reading. A few minutes later she signed a nondisclosure agreement, pushed it across the table and stood up, her heart beating wildly: she was finally free. Maintaining her composure, she nodded at the two men. "I would say it's been nice working with you, but that would be a lie. Thanks for living up to our bargain."

The two men watched her leave, then Hal looked at Ron. "She's really pissed."

"Yeah. Hope we don't have to activate her any time soon."

"You think she knows we'll recall her if we need her?"

Ron shrugged. "She's smart. I'd bet on it."

SHELBY ARRIVED JUST as a burly police officer was manhandling Jonathan into the rear seat of a police car in handcuffs. She pointedly ignored his venomous glares and the barrage of vicious threats he screamed after her as she entered the house. Masha arrived moments later, and joined the younger woman as they waited for the officers to finish taking pictures and completing statements from Lisa and the boys.

When Shelby saw Jason's black eye, she was filled with a raging desire to march back outside and give Jonathan one to match, but she controlled herself. Listening as her mother gave a straightforward account to the officer without any effort to protect her husband or excuse his actions, she was consoled that this time—at last—he wouldn't escape justice. Deep down, she was simply glad that there had been no worse injuries, for she had no illusions about what the man was capable of.

Kim came running into the house just as the officers were leaving and, quickly taking in the situation at a glance, she drew Lisa aside, laying a sympathetic arm over her shoulder as the two spoke softly. With a reassuring glance at the others, Kim led Lisa into one of the bedrooms. Shelby relaxed, knowing her mother would get both solid support and sound advice from her friend, and turned her attention to her brothers.

"You might want to put some ice on that shiner," she suggested gently to Jason, who nodded and headed for the kitchen. Shelby turned her attention to her younger brother. The devastated look on Jimmy's face worried her. "Hey, are you okay? He didn't hurt you, did he?"

He couldn't meet her eyes. "I—I couldn't stop him, Shel. He threw Mom like she was a rag doll and I didn't even try to stop him."

Shelby was startled to hear the self-loathing in his voice. "Jimmy, he's a full-grown man, and he was completely out of control. There is no way you could have stopped him!"

"Jason at least tried!" the younger boy blurted, the tears now clearly visible.

Before Shelby could answer, another voice broke in. "You would've too, bro. You were still in shock. Don't blame yourself, kid. Besides, if you hadn't made the phone call, who knows what the hell he'd have done to all of us, right, Shel?"

Both boys looked to their older sister as she reluctantly nodded. She didn't want to traumatize her brothers any further, but after what they'd already seen, she knew she couldn't sugar-coat things either. She suspected that the whole family was going to need some intensive counseling after the events of the day, but at least now the healing could begin. She was saved from further questions when Lisa and Kim returned to the living room.

"Mom?" All three siblings asked together, then grins broke out all around as Lisa made a comical face at them. The grins quickly faded, though, as Lisa gestured Kim to a seat and pulled up a dining room chair for herself.

Lisa first looked apologetically at her daughter, and an unspoken communication told both that many words would be exchanged in the future, but for now the older woman had to concentrate on her sons. Shelby acknowledged that necessity, and gave her mother a supportive smile. There would time enough for them to heal their relationship, but her brothers were so new to the understanding of their father's violent nature that they needed reassurance that this was neither the end of their lives as they knew them, nor of their family.

Shelby, her mother, and her brothers all talked over what had happened, gently guided by Kim, who directed the family into more positive avenues of thought when emotions threatened to run too high. None of them would forget the past, and there were still things that would definitely have to be dealt with, but by the time the analyst felt comfortable leaving, all four were starting to contemplate a brighter future. Lisa had even agreed to Kim's suggestion that both she and the boys see a psychologist for some counseling. After two hours of intensive conversation, Shelby rose to leave, Kim having departed ten minutes earlier.

The analyst felt as if a huge weight had lifted from her shoulders, almost giddy with relief. Stretching a little, she was about to ask Masha if she could offer her a ride back to the apartment when her mother looked up and extended her hand.

Shelby crossed the small distance between them and gladly took the proffered hand.

"Thank you so much for being here, honey," Lisa said with a sad smile. "I know how tough this has all been on you, and I'm so sorry..."

"Shhh, it's okay, Mom," Shelby assured her, giving her hand a gentle squeeze. "We'll talk later, but for now I just want you to get a good night's sleep."

Lisa nodded wearily, then with an obvious effort asked, "I forgot to ask, how's Kr—uh, Nata—your partner doing?"

Fighting back the grief that threatened to overwhelm her, Shelby forced a smile. "She's still involved in the case, Mom. Can't tell you much more than that at the moment, though."

Lisa nodded understandingly. Shelby turned back to Masha, who had been watching the events closely. The analyst wasn't sure how much Kris' mother understood, but the older woman had provided a solid, comforting presence, and to her surprise, Lisa had responded positively to Masha's few, quiet words. She was half-amused at the irony that her and Kris' mothers seemed to get on so well.

"Are you ready to go, Masha?" Shelby asked.

Instead of answering, Masha went over to kneel beside Lisa. "I stay? I help, yes?"

Shelby fully expected her mother to refuse politely, but when the Russian woman laid a worn hand on the American woman's face, Lisa just nodded.

"Thank you, Masha. I would appreciate the company."

Shelby felt a rush of gratitude to the kind foreigner. She had been feeling slightly guilty about having to leave her mother alone, but her need to refine a strategy to help Kris overshadowed everything else. Certain that her family was in good hands, she bade them all goodbye, hugging the boys and giving her mother a fierce embrace that conveyed more than words ever could.

Walking out to her car, Shelby was flooded with wildly fluctuating emotions. Relief, anger, fear, worry and grief wracked her – all compounded by the dread of spending her first night alone since Kris had been gone. Sliding in behind the steering wheel, she dropped her head on her hands, and for the thousandth time, the same question assailed her: *Kris, where are you?*

KRIS RANG THE doorbell, though she didn't expect an answer. When the taxi dropped her off in front of the building, she hadn't seen her partner's car or the Taurus she'd rented. Turning her key into the lock, she entered and looked around. While she couldn't wait to see Shelby, she was nervous about seeing her mother. It seemed so strange to have a mother again. What would Masha think of her? Could they recapture the relationship that had been stolen from them so long ago?

Pushing her concerns aside, Kris picked up Stormy and gently hugged her despite the young feline's mewling protest. "What? You didn't miss me?"

The operative set the kitten down, walked over to the couch, and picked up the neatly folded sheet at the end, smiling at the sight of the unicorn on the floor next to the couch. Knowing her partner would've insisted on sleeping on the couch, she inhaled deeply of the linen and was rewarded by the faint scent of Shelby's bath oil. In the absence of the young blonde, Kris hugged the sheet close to her.

During the long days in isolation, she'd hungered for Shelby's presence, half-convinced that she'd never again feel her partner's touch. Repeated requests to use the phone had been denied, so she'd dwelled on her memories, lingering over every conversation, recalling each nuance of expression on that animated face, and tormenting herself with an intense longing for the feel of the other woman's body pressed against her. Kris had spent hours projecting her overwhelming love, hoping that somehow Shelby could feel the message of her heart through the distance separating them.

The tall woman sighed and sank down to the couch, the sheet still clutched tightly against her. She would have to wait a little longer. A few minutes later, she laid the cloth down and began pacing around the apartment, finally coming to a stop in front of the balcony door, her eyes riveted on the partially filled parking lot.

SHELBY DROVE HOME slowly, in no hurry to return to her empty apartment. She didn't even have a picture of Kris; all she had were her memories. Reaffirming her resolve to confront her superiors on Monday, she parked the car and started towards the apartment.

Kris had been standing at the glass door for an hour, stoically watching as the lot filled up. It was dark out, and she was now unable to identify the make of each car until the driver turned off the lights and got out. Checking and eliminating each vehicle, she maintained her vigil.

Kris watched another car pulled in and park, refusing to get her hopes up again. But when her partner was the driver that got out, she didn't even wait to see her close the car door. Kris was out of the apartment and bounding down the steps two at a time, a big grin on her face as she ran across the parking lot. Shelby recognized the familiar figure racing towards her and broke into an all-out sprint of her own. As they came together, Kris threw her arms around Shelby, drawing her into a bear hug. Shelby embraced her in return, her heart leaping for joy, tears of happiness falling freely.

"I was so worried."

Kris murmured, "I missed you so much."

Neither wanted to relinquish her hold on the other, and they walked to the building with their arms wrapped around each other's waist.

Kris suddenly realized her mother hadn't gotten out of the car with Shelby and looked back towards the lot. "Where's Mom?"

"She's spending the night at my mother's house." Shelby laughed delightedly at the raised eyebrow and quizzical expression on her partner's face, a look she had despaired of ever seeing again. "It's a long story."

Kris smiled, relishing the sound of her partner's laughter. "I'll just bet it is."

The door was no sooner closed than the women embraced again. Shelby pulled Kris' head down and met her mouth for a deep, passionate kiss which her partner returned with equal fervor. "I'm so glad you're back."

Kris led Shelby over to the couch, sharing kisses with her along the way. Sitting down, she pulled her partner into her lap, wrapping strong arms around her and lowering a hungry mouth to the anxiously waiting lips. Her heart was beating so hard, she was sure Shelby could feel it. "I love you."

Shelby sighed contentedly. "I love you, too." She turned serious eyes toward Kris and though unwilling to break the spell, voiced her worst fear. "Did they give you the deal, or do you have to leave again?"

"No. No. No." Each word was punctuated with a kiss. "I'm here to stay, for as long as you want me."

Breathing an audible sigh of relief, Shelby said, "Forever. I want you to stay forever."

Kris wrapped her arms around her partner, pulling her close. "I'm glad you do, because that's what I want too."

After sharing another kiss with her love, Kris' curiosity got the better of her and she asked, "How did my mother end up at your mother's house for the night?"

Shelby shook her head. "In a word, Jonathan."

Kris raised an eyebrow, concerned. "What did he do this time?"

Shelby gave the operative a thumbnail sketch of everything that had happened that day, then asked with uncertainty, "Do you want to go see your mother now?"

The operative glanced around the room. She did want to see her mother, but that visit could wait until morning. "It's late. Why don't you call your mom and ask her to tell my mother that I'm fine and that we'll stop over in the morning to pick her up."

Shelby waited until Kris turned back to face her. "You don't want to talk to her on the phone either?"

"I do, but I don't. I'd rather talk to her face to face."

Grasping her partner's hand, Shelby asked, "What's wrong?"

Kris sighed. "I don't know what to say to her. She always hated government agents. They used to plant them among the people. We lost a close friend because of them. She'll hate me because of what I am."

Shelby shook her head. "Oh, sweetheart, your mother doesn't hate you. She loves you. She knows you're a spy, and she's okay with that."

"How can you be so sure?"

"You were the one thing we had in common; we talked about you a lot. Trust me on this: your mother loves you very much."

"She never visited." At Shelby's puzzled look, Kris added, "When I was at the training center, she never came to visit."

"Maybe she couldn't. Ask her, Kris. I bet she has a good reason."

Kris smiled at the conviction in her partner's voice. "You're probably right."

Shelby reached for the phone, dialed her mother's number, and then quickly relayed Kris' message before telling her mother she'd talk to her in the morning. Mission accomplished, she settled back into Kris' lap.

Kris brushed her fingers across Shelby's face. "I'm glad we're alone tonight."

Shelby lifted the hand from her face and kissed the palm. "So am I."

The operative smiled. "Where do you want me to start?" She chuckled at the blush that crept over her partner's face. "I meant, about the case."

"Oh." Shelby feigned disappointment until Kris leaned down and kissed her pout away. "What happened to you? Is everything okay now, even though Sergei died? And why did Gregor kill him?"

"Gregor wasn't as stupid as I thought. He was working his own agenda. He knew Sergei planned to eliminate him, but he had no real desire to defect. He only requested political asylum out of desperation. With Sergei out of the picture, no one in Russia would know of their rift and he would be in line for a promotion. Naturally, he withdrew his request for asylum."

Shelby shook her head. "I never would've guessed he would kill Sergei."

"Neither did I. He was looking out for himself and got lucky." She shrugged. "Happens sometimes. People get more than they deserve." She gave Shelby's shoulders a pointed squeeze.

"What about you? Are you legally an operative now?"

"No. I'm officially retired." Kris rubbed Shelby's back in a gentle circular motion. It was time to tell her partner the rest of the tale. "It's a long story, but I'll try to make it short. About eight years ago, a top-secret organization that reports directly to the president managed to infiltrate the Russian mole infrastructure here in the States. My name was uncovered and I was contacted. They wanted me to double. I refused."

Shelby gazed at Kris. "I'm surprised they didn't deport you."

"Yeah, me too. The only reason they didn't was because I hadn't ever been activated. They wanted to find out who was running the double agents here, so I got offered a deal: when I was activated, I was supposed to notify them with all the details of who contacted me and what they wanted me to do."

"What was in it for you?"

"I would get political asylum, but my career would be over because the bottom line is—I am Russian. I didn't have much choice, so I agreed. As the years passed, I was glad I wasn't activated, because I didn't know what I'd do when actually faced with the dilemma."

"But if you were granted political asylum..."

Kris shrugged. "It wasn't that. I didn't really know anyone or have any friends here in the States. Even though I love this country, I've spent little of my adult life living in it. So I strove to be the CIA's best operative. That way, I figured I wouldn't be recalled, and it would have the added benefit of making it extremely difficult for the Russians to find me in the field. It worked for a long time." The operative smiled at Shelby. "Until you came along, and found a pattern that got me recalled."

Shelby turned puzzled eyes on Kris. "I don't get it. If you were working for some special agency of this country, then why didn't you just contact *them*? They could've rescued your mother and none of this would've happened."

"I tried to contact them a couple of times; they never responded. Turned out that Michael worked for them, too, and they suspected him of being a traitor. They knew what was going on and just let it play itself out to try and get the leverage they needed to turn him." Kris shrugged. "They got what they wanted. We were used, but it did turn out okay."

"So you don't owe them anything more, right?"

Kris sighed. "Supposedly not. But I wouldn't be the least bit surprised to be reactivated if they decide they need me for something."

"That sucks!"

"I know, and I would fight it, but it is an outside possibility. And, as an independent contractor, they'd have to pay me pretty well."

Shelby nodded. "Well, it's a good thing they released you, because I was going to talk to Earl and Dennis tomorrow and just happen to mention what a field day the press would have if they ever found out about this case. No way was I going to let you just disappear."

Kris shook her head, marveling at her partner's tenacity, loyalty, and love. Exposing the whole affair to the press would've been career suicide. She knew that, and Shelby had to know it too. Yet there wasn't even a trace of hesitation in her voice, and that overwhelmed the agent as nothing else ever had. Shaken by the intensity of her feelings, Kris responded instinctively, gathering her lover in her arms and brushing soft lips with a gentleness that none of her handlers would ever have suspected she possessed. Words being superfluous, they just rested easily in each other's embrace, swaying slightly as two pairs of eyes closed in contentment.

Finally, Kris pulled back enough to smile mischievously. When Shelby cocked her head questioningly, she teasingly asked, "So, it occurs to me that we have the apartment to ourselves tonight. Or were you expecting company?" There was no mistaking the underlying desire in her voice, and Kris could see the instant response in the other woman.

Smouldering green eyes met blue, and Shelby shook her head slowly. "No, it'll just be you and me. Think we'll be able to find something to do?" She smiled and softly brushed the tips of Kris' breasts with her fingers. When her partner took a deep breath, Shelby's fingers revisited the now-erect nipples.

Kris grasped Shelby's hand and raised it to her mouth, kissing the palm. "You are a tease."

Shelby innocently commented, *"Moi?"* She chuckled. "Payback time."

Nodding in understanding, Kris grinned. "I think I'm gonna like this payback." She kissed Shelby lightly. "Let's get more comfortable. I hate this institution clothing they gave me."

Shelby made a point of looking at her partner's plain blue blouse and slacks. "Oh, I don't know; they aren't so bad. Or maybe it's just that I like what's in them."

Laughing, Kris said, "Is that right?" She shifted her partner off her lap, stood, and offered her hand.

Accepting it, Shelby eagerly followed the operative into the bedroom, feeling the desire surge through her body as her green eyes hungrily raked the tall form preceding her.

Turning, Kris drew the blonde into her arms, marveling at how the shapely body melded so perfectly with her own. Her heart raced as she inhaled the scent that was uniquely Shelby's and she tightened her embrace, passion and peacefulness vying for supremacy in her raging emotions. Nuzzling the fragrant golden hair, she whispered, "I love you, you know. No one's ever made me feel like you do. With you in my arms, I feel like nothing can touch us, no one can hurt us; I've never been happier in my life."

Her face buried against Kris' neck, Shelby smiled a radiant smile of contentment. She knew exactly what her partner meant. She never wanted to move, never wanted to break the enchantment of being in this woman's arms. Then she felt Kris' hands begin to stroke her back and heard the other woman's voice, husky with desire.

"I'd like to make love to you."

Shelby's skin was contracting with each movement of her partner's fingers, fueling the fire already burning hotly within her. Her voice sounding strange to her own ears, she breathed, "God, yes!"

Kris took a deep breath to slow her racing desire. She wanted this to be special for Shelby, didn't want to rush. She unbuttoned each button deliberately, taking her time, fighting the urge to hurry.

Parting the fabric, she eased it over her partner's shoulders and let it slide to the floor. Leaning forward, she shared a kiss with Shelby.

Utterly captivated by the blue eyes burning into hers, Shelby's hands fumbled with the buttons on Kris' shirt, her fingers not cooperating as her body thrilled to the magical feel of her partner's touch on her exposed skin.

Shrugging off her unbuttoned blouse, Kris reached behind Shelby and unfastened her bra. Within seconds it joined the growing pile of clothes on the floor, and Kris paused to admire the firm, full breasts before softly kissing each erect nipple.

Shelby sucked in a breath, arching into the sensations elicited by the warm lips. She slid her arms around Kris, undoing and removing her partner's bra, brushing her fingers across the bare breasts in front of her.

Kris struggled to control her desire. Wanting to just rip the rest of their clothes off, she murmured, "You have no idea what you're doing to me," and ran her fingers down the middle of her partner's abdomen, stopping at the top of Shelby's shorts.

"I hope it's the same thing you're doing to me." Shelby reached over and grasped the elastic waistband of the uniform slacks that Kris had worn home, tugging downward.

Kris smiled and winked. "I'll get these if you get yours."

Shelby returned the smile. "Deal."

Within seconds, the two women stood face to face, each admiring the other's shape and substance.

Kris closed the minute distance between them and embraced Shelby, electrified by the feel of the younger woman's skin against her own. "Mmm." She lowered her mouth to Shelby's neck and left a path of wet, warm kisses in its wake.

Shelby felt a flicker of uncertainty. She wanted to make love to Kris, but was suddenly overcome with doubts about her inexperience.

Sensing her unease, Kris gazed at Shelby. "If you're not ready, we can wait."

Looking into the concerned blue eyes, Shelby shook her head. "No. I'm ready. That is, I want to." Flustered, she tried again, "It's not that. It's just, I feel like...I don't know, really, what to do. I've never made love to a woman before."

Kris smiled warmly. "You've been doing just fine." She lifted Shelby's hand and kissed the palm. "Let me show you?"

Shelby gazed into the ardent blue eyes and nodded. "I want you to teach me how to make love to you."

Her partner's words acted as an aphrodisiac, and Kris guided Shelby towards the bed, pulling the covers down, then joining Shelby, who slid over to the center of the bed, opening her arms as her lover moved smoothly into them.

Shelby's body thrilled to each caress of her partner's hands and to the mouth raining kisses upon her, feeling the love behind each touch as the sensations in her body continued building. Time became meaningless as her body soared toward release, until, breathless, she begged, "Kris, now."

When her partner complied, Shelby plunged into a blissful idyll, her body convulsing as waves of pleasure rippled through her.

She felt Kris enfold her, holding her tightly until she finally stilled. Looking up at her partner with dreamy eyes, she whispered, "Oh, my God."

Kris smiled, brushing the bangs from her partner's forehead before kissing it. "I take it you liked?"

Shelby, drained, chuckled weakly. "You have to ask?"

"I wanted it to be special."

Looking into the serious blue eyes, Shelby assured Kris, "It was. You took me to a place," she struggled to find words to convey the depth of her feeling, "that I've never been before."

Smiling contentedly, Kris gazed at her partner. "I'm glad."

Shelby reached over and brushed her fingers against Kris' nipples, smiling as the flesh puckered at her touch. "I want to do that to you."

Kris' desire flared at the seductive words and she sucked in a breath when Shelby's teeth grazed one of her erect nipples.

"So, what do you say?"

Nodding, Kris said, "Yes, please."

Shelby urged Kris onto her back, then positioned herself over her partner. She gazed into the blue eyes, seeing the vulnerability so carefully hidden from the world, and her heart melted.

Cherishing that trust, Shelby began a slow exploration of her new lover's body, her nervousness forgotten as Kris eagerly responded to her touches, her body pleading for more until time lost all meaning in the consummation of their love.

THE NEXT MORNING, Kris and Shelby departed for Lisa's house at 10:00 a.m. Kris was quiet most of the trip, deep in thought. She was happy her mother was alive, but still had no idea how to relate to her. They were worlds apart. Shelby now knew her mother better than she did. *How do you recapture a bond that you thought was gone forever? Will my mother accept me for who I am?* These and many other questions haunted her.

She thought about what Shelby had said about how much Masha loved her, but it was hard to wrap her mind around that. She loved the mother she treasured in her memory, but was she still the person

Kris remembered from childhood? She found herself nervously excited, and was thankful for the comforting feel of her lover's hand resting on her thigh, soothing her roiling emotions.

Shelby squeezed Kris leg when they pulled into the driveway and parked. "Ready?"

Kris quirked a tentative half-smile. "Ready as I'll ever be." She followed Shelby to the door, watched her partner knock, and then followed her into the house.

Watching out the living room window, Lisa saw Shelby's car turn into the driveway and hurried to the kitchen to greet her guests. Masha indicated she would wait for her daughter in the front room, wanting some privacy for their reunion.

Lisa smiled at Kris as she and Shelby entered. "She's in the living room."

Kris nodded, steeled herself for the reunion, and left the kitchen.

Shelby hugged her mother. "Your lip looks better today; that ice helped."

"Yes, it did. Jason's eye looks worse, though. I even put raw steak on it, but it didn't do much good."

"How is he?"

"He's fine. I'm more worried about Jimmy. He seems more himself today, but he just adored Jonathan. This is all my fault."

"Mom, it's over now. Blaming yourself isn't going to accomplish anything."

Lisa sighed. "I know. I just wish..."

Shelby sat down at the table with her mother. "I'm proud of you."

"Why, Shelby? I let you down, over and over again."

Reaching for her mother's hand, Shelby said, "Because you're standing up for what you believe is right. It's not easy to do that. I respect you for admitting you made a mistake. I love you, Mom."

Lisa wiped the moisture from her eyes. "I love you, too. Thank you for not giving up on me like Ann did."

Shelby smiled. "Oh, I think she'll be back to visit soon." She decided to call her sister and invite her to come and stay for a while. "You'll see."

KRIS STOOD JUST outside the living room doorway, gazing at her mother watching TV. She stepped into the room and cleared her throat.

At the sound, Masha glanced up, and a tentative smile lit up her face as she rose to greet her daughter. They both stood there awkwardly until Masha took the initiative, speaking in their native language. "I've missed you so much. We have been cheated out of so much, you and I."

Kris nodded, the sound of her mother's Russian words taking her back to her childhood. This was the mother she remembered, a woman who dived right into the crux of the matter. "Yes, we have. For so long I thought you were dead." She glanced away, trying to find words to express her feelings.

Masha closed the distance between them and wrapped her daughter in a hug. "I don't know if you want me in your life, or if you blame me for what has happened to you because I let the Center take you. You are my daughter, and nothing can change that; I will love you no matter what you decide."

Kris returned her mother's hug. "I love you, too, Mom, but I've—I'm not the daughter you remember."

Masha smiled gently, sensing her daughter's unease. "No, you're not. And I'm probably not the mother you remember, but that doesn't mean I love you any less." She nodded at the couch. "Come, let us sit."

Once the two women were seated on the couch, Masha said, "When I was locked in that room, I had a lot of time to think. When they told me I was going to see you, I didn't believe them; I thought it was a trick of some sort. Then when I realized you really were alive, I knew you had to be very important for them to bring me to America."

"I just wish you hadn't had to go through that. You were Sergei's trump card. He wanted information and I wasn't being very cooperative." Kris gazed at her mother. "I'm glad he brought you here, though."

Masha reached over and grasped her daughter's hand. "I was treated fine. It was you I was worried about. Once Shelby told me you were Russian agent, then all the pieces began to fall into place—why they wouldn't let me visit, why all my letters were returned, everything."

"You came to visit?" Kris gazed into her mother's eyes. "I never knew that."

"Oh, Natasha, of course I came. I was turned away at the gates. They said you had broken the rules and were not allowed visitors. I came very single week until they told me you died. I never deserted you."

Her last doubt buried, Kris embraced her mother. They had a lot of catching up to do, but they had plenty of time to do it.

Masha looked at Kris curiously. "So, they taught you to be spy?"

Kris nodded. "Yeah. I was brought over here when I was ten and raised as an American."

"The Americans know you are Russian, yet you are free."

Kris smiled. "Yes. I made a bargain with them a long time ago and have been granted citizenship, but my name is no longer Natasha. My papers reflect my American name—Kris Bartley."

"You are still Natasha to me."

Kris chuckled. Her mother hadn't lost any of the feistiness she remembered from her childhood. "Yes, Mother."

They began to converse a little more freely and started slowly rebuilding a relationship lost long ago. An hour later, Shelby glanced into the living room, smiling when she saw Masha and Kris engaged in a conversation that she would've bet was laden with childhood memories, judging by looks on their faces.

Just as she began backing out of the door, Kris spotted her and gestured for her to join them. She reached out, grasping her partner's hand and with a smile reverted to English. "Shelby believed in me. If it weren't for her," Kris paused, searching for a way to explain the analyst's importance to her.

Masha smiled and commented, "Shelby loves you."

Kris' jerked her head around to gaze at her mother. Then she looked at Shelby. "What did you two talk about while I was gone, anyway?"

Shelby was lost because Masha had spoken Russian. "What did she say?"

"She said you love me."

Shelby grinned. "Oh, that. I do. She figured it out by herself."

Masha picked up enough of the English to know that she'd shocked her daughter by revealing what had been obvious to her. Watching them interact now, she knew that her daughter felt the same way about the American. Straight to the point, Masha said, "Good. You love her, too."

Kris' face reddened and Shelby chuckled, not needing a translation of the words this time. "I think she's got your number."

Her mother always had been able to read her, and Kris realized that their long separation hadn't changed that. It was hard to believe that her life had changed so totally in the matter of a few weeks. Her mother was back in her life, and the woman she loved with all her heart was at her side.

Epilogue

IT HAD BEEN two months since Kris had been released, and her time alone with Shelby had been very limited. They had stolen moments whenever they could, relishing each second they spent together. Now Masha was going to stay in New York for two weeks to visit a friend who had emigrated from Russia for political reasons. This was her second visit, and she'd expressed a desire to find a place to rent in the Russian community, intending to use this visit to do that. In Russian, she had already told Kris that she expected to see them at least once a month if she did find a place, or they could expect her on their doorstep. Shelby chuckled when Kris relayed the message and hugged Masha, promising, "We would miss you too much if we didn't." Shelby had grown very fond of Masha, and was glad they were all starting a new in their lives. Kris hugged her mother goodbye and joined Shelby in the car for the long ride back to northern Virginia.

Later that night, Shelby glanced at Kris and smiled. "Wouldn't it be fun to go on a vacation?" Laying her head back against the couch dreamily, she thought out loud. "Maybe California, Florida, or even Myrtle Beach. I've still got more than thirty days of leave time left. You could take a hiatus from setting up that electronics business. With that big severance check you got, we could afford it."

Without answering, Kris stood up and walked out into the kitchen. Shelby's eyes followed her. "I guess that means you don't want to?" she called, disappointed. Her partner returned and handed her an envelope. Shelby opened it, perused the contents, then jumped up off the couch and hugged Kris. "Key West! Here we come!" After giving the operative a big kiss, she asked, "And just when were you going to tell me about this?"

"I was going to ask you to go to dinner tomorrow night and give you the tickets then. I picked Key West because I was there on a case once, and I just loved it. They have the most gorgeous sunsets I've ever seen. I wanted you to get the chance to see it, too. I hope that's okay."

"Okay? Are you kidding? I'm thrilled!" As Shelby began energetically expressing her delight, Kris moaned softly. Suffused with pleasure, the tall woman felt a brief flash of gratitude for everything that had brought her to this place and this woman. All the deceit, betrayal and violence – none of it was important if she could spend the rest of her life with the blonde whose eager lips were erasing everything from her mind. Smiling with delight as her lover pushed her back onto the couch, Kris let the past go. Shelby was her future, and that was all that mattered.

THE END